DEDIC

This book is dedicated to my wife, my children, Joey, Jay, and Jenny. Without their love, help, encouragement and assistance—the stories in this book would never have been memorialized.

FOREWORD

I began this book not knowing if there would be any interest in the tales I had to tell—why they were any different from the stories created by people today. Then an afternoon conversation with my oldest son gave me the answer.

We were talking about the way people communicate, and he remarked, "People just don't stay in touch the way they used to. They'll call, or email, or text each other. A close friendship can survive on a diet of phone calls and abbreviated code text words for months".

My stories are born of *personal* interaction with people. Some of them come from a time when the military draft was still mandatory, many homes didn't have a phone, a TV, or a radio that reached beyond local stations. Not every family had a car, and if they did, trips were relatively short. This was usually due to the conditions, or lack of, local roads. One might get to his destination faster by walking—somewhat safer too. A child's trip to school most often involved walking. It was an adventure that involved railroad land, dirt roads, foot-bridges over creeks—in all manner of treacherous weather conditions. Even small communities, places that today would be referred to as mere 'neighborhoods', had their own schools, stores, doctors, churches.

These things forced people to rub shoulders with each other on a daily basis. Most summer evenings found folks on their front porch catching up on the plight of local heroes, scoundrels, and fools. In short—people personally *talked* and *listened* to each other. The stories exchanged served two purposes. One was to pass information—word-of-mouth was the email of that time. The second was to entertain.

Even 25-30 years later, as I spent my days working in the corporate world, I still listened to what people said—and watched what they did. Some small thing I saw or heard might later become the genesis of one of my stories.

From this life-time background I learned how to *listen*, absorb information, make up, and *tell* stories. If readers are disappointed or offended by the language in my stories—I do not apologize. I'm not perfect—neither are the people in my stories. They are, after all, just stories—they are my stories—so I get to tell them the way I want.

To my family, friends, co-workers, teachers—even the one who forecast no future for me beyond pumping gas or digging ditches—my thanks for making my life so rich and full. I apologize for all the times I must have tried your souls.

Acknowledgements

My heart felt thanks to my son, Joey, who did the art work for the cover of this book and did unending work to convey my manuscript to the publisher in a publishable form.

My undying gratitude to my long time friend, Darla Jane Owens. She introduced me to the various formats used in printing anything written--and spent some long hours converting this book from its original format to one used by most publishers.

Between Joey and Darla, I learned that writing a book is one thing. Doing it in the correct format for publishing is another thing. Between them, they made my raw manuscript into a book.

Table of Contents

METHODIST CHURCH IN CENTER OF CAMP
COAL TIPPLE IN BACKGROUND

PAGE COMPANY STORE

HOMES OF CAMP RESIDENTS

PAGE CAMP KIDS & HOUSES

PAGE, VIRGINIA

Nestled in the mountains of southwestern Virginia were, at one time, some of the richest coal fields in the United States. By 1960, most of the economically accessible coal had been mined out. Coal mining companies, people who worked for them, and some of the towns which existed around mines have disappeared. Acres of land, once host to businesses, homes, and schools has been abandoned and reclaimed by nature. Memories and old photographs are often the only evidence these places, things, and people ever existed.

Ah, but exist they did. During the 1930s, 40s, and late into the 50s the people, towns, schools, and businesses existed with a passion and enthusiasm that created many stories. Some stories were born around a 'coal camp town' called Page, Virginia.

 Towns built around coal mining operations, were called ' Coal Camps'—even if they had a U.S. Post Office officially making them a town on the state map. The word 'camp' stemmed from the practice of mine workers, when they first established a new mine, of initially living in tents—or 'camps'. Even after normal houses had long replaced the tents, the town was still called a 'camp'.

As a mine became established and was producing a steady stream of coal, the coal companies built houses, paved some streets, built and stocked a company store. Some even built and staffed a doctor's office. So, what was called 'Page Coal Camp' was actually a rural town—even if it had dirt streets and was built on the side of a mountain.

Page had approximately 60-65 'Company' owned residential houses. Page Coal Company rented these homes to their employees. The rent was low. The 'Bosses', or management staff of the coal company, were furnished homes rent free. Water and coal, used for heating, was also free. Page had a population of 400-450 souls, give or take a few.

The people in Page and surrounding areas were hard working and honest. Some had little formal education—the very educated were in the minority. A few actually passed their teen-age years only rarely setting foot outside the county. Church was the major source of social interaction for many. The one local movie theatre was attended mostly by the younger set.

Most of the towns, 'camps', or communities had public schools, within a one mile radius. Travel to and from school was by foot. Very few rural elementary schools had a separate room for each grade. Some schools had only one or two rooms, shared by grades 1 thru 6. Heat came from a pot-bellied stove that burned coal or wood. An open window or door provided ventilation on the warmer days. When you reached the seventh grade you were bused 4-5 miles to the local high school.

PAGE CHARACTERS

Some of the people who lived in Page were—well—unique. It could be argued that some of the residents of Page Camp were more bizarre than unique. Those of a kinder nature would say these people just had 'their own way' of doing things. Those less forgiving said they were 'crazier 'n hell'.

Each individual decides where the acts or habits of others fall on the scale of acceptance. Here are some stories about Page 'characters'. You make up your own mind.

AUBREY COMPTON was a miner. He lived in Page. His was a relatively small house. His large family made it a crowded house. In addition to 6 children, Aubrey provided a place in his home for his Mother, known to all as 'Ma' Compton. Providing for such a large family left Aubrey with limited money for automobiles.

Aubrey had penchant for the HUDSON automobile. Eighty percent of cars in Page were Fords, Chevy's or Plymouths. Aubrey—well he just had a thing for the Hudson. *Used*

Hudsons, to be exact. The expense of caring for his large family kept ownership of a *new* Hudson out of the picture. Aubrey bought a used Hudson, and rode it until its engine and body were pretty much history. Then he bought another used Hudson, and cannibalized parts from the two cars to keep *one* running.

Aubrey was good mechanic. He had to be to keep one of his used Hudsons running. He wasn't that diligent when it came to body repairs. Oh—he would take some tin snips— cut up a metal 3lb. coffee can—make it into a piece of small sheet metal—use screws and the coffee can metal to cover a major 'rust' hole in the body. He would also do a little 'innovative' painting—by pouring paint into a manually operated *Black Flag* insect pesticide sprayer and manually pump that insect sprayer until he had a repaired or replaced car part completely painted. He once painted an entire Chrysler for his brother with that *Black Flag* insecticide sprayer manual pump can. Granted—when he finished painting with that insect sprayer, the finished car looked like he had finished it with a cinder block or a whisk broom. On the other hand, the entire car was all the same color.

The body defects that couldn't be cured with a piece of coffee can metal or coat of paint from Aubrey's hand sprayer—well, they gave Aubrey's cars *character*.

When the floor board in Aubrey's Hudson finally rusted and rotted completely away, no repairs were made. I once rode, for miles, in the front passenger seat of his Hudson with no floor board beneath my feet. Looking down, I watched the highway sliding by at 45 mph beneath my dangling feet. The soles of my shoes were no more than 10 inches from the surface of the road.

Of course, I had choices. I could try to find some part of the interior of the car to brace my feet on—like the dashboard. But there was no guarantee the weight of my feet on the dashboard wouldn't break it away from the engine firewall and cause it to fall through the missing floor to the highway. I could have hung my feet out the open window of the car door—but, I had no guarantee they wouldn't hit some roadside mail box and tear them off. I could have tried to cross my legs, pull my feet beneath me, and sit on them—but, my shoes were muddy and Aubrey wasn't likely to show any restraint if I got mud on his car seat. Or—I could just let my feet dangle straight down and hope we passed over no raised object in the road that would catch and rip off my feet.

Those old turret top Hudson sat a little higher off the road than most cars. I decided to take my chance with dangling feet. I got lucky—arrived home with both feet intact and working properly.

J. HOUSTON BLAND was a devout man. J. HOUSTON lived in the lower quadrant of Page with his wife and five children.

It was never clear what the 'J' in his name stood for. But,

everyone used the initial when addressing him. No one ever heard him called by any name except J. Houston.

J. Houston worked hard in the mines. He treated his family well. He stuck close to home when not working. On Sundays church attendance was an absolute must for J. Houston and his entire family. On Sundays the Missus saw that their 5 children were bathed, properly dressed, and, with Bibles in hand, crammed into the back seat of J. Houston's black, 1941 Plymouth 4 door sedan.

With the Missus sitting up front, J. Houston went through the ritual for getting any car of that era started on cold winter mornings. He pulled the manual choke as far out of the dashboard as it would go. He pumped the gas pedal with his foot several times. Finally, he pushed the starter button on the dashboard. If J. Houston was lucky, the car would cough to life as a thick stream of blue-white smoke belched out of the exhaust.

J. Houston rarely had any luck with that old Plymouth on cold winter mornings. It was in the dead of winter, and the temperature was well below freezing. The starter growled, the motor slowly turned over a few times, but didn't come close to starting. J. Houston hopped out of the car and went under the hood. The battery and radiator both were nearly frozen solid. The car's motor oil was as thick as jelly.

Most people would have given up on church for the day and gone back to the house for some private devotions. Not J. Houston Bland. Ol' J. Houston had the Missus take the kids back to the house for the moment.

J. Houston gathered some newspapers, kindling wood, kerosene, and walked back to his trusty '41 Plymouth sedan. With the hood raised for ventilation, J. Houston got down on his knees, reached under his car, and carefully placed the paper and kindling wood in a neat pile on the ground beneath his car motor and radiator. Then he poured a cup of kerosene on the paper and wood. Satisfied with his preparations, he tossed a lit wooden match under the car on the kerosene soaked paper and wood.

Having never seen anything like this, a neighbor asked J. Houston what he was doing.

""-thawin' her out, buddy", said J. Houston. "All I need to do is get the bat'try, radiator, and motor warmed up a little bit—get that oil thinned out, and she'll start right up."

No one said anything. Those standing around the car looked at each other, then at J. Houston. With the paper and wood soaked with kerosene, fire blazed up beneath the hood around the motor.

Those standing close to J. Houston's car began running. They wanted some distance between them and J. Houston's car before that fire burned through the rubber line carrying gas from the gas tank to the motor. No one stopped running until they had a building or object between them and J. Houston's car. All were yelling for J. Houston to run—get away from his car—before it exploded and he celebrated his Sunday by burning to death when his car exploded in flames.

Ol' J. Houston stood right next to his Plymouth, watching flames shoot up through the engine compartment from the ground. With a satisfied smile on his face, he held his bare hands over the car engine to catch some of the heat from the flames that found their way up through the engine compartment and danced toward the upraised hood of the car.

Miraculously, the car did not catch fire. No explosion occurred. In 3-4 minutes the fire had died down. Unbelievably, there was no damage at all to the car. J. Houston reached under the car with a wooden stick and knocked the remainder of the burning kindling wood from beneath the car. He took his foot and kicked the few remaining embers away from his car. Satisfied that he had all the flames extinguished, he crawled in the car, pushed the starter button, and the car belched a stream of blue-white smoke out the exhaust as the engine sputtered and roared to life.

Everyone who witnessed that 'auto warm up' exercise was astounded—except J. Houston. He slammed the hood of the Plymouth shut, yelled for the Missus and kids, crammed them in the car, and headed off to church.

As J. Houston drove off, one of neighbors standing nearby

summed up things neatly.

"Well, I guess the Lord really did want ol' J. Houston to show up at that church today. Otherwise, that ol' piece-of-junk he drives would have caught fire and blown ol' J. Houston straight up to the Lord".

STATLER 'PREACH' STEVENS was a mine foreman for Page Coal Co. He lived in the central part of the camp, where most of management for the company lived. Most everybody called him 'Preach'. It was doubtful that everyone living in the camp knew his real first name.

The older people in the community said 'Preach' got his nickname when he was 8-9 years old. By their account, 'Preach' had attended Sunday services at a local Pentecostal Holiness Church. To show passion and enthusiasm in his sermon, the pastor of that church shouted most of his message—at the top of his lungs. He reinforced his message by swinging his arms in the air, kicking his feet, and doing a little soft-shoe dance at the altar. All of this left an impression on 'Preach'.

On his way home from the church service 'Preach' came up on a group of men playing poker with gambling cards on an old blanket they had spread out along the side of the old dusty, rut filled road. With the Pentecostal minister's railings about sinners still firmly fixed in his mind, 'Preach' jumped on a nearby tree stump and began to preach a sermon on the wages of sin—like playing cards. As did the good Pentecostal minister, 'Preach' delivered his 'hell fire and damnation' sermon at the top of his lungs—and even threw in a little dance on that stump. From that day forward, Statler Stevens was called 'Preach' Stevens.

The name 'Preach' stuck. His enthusiasm for *all* the lessons found in the Pastor's message did not. Preach, over the years, developed a fondness for the 'spirits' found in a bottle. More specifically, those bottles emblazoned with labels like JOHN PAUL JONES or FOUR ROSES bourbon.

'Preach' was respected as a good worker, a good husband, and a good father. An affable man, he was popular with adults and children alike. He was easy to talk to, and pleasant to be around. Don't misunderstand—'Preach's' fondness for bourbon did not mean he was a 'falling-down drunk'. Not even close to it. And he never let it interfere with his work. But, when holidays or weekends came, like most other men in Page, 'Preach' indulged in the spirits— heartily.

One winter evening there was a foot of snow on the ground in Page. The road through the center of the town sloped downhill at about 15 degrees. Children had been sleigh riding down this road all day. By nightfall they had the snow packed tightly to the ground. This, combined with the freezing temperature, made that road a lightning-fast sleigh run.

As it grew dark, porch lights were turned on, some fires were built along the road. The hill was filled with children and adults having a fine winter night of sleighing in Page.

The adults were out in numbers that night. There were more people than there were sleighs. Some of the adults were too big for the sleighs. Not to be denied the fun of sliding down that long road, the men brought out shovels they used to shovel coal into the furnaces which heated their homes. 'Preach', fueled by half a pint of FOUR ROSES bourbon, was one of those who walked to the top of this sleigh run with a coal shovel in hand.

The road used for our sleigh run was around 250-275 feet from the top to the bottom. At the bottom, the road ended in an intersection with another road that forced a turn 90 degrees to the right or left. The kids in the camp were good at making these turns—even on lightning fast sleighs. They had mastered the art of shifting their weight, positioning their bodies on the sleighs, and making the sleigh's runners bite into the snow for those sharp turns. If you missed the turn at the bottom of the hill, you barreled straight ahead for 30 feet, shot out over a high rock wall, into the air, and plunged 8 feet to the ground. It happened to a few sleigh riders—none enjoyed the experience.

The conversion of a shovel to an imitation sleigh was simple. You placed the shovel handle between your legs, sat in the shovel scoop—lifted up your feet, leaned back, pushed off with your hand to gain momentum, and went sliding down the hill. Actually, a shovel worn smooth can slide faster than a real sleigh. The trick is in the navigation of the shovel. Leaning the body and weight shifting are the only means of guiding a shovel. The shovel handle was good for little beyond holding on to for balance.

'Preach', emboldened by a snort of FOUR ROSES, skipped the customary 'practice' run from a lower point on the sleigh run. He took his shovel to the top of the hill, plopped down on it, and with a loud whoop, announced the beginning of his run down the hill.

"Look out boys! I'm a-comin' down! Whoooeeee!"

'Preach's' shovel must have been really smooth. He shot away from the top of that hill as if he had been shot from a cannon. He was virtually skipping over some of the uneven places in the road as he rode his shovel down the hill. Half way down the hill it became obvious 'Preach' had no control over the direction that shovel moved—period. He was holding on to the shovel handle with one hand. His other hand was holding his hat on. Preach was oblivious to his lack of control. His whoops of joy communicated his pleasure as he rocketed down that hill.

"Whoooeeee! Heee--hiiiii!"

'Preach' didn't see it coming. A little past half way down the hill, his shovel slid to the left and off the regular sleigh track on the hill. He had to be traveling 15 mph when he ran straight into a big wooden utility pole. To see that pole in the dark would have been tough—even if you were walking. Traveling at the speed Preach was moving on that shovel—seeing that pole in time to avoid it was impossible. 'Preach's' shovel handle hit that pole first—dead center. The impact of the collision rammed that shovel handle backwards into 'Preach's' groin. Then 'Preach's' body lifted off the scoop of the shovel and flew through the air until his forehead hit the utility pole.

'Preach' was unconscious when the first people got to him. They rubbed snow on his face to bring him back to consciousness. From 'Preach's' standpoint, that probably was the worst thing they could have done.The pain from his mashed groin was almost unbearable. His screams and curses conveyed the intensity of the pain from his abused testicles. 'Preach' would later describe his pain by saying his testicles hurt so bad they felt like they had 'swapped sockets'.

It took six men to carry 'Preach' to his house. Doc Moore was called to administer a pain killer. 'Preach's' recovery caused him to miss 3 days of work. In the winters that followed a lot of kids rode shovels down that road in the winter—but not Preach Stevens.

~

HOWARD MESSALL is a 'must' in any discussion of Page characters. He and his wife would be at the top of the list if spousal abuse was one of the criteria for inclusion in the Page 'characters' club. Don't jump to the usual conclusions when you read the words 'spouse' and 'abuse' in the same paragraph.

Howard Messall, his wife Eve, and their son Dodie (emphasis on the letter 'o') lived in a house in the upper quadrant of Page camp. That is to say, he lived in the top 'ring' of houses—that could only be reached by climbing a long pair of wooden stairs up a steep embankment from the paved highway running around the upper perimeter of Page. Howard was a motorman in Page's No. 1 mine. Howard stood about 5'6" and weighed 130 lbs., if you included his clothes. Not physically imposing, as the average man goes. His wife, Eve, was 5'10", and wound up the scales to l70-l75 lbs—closer to 175, truth be known.

Howard was a rather passive and quiet man, except when he got liquored up. Consumption of the better part of a fifth of JIM BEAM sour mash bourbon on Friday night or Saturday afternoon would seriously warp ol' Howard's understanding of his physical limitations. He believed himself to be a world-beater on weekends, when he had fortified himself with half-quart of JIM BEAM.

Eve was a polar opposite of Howard. Saying she was assertive was an under-statement. She had opinions on everything, and loudly verbalized them—regardless of your lack of interest in what she had to say. Most of Eve's opinions were, blatantly biased, had no basis, grossly mis-informed, liberally laced with profanities, and outrageous. Everyone but Eve knew this. Eve knew some of her ridiculous views, delivered in her fog-horn voice, couldn't hold water—but, she didn't really care. She was far more interested in gaining recognition than claiming accuracy.

Howard and Eve had one child. They called him Dodie. His real name was thought to be Donald or Ronald or David—but no one cared enough to ask Eve and get one of her famous 'chewing outs'. Eve wasn't much on sharing information about 'my personal biznis'. Dodie was 7-8 years old and an undisciplined, obnoxious, little turd. Eve gave him anything he wanted, let him believe he could do or say anything he wanted, defended anything he did, no matter how offensive it was. In short, he was a miniature version of Eve. Most of the kids in Page beat the crap out of Dodie when Ethel wasn't around—just to even the score for some offense he committed when she <u>was</u> around and wouldn't let them work him over.

Let me offer an example that puts Dodie and Eve in the proper light. I was working at the company store. It was close to quitting time. In keeping with the daily closing ritual, I was sweeping and picking up trash along the sidewalk in front of the store. Flem VanDyke was sitting on one of the benches in front of the store. Flem was not a talkative man. Nor did he see a lot of humor in life. He had little patience with things not to his liking. He was a grizzled veteran of World War I, with a face and voice that made you think twice before even speaking to him. Dodie had just bought 5 pieces of bubble gum in the store, and stuffed every one of them in his mouth at once. Excess was Dodie's middle name. He worked all that gum together in his mouth and blew a huge, multi-colored bubble out of his mouth. It was a disgusting sight.

Ol' Flem gave Dodie a withering glare and said, "HEY! Boy!

Stop that! Ever time I see you blow one of those bubbles I think your guts are coming out!"

Dodie, turned to Flem, stuck out his tongue at Flem, and blew another big gum bubble—not 12 inches from Flem's face. Ol' Flem jumped up from that bench, lunged toward Dodie, and bellowed, "Get th' hell outta' here!"

Dodie, true to form when Eve wasn't around to protect him, began screaming, crying, and running for home. Flem sat back down. I quietly eased over to the store's loading dock and waited for the show-down I knew was coming. No more than 2-3 minutes passed before Eve came tearing around the corner of the store with Dodie in tow.

She began yelling at Flem. But, she met her match in Flem. I had heard stories about Flem, when he was an army Sergeant and leading troops in battles through the Argonne Forest of France during WW I. His willingness to fight was legendary. In the next few seconds he confirmed his willingness to do battle. Flem and Eve called each other every profane name I ever heard—and some I hadn't heard.

They threatened to beat each other—re-arrange each other's faces—kick each other's asses. They punctuated their threats with taunts of 'go to hell' and 'kiss my ass.' Ol' Flem was one rough looking rascal, even when he wasn't angry. When he was angry, his face took on a look that can only be described as the absolute definition of vicious. When Flem tired of exchanging threats and curses, he moved toward Eve and told her he was going to settle the matter by 'throwing your lard-ass ass off the bridge' next to the store. Eve knew he meant it. That was enough to cause Eve to back off and take Dodie home. But—she took Flem right to the brink of throwing her off a 30 ft high bridge before she 'blinked' first.

Back to Howard and Eve. Come weekends, Howard would announce his intention to attend a Union meeting, shooting match—anything away from Eve. He decked himself out—best clothes, dress boots, and $12 felt, snap-brim dress hat. Invariably, Howard was falling-down drunk when he returned home. It was all he could do to climb those steps from the road to his house. He literally crawled up those 30 wooden steps—on his hands and knees. Next door neighbors cheered him on as he struggled up the steps. Once he cleared the top step and staggered into his front yard—the action began, and the routine seldom varied.

Eve met Howard in the front yard. She let Howard have it for violating her standing rule of 'no likker drinkin'. She yelled at him, cursed him, and cuffed him about the head and shoulders with her fists. Emboldened by the quart of bourbon in his belly, Howard would over-estimate his physical strength, draw a verbal 'line in the dirt', and dare Eve to cross it.

"I'll do what I dam well please, and give you a good ass-whuppin' if you say one word about it", he snarled.

From this point on, things always went badly for Howard. Eve was bigger, stronger—and sober. Howard--? He was hardly able to stand up-right—let alone mount a physical defense in his own behalf. First, Eve would jerk his good $12 dress hat off his head. Then she would jam his old, soiled every-day hat down on his head until his ears were pushed down. Then she drug him across the yard, stood him up-right at the top of the steep embankment that dropped to the road, and gave him a kick in the rear that sent him tumbling, rolling, and sliding 30 ft down that bank to the road.

To the cheers of the neighbors, Howard would pick himself up and stagger out of the road. Once again, he crawled up those 30 steps to his front yard. When he reached his front yard, his neighbors would give him another round of applause and cheers. Howard would acknowledge their encouragement with a wave of his hand—collapse—and pass out in the front yard. Eve wouldn't let him in the house until he sobered up—even if he had to lay in the yard all night to do so.

Eve's final penalty for Howard's 'likker drinkin' was to come into the company store—buy anything she wanted—and sink Howard another $20-25 in debt. To give this scale, a miner's pay for an <u>entire</u> day's work in the mines was $22 in the late 1940s.

Howard and Eve exercised their 'test of wills' twice a month for—years.

A HOME-MADE CAR

Growing up in rural coal towns involved a lot of devise-your-own-entertainment. Page, Va. was no different. There was the *REX* movie theatre, four miles away, which showed movies Friday night thru Sunday afternoon. For high school kids, the local high school held folk dances one Friday night each month for 6-7 months out of the year. A few times each year someone's parents threw a birthday party for their child—if you were a friend you were invited. The Methodist Church held two hour MYF social gatherings for young people one evening a week throughout most of the year. These things helped—but they didn't come even close to filling in all the days and hours that passed with no planned entertainment for the boys in Page. No—any way you looked at it, we had to rely on our own ingenuity for a good bit of our entertainment.

There were no libraries, save the one at the high school. Until the mid l950s, there were no TVs. There were a few night clubs and dance halls featuring local bands scattered along the busier highways. They were of no use to young boys. Our parents would have 'busted' our tails good had they heard we were even close to one of these places. Even if we had been allowed in or around one of these night clubs, no kid I knew was anxious to go to one and risk getting in harm's way—although, the nightly 'action' at one of those places might have been the best evening show in the area.

Most evenings at these dance hall/bars weren't complete without a fight. People drank too much of the 'spirits', passions ran hot, and lack of restraint was common place. The end product of all this was predictable. People were popped in the head with wine bottles—chairs were broken over the backs of unsuspecting customers—every man on the premises carried a knife or gun, and was likely to use either with little provocation. On rare occasions men would let their emotions lead them to settle a disagreement with pistols. The man who finished their shoot-out in second place was carried away in a body bag. The man who finished in first place was carried to jail in the back of the Sheriff's car. The winner, in one such case, defended himself against a charge of murder by telling the jury he killed the other man, "—because the card-cheatin' SOB deserved a killin'—". Oddly, the jury agreed with his defense and found him innocent of all charges.

No, kids didn't want any part of the night club/dance hall 'action'. Anyway we looked at our situation, it was up to us to find some other way to fill our leisure time.

The norm was to play cowboys and Indians; make a homemade basketball goal and play basketball; find some flat ground for a football game; do a little hunting if you were big enough and could get somebody to let you tag along; or, a dip in a swimming hole built by damming up a creek with a felled tree and 'borrowed' barn boards. These things grew boring after a few weeks. There was always a search on for something new. Like the summer Walter Sawyer led a group of us in the restoration of that old abandoned Oldsmobile car setting in the 'bottom' below Page camp. A 'bottom' was what we called a piece of flat land, along a creek, at the base of two mountains. Such land was at a premium in the mountains surrounding Page, Va.

That ol' Olds, made in the late 1930s, had been setting there, abandoned, for over a year. For reasons unknown, someone had re-moved the body from the Olds. They took every piece of sheet metal off that car. Strangely, they left the seats, still bolted to the floor of the car. The steering wheel, motor, wheels, and tires were there too. Yes sir, to a bunch of 10 - 12 year old kids looking for fun—having a running car in our possession for the summer was as good as it got in 'kid-dom'. Well—a car that could be a <u>running</u> car with some effort on our part.

Walter Sawyer was the oldest one of us. His Dad was a machinist. He was a darn good mechanic too. He taught Walter a lot. Walter's nifty ability to 'fix' mechanical things put him in high esteem among kids our age. It was Walter who, after a swim in the creek, pointed out the possibilities in the remains of that old car. Until he assured us we could get it running, we had looked at the cannibalized old car as just so much scrap iron with no possible value to us.

There was some open land in the 'bottom' between the railroad rails and the creek where Walter said we could drive it—maybe even take the car for a one mile ride up the tracks where the rails came to an end. Why, by the time summer was over, every last one of us would know how to drive a car, according to Walter. No more walking to get to places we wanted to go, no more begging parents to take us, no more hitch-hiking. We would just use 'our own car'

Of course, it was a wild-eyed pipe-dream that only kids could believe. The important thing was our *belief*. For a kid, belief in possibilities is the fuel that drives them to work on ideas and dreams until they become realities— with all the rewards that come with them. Having a real car— feeling the pride and joy of driving a car—it was a project with no down-side. For kids who had, up to this age in their life, only built and driven home-made wagons made of old boards, bolts, rope, and scavenged wheels— who had used their own energy to get a bicycle to move— well, this was heady stuff. Just the possibility of 'moving up' to ownership of motorized transportation was simply too great to be ignored. Nearly every boy in the neighborhood signed on for the project—enthusiastically.

Walter was in charge. He assigned everyone a task. He had boys pumping up the car tires with a bicycle hand pump. It took hours to pump up those four tires. They leaked air so we had to pump them up 'tight' again every 3-4 days. We didn't know, or care, anything about proper air pressure in the tires. The boys on 'tire detail' took turns pumping up those tires until they were so tight it felt like we were kicking a rock when we kicked them.

One or two boys were put on 'gas detail'. They scrounged

three gallons of gasoline by using a siphon hose to suck it out of the auto gas tanks of local neighbors. Walter, always a thinking man, told the 'gas detail' boys not to siphon more than a couple of quarts of gas from any one car—so the car owner's gas gauge wouldn't alert him to the loss of gas from his car.

Hunting for a battery, looking for used spark plugs, pilfering ginger from some mother's kitchen for use in plugging the holes in the old car's radiator, finding a cake of Octagon laundry soap to rub over and seal holes in the gas tank, locating and 'borrowing' some automotive electrical wire to splice the car's electrical system back together—all of these task were assigned to various boys involved in the resurrection of 'our car'. No one complained—everyone took on his assigned tasks with fervor—motivated by Walter's promised rewards from the end product of our work

We worked on the restoration of that old car for three weeks. Every moment we could spare from our daily chores and any leisure time we had was used to fix something on the car. Everyone was sworn to secrecy. No one believed, not for one second, that any parent in the entire neighborhood would, voluntarily, let us restore that old car and ride it around the bottom while hanging on to the open seats.

Besides, we wanted to see the looks on their faces when our ingenuity brought that old piece-of-junk car to life. Once we had that thing running, we were sure all would be forgiven by every parent in the camp. Well, we weren't so naïve that we thought awards would be handed out. But, we reasoned, we wouldn't get paddlings either. Some things done by kids in our neighborhood, as with kids most other towns, were done with an eye toward how far we could go without having a parent bring out the paddle, switch, or belt to drive home their feelings about unacceptable behavior.

At the end of three weeks Walter announced we were ready for a trial run. With Walter at the steering wheel, all of us piled on the front and back seats of the Olds. Don't ask me how, but there were 11 of us piled up on that car. Some of us sat on the laps of those sitting on the seats. Walter, Harold, Goat, Bob, Jack, Mule, Jitterbug, Abner, Eugene, Tommy Joe, and 'Greasy'.

The heart of every boy sitting in or hanging on to that old wreck of a car was pounding as we held our breath and waited to hear the car motor come to life. Every eye was glued to Walter's hands as he touched the naked ends of the starter button wires together and,—and nothing happened. He continued to brush the two wires together feverishly—without a feeble spark from the wires. Not a peep—not even one slow growl from the motor.

We piled off the car, mumbling to ourselves. The older and more worldly of our gang of boys uttered a few curses. We looked to Walter with questions in our eyes. Walter, we thought, knew everything about cars. He had directed the construction of the car—every step of the way. So why wasn't it running?

Walter tested the battery. It was dead. Having 'borrowed' it from the floor of Cameron Sauer's garage, we had assumed it was a 'live' battery. We never once considered that the battery might be dead. We were trying to put together a running car. The last thing we wanted to do was trouble ourselves with possible negatives.

But, reality reared its ugly head. The battery was dead. There was no way we could 'borrow' a 'good' battery from someone's car in the neighborhood and just assume he wouldn't notice the absence of the battery when his car didn't start the following morning. Siphoning 20 cents worth of gas out of a neighbor's car was one thing. The disappearance of the gas would most likely go unnoticed— and wouldn't cause any probing questions if it was noticed. A 'borrowed' battery was another thing. The owner of the missing battery wouldn't let that slide. Gloom descended on the boys. Three weeks of work— down the drain—for nothing.

Walter rallied us. He stepped away from the battery and spoke with the voice of authority that the oldest boy in the crowd always seems to have.

"Boys, this ain't no big problem. All we got to do is get the motor in this car a-runnin' is to get it a'movin' at 5-10 miles per hour, put it in second gear, pop the clutch, and the motor in this thing will start right up. Yes sir, we get the motor runnin'—it will charge that battery right up in less than 5 minutes. Once we get the battery charged—we can start it with them there 'starter wires' any time we want to."

Mule, ever the cynic in our group, spat on the ground in front of the car, turned to Walter, squinted his eyes, and said to Walter. "Walter, how'n the devil we ever gonna' get this thing up to enough speed to turn the motor over? Huh? Look around you. The ground is flat. We're in a bottom. This thing ain't run for a year. We can't push this thing fast enough get it up to 2 miles an hour—let alone 5-10 miles an hour. Even with ever last one of us a-pushin' this thing up and down this bottom—we ain't never gonna' get up enough speed to kick its motor over so it can start on its own."

Walter considered this. Mule had a point. Besides, if we pushed it too far along the bottom we would have the car right up against the railroad or the coal tipple. The railroad or tipple bosses would be all over us. We weren't supposed to be near either one of those places. Being caught near the tipple or railroad was sure to get you reported to your parents—and that would cost us a spanking, for sure.

Walter was the last one of us to admit defeat. He leaned against the car, said nothing as he gazed at the land around us. Suddenly his face lit up.

"By golly, its right in front of us, boys", he answered as he pointed to the other side of the creek. "All we got to do is take 'er up that No. 2 mine road about 250 feet, turn 'er around at the slate dump, give 'er a 'poosh' to get 'er rolling down that road, get 'er up to 5-10 miles an hour, pop the clutch out, and we'll have a-plenty of speed to start the motor in this here car. Once we get 'er started a-runnin', that the motor will charge that bat'try right up—and we can use the bat'try to start 'er up after that! "

All of us looked at the rutty, dirt road sloping up the mountain on the other side of the creek. It wasn't real steep—but—it was still uphill, at a pretty good angle. There was a lot of skepticism in our faces as we looked at Walter. We would have to push the car 100 feet to the one lane bridge crossing the creek. No problem there because the road from the car to the bridge was slightly downhill. We'd have to be careful getting the car across the bridge. It was a wooden, narrow, one- lane bridge with no side rails. To get on the bridge from either end required a sharp right angle turn. Yes sir, a full 90 degree turn.

In the 1930s and 40s no one took the time and trouble to build diagonal bridges across streams. To compound matters, the highway department did not waste money on wide sweeping turns in the roads approaching the ends of bridges built straight across a creek or river.

Having no other alternative ideas for starting the car, we couldn't afford to think negatively. Pushing the car across the bridge was a minor thing—in the overall scope of things. BUT, pushing it 250 feet up that rutty, rocky, road—some of the boys mumbled serious doubts about our ability to do it. If we boys thought we were going to just throw in the towel on 3 weeks of hard work on that old car, Walter firmly disabused us of that idea

"Wait a minute! You boys ain't got your thinkin' caps on! We ain't got nothin' here but a motor and two seats mounted on a skinny little frame that's a-settin' on four wheels. Them seats don't weigh a 100 lbs. That skinny frame can't weight more'n 200 lbs. Them wheel bearings is greased so good they're slicker'n snot on a door knob. Them tires is pumped up so tight they're harder than a rock. They ain't no 'drag' in them wheels a'tall. And if all 'leven us can't push a motor and two seats a-settin on wheels up that little dirt road, well bygod,—the whole gang of you ain't nothin' but a bunch of 'weak sissies'!", declared Walter as he slammed his hand down on the seat of the car with an air of finality.

No boy in that coal camp wanted to be called 'weak' or a 'sissie. A name like that stuck with you like tar—for years. We all began pushing. To our amazement, Walter was right. It wasn't that difficult.

With Walter steering, we had the car safely across the bridge in a minute or two. Walter, jumped to the ground, steered the car with one hand and used his free hand to join the other ten of us in pushing the car up the road. All of us were yelling at each other to push harder. In another 5-6 minutes we had that car 250 feet up that rutty, rock filled road and resting in the 'turn-around' portion of the road where coal company trucks dumped slate and rocks from the mines over the side of the mountain.

The second we had the car securely resting on the level ground of the 'turn- around' every one of us dropped to the ground on our knees or butts to catch our breath. We had, as Walter said we could, pushed that car up that hill. We were covered in sweat, breathing fast, exhausted— and smiling proudly.

After lying in the shade of a nearby oak tree for a full five minutes, we slowly got to our feet and walked across the road to a stream of spring water that constantly flowed out of crevice in the mountain. All of us took turns drinking the cool water and holding our heads under the stream cascading from a piece of pipe someone had driven into the crevice to make the water easier to catch in a jug or bucket.

The rest and water left us feeling refreshed—ready to take our maiden ride on our very own car. We pushed the car back and forth on the flat ground until we had the front of the car pointed back toward the road—ready to begin its down-hill trial run.

Walter gave his 'We're 'bout ready to roll boys' command from his seat behind the steering wheel. He had the clutch pedal shoved all the way to floor with his left foot. He shoved the gear shift handle upwards into second gear and grabbed the steering wheel in a white-knuckle two handed grip. As prepared as he was ever going to be, Walter gave his final instructions before we started the car in motion.

"Everybody—except Harold, Mule, and Greasy—get on the car and take a seat. Harold, you, Mule, and Greasy 'poosh' on the car until you get it out of this here turn-around, over to the road, an' get it to rollin' down the road. Now, once you get 'er to rollin' downhill—you jump on the car real quick. You ain't gonna' have much time to jump on 'fore it commences to pickin' up some real speed. So when you jump on—if you can't find a place to sit—just find somethin' to stand on—somethin' to hang on to—and I mean hang on tight!"

Once we got it out of the flat turn-around, the car began to roll easily and quickly down the one lane, dirt road. The three of us jumped on. There was no place to sit. All three of us stood on bare sheet metal that served as a floor of sorts between the front and back seats. There was nothing to hang on to but the backs of the front seats and each other, so we satisfied ourselves with those weak grasps to keep our balance and not fall off the car.

The feel of the wind moving across our faces as the car picked up speed and rolled down the mountain road was indescribable. There were shrieks and shouts of pride and pure joy from every one of us.

After 25-30' feet, Walter popped the clutch. Nothing. He rammed the clutch back to the floor with left foot and pumped the gas pedal with his right foot. The car picked up speed for another 30 feet, and Walter popped the clutch again. Nothing. Not one click, whine, growl, or popping sound from the car motor. We seemed to be literally flying after traveling 100 feet down the road. But then, moving in open air with nothing but a set of wheels under you makes any speed feel exaggerated. That's what we were telling ourselves.

By now, Walter was popping that clutch in and out, stomping the gas pedal, with every 10 feet we traveled. The car was moving even faster and bouncing up and down over the ruts and rocks in the road. Still, Walter had no luck getting the engine started. We could, at last, hear the motor coughing, chugging, and laboring but it never came close to starting or running—despite Walter's frantic efforts with the clutch and gas pedals.

"Walter, this thing ain't a-gonna start this time. Put the brakes on! Stop this thing! We'll push it back up the hill again for another try", said Mule.

We were no more than 75 feet from the bridge and must have been rolling at a speed of 25-30 miles per hour by then. Walter stomped down hard on the brake pedal. The brake pedal went all the way to the car's floor. Nothing happened. Walter feverishly stomped the brake pedal—again and again. Not only did the car not slow down—its speed was actually increasing. It became horribly obvious to all of us that the car had no brakes. We had never checked them before. Our priority had been to get the car to move—not stop. We couldn't have discovered the lack of brakes at a more dreadful moment—but, it was what it was.

The car and that narrow, right-angle bridge were fast approaching a meeting—a meeting that was dead certain to produce unhappy results. Walter had a better chance of climbing a greased pole with his fingers cut off than he did of safely crossing the bridge in our old out-of-control car. Staying on the car with Walter to show loyalty and trust in his ability to negotiate the turn and cross a rickety, narrow wooden bridge—that was one thing. Staying on the car with Walter when our chance of <u>surviving</u> the attempted crossing of that bridge was next to <u>zero</u>—now that was another thing.

We could have stayed on the car and prayed for a miracle. Kids know God doesn't answer every prayer with a 'yes'— especially pleas to defeat the laws of gravity by holding a speeding car upright on an impossible turn. In a situation like this, with their own hides at stake, kids will usually opt for some action to help themselves and ask later for forgiveness for their lack of faith. From our viewpoint, parting company with Walter and the car *before* we got to that bridge seemed the better choice. Without a word to each other, we all began jumping off the car.

Those who jumped to the left only managed to get one foot on the ground before the forward momentum of their body hurled them through the air, into the dirt drainage ditch 2 feet deep. They tumbled and rolled head over heels for 8 to 10 feet before they rolled to a stop—either face up or face down in that dry, rocky ditch.

Those who jumped from the right side of the car fared worse. They barely got one foot on the ground beside the road before the momentum launched their bodies through the air, and down a steep, dirt embankment. They tumbled and rolled 20 feet down the steep hill until they came to a stop in the water of Garden Creek.

Both sides of the road were filled wild black berry vines with sharp briars. Regardless of which way the boys jumped, most of them were going to do some of their rolling and tumbling through briars on those berry vines.

You could hear screams and cries of pain from the boys within seconds of their jump from the car. It was summer time—a time for wearing as few clothes as possible. That left a lot of skin exposed. Rolling, tumbling, sliding, over and through rocks, briars, and hard-packed ground instantly reduced our clothes to tattered rags. The bare portions of our bodies were torn and bleeding from briar cuts and abrasions. Some of the boys were crying or moaning from the pain of bruises, contusions, and, for all we knew, broken bones.Walter and his brother Jack never jumped. Walter would, later, say he never jumped because he believed the car engine would start if he kept popping the clutch. Ever the realist in our group, Mule looked him in the eye and asked what possible use a running motor would have been to him when the car reached the bridge doing 25-30 mph with no brakes.

When the car reached the bottom of the hill it had to be doing 25-30 mph. No one had ever negotiated the turn onto that bridge at more than 5-10 mph. When it became obvious, even to Walter, that pumping the brake pedal would not slow the old car, he turned the steering wheel to the right as hard as he could—just as the road made a 90 degree turn to the right to meet the bridge. The tires, almost bare of tread, tried to bite into the dirt road and turn right, but the car's forward momentum was just too much. Dust and dirt flew into the air from the skidding tires. The car's suspension system made stressful, popping sounds as it labored to keep the car upright.

Those of us least injured from our jumps were able to see the car sailing down the road to the bridge. We watched in horror at what happened. The car's speed was just too great and the tires too bald to allow the car to make a successful turn onto the bridge. Mule and Greasy, still on their knees from their tumble down the ditch, watched, frozen in fear, as the car shot straight ahead, off the side of the bridge, into the air, and gravity began pulling it down to the creek 20 feet below.

First, the front of the car dropped out of sight below the edge of the bridge. When the front of the car, bearing the heavy motor, fell toward the creek first it caused the middle and rear of the car to flip straight up in the air—completely off the bridge. This caused the seat Walter and Jack were sitting in to become a literal catapult. We saw Walter and Jack propelled out of the car seat, into the air, and out of sight as gravity pulled them 20 feet to the creek below. Then the rear of the car flipped upside-down and disappeared below the edge of the bridge. We only heard one big splash when the car hit the creek. We couldn't see Walter or Jack—nor hear a single sound from them.

Those of us able to move and not nursing crippling injuries quickly hobbled and shuffled down to the bridge. On the way there Greasy had the sick feeling that nothing but bad news was waiting for him. The water in the creek was seldom more than a foot to eighteen inches deep—and filled with big rocks. Walter and Jack—thrown up in the air from those seats—dropping 20 feet or better to a landing in 18 inches of rock-strewn water—they didn't stand a chance. If the fall hadn't killed them, the car falling on top of them almost certainly would have.

Their mourning for the loss of Walter and Jack was short lived as their thoughts swiftly turned to what the cost to each of them, personally, would be for being involved in this disastrous venture. He figured a sentence to a Boys' Penitentiary was almost certainly in his future—if his parents didn't kill him first with a belt or paddle. He wondered how many years he would have to stay in the penitentiary when loss of life was involved.

Mule, Harold, and Greasy got there first. They ran onto the bridge, looked over the edge—and saw Walter and Jack slowly wading out of the creek. Greasy didn't believe he had ever been so happy, before or after that day, to see two people alive as he was at that moment. Had it not been for knees and legs sprained and bleeding, all of them would have celebrated their survival by running down the bank to help Walter and Jack from the creek.

The car lay on its top in the rock filled creek just below the bridge. Actually, the car was resting on the upright portion of the car seats. Except for the bent and crushed car seats, the old car looked none the worse for its fall from the bridge.

Some 25 feet south of where the car lay in the creek was the reservoir dredged out of the creek by the coal company that operated a nearby coal processing tipple. The reservoir was maybe 20′ wide by 8′ deep. The company used this pool of creek water to pump water for cleaning coal it processed in the tipple.

Fate, and the laws of physics, had slung Walter and Jack's bodies away from the falling car and into the creek reservoir where there was enough depth to the water to easily cushion their fall. This had saved Walter and Jack's lives. Ironically, they were the only two or the eleven of the boys with no injuries. They didn't have even a scratch on them—from head to toe. The whole thing had been no more than a dive into a swimming pool for them.

The Superintendent of Page Coal Co. was beside himself with anger. The tipple boss wanted to beat every one of our butts with his mine belt—right on the spot. They both appeared at the creek edge while Walter and Jack were wading out of the creek. Their hair plastered to their heads, their clothes dripping water, their shoes missing, they stood there without a word as the Superintendent delivered a long list of punishments he intended to dish out to every one of the boys.

I don't know how word traveled so fast, but parents were there in minutes. Even parents who had no kid involved with the car showed up. Within 10 minutes of the car plunging off that bridge there were so many adults standing along the creek bank it looked like a scene from a Sunday afternoon baptism by a country church.

The things that saved most of us from being paddled— right on the spot—were the cuts, ugly abrasions, bruises already turning blue, and big lumps or knots on our bodies. That and all of us exaggerating our injuries and pain. There were parents strung out up that road and down in the creek—picking up boys from ditches and a foot of creek water. The queries from our parent were loud and pretty much limited to three questions.

"Where do you hurt?", "What on earth were you thinking about to do a fool thing like this?", and "Have you lost your mind—pulling a stunt like this?"

Given the obvious wreckage of our bodies, none of us could claim not to have been involved in the car ride. The younger boys, however, did minimize their blame by saying the older boys talked them into the whole affair. First, they figured we older boys were already in so much trouble that being accused of leading them into the project couldn't compound the depth of our trouble that much. Secondly, it was the only tale they could come up with that was half-way believable. The older boys offered no defense or excuses. Given the state of mind of the parents around that bridge, their chances of finding a sympathetic ear on any parent was somewhere between nothing and less than nothing.

Two of the boys had to be taken to Doc Moore for possible internal injuries. One of them was sent to the hospital where an x-ray confirmed a fracture of his arm. Other than those two, we had to make do with the salves, iodine, rubbing-alcohol, or whatever else could be found in our parent's medicine cabinet at home. None of them offered any aspirin for the pain. I guess they felt some pain was warranted—and it took the place of what we would have suffered from a spanking.

The coal company had one of their bull dozers pull the car out of the creek. The car was pulled back to the place where it sat when we started work on it. It was turned upright, its wheels taken off, and dropped to the ground on its frame. That pretty much guaranteed there would be no future 'test runs' in it. The machinist on duty at the tipple had to re-weld the pipe that carried water from the creek to the tipple. The Olds, well it was taken away, eventually. Nobody knew who it belonged to. No kid involved with the car was about to ask a parent where the car was. Word got around that the company put it on one of their trucks, hauled it to Lambert's junk yard, and gave it to him for scrap metal.

No matter. Up to the point where we discovered the car had no brakes and had to bail out of it—it had been a great 'home-made' car and an exciting ride—short lived as it was. Since that summer of the late '40s, I have owned many vehicles. I remember very few, if any, of them as clearly as I do the 'Home-Made Car'.

COOK SCHOOL

COOK SCHOOL

On a 7-8 mile stretch of Garden Creek, from Clell to Oakwood, there were three rural elementary schools. Each constructed of wood, painted white, and contained from one to several class rooms.

At the head of Garden Creek was HALE SCHOOL. In the middle area of Garden Creek was COOK SCHOOL. The lower part of Garden Creek was served by the former TMI (Triangular Mountain Institute) ELEMENTARY SCHOOL.

Kids living in Page, and some other areas above Page, attended Cook School from grades one thru six.

The elementary schools were built within 'walking distance' of the neighborhoods served. As a rule, 'walking distance' meant no more than a mile—but, you wouldn't find this guaranteed in writing. In the case of the kids in Page camp, walking distance was about one mile—each way. In the 1940s, closing schools for 'snow days' was a concept not yet formalized. Except for snow falls measuring a foot or more, classes were held. No need to be concerned about the possibility of school buses wrecking on slick roads—because there were no buses for the rural schools.

To be fair, the rules about walking to school were informal. You could walk on a county dirt road, or along-side the railroad. It was 1/5 of a mile further by the county road, which was always muddy or dusty. Students shared the county road with coals trucks, which left a fine layer of coal dust or mud on you as they roared by.

The path beside the railroad tracks was everyone's path of preference for walking to school. It was level, never muddy, and was a shorter walk. On the other hand, it was strictly against railroad rules for anyone, except railroad and mine employees, to walk along the railroad tracks.

The railroad tracks were patrolled, irregularly, by the railroad company section boss, Mr. O.V. Bostick. Ol' 'Boss' Bostick was fearsome—even to look at. He had dark eyes—black as night. His long upper lip was covered by a brushy mustache. No kid had ever seen him smile. He wore a big Stetson hat that made him look even taller than his 6' 4" height. If the man had an ounce of the milk of human kindness in him, kids caught walking along those railroad tracks never saw it.

We had it on good authority (the older kids) that 'Boss' Bostick would have all those caught walking on railroad property put in jail. He rode this motorized car up and down the rails as he patrolled the tracks for miles in several directions. We never knew what his schedule was, nor when he might come rolling up the track in his little 'Orange Blossom Special' motor cart and find us walking to school or home on railroad property. The older kids swore he would 'snatch us up—throw us on his motor cart—and take directly to the county jail'—before our parents even knew we were gone.

No kid, even those feeble of mind, wanted to be caught or captured on railroad property by 'Boss' Bostick. We knew it was against the rules to be on railroad property. But, we felt sure kids *must* have the right to *try* to walk along-side those rails. Not only that—we were just dead certain we could avoid discovery or capture, by 'Boss' Bostick, while walking along-side the tracks. Unless you were, at the very least, in the fifth grade, we couldn't even spell 'trespass'— let alone wonder if you were guilty of it.

In our daily walks along the tracks—even if we were talking and laughing with each other—we always kept one ear 'cocked' for the approaching sound of 'Boss' Bostick's little motor car. We could hear its familiar 'putt-pop-putt-pop' sound, even before it rounded the nearest curve and came into sight. When we heard the sound of that motor car, boys and girls alike, dove over the high dirt bank that led from the railroad bed down to the creek.

We slid and tumbled eight or nine feet down that steep bank to the creek, which was normally about a foot deep and ten feet wide. It was filled with big slippery rocks. We tried to jump from rock to rock in the creek to reach the other side of the creek without getting our feet wet. Very few of us were ever successful at crossing the creek with dry feet. The rocks were unstable and slippery. Between the first step onto a rock in that creek and land on the other side, you were going to get one or both feet in that water The creek's water temperature varied from cool-to cold-to freezing—depending on the time of the year. Fear of taking a one way ride to jail on 'Boss' Bostick's little motor car helped us ignore the bite of that cold water if we got one or two feet wet while trying to reach private land on the other side of the creek. On days when we crossed that creek, 15-20 kids sat in class that day with one or two wet feet, socks, shoes, and pants legs. Uncomfortable—yes. But, preferable to an unsolicited ride to jail on 'Boss' Bostick's little motor car.

Most of the owners of private land across the creek from the railroad tracks were kind enough to let us traipse through their farms until we reached the school play-ground. They understood our predicament—except for Garfield Coleman's mother. His mother was about 75-80 years old. She lived with Garfield and his family in their big, old white farm house. 'Ma' Coleman, as she was called, was, in her neighbors' words, 'not right in th' head'. Believe me, those words described her mental condition and attitude in the kindest possible light. That old woman was viler than a cake of home-made lye soap.

'Ma' Coleman assumed anyone she saw on any part of their farm was there to 'do me harm'. She never asked, nor cared, if Garfield had given permission for people to walk on his property. If 'Boss' Bostick's sudden arrival caused us to make one of our 'emergency evacuations' from the railroad, through the creek, and onto Garfield's cow pasture—well, 'Ma' Coleman was apt as not to bear down on us with a load of buckshot from the 12 gauge shotgun that was never far from her hands.

Thank goodness we were a hundred yards away from 'Ma',

and her aim was poor. Still, with buckshot cutting through the air around us, we were left with no option but hopping back on the creek rocks—which was neutral ground for everyone—and walking on creek rocks in the creek until we reached other property or the school playground.

Cook School was a one room school, measuring no more than 50' by 50'. There was a green burlap curtain, hanging from the ceiling to the floor that divided grades 1 thru 3 from grades 4 thru 6. Flossie Murray, a nice lady, taught grades 1-3. Hettie Kane, a good teacher and strict disciplinarian, taught grades 4-6.

There were two old cast-iron, *Burnside* brand, coal stoves that provided heat on both sides of the curtain during the winter. The teachers were, personally, responsible for starting and maintaining the fires in those wretched old stoves. They neatly side-stepped this job by paying one of the older boys $5 a month to get to the school a half hour before class time and start a fire in those old stoves.

 The stoves were located in a corner on both sides of that deteriorating old burlap curtain. Those seated closest to the stove, literally, had red faces, from the heat coming off those stoves, within an hour of the beginning of classes each morning. The unlucky students seated the greatest distance from the stoves didn't feel any real heat from those stoves until early afternoon—about one hour before classes were dismissed for the day. They just kept their coats on all day.

Seating was a random collection of single and double desks. Desks, with broken seats, had a 'saw-horse' for a seat, made of pieces of raw 2"x4" lumber. The writing surface of the desks had so many initials or names carved in them they were almost useless as a writing surface without 5-6 sheets of paper beneath the sheet you were writing on. The double desks were favored by those who were 'slow learners', or those who saw studying and homework as an unfair infringement on their pursuit of a work free life. They asked the teacher to partner them at a double desk with someone who actually did home work assignments and studied the school text books. They were content with copying their desk-partner's work or learning what they could from mentoring by a desk-mate.

Not to imply that discipline was completely absent at Cook School. Offenses such as fighting, smoking, cursing, hitting a girl, sassing the teacher—and a litany of lesser offenses— resulted in a 'paddling' by the teacher. 'Paddling' is a kind word—'horse-whipping' might be a more accurate description—especially by those on the receiving end of this punishment. Laws against corporal punishment were non-existent at Cook School. The punishment was administered by means of a wooden paddle, a miner's strop (belt), or several switches braided together.

If the teacher elected to go with switches, she would send the person to be punished out to the wooded area on the edge of the playground to select the switches and braid them together. This was done to give the 'rule breaker' time to consider the pain he was about to feel for his misdeeds.

I never saw a girl receive a spanking. At worst, the teacher might smack a girl's hand with a wooden ruler. The reason for letting the girls off with softer discipline seemed to be rooted in the theory that the humiliation of <u>any</u> public punishment, however light, was enough to deter the girls from repeating their offense.

Besides, just 'flogging' the boys gave the teachers a crowded disciplinary agenda. Hardly a day went by when Miss Hettie didn't feel the need to flogg some male student for violating the rules. When a boy committed a punishable act Miss Hettie would bellow the name of the boy, tell him to come to the front of the classroom and 'take your *tea*'. Translated, that meant he was to come to the front of the classroom, bend over, and take a firm hold on the chalk tray at the bottom of the black board. Then Miss Hettie used belts, paddles, switches—or whatever her disciplinary-tool-of-the-day was—to raise classroom punishment to an art form.

Every boy had his own way of handling the pain of the punishment. <u>Some</u> held on to that chalk tray with a white-knuckle grip and gritted their teeth to keep from yelling or crying. To yell or cry was seen as a sign of weakness. Others would start screaming and shrieking when the first 'swat' of a belt or paddle landed on their buttocks.

Earl and Bill Wright were masters of ear-piercing screams and 'Oh God, you're killin'me' wails.A paddle, belt, or switch barely made <u>first</u> contact with their back-sides before they let out screams that sounded like abused pigs squealing. It worked. The sound was so shrill and curdling that the master disciplinarian, Miss Hettie, rarely got in more than 3 or 4 good licks on either Earl or Bill before she stopped. Judging by the hideous screams coming out of those ol' boys, Miss Hettie probably figured she had already done some permanent damage to their backsides.

"Let that be a good lesson to you! Now you go back to your desk, sit down, and behave yourself", barked Miss Hettie after she had given Bill or Earl a dose of 'tea'. Earl would continue to wail and moan as he walked back to his desk. When he passed my desk he would look at me, wink, smile, and then give out another mournful wail for Miss Hettie's benefit.

Then we had a group of boys labeled as 'spinners. They were boys who declined to grip the chalk tray and grit their teeth in silence while Miss Hettie flogged them. They would stand up-right at the front of the class room. As Miss Hettie swung the paddle, belt, or switch toward their backsides they would quickly run in a circle—to lessen the force of the blow of Miss Hettie's 'disciplinary tool' with their backside. Miss Hettie would grab their left arm, try to hold them still, and swing her, paddle, belt or whatever with her right hand. She was never able to hold the student still while she flailed away at him. He moved in an ever faster circle—Miss Hettie moving with him, flailing away—until both of them were fairly 'spinning' in a circle. I guess 'spinning' had some benefits. It did lessen the impact of the application end of the paddle/belt with the butt of the boy being punished—

and it quickly wore Miss Hettie to a frazzle—chasing that boy around in a circle while trying to give him his proper dose of 'tea'. She would give up a minute or two earlier than she might had she not exerted so much energy spinning in a circle with the student receiving her 'tea'

Some older students—15-16 years old and still in the sixth grade—upon hearing Miss Hettie bellow for them to march up to the front of the class room and 'take your tea'—would opt for 'desertion'. They would run to the back of the classroom, throw open a window, leap through it, and go running off across the playground, the creek bridge, and up or down a road until they were out of sight of the school. This method of avoiding 'tea' was a personal favorite of John and Emory Holton. They saw no shame in fleeing from pain.

Their escape was only a temporary reprieve. Miss Hettie would send word to their parents of their unauthorized flight from the school grounds. Parents of students of this age would do one of two things. They would (1) haul their son back to school the following morning for Miss Hettie to give him 'the whuppin' he's got a-comin' to him'—(2) the parents decided, having only reached the 5th or 6th grade by 16 years of age, their son would be 27-30 years old when he finished 12 years of school and send word to Miss Hettie that their son was dropping out of school 'to work full time'.

It didn't take long for those who 'took their tea' weekly, if not more often, to find a solution for the pain involved in the floggings they were taking.

If there was a 'master' at scheming ways to aoid the pain of 'tea' in school it had to be Harold Sarver. He gathered 15 or so boys around him shortly after one fall school term began. With that maniacal grin that was his trademark, he spoke to the boys in a conspiratorial whisper.

"Boys—getting the stuffin' beat out of you is one thing. Having to feel the pain of it is a 'nother thing. Now lookie' here—all of us is gonna' have to join th' Let-Go-Of-The-Pain Union. You join this union by gettin' some old newspaper at home—fold it just so—and stick it down in the seat of your britches. If Miss Hettie wants to beat on something that bad—let her beat on yesterday's news paper."

Boys began coming to school with old newspapers stuffed in the seat of their pants. All boys caught on. Even those who got rare or infrequent spankings began showing up school, every day, with yesterday's newspapers neatly folded and stuffed down in their pants. Miss Hettie was not a fool. Earl, Bill, Jessie, Goat and a few of the other boys were not 'thinkers'. With boys like them involved, something was bound to go wrong with the plan to avoid pain via newspapers stuffed in the seat of trousers.

The first time she laid that belt across Earl's 'papered' tail he didn't squeal in pain—even flashed a big toothy grin. Earl wasn't very smart—Miss Hettie was. She smacked his behind with her hand and felt that newspaper. She made him pull the paper out of his pants, flogged him with that big belt, and we were back to Earl's unearthly shrieks.

Right after she gave Earl his 'tea', Miss Hettie immediately called all boys to the front of the class room and checked all for a 'papered' behind. Except for 1-2 boys who just never committed disciplinary offenses, every boy was very well 'papered'. She collected enough newspapers out of our pants in one afternoon to start a fire in that miserable old class room stove every day for a month. Harold Sarver and Gene Snyder, who got a dose of 'tea' weekly, were foot stomping mad about the exposure of the 'padding'. They beat ol' Earl half to death on the playground during the next recess period for giving away the secret for a pain free paddling. Of course, recess was followed with Harold and Gene getting a dose of 'tea' from Miss Hettie for beating Earl. The disciplinary routine returned to normal.

Entertainment at the school was self-devised. We played ball, built forts with rocks gathered from the creek, played tag, etc. Over time, we tired of these same games. Something more adventuresome was called for. One of our diversions was to catch someone inside one of the outdoor toilets, get two or three boys together, running three abreast, make a full-speed run at the 5'x5' wooden outhouse, and turn it over with the user in it. The girls became so nervous about using their outhouse they had a friend stand outside and shout a warning if they were about to be turned over.

The girls, hearing a warning from their friend 'standing watch' outside, would come lunging out the door of the toilet, their 'dignity' protected by one hand holding up outer garments, their other hand being used to undo the latch-lock on the door as they fled the little wooden outhouse before their tormentors could turn it over with them still inside. Most of the time they never got out before the little wooden toilet was overturned. At the very least, the warning gave them enough time to grab something and brace themselves until the building came to rest on its side.

Usually, the boys who turned over an outhouse got a big laugh out watching the occupant, be it a boy or girl, come staggering or crawling out of that overturned wooden outhouse—trying to button or zip up their clothes as they did so. It didn't always work out that way.
No doubt, every student in school remembers the time some boys turned over the girls' outhouse while Della Mullins was using it. At 5' 11' and 170 lbs, Della was bigger than most of the boys in Cook School. No one in school wanted to cross swords with Della. The boys didn't know Della was in that toilet when they turned it over. When Della came crawling out of that outhouse, pulling up and zipping her slacks—she had pure fire in her eyes. The closest person to her was Jessie James Barnes. Della, wrongly, assumed Jessie was one of those who turned the outhouse over with her in it. She grabbed Jessie by the shirt collar, lifted him halfway off the ground with one hand, and began slapping his face back and forth with her other hand. She shook him like a rag doll. When she finally had ol' Jessie crying and yelling for the teacher to help him, she threw him down on the ground, kicked him in the rear, called him several unmentionable names, and stomped off across the playground.

Probably—years later—most of the students couldn't, from memory, tell you who was in the toilets when they were overturned—except for the time Della was in that toilet. I daresay every last student will remember the fateful day that toilet was overturned with Della Mullins in it and she pulverized poor ol' innocent Jessie's face.

Turning over an outhouse always resulted in a dose of 'tea' for the offenders. Some of the older boys considered it a small price to pay for some relief from the boredom of the usual games we played.

Providing food and water at school a simple matter. Students carried their lunch from their home in a used paper grocery bag, or a tin lard bucket. No one had heard of the problem with cholesterol, found in lard, at that time. The majority of food was cooked by frying it in lard. The lard came in one quart tin buckets. When all the lard had been used, the bucket was washed out and became a child's lunch pail. Most of us ate sandwiches or milk with bread crumbled in it. Eating what you preferred was no problem. At lunch time every student traded food items in their lunch pails until everybody was fairly satisfied with what they were eating.

Water was supplied by the School Board. That is, they drilled a well and placed a hand pump over it. Vigorous pumping of the well handle would bring water up from the well. They also furnished a two gallon water bucket and a metal water dipper with a long handle. The dipper was always left in the bucket of water drawn from the well. Any student who wanted a drink of water simply walked up to the bucket of water on a table, removed a dipper of water from the bucket, and drank from the dipper. All students drank from the same dipper.

If you were squeamish about drinking out of a dipper used by 50-60 other people you could fashion a cup out of a piece of lined writing paper. Some people became artists at making paper cups that didn't leak down your shirt sleeve while you drank. It never occurred to any of us that the water might contain more bacteria or germs than the dipper. Water testing, in those times, was done by taste or smell. If you could not taste or smell the water it was considered fit for consumption. It was a miracle the water coming out of that old hand pump was as odor free as it was. Much of the water pumped out of the ground in coal fields smelled like sulfur (rotten eggs).

Thus was life at the rural school 'up Page hollow' called Cook School. Years later, after graduation from college, I reflected on the probability of students in a school like Cook School getting an elementary education that would prepare them to successfully cope with and complete studies at the high school and college level. The truth was, those who had parental encouragement and truly wanted to learn— learned well at Cook School.

As nearly as I can remember, the last time I saw Cook School was late in the 1960s. While visiting my parents, I drove up to the school. The school was no longer in use. Students from that area were being bused to a new elementary school on Garden Creek.

Some 20 years later, I paid another visit to the old school—only to find it was no longer there. The school had been torn down. The only part of it left was a few foundation stones. Trees and brush grew where the school, water pump, outdoor toilets, and playground had once been. Nature was fast reclaiming the land. Had I not attended school there in years past I probably wouldn't have known there had ever been a school there at all. The photos I took during my visit there in the 1960s are among the few pieces of evidence that Cook School ever existed.

Over the sixty some odd years that have passed since I attended Cook School I managed to keep track of some of my classmates. Some of us on to become school teachers, draftsmen and designers of naval ships, designers and builders of custom homes that were show places, corporate managers, and one married a doctor. Some found happiness in continuing to live and work all their lives within a few miles of Cook School.

In the mid 1990s, a national newspaper published the names of the ten wealthiest people in the state of Virginia. In the number one position on the list was the name of one of the boys who attended school with me.

Not a bad record for a group of kids who passed through a little country school called Cook School.

THE INTRUDER

Wallis Malcolm worked as a coal loader in the No. 2 mines for Page Pocahontas Coal Co. He was a hard worker; had a ready smile; and not a lot to say about anything; was 30 years of age; had served three years in the Army. Two of those three years were served in the Europe during WW II. When Wallis was mustered out of the service, he managed to bring home a machine gun he had picked up after a battle in Europe. He never planned to use it. He was just fond of that particular gun and thought of it as a souvenir of his days in WW II.

Wallis and Janet rented a home located on the bottom row of houses in Page. There was open land behind their house, a railroad, and finally the creek. There were houses on either side of them and a road ran in front of their house. People living around them were came and went at different hours because the mines ran 24 hours a day. Children ran about, playing, until forced into bed at night.

Wallis was on the night shift 3pm till 11pm. Janet was a nervous woman. Behind her back, some of the camp wives called her a 'fraidy-cat'. Janet had no children. Before marrying Wallis she had lived her entire life with her parents. She seldom spent time away from her parents. She never spent a night alone before marrying Wallis. Her parents' home was in a quiet, rural area. She never heard strange noises at night there. What one did hear in her home was gossip—about homes being broken into by thieves, who also sexually assaulted any woman alone in these houses. Rumors claimed the trauma of the assaults on these women often cause insanity and commitment to the 'looney bin'—the Insane Asylum in Marion.

These grim 'gossip' stories prayed on Janet's mind every night Wallis was at work. The grinding and squeal of the nearby coal tipple sounded, to her, an awful lot like some poor woman's screams because of unspeakable sexual acts by an intruding man of low morals. Those car doors slamming in the road outside, she thought, could be from the cars of 'low-minded' men— coming to pillage her body. The carefree shrieks and yells of children sleigh riding in the road outside sounded dreadfully like the cries of some poor woman trying to defend her body from plunder. Janet lost more of her grip on reality as she listened to these sounds each night.

One week it had snowed heavily, melted a little during the day, and froze with night fall. Janet and Wallis had one of the 'deluxe' houses in Page. That is, it had a front porch. The roof of the porch was made of tin. There were no gutters. Snow, rain, ice, just dripped onto the floor of the front porch or the yard.

Wallis wasn't home, as he usually was, by 11:30 that night. He, in truth, was working overtime. Most every miner's wife knew overtime was involved when a husband didn't walk through the door within an hour after their work shift. Not so with Janet. Night after night, alone in the house, she sat in the dark and listened to strange noises that bode her no good tidings—and, now, her husband had failed to come home. Her mind was close to overload.

The Gods of Darkness had more trials for Janet. The large icicles that had formed on the edge of her roof over the front porch had been loosening all evening due to rising temperatures and the heat rising through Janet's un-insulated living room ceiling. In tandem, 3 or 4 of the two foot long icicles broke off the roof and fell on the wooden floor of the front porch. The falling icicles made a loud noise and shook the front wall of the house.

That was it! Her worst fears were now realized! In her mind, some of those men of 'low morals' had way-laid her husband so he couldn't defend her. In her mind, those men were here! Right on her very porch! Getting ready to break down her door and have their way with her! By god, they weren't gonna' take their pleasure with her! Not without a fight! She wasn't spending the rest of her life at that Marion 'looney-bin'—walking the halls all day in a night-gown, hair not combed, no make- up on, drooling while she mumbled to herself! Not without a fight, she wasn't!

Screaming defiant threats and curses, Janet ran to Wallis's gun cabinet and yanked out his WW II trophy machine gun. Though he had never fired it since be bought it home, Wallis kept the gun cleaned and loaded. You just pointed and pulled the trigger. Janet shouldered the weapon, stood in the middle of the living room, and screamed through the wall at those dirty, rotten, God-less 'Intruders' she just knew were on her front porch, making ready to break down her front door and 'have at her'.

"You low-minded trash ain't gonna' rape me! Not before I get a few of you! I ain't windin' up in Marion because of the likes of you filthy animals!"

With that, she squeezed the trigger, and sprayed bullets back and forth, across and through the front wall of her living room. Her continual screams rose above the deafening clatter of the powerful gun as she poured an endless barrage of bullets through the front wall of her living room.

The big caliber slugs cut through the sheet rock and lap-board siding on the front of the house with the ease of water through a wire screen. The glass in the two living room windows flew out of the frames so fast and with such force it crossed the front porch and landed in the front yard with hardly a shard on the porch. The front door was blown off its hinges, hit the front porch floor once, and bounced 10' into the front yard before it came to rest. Even then, smoke still spiraled upward from the holes the bullets left as they passed through the wooden frame of the door. Some of the slugs that passed through the living room wall struck the 4 x 4 posts that held up the front porch roof. The posts were no match for those machine gun bullets. Some of the posts were literally blown into the yard. Some were cut in half, as if a chain saw had been used on them. Only one post on the northern end of the porch was undamaged.

One post, alone, was not enough. With three of the four posts gone, the porch roof sagged, groaned, swayed, and began its inevitable fall. The porch roof's ceiling rafters were tied to the front wall of the house, so the roof couldn't fall straight down to the porch floor. After Janet's barrage took out the third of the four poles she ceased fire—because she had emptied the machine gun of all its bullets. With the deafening clatter of the machine gun stilled, Janet heard nothing but quiet. She felt sure her intruders were dead or running for their lives.

Then, in the few seconds of silence that followed Janet's 'cease-fire', the porch rafters gave up their support of the roof. But, being tied to the front of the house, the rafters acted as a hinge and caused the entire porch roof to swing back against the front of the house. With a final *whhooooosssh*, the falling roof swung back and slammed into the front of the house.

Janet, who only seconds ago believed she had successfully defended her body and home from being pillaged, now believed the sound of the porch roof's final collapse was the sound of surviving Intruders coming for her again.

Janet grabbed Wallis' Smith & Wesson six shot revolver sent all six of the bullets in the gun through what remained of the living wall and the fallen roof of the front porch. Every bullet from the pistol was fired along with shouted words of profanity that Janet had only heard, but never used before. These were desperate times. She felt the curses might convey her resolve to resist an unsolicited sexual encounter with 'Intruders'—just in case the bullets she had put through that wall didn't lend sufficient clarity to her message of 'no sex'.

Having no more ammunition, the adrenaline drained from her body, Janet collapsed on her sofa, and began to cry. Between sobs, she mumbled threats of using other guns in Wallis' gun cabinet.

It was after mid-night when Janet initiated her one-woman defense of body and home. Except for the sounds of the coal tipple running, the camp, as usual, was rather quiet. Most people not working were in bed. That is, they were before Janet started stitching the front of her house with high caliber machine guns slugs. By the time the last sound of her assault had died away, there were lights on in houses all around her. No one rushed to her house to inquire after her welfare and the cause of the destruction to the front of the house. Fact was, most neighbors felt Janet was 'odd—not right in the head'. Most people around the camp dealt with Janet from a distance, even in the best of times.

After thinking about it for a minute, Fred Childs, Janet's next door neighbor, sent his boy, Mose, over to the camp Superintendent's house to fetch him to the scene. Fred had spent some time in the army. He recognized the sound of a machine gun and knew very well the damage it could do. He didn't know how many rounds Janet had left in that gun. No point in him getting killed trying find out what had set that crazy woman off this time, he decided. Let the Superintendent do it. He got paid oversee this camp—so 'let ol' 'Boss Jack' do it', he thought.

The coal company Superintendent, Jack Carson, was not happy to be called out of bed after midnight. Jack was not a man with a great sense of humor. Running the entire mining operation of Page created stress that offered few reasons to see a lot of humor in life.

Jack had even less reasons to smile when he saw Janet's unauthorized 'alterations' to the front of the company owned house she and Wallis were renting. Jack was also not a man to back down from a situation. Of the old adage, 'sooner or later', Jack chose 'sooner' every time when it came to addressing a problem.

Jack sent Mose back to his house to tell his wife to call the foreman of No. 2 mines and have him send Wallis home immediately. Then he walked slowly and deliberately to the edge of the Malcolm's front yard. He could hear Janet inside the house, crying softly and mumbling to herself. He spoke loudly through what was left of the living room wall to Janet.

"Janet, this is Jack Carson! I don't know what in the name of God has got into you, but I need to talk to you—right now! Now, Janet, you know me. You know who I am. You know I ain't gonna' hurt you. So, I want you to put your gun down, right now! I want you to come on out here where we can see each other—and talk to me. I've sent for

Wallis. He'll be here in a few minutes. Ain't nothing to be scared of. You come on out here and tell me what your problem is. If you don't—I'm a-gonna' have to come in there. If I have to come in there and get you—ain't neither one of us gonna' be happy about it."

Fred Childs had been hiding around the corner of his house, listening to Ol' 'Boss Jack'. Hearing Jack's vow to enter the house, Fred jumped up from his crouched position and peeked the corner of his house.

'WHAT!', Fred thought. 'He's goin' *in* that house? In there with that crazy Janet—who done already used that machine gun to turn the front of her house into a pile of kindling wood? Sheeit—ol' 'Boss Jack' was as crazy as that half-wit Janet! Hell—he's *crazier* than Janet!'

Jack moved a few steps toward his back porch steps. Fred shook his head in disbelief. 'This story ain't over yet—and it don't look like it's gonna' have a quiet ending', he muttered to himself. 'How 'n hell', Fred asked himself, 'did that man ever become Superintendent? One thing for sure', he told himself, 'come daylight tomorrow, the company will be looking for a new Superintendent. Cause I'm looking at a dead man walkin'! The minute 'Boss Jack' sets a foot on those back steps, ol Janet will fill him so full of holes you'll be able to read a newspaper through him.'

Fred stuck his head through the back door of his house and whispered to his wife.

"Christ sake, Naomi—lay down on the floor. I mean as flat as you can get on that floor! Get the kids down there too! The minute ol' 'Boss Jack' sets foot on those back porch steps, Ol' Janet' is gonna' let go with another round of bullets. She'll 'stitch' 'Boss Jack' so full of holes he'll look like Swiss cheese! When Janet uses that machine gun to 'dance' 'Boss Jack' off her back steps a few stray bullets will almost sure as hell hit our house. I sure do wish that 'radio preacher' you are always sending money to was here right now—to pray us out of this mess!"

Just when 'Boss Jack' was about to step up on Janet's back porch steps, a truck pulled to a sliding stop in front of the bullet riddled house and Wallis jumped out. He stood looking at the front of his house in shock. Jack took Wallis aside and held a conversation with him that no one could hear. Wallis nodded and then called out to Janet.

At the sound of his Wallis's voice, the back door slowly opened and Janet cautiously peeked out. When she saw Wallis, Janet walked out on the back porch, sobbing, and held out her open arms to Wallis. As Wallis stepped up on the back porch Janet began to wail incoherently about men trying to attack her and how she had fought them off with his guns. Wallis comforted her and led her back into the house through the back door. It was the only way in or out of the house, for the moment, save for a few good windows.

Not a lot of detail came out in the days that followed. Wallis took Janet to her parents' home the next day. Jack

Carson demanded he take his machine gun out of Page too. A week later, Wallis moved his furniture to a house several miles from the camp.

Wallis worked on in Page mines for several years. Jack Carson continued as Superintendent of the mining camp of Page for another 10-15 years. Fred Childs never stopped telling people how close 'Boss Jack' was to 'meeting his maker' when Wallis showed up. No one ever saw Janet in Page again.

AVOIDING THE WAR

Trig Saunders was born, raised, and lived his entire life in Burton Hollow off Garden Creek. Burton Hollow was reached by a dirt road, along a small stream, that ran three miles to the top of the mountain. Most of the people living there were, in some way, related to each other.

Trig could read, write, and count—barely. Most information in Trig's brain was received through his ears. Trig was satisfied with the spoken word as a medium of learning—preferably from those he knew and trusted. News and information of value to him was generally limited to (1) the needs and welfare of his immediate family (2) the price of gas and tires for his log hauling truck (3) who was paying the best price for 'saw logs' delivered (4) hunting and hunting guns, and (5) the weather.

Most other information, to Trig, was irrelevant and a waste of time. There were no TVs in the area during the early '50s. Except for the country music broadcast on the GRAND OLDE OPRY radio show on Saturday night, radios were of no use to Trig. What little he heard on a radio, other than country music, didn't interest him at all. Newspapers printed news that had nothing to do with him—the print was so small it was hard to read—and they charged a nickel for a newspaper. 'Dam waste of hard-to-come-by money', according to Trig.

No, Trig considered himself to be a man who confined his

intake of information to *essentials*. Not to say Trig was a man to belittle *good* information. Actually, Trig prided himself on being an authority on any subject in which he had an interest. Regardless of whether the subject was about recognizing good and valuable timber, how best to care for a truck, or the best way to position your body to get off a 'balls-on-accurate' gun shot at wild game.

Moreover, Trig insisted on being recognized as the voice of authority when he spoke. He demanded everyone's full attention, be his audience one or ten people. It never occurred to him that most people considered him to be illiterate, and only listened to him because it took less effort to listen to him for a moment than try to explain to him why he was wrong. Clyde Allen said he only listened to Trig's b. s. was because 'he's so stupid he's interesting'.

It had rained hard the night before. Trig pulled into Joe Boxley's service station to fill up the gas tank of his big truck. He had a huge load of massive oak logs on his truck. He was making his usual run to a wood processing plant in Aberdeen. While Joe was pumping gas into his truck, Trig drifted over to a group of 7-8 men standing in the office of the service station. He began telling them how he had killed a 'coon' last night. One or two of the men glanced backwards at Trig. That was enough to make Trig believe he had the attention of the entire group. Trig began his step by step account of killing the coon—with one shot.

"My dogs done tree'd this 'coon' up this big ol' poplar tree. I seen 'im—a-way up in that there tree", said Trig. "I got down on my one knee—jes' like this."

Completely oblivious to the thick layer of doughy mud on the ground from last night's hard rain, Trig dropped to his right knee. The leg of his overalls sunk into the black mud. One of the men looked at Trig, looked at the leg of his overalls soaking up the wet mud, and shook his head as he turned away from Trig. 'Ig-n'rant fool', he thought.

"Then—I done 'scotched' my other foot real good and lined up my rifle—."

Trig stopped in mid-sentence when he realized not one man was facing him—let alone listening to him. He stood up quickly and strode toward the group of men.

'Bygod, he thought, 'I'm a-gonna' find out why ain't nobody a-listenin' to me—why they ain't a-showin' me no respect. Ain't a better hunter in this county—and they got no call to be treatin' me like this.'
As Trig got close to the group of men, he could hear a man's voice talking in a forboding tone. A tone that Trig interpreted to mean 'bad news.'

"Who's that a-talkin'?" demanded Trig.

"Trig—be quiet! We're trying to hear the radio—about the war that's done broke out", said Louie Stone.

The word 'war' got Trig's full attention. He listened intensely to the radio announcer's grave voice as he relayed the decision of President Dwight Eisenhower to send the U.S. Marines into Lebanon to put down an outbreak of war between the citizens of Lebanon. Trig listened without a word until the newscaster concluded the news bulletin.

Trig listened as the men began discussing Eisenhower's decision to send the Marines into Lebanon to put a quick stop to the fighting and shooting before it spread. As they talked, Trig's mind began to process what he had heard on the radio—and what they men were saying now.

'Wait a minute', he thought. Anger began to swell in him. 'Wait jes' one minute! War in Lebanon? That's plumb crazy, he told himself.' He had to get something straight with the men around him.

"Hold on there, boys! Where'd that radio fella' say that there war was a-goin' on?" asked Trig with his eyes narrowed to slits.

"Over in Lebanon—you heard him", said Aubrey.

"Aww—hail far! If'n that don't beat all!" snarled Trig, as he slammed his hand down on the table. "Them fools—a-fightin' 'mongst themselves—an' they ain't got nuthin' that anybody wants! Hail—'cept for the court house, a grocery store, a Ford dealer, and a res'trant—they ain't got nuthin' in that whole town worth a hoot! Leastways—nuthin' worth fightin' for! Nuthin' but a bunch'a ol' poor-boy farmers scratchin' 'round in some ol' worn out dirt!"

The men stared at Trig with a puzzled look. His angry outburst was so unlike Trig's usual laid-back attitude. He usually didn't know, or care, about world affairs. They stared quizzically at Trig as he paused in his tirade.

"Trig", said Joe Boxley, "What'n the Sam Hill are you goin' on about? What do you know 'bout Lebanon anyhow?"

"Wha'd you mean, 'wha'd I know 'bout Lebanon'? How'n hail do you think I get logs to Abin'don? Huh? I go through that there town 5 days a week! Why, I drive smack-dab through the middle of that there lil' piss-ant town, on Rt. 11—ever day! It's the quickest way to get to Abin'don from here. An' I'll tell you 'nuther thing—Mr. Joe Boxley. I even *stop* in Lebanon sometimes—to eat lunch! Yeah—right next to—*gawdamighty*, what'r they a-thinkin' 'bout! Lost their fool minds!"

The men began to smile. Joe wanted to explain to Trig that the Lebanon involved in this war was a nation thousands of miles away, across an ocean. While he tried to think of a simple way of explaining that the nearby town of Lebanon, Va., some 30 miles away from where they were standing, was still very much at peace, Trig began ranting again.

"Well, bygod, I ain't a-gonna' get involved in no daggon' war! It ain't none of my business—so I ain't driving through there—let them fools shoot my truck all to pieces—maybe kill me in the bargain! No sir—I make a livin' with my truck! I worked hard to git it! I'll not have those fools destRayin' it! Tell'ya' what—I'm goin' down to Vansant, take Rt. 83 over to St. Paul, and hook up with Rt. 11 at Hansonville. That's a good 8 miles west of Lebanon. It's maybe 20 miles further to Abin'don that way, but it beats gittin' caught crossways in a shootin' war an' shot to pieces by a bunch'a fools a-fightin' over nuthin'!"

"Trig—let me talk to you for a minute about this war in Lebanon", said Joe Boxley.

"Naw—naw, I ain't really got no time to talk to you right now, Joe. I'm already late on this here run to Abin'don. On top'a that, I gotta' drive way 'round by St. Paul. That'll take me an ex'tre hour. I'll talk to you 'nuther time", said Trig as the engine on his big truck roared to life.

Some of the men moved forward, waving to Trig to stop his truck. They were shouting for him to stop—that he need not take the long way to Aberdeen. Trig motioned them out of his way as his truck rumbled on to the highway.

"Let him go", said Joe. "Poor ol' hard-headed, ign'rant rascal never did have sense enough to listen to reason. Just have to let him learn his lesson the hard way."

The men stood in the work bay of the service station and watched Trig and his truck load of logs begin a long drive to Aberdeen—by a route he was sure would safely avoid a raging war being fought on his normal route of travel through southwest Virginia.

Trig continued to use this round-about route to Aberdeen for a month, until Joe Buford borrowed a globe of the world from the local elementary school and used it to convince Trig (1) there existed, across an ocean, a nation called Lebanon, which was at war (2) Lebanon, *Virginia* was not at war—and never had been.

BO PEEP

In the summer of 1956, I came home from college looking for a summer job. My Uncle Vern was a senior member of the Virginia House of Delegates. He had a work program set up with the Buchanan County Division of the Virginia Dept. Of Highways that provided summer jobs for 5-6 boys who needed to earn money for college tuition. I got one of the jobs. The highway department assigned me to the 'bridge gang'. It was on this bridge gang that I met and worked with, Bo Peep Dawson.

Bo was 25-26 years old. If he had a legal name other than Bo Peep, none of us knew what it was. When asked, Bo said it was the name by which he had been called all his life. Actually, he said, most folks just called him 'Bo'—and that was ok by him.

Bo recalled his mother saying she bought a bottle of household ammonia with a brand label of 'Bo Peep' on it right before he was born. She thought the name had 'a real nice ring to it', so she named him Bo Peep. 'Maybe, your mom told you she saw the name in a book of nursery rhymes—not on a bottle label', we suggested. Bo brushed aside that suggestion with a quick shake of his head.

"Naw, we didn't have hardly no books a'tall around our house—couldn't afford 'em. Didn't nobody read 'em no how. Naw, momma tol' me she got my name off an ammonia bottle."

Bo was easy-going, honest, hard-working, —and extremely frustrated by having very little or no sex in his life. Bo was only interested in dates with girls that led to sex within minutes—if not sooner.

Oh—I should mention that Bo was illiterate. He could not read, write, or count—not even money. Because of these handicaps and his meager social skills, his first date with a girl—if he actually got a date—was usually his last. Bo's simple views, poor people skills, and lack of training in acceptable 'dating rituals' saddled him with a disastrous, 'let's do it' approach to girls—15 minutes into the date.

He didn't see the need for subtlety, compliments, patience, and gifts as a part of the dating ritual. In his mind, these were time wasting preambles. In his view, the cause for any meeting between single boys and girls was to satisfy their sexual needs. He was certain female sexual appetites matched his—so why not see to each other's mutual cravings by, 'jes' gettin' butt nakid an' a-doin' it to each other—rat-cheer, rat-now'.

So far, Bo's approach had led to a nothing from the girls except an outraged 'NO!' A few punctuated the 'NO' with profanity. Those highly offended slapped his face.

The men in our bridge-gang decided to become mentors to Bo in his quest for a successful relationship with girls. We decided our tutoring would have to include some training in basic reading, writing, counting, as well as social skills. Our amateur 'training' and Bo's habit of putting his own 'twist' on our training led to some interesting incidents that summer.

There were 6 men and a foreman in our bridge work-gang. We repaired worn bridges and built some new ones. Most of the bridges we repaired were in rural areas. Nearly all were made of steel with wooden floors. The work truck would drop us off each morning at a bridge over some river or creek with our tools and a flat bottom river boat.

One or two of us would work 'top-side'—standing on the floor of the bridge. The rest of us would carry our tools and the boat down a river bank to the river's edge. We'd use the boat to float men and tools out to the steel support columns rising from the river bed to the underside of the bridge. We'd anchor the boat, climb up the lattice work of the supports, set up work cradles on the 'under-side' of the bridge floor, hook up our safety harnesses, and go to work on the bridge floor. It took a while to get that boat in the water, row it out to the support columns, climb those columns, haul up our tools, and get a work platform set up under the bridge. Once in place, we stayed there except for our lunch break or a call of nature.

About two weeks into summer, we were assigned to repair the Bill Yount Bridge over Dismal River. The bridge was about 30 feet above the river and 75-80 feet long. It was an old single lane bridge with a lot of broken and rotting floor boards which were bolted to steel girders.

On one end of the bridge the road began its run up Bill Yount Mountain. There was also an old, unpainted house with a small yard setting on a hillside near that end of the bridge. The family living there included two girls in their late teens or early twenties. The other end of the bridge ended perpendicular to Dismal River Road. You could go right or left on Dismal River Road, or straight across the road into the dirt parking lot of W.W. Wilson's General Merchandise store.

W.W.'s country store was an old, white, clapboard building. It covered some 30 x 30 feet of uneven wooden floor, with the only illumination inside the cavernous old store provided by two bare light bulbs hanging from the ceiling. Mr. Wilson's name was painted across the front of the store above the front porch roof in faded, black letters—three feet high.

W.W. was the owner and sole employee. He was 80 years old—so he said. Judging by his shriveled body, watery eyes, and pace of movement, most of us thought he had long since passed his eightieth year of life on this earth. But, he was a genial fellow, always had a smile on his face, honest to a fault, could add and subtract in his head faster than most of our crew, and welcomed us to his store every time we darkened the door.

As the weeks wore on, the work on the bridge progressed. We took our 40 minute lunch breaks on the porch of W.W.'s store. We devoted part of every lunch break to improving Bo's education and social skills. As we washed down our lunches with a cold Pepsi from W.W.'s cooler, we taught Bo to write his own name, drilled him in the proper rituals for dating girls, and W.W. taught Bo the basic skills of counting money. W.W. brought out a dozen items from the shelves of his store—lined them up on the porch of the store—and placed coins, or combinations of coins, that would buy these items in front of each of the items. He continued doing this until Bo could place the right coin or combination of coins in front of each item he wished to buy. Bo learned to count money this way and could recognize numbers and coins up to one dollar.

We didn't have enough time to teach BO the entire alphabet. Using an old broken tree limb, and the dirt in W.W.'s parking lot, we taught Bo the letters in his name by having him draw the letters in the dirt. At the end of 2 weeks, he could print his name in the dirt in front of W.W.'s store porch. Not a demanding leap in reading & writing when your first name is 'Bo'.

To increase his chances of having successful dates with girls, we hammered into Bo the time honored customs of talking to girls about things that interested *them*—taking them places *they* wanted to go—giving them gifts likely to please *them*. We had him memorize his 'new' motto— 'If *she* isn't happy, *you* won't be happy'. Not until you have spent 2 weeks doing these things with the girl will you try to even *kiss* her, we told him. Don't even *think* about mentioning sex until you have dated her for 3 months— maybe even longer, we cautioned.

After several weeks of lunch time coaching, we could see a visible change in Bo. Seeing his pride in being able to endorse his pay check by printing his name was our reward. To see the smile on W.W.'s face when Bo laid a dime on the counter to pay for his Pepsi told us how proud he was to have played a part in Bo's 'formal' education. Several weeks into his 'training', Bo had not yet found an opportunity to test his new social/dating skills.

We had been working on the Bill Young Bridge for three weeks. The heat of each day registered in the high 80s or low 90s. Each day, beginning no later than 10 am and continuing steadily until our 4:30 pm quit time, the two girls living in that old shack of a house at the north end of the bridge would go through their day-long sun bathing ritual.

They were truly blessed with voluptuous bodies, and were proud of what genes and nature had done for them. Every morning the girls would parade into their front yard, spread a raggedy old quilt on the grass, rub tanning oil on their bodies until they glistened, and lie there soaking up sun. They turned from their backs to their stomachs, and again to their backs, every 5 minutes. They stood up every 15 minutes to stretch their bodies into provocative poses and adjust their bikinis. As the day waned into afternoon and the heat of the day increased, they sprayed water on each other until their brief two piece bathing suits were plastered to their bodies

It was quite a show and a periodic relief from the grinding, hot, work on the bridge. We were satisfied to sneak an occasional glance at the girls, and considered them 'eye candy'. All of us except Bo.

We had to, repeatedly, prod him to keep his mind on his work and stop staring at the girls before his lack of attention caused one of us to drop 30 feet into the river. One afternoon he almost fell into the river when he released his safety belt so he could lean out further and get a better view of the girls spraying water on each other. That near accident cost Bo a string of profanities from our boss, Buck Blevins. Truthfully—Buck's curses and threats had but a short term effect on Bo's obsession with watching the girls.

The daily sounds and routine of our work were broken by Bo's constant, mumbled comments to himself as he squinted at the girls from his perch on our work cradle hanging beneath the bridge. His mumbling alternated between pleas to God and petitions to the girls for some relief from the frenzy of sexual frustration the girls were drowning him in. The last few words of his sing-song pleas were muttered loudly.

"Lawd, have mercy ON MY SOUL! Ohhh girls—won'cha have a lil' mercy PLEASE! Lawd—those wimmen are a-drivin' me right into a NERVOUS BREAKDOWN! I do b'leve that woman has done TOOK HER BRA OFF! I'm jist—tore ALL TO PIECES! That there woman is a-gonna' keep on till she messes up MY MIND! LOOKA' YONNN-DUR'! The one with the black hair done shook HER TAIL AT ME! Sum'body sure oughta' make her stop a-doin' that! You think her Daddy's in the house? You think he's got a gun?"

After a couple of days at the bridge we just answered Bo with grunts of 'yeah' or 'I dunno'. I doubt Bo was actually listening to our answers. He was too busy fantasizing about the girls and talking to himself to hear anything we had to say. Occasionally, we had to yell at him when his lack of attention almost got one of us knocked off the work cradle and into the river.

One afternoon, in our fourth week at the bridge, the girls—their skimpy bathing suits—it just became too much for Bo to deal with. He was working on the underside of the bridge with me and two other men. Without a word, he disconnected his belt and climbed down the bridge support column to the river. He jumped into our work boat and rowed it to the river bank. No one said anything. We assumed Bo was answering a call of nature. Bo tied up the boat on the river bank, crawled 30 feet up the bank, and walked across the road to W.W.'s store. At this point we began to give each other 'where is he going' looks.

In less than a minute, Bo came out of the store. He had a small brown bag in his hand. He crossed the road and walked onto the top side of the bridge. Still without a word of explanation, he walked right over our heads. His eyes were glued to the girls in their yard on the other side of the river. Buck, our boss, spoke up first.

"Bo, I'd like to get this bridge floor finished—this month, if you don't mind. Where n' hell you goin'? That's right, boy, I'm talkin' to YOU!"

As Bo walked above our heads we talked to him through the cracks of the bridge flooring.

"Bo—my good man. What's in the paper bag? Where're you goin'? Bo, you better answer ol' Buck. He's already in one of his 'moods' today—and you takin' a walk during work hours ain't helpin' his disposition a-tall", said Chester.

"Bo—! Hey, lame brain! I hope you ain't figurin' on talkin' to them girls!" said Shorty, whose approach to people didn't include the use of subtlety. "Listen to me, you half-wit! Their daddy might jes' be in that house—and he might jes' have a gun. Don' go in that there yard without askin' permission first! Dammit, Bo, are you listenin' to me?"

Through all of this, Bo never uttered a word. He never broke stride. He never took his eyes off the girls on their blanket. Without hesitation, Bo walked across the yard of the leaning, ramshackle, old house until he was standing right over the girls and their blanket. They stood up, smiled at Bo, adjusted their bikinis, and began talking to him. We were too far away to hear the conversation between Bo and the girls. All we could do was watch. Not a one of us made a sound or took our eyes off Bo and the girls. Considering Bo's lack of restraint around girls, none of us had a good feeling about his visit with these girls.

After a brief conversation with the girls, Bo got a sly grin on his face and handed the little brown bag to one of the girls. She took the bag, opened it, and peered inside. With a look of disbelief on her face, she handed the bag to her sister. While her sister was looking inside the bag, Bo pointed to their blanket, began talking so rapidly his words sounded as if they were running together. He began to unbutton his shirt as the grin on his face stretched from ear to ear.

Suddenly, the second girl's head snapped up from that little brown bag. With a look that clearly telegraphed surprise and anger, she jammed one hand down on her hip, while passing the bag back to her sister. After the girls exchanged disbelieving looks, their mouths began to open and close rapidly. Their voices rose to a shout. We didn't have any problem hearing *their* end of the conversation. If their salty language could be taken as an indicator, those girls weren't 'well-bred young ladies'—as defined by Miss Manners' *Rules of Etiquette*.

They raised the use of profanity to an art form as their shrill voices filled the air. Their condemnation of Bo, whatever was in that little brown bag, and Bo's proposal to them was made crystal clear. They pointed fingers at him, punched the air with their fists, and waved their arms wildly in the air. When they walked close to Bo their faces, just inches from his, bobbled rapidly up and down. You could read the obvious anger and aggression in their expressions—even from our work site 150 feet away.

Bo, stunned into silence at first, became irate and indignant. He responded in like kind to the girls' profanity, anger, shouts, and hostile gestures. After one final angry reply, Bo made a gesture at them—a gesture communicated through the extended middle finger. He turned on his heel and stomped out of their yard to the road. One of the girls, screaming cuss words, took the little brown bag and its contents and threw it with all her might at Bo's back as he walked away. The bag bounced off Bo's shoulder. He didn't look back at the girls or give any indication that he knew or cared about being hit by the bag.

Hands stuffed in his pockets, head hanging down in disappointment, brow wrinkled in puzzlement, Bo walked back across the bridge without a word. He gave no indication he heard one word of the questions we shouted to him as he re-crossed the bridge.

"You want to tell me what n' hell that was all about?" said Buck as Bo passed him on the bridge top side. "What'd you do? Huh? You better by-god answer me, Bo! If those girls complain to my boss an' he gets in my face—so help me god, I'll transfer your ass to the brush gang! An' you can mark that down, boy!"

The absolute worst of all highway jobs was the 'Brush Gang'. Cutting roadside brush, briars, poison ivy, and trees with a heavy brush axe—mosquitoes, big enough wear tennis shoes, eating you alive—snakes, just waiting to sink their fangs in your leg. The misery of a job on that gang was almost beyond description.

Then Buck turned his anger on the rest of us. His eyes were blazing as he pointed his finger at the rest of us.

"I lay this whole thing your door! You and your 'trainin' of Mr. 'Half-Wit' Dawson here, on how to socialize with girls! Oh yeah—the whole lot of you! And now look at what I got on my hands! Oh boy—if this ain't a 'Frosty Friday'! I just hope that shack those two sunbathin' hootchie-coochies live in ain't got a phone in it. If it does, they're on that phone right now—and, likely as not, there'll be a Sherriff's car a-pullin' up here inside of 30 minutes! Tell you one thing—if the Sheriff does come a'callin'—I'm tellin' him to take every last one of you in with Mr. Romeo Dawson! Yessir—let you see how you like trainin' Mr. Romeo from inside a jail cell!"

"I didn' do nuthin' tuh' 'em, Buck! Even tuck 'em a gift— and look what it got me. You try to be nice to some people—they don't 'preciate it! Treat you like you ain' no better 'n a chicken in th' middle of the road at rush hour!", said Bo, as he retraced his steps down the bank, jumped into the boat, paddled to mid river, and made the high climb back up to our work area under the bridge.

Chester, in his usual calm and unhurried manner, spoke quietly to Bo.

"I know you wouldn' deliberately do nuthin' mean to nobody, Bo. I know your heart's in the right place. You wanna' tell us what went on in that yard over there, Bo? From our viewpoint under this here bridge—didn' look like things went real well for you. Maybe we could hep' you—if you was to tell us what happened with them girls."

"I done jus' like you boys taught me. You seen me—I brung 'em girls a gift. I bought a nickel's worth of peppermint stick candy—five sticks it was—from ol' man W.W.—for 'em girls. I acted real nice. I walked up in their yard—and I first talked to 'em—you know, socialized. Jes' like you boys tol' me to, Chester. I tol' 'em girls, I says 'I purely admire you ladies. You're mighty fine lookin' wimmin'. You sure do fill up 'em lil' bitty bathin' suits yuh' got on. An' you girls strut around this yard prettier 'n any show-hoss I ever seen'. I did jus' like you boys taught me, Chester—took time to butter 'em up 'fore I got down to bizniss."

"And one of 'em says, 'Oh, thank you. You're so nice. What's your name?' I tol' them my name—then I figured we'd done 'bout enough talkin' and socializin'. So I gave 'em that bag of peppermint stick candy and tol' 'em I bought 'em that candy, to 'do it' with me—and did they wanna' 'do it' on their blanket there in the yard or go in the house."

"Then, for no reason a-tall, they flew mad at me. Started cussin' at me—asked me what kinda' girls I thought they was. I tol' 'em I didn' know—I jes' met 'em. They yelled at me—tol' me 'at they didn' know who 'n hell I thought I was—that I mus' be stupid, and to get th' hell outtta' their yard. Said they didn' want nothin' to do with me. So I told them to take that candy and stick it up their 'nigh-way'! Then I walked off, and they throwed that candy I bought 'em at me and hit me in th' back! 'Em girls must be crazier 'n hell—'ats all I can figure out."

Our first impulse was to laugh uncontrollably. An offer of five cents worth of hard, stale, candy for sex with two girls. Knowing Bo would not understand and be hurt by our laughter, we smiled, sympathized with him, and told him some women just need a little more pampering than others. The work gang kept quiet until we dropped Bo off that afternoon at the highway shop. Then we doubled over in laughter for 5 minutes.

Despite the set-back with the sun-bathing girls, we continued to coach Bo. We told him one of the best places to meet girls was at church 'tent-meeting revivals'. Summer was the time tent meeting revivals took place nearly every week in dozens of communities and towns throughout the county. They usually lasted a week.

Parents who limited the places their daughters were allowed to go on their own or, worse, never let them out of their sight, would bring these daughters to a religious revival held in an open field under some old army surplus tent. These same well intentioned parents assumed that any male attending these revivals was trustworthy and of high morals. Within bounds, they would entrust their daughters to these men—un-chaperoned. Bo found the idea appealing.

When ol' Bo showed up at one of the 'tent meeting revivals', one girl caught his eye right off. According to Bo, 'she had dark hair, real white skin, brown eyes, and was just put together real good'. Her name was Vicey (pronounced vY-cee)

Bo attended the revival nightly, from Monday through Thursday. He practiced self-restraint where his sexual urges were concerned, even though it tested every fiber of his being. He met and chatted with Vicey's parents each evening. He sat next to them at the revival, singing, shouting, and showing unbridled exuberance for the sermon throughout each service. At the end of Thursday evening's service, Bo asked the parents if he might walk their daughter home. He received their approval.

Walking a girl home in the mid 1950s in a rural area often meant walking along unlighted dirt or gravel roads. Sometimes the roads were little better than goat paths. Bo knew the area well. He knew of several good spots alongside the road where sweethearts could stop to 'pleasure' themselves. As Bo walked along that dirt road he was unsure of the best approach for taking his relationship with Vicey to the next level. Bo's worries over how best to gain carnal knowledge of Vicey were wasted. As it turned out, Vicey was 22 years old and had, despite her parent's close oversight, enjoyed sexual relations with several partners before Bo came along. In fact, she had a lusty appetite for the physical side of romance.

The following day, during lunch on the porch of W.W.'s

store, Bo related his story of that walk home with Vicey. As Bo told it, this is what happened.

They had walked half a mile when Bo could contain himself no longer. Bo made his move.

"I sure would like to kiss you!" Bo said.

"OK, but let's go over there in the woods!" Vicey said, as she led Bo to an area under some trees just off the road.

Bo's kiss was accepted and returned with enthusiasm by Vicey. While Bo was pondering his next move, Vicey became impatient

"She done grabbed me, kissed me again, and rubbed herself up against me real hard!" said Bo.

Bo must have still appeared uncertain, so Vicey took the lead. In less than a minute their clothing was off and used to form a blanket on the ground. Bo thought he had truly found a heaven on earth. Vicey's participation in their love making was total and unbridled. Bo and Vicey made love vigorously, for what Bo said was 'a right good while'.

"I couldn' hardly keep up with her she was a-movin' so fast. She kep' on hollerin' and yellin' and a-goin' at me till I was near wore plumb out. That woman must surely like God—'cause she kept on a-yellin' his name while we was doin' 'it'", said Bo, shaking his head as he recalled the moment.

His lust satisfied, Bo immediately thought of the time that had passed and wondered if the parents were concerned that Bo and their daughter hadn't arrived at their home yet. Even worse, he thought, what if they are out a-lookin' for Vicey and find us here in the woods with no clothes on.

Bo jumped to his feet, began putting on his clothes, and, repeatedly, urged Vicey to do the same. Bo's new love-mate had other ideas. Vicey wanted to savor the moment, bask in the afterglow, take a few moments to regain her breath.

"I'm tired. And it feels good just layin' here and restin' a while. Ain't you tired?" said Vicey.

Vicey continued to lie there, sighing, making low, moaning sounds, and begging Bo to rejoin her on the ground.

"No! We ain't got no more time to be a-layin' around and a-doin' 'it' no more! Your folks are prob'ly out a-lookin' for us right now! C'mon now, git up from there and put your clothes on. We gotta' go!" Bo pleaded.

"No! I'm tired. I done tol' you I'm not getting up till I rest a while!" said Vicey as she reached up to pull Bo back to the ground.

Bo used her outstretched hand as an opportunity to pull her to her feet. He pulled on her arm and had her halfway into a standing position when Vicey realized Bo's intentions didn't include more sex.

"She turned on me", lamented Bo. "She let her whole weight sag on her arm and started kickin' at me. She tried to kick me in th' balls. So I jus' let go of her, and she fell back on the ground!"

"I told you I don' wanna' get up! I'm gonna' lay here 'til I am dam' good and ready to get up! Don't you pull on me no more neither!"

Bo was frantic. He knew had to find some way to persuade Vicey to get up and go home before her parents found them. He knew if her parents found them—with vicey naked—. Well, they might 'whup' her—he reckoned—but it was just about a sure fire bet her Daddy would kill him

When he got to the point in the story where Vicey kicked at him and refused to get up, Bo paused as if he had concluded the story. All of us had become so engrossed in the story that we had stopped eating and were giving Bo our full attention. Even W. W. was sitting on the porch— not moving a muscle—all ears.

"Well, what th' hell happened then? When she wouldn' get up, what did ya' do? Don't tell me you stood there like a dummy till her parents found you!" said Buck.

Bo may have been illiterate, but that didn't mean he couldn't solve problems.

"Naw", said Bo. "I raked me some old dead tree leaves up around her. Then I took my Zippo lighter and set them leaves on fire. I had a ring of fire burning around her. She come off that ground real quick then—yessir!"

None of us could believe our ears. We looked at each other. Initially, we thought Bo was fantasizing. Then, on second thought, we knew Bo had so little guile that he would tell the truth before taking the trouble to concoct a lie. The latter required too much thought and work.

I don't think the bridge gang laughed as hard through the remainder of the summer as we did at that particular moment. Bo went on to tell us that Vicey did put her clothes on, cursing him loudly as she did so. She refused to let Bo walk her the rest of the way home and promised to have her Father give him a 'whuppin' if he showed his face at the revival meeting' the following night. Bo took her at her word. He didn't show up for that revival, or any others that summer.

We continued to work with and coach Bo for the remainder of the summer. It is with pride that I say Bo could print his name, read a little, count numbers/coins up to a dollar, and count out small amounts of money when I went back to college in September of that year.

The following summer I got a better paying summer job with a construction company. When I finished college I accepted a job on the other end of the state. As years passed, on visits back to my parents' home, I would occasionally see some members of the bridge gang while in town. But I never again saw Bo Peep Dawson. I regret that. I would have enjoyed talking with Bo again.

As decades passed, in moments of fanciful imagination, I wondered if I went down to the Bill Young Bridge and stood there a while—would Bo come along?

Nah—not likely. Maybe my memory of the 1950s version of Bo is better—for him and me.

THE HOME PLACE

Our parents began married life with little money. Not too long after I was born my two sisters were born—with my brother coming along 12 years after me. My Dad was trying to work his way up in the world of retail stores that belonged to coal mining corporations. Managing stores didn't pay a lot of money in the early years in 1930-40-50s.

After clothing, feeding and educating us, Mom and Dad managed to save a little money each year. The operative word in the previous sentence is 'little'. We lived in rental houses—the years rolled by. My parents were in their late 40s when a nice piece of available residential property and my parents' savings matched to the advantage of everyone involved.

My parents became the owners of one of the better homes in the area. A large white house with a garage setting above the road, it became known as 'The Home Place' to our family. It came with 7 acres, a second smaller home complete with the same family who had rented it for years, a chicken house, a lawn that covering three quarters of an acre, English Boxwood shrubbery, towering oak trees, and a flourishing mass of wild roses covering the bank between the lawn and highway. As well as I can remember, my parents paid $7200 for the entire thing.

On Labor Day of 1954, more than half way through my Dad's life span, we moved into the first and only home my parents ever owned. The whole family was proud of that home, but none more so than my parents. They adored that home, cared for it lovingly, and worked tirelessly to improve it. Someone was perpetually mowing grass, whitewashing trees, painting the inside and/or outside of the house, polishing hardwood floors, closing in a porch, pouring concrete walks, raking leaves, or sweeping the driveway. Even after growing up and moving away from home, my siblings and I knew that a return home, just for a visit, would, involve work on some project around the house.

Even after my Dad retired, he wore out two brooms a year with his daily routine of sweeping every last foot of our 90 foot driveway—all the way down to the highway. Not an acorn, not a leaf, not even a single dime-sized pebble was allowed to rest on that driveway between dawn and dusk. My Mom, who continued to teach school for several years after Dad retired, would sometimes reach for her Windex and roll of paper towels—only to find both totally depleted. While she was at school, Dad would, in a month's time, run through two big bottles of Windex and half dozen rolls of paper towels as he cleaned glass inside and outside the house.

This went on for 7-8 years before Dad died of a heart attack in his early 70s. Mom lived on in the house and continued to meticulously care for it until she retired three years later. The years were close to the mid-1970s. Her energy for maintaining the house at the level she and Dad pursued for years was fast waning. Coal mining companies, at that time, were buying residential property in the area—for use in mining coal or for storage. Mom sold the home-place to a coal mining company for a good price and moved to the other end of the state.

Soon after the mining company bought our home place the demand for coal dropped drastically. The mining company put their ambitious plans for using our home place as a drilling site for coal or a storage site on hold. Someone approached the mining company about renting our house on a short term basis.

They rented the house to some family—and later to other families. None of the tenants took good care of the house. After 3-4 years the mining company rented the house to a building contractor named Freddie Mosely. Freddie and I had been class mates in elementary school. He was a good man—reputed to be one of the better home builders in the area. Freddie had married a very pretty girl from that area. They had one child—a daughter. The daughter was to be the only child they would have. She was 9-10 years old when Freddie and his wife rented our old home place.

Freddie and his wife had been tenants in our former home for a year when problems began to surface in their marriage. Freddie suspected his wife having an affair with another man. Whether this was true or not depended on who you asked. Over a period of months, Freddie's wife, so he said, increasingly rebuffed his efforts to have intimate relations with her. Finally, they stopped sharing the same bed altogether.

Freddie openly accused his wife of having an affair with another man—or men. She denied any relationship with any man outside their marriage, sexual or casual. She did admit to no longer wanting to be married to Freddie. She was more interested in a separation—one which included Freddie moving out of the house, immediately. Hostilities between the two came to a head one evening. After an argument filled with fiery accusations, and passionate denials, Freddie packed his bags and moved out of the house.

Freddie became obsessed with the idea that his wife was sleeping with another man. He had no hard evidence, but he just couldn't let the suspicion go. It was on his mind, night and day. He knew she wasn't going to voluntarily confess to adultery. That meant he had to 'catch her in the act'. This would force her admission of betrayal and keep her from 'taking everything I got', daughter included, in a divorce court. In Freddie's mind, it was one thing for his wife to sleep with another man while living under a roof provided by him—quite another to rub his nose in it by taking sole custody of the daughter he dearly loved.

When not working, Freddie gathered evidence that would prove his wife's infidelity. After several months of secretly following his wife at night and on weekends, following up on tips and allegations from friends, he believed he had enough hard evidence to confront his wife. Since she wouldn't see him, he called her, laid out his evidence of her infidelity, called her unkind names, and voiced his intentions to take revenge for her betrayal and lies. His wife denied any and all allegations, called Freddie names that questioned his manhood, told him she wasn't worried about his threats, to bring them on, and hung up on him.

This is where events began to spin out of control. Freddie and his wife both purchased .22 pistols and kept them on their person at all times—fully loaded. Freddie made the first move. Late one winter afternoon he went to his house—our old home place—on which he was still paying the rent. He got there before his wife got home from work. He talked to his daughter, put her in one of the bedrooms in the rear of the home, and got her promise not to come out of the bedroom until he and her mother had 'settled some things between us'.

Freddie went outside the house and found a hiding place where he believed his wife would not see him when she came home. That would give him the advantage of making the first move—whatever that move might have to be. He had to find a way to talk to her.

As she left the highway to enter the house's driveway, Freddie's wife saw his work truck secluded in the trees on the other side of the highway. Freddie's wife may have been a number of things, but a shrinking violet wasn't one of them. When she saw Freddie's truck she raced up the driveway, jumped from her car, pulled her pistol from her purse, flipped off the safety, and ran toward the front door—gun in hand.. She couldn't see Freddie, but she knew he was somewhere on the premises—and was sure he hadn't come bearing gifts. She didn't intend to go quietly into the night.

When he saw his wife racing for the front door, pistol in hand, Freddie knew she had discovered he was there. For all he knew, she might know where he was hiding and was making a move to take him out. His plan had been to confront her verbally—using his pistol only if she 'got ugly' with her pistol. Events were moving too fast for Freddie to think rationally. The sight of his wife running, pistol in hand, told him she wasn't in a mood to see or hear his damning evidence of her infidelity, let alone show a little restraint with her gun. He quickly decided not to take a chance on her 'dropping' him before he could confront her with his evidence of her marital betrayal.

In haste, Freddie fired the first shot, 35 feet away from a petite woman who was running. His bullet hit the wood siding of the house three feet from the front door. His wife returned fire just before diving through the front door and slamming it shut.

Freddie heard the lock turn in the front door. The fat was in the fire now. He knew he had virtually no chance of getting inside the house now without his wife ventilating his body with bullets. Worse still, he didn't know exactly *where* in the house his wife was. She could be looking at him right now—peeking at him from the corner of some window—lining up a shot at him. To try and locate his wife's location *in* the house Freddie began running around the outside of the house, in the yard. As he ran around the house he looked through the window of each room he was running past. His wife, wanting to know exactly where Freddie was *outside* the house—lest he find some way to sneak in the house unbeknown to her—began matching Freddie stride for stride— as she raced around the <u>in</u>side of the house.

As each of them ran past a window of some room in the house, they could, for a second, see each other. During these split-second sightings, they fired shots at each other, on the run. In the openings moments of this on-the-run gun battle the only casualties were window panes. They were fast shattering panes of glass in every window in every room of the house.

It was inevitable that the odds would work against both of them. On his third trip around the house Freddie drew first blood, nailing his wife with a shot as she ran past the living room window. Despite being shot, she was still able to run. Less than a minute later, she got off a shot which hit Freddie in the shoulder as he passed the dining room windows. The shot momentarily dropped Freddie to his knees, but he got up and continued his run around the house—searching for any sight of his wife as he passed each window.

In the next few minutes, while emptying their guns three times and blowing out 25% of the glass in the windows during multiple trips around the house, they both put two more bullets in each other before collapsing—she on the living room floor— he in the front yard. Both were still conscious, but bleeding badly. When the firing stopped the daughter raced out of the bedroom—saw the damage her parents had done to each other—and quickly dialed 911.

The Rescue Squad got to the scene quickly, loaded both of them into the ambulance, and raced to the new Granby Hospital, 14 miles away. Granby is a small town. There was only one doctor on duty in the hospital ER when they wheeled Freddie and his wife into the ER. The doctor took some quick x-rays, made a quick diagnosis of both and offered his assessment.

"I can save her. Him—no chance. He's got a bullet lodged near his heart and has already lost too much blood."

They immediately wheeled Freddie's wife into the new hospital OR and began surgery. Since there was no other doctor on duty at the new hospital and Freddie was still alive—they loaded him back into the ambulance and took him 5 miles to the **OLD** Granby hospital. The old hospital was still in operation—just not as well staffed and equipped as the new one.
On duty at the old hospital was a doctor of Palestinian nationality. As they wheeled Freddie into the hospital, the Palestinian doctor took a quick look at him and the x-rays they had carried from the new hospital.

"Yeah—I can save this guy", said the Palestinian doctor. "I grew up in a place where there is always a war going on, shootings, gun-shot wounds—I've operated on a bunch of people in this guy's shape."

They wheeled Freddie into the OR of the old hospital and the Palestinian doctor went to work. The bullet was lodged too close to Freddie's heart for the doctor to crack his chest in the traditional way of accessing the heart. It would take too much time. Freddie didn't have that much blood left in him for the usual precautions doctors followed for operations like this. Besides, he had two more bullets in him that would have to come out.

The doctor used a long thin wire with a clasp on the end of it, went through Freddie's groin, worked his way internally up to his heart, grabbed the bullet with the wire and extracted it in relatively little time. He gave Freddie blood while he removed the other two bullets from him—and Freddie lived. He was the beneficiary of the skills of a doctor from a land thousands of miles away where people had been shooting and killing each other for centuries. Their refusal to find peace with each other had left this doctor with skills that saved Freddie's life.

Freddie's wife? She didn't fare as well. She died on the operating table. The doctor operating on her hadn't anticipated the severity of the wound to her liver. She bled out on the operating table before they could stabilize her condition.

Freddie recovered enough to leave the hospital 45 days later. The county's Commonwealth Attorney charged him with the murdering his wife. He was tried, convicted, sentenced to life in prison. He was in his mid-30s. Freddie's crime was one of passion. He was no real threat to others or even a threat to escape the bounds of wherever they imprisoned him. So—he was sent to a County Prison Farm—a medium security prison. He spent the next 20 years tending a dairy herd, large fields of vegetables, and fruit orchards that provided a good part of the food for those sentenced to the farm prison.

Freddie's family, known and respected in the county, worked tirelessly for Freddie's parole from the day they put him in prison. Their campaign for his release included button holing every politician from the local, to state, to national level. They hammered on his late wife's infidelity as the motivator of the shoot-out—her response in kind to every shot Freddie fired at her, as opposed to calling 911 for police protection during their 10 minute gun battle—and Freddie's young daughter being without the benefit of either parent in her young life.

After 20 years most resistance from any source melted away and Freddie was released from prison on parole. He was an elderly man when he walked out of prison. He kept to himself for the most part. Never a man of many words, he said nothing to anyone about the gun battle, his time in prison, or much of anything else. He got a job as a carpenter, led a quiet life, with little contact with any one beyond his family, his daughter, and the family his daughter now had.

After the incident between Freddie and his wife, the mining company who owned our old home place repaired the damage done by the gun fight and rented it to others. Over the next 20 years the house was rented to a succession of people, none of whom took care of the house or grounds. The mining company spent little or no money on upkeep of the house.

Paint eventually flaked off the board siding of the house until there was more wood showing than paint. The corners of the house began to pull apart at the foundation. The sides of the old home place appeared to be sliding across the yard in four different directions. The lawn and English boxwoods my parents had proudly and lovingly cared for over 20 years disappeared into a morass of weeds. The gutters sagged, and then fell to the ground. Tenants used the lawn for additional parking until it became filled with muddy ruts. Spare car parts could be seen lying in random spots on what remained of the front porch and driveway. An old abandoned soda pop cooler was discarded at the foot of the driveway alongside the highway. It was an eye sore until it, too, became hidden by weeds grown out of control.

One summer day a County Deputy arrived at the house to serve a warrant on the present tenant of the house. There was no answer to his knock on the front door. On the off chance the subject of the warrant might not have heard his knock or was hiding in the house to avoid service, the Deputy leaned out over the front porch railing and looked through the big double windows of the living room.

To his amazement, he saw a moonshine whiskey still, fully operable, taking up most of the entire living room of the house. It was fueled by propane gas and was being vented through the living room fireplace chimney.

Production of illegal whiskey wasn't the purpose of the warrant the Deputy was trying to serve. Whatever the cause of the warrant he had in his hand, it quickly became secondary to what he saw through the living room window. He called his office, had another Deputy run over to the Judge's Chambers and get another warrant that would let them enter the house, seize the still, and arrest the operator.

He waited at the house until he was joined there by several other Deputies and a member of the federal ATF force, who happened to be in town on another matter. They forced open the front door of the house, went in with guns drawn—and found no one in the house. Just a few items of personal property, the whiskey still, several 100 lb bags of sugar, several bags of ground corn, 6 barrels of cooked sour mash, and numerous jugs of moonshine whiskey.

Always looking for favorable publicity for law enforcement, the Deputies notified a cameraman for the local newspaper. With the photographer clicking away, the deputies cracked open the top of one of the barrels of used, bright yellow sour mash—and let him photograph them pouring the river of yellow sour mash down the front porch steps of our old home place.
The picture was featured on the front page of the local paper. I got an email of the picture, along with a rhetorical question asking 'do you know this place'?

I'm glad my parents weren't alive to see the end product of 20+ years of labor, money, and love poured into the home that stood as one of the proudest accomplishments of their married lives.

There is an old adage which says 'You can't go home again'—or something like that. I used to doubt the unalterable truth of those words. When I saw the picture of the sour mash running down the steps of our home place—already in a near state of collapse—I found myself agreeing with whomever penned that bleak appraisal on the chances of anyone 'going home again'.

Actually, who would <u>want</u> to go back to a house that was no longer a 'home'????

THE CON ARTIST

The town of Oakhurst was no different from hundreds of other towns when it came to having town characters. Toodie Sizemore was one of the characters in Oakhurst. He may have been the leading character in town.

Toodie probably had a legal name, but no one seemed to know what it was. Even his Mother called him Toodie. He was short and stocky. We wondered how Toodie came by his name. We wondered, but none of us had any intentions of approaching Toodie's mother, Mrs. Sadie Sizemore, for an explanation of his name. Her prickly temperament was well known around Oakhurst.

I suppose this would be a good time to mention that Toodie was mentally challenged. Toodie, on his best days, had the I.Q. of a child of eight to ten years of age. He could be trusted alone. He could make some decisions, generally knew right from wrong, and was fairly trustworthy. On the other hand, he still had the mind of a young child. He would do things on impulse. He might yield to his hunger and eat something in a store without paying for it. He might dart in front of a moving vehicle without first looking. Acts that were not premeditated but caused concern.

While Mrs. Sizemore wasn't particularly known for her warmth and charity toward people in general, she loved Toodie. She treated him with love, tolerance, and respect.

She was also very protective of Toodie. Woe be unto the person who ridiculed, teased, or abused Toodie.

The town sort of adopted Toodie. He had lived his entire life there. Most everyone knew and liked him. Toodie walked everywhere. The Sizemores didn't own a car. As Toodie walked by houses, the town's inhabitants would speak cheerfully to him and sometimes offer him money.

The merchants in town gave Toodie simple jobs to do. He would sweep floors, pick up trash in the parking lots, wash windows, and make daily trips to the post office to pick up their mail. Besides earning a little money doing these jobs, they gave Toodie a feeling of importance, trust, and belonging in the community.

Admittedly, the merchants had to keep a rein on Toodie. He fancied himself a cowboy. He loved to play games of cowboys and Indians. While working in the stores, Toodie would, periodically, pull his ever present bandana from his neck up over his nose and go galloping down the store isle at break-neck speed. While running, he would slap his thighs with his hands and yell 'Hi-Yo Silver'. The local merchants put a quick stop to his fantasies inside the stores, but they let him 'ride his horse' to the post office to get their mail. Toodie's horse was a broom stick from which a local carpenter had removed the broom straw and replaced it with a horse's head carved from an old piece of white pine board. The merchants even gave Toodie an old canvas bag, once used by a news-paper delivery boy, and let him carry their daily mail in it. With the strap of the bag flung over his shoulder, and both hands firmly on his stick horse, Toodie, happily delivered mail from the post office to some of the merchants in Oakhurst.

Toodie had no idea he was mentally challenged. He believed himself to be just like every other soul in Oakhurst. No one saw any reason to disabuse Toodie of that notion. Then, one day during the time of the Korean War, the military Selective Service System changed Toodie's life.

In the early 1950s, the military draft law was in effect. Every male eighteen years of age had to register with the Military Selective Service System. They went to the local county court house and, by law, registered to serve two years in one of the branches of the military services. The system was supposed to exempt any male mentally or physically unfit to serve. As with most government agencies, mistakes did occur. Like the mistake they made when they sent Toodie notification to report to the Bristol, Va. Induction center for processing into military service.

Despite the best efforts of Toodie's mother and a letter from Dr. Coleman, Toodie was registered in the system as an able-bodied male fit for military service. Once in that system, short of failing a physical or mental exam at the induction center, it was almost impossible to convince the military draft authorities of their error. The examiners at the induction centers were universally suspicious of people claiming physical or mental disability. Especially when our Army was involved in a shooting war.

Toodie and twenty other boys climbed aboard an old bus bound for the army induction center in Bristol at 6 a.m. on a rainy, autumn morning. The darkness of the hour and the pouring rain were compounded by the wailing cries of Mrs. Sizemore as she put Toodie on the bus. Toodie thought the whole thing was a hoot. He was in the full throes of that high pitched maniacal laugh of his as the bus pulled away from its loading area in front of the Brown Horse restaurant. Toodie was looking forward to the trip. He seldom got to go anywhere outside of Oakhurst. He was ecstatic. The same couldn't be said of Mrs. Sizemore. She railed against 'those bastards down at the draft board' to any willing ear as the bus pulled away.

 Other parents, who had come to see their sons off, tried to comfort Mrs. Sizemore. They offered assurances the induction center would quickly recognize Toodie's 'backward nature' and quickly send him home. Mrs. Sizemore wasn't so sure of this. She feared the induction center personnel were no less likely than the local draft board to push Toodie through the system and induct him into the army. She had nightmares of the Army shipping Toodie to Korea, giving him a rifle, and turning him loose to fight in the Korean War. "Once that happens", she wailed, "Toodie will stand up and yell 'Hi-Yo Silver'. Some China-man will 'line up his sights' on Toodie and shoot him down like a dog—or Toodie will haul off and shoot somebody on our side, because he don't know no better. Then, the army will take Toodie out back somewhere, stand him up against a wall, and shoot him for killin' one of our own".

Two days later, the bus stopped in Oakhurst and Toodie stepped off. He had a grin that went from ear to ear. Toodie walked from the bus straight into the local grocery store, grabbed a broom and began to sweep the floor.

"Toodie", said the store manager, Bob, "it's good to see you back in town."

"I'm glad I'm here. Yessir. I feel good when I'm here. Bob, you're standing on the floor. I can't sweep the floor if you stand on it. I have to sweep the floor and go get the mail, Bob", said Toodie, as he tried to get Bob to move off the floor of that isle.

"Oh, okay, Toodie", said Bob as he stepped aside. "I just wanted to ask you how things went for you at the induction center. Are they going to take you into the Army?"

"Naw, they ain't gonna get me to go in no Army. I talked to some boys down at that ducshun' center. Em' boys told me if the army sent me to some place called Ko-rea –that 'em people over there would shoot my ass off. I ain't goin' NO place where they shoot my ass off."

"Well, how did you get out of being inducted in the Army? They don't just turn you loose because you tell them you don't want to go some country where there is a shooting war going on."

"Naw. They didn't jus' turn me loose. I fooled 'em, Bob. When they 'zamined me I acted like I was cwazy. "(Toodie had trouble with the letter 'r').

"Did they believe you?"

"Naw—not at first. First, they say they gon' lock me up if I don't start actin' right. Then they made me take my clothes off, like when you're in the hospital. But, I wouldn't give 'em my cowboy mask. While I was nekid I put my cowboy mask on and ran up and down the floor in that room till they grabbed me and made me stand still. They had this Army po-leese-man come in the room. He had a gun an' a billy club. He grabbed me, put his face right against mine, and he say to me, 'Boy, you open your mouth or get out of line one more time I'm gon' throw your ass in a jail cell till you get thuh' picture'"

"What happened then?"

"Not sure. Some doctors talk to me. They ask me lots of questions. But, I fooled em. I tol' 'em I don't know no answers to none of 'em questions they ask' me. I acted like I don' know nothin'. They showed me a bunch of pit'chers'—of nothin'. Asked me what those pictures was. I tol' 'em I couldn't un-'erstand none of 'em pit'chers. This morning some so'jer take me back to the bus station and put me on a bus that brought me back here. I done fool 'em. They thought I was cwazy, Bob. Huh-huh,ha-ha,Ha-Hi-HIEEE."

So ended the tug of wills between the draft board and Toodie Sizemore. No doubt the army would not have discovered Toodie's mental challenge without a charade by him. But, the story is made all the sweeter by Toodie's efforts to help them reach their decision. His belief that he narrowly saved himself from having his 'ass shot off in Korea' is the icing on the cake.

Toodie lived out his life in Oakhurst. When he passed away, in his mid-sixties, his loss was felt throughout the town. In fact, most people felt Toodie was one of those people who leave such vivid memories they never die.

THE PHONE CALL

Harve Vencil was a life-long resident of Garden Creek. His education ended somewhere in elementary school. Harve was not a well traveled man. He knew little, and cared less, about events that occurred more than a few miles from his home.

Harve was, to a degree, an honest person. That is to say, he would not steal *outright* from you. He had worked for most of the things he and his wife had accumulated in their 50 some odd years of life. On the other hand, Harve was recognized as *one* of the biggest liars in the county. Some said he was at the *top* of the list of liars, and <u>way</u> ahead of whoever was in second place. Harve had lied for so long it became second nature to him. Those who knew him best swore that Harve would climb a tree to tell a lie before he would just stand on the ground and tell the truth.

Harve held several menial jobs over the years. He had hand-loaded coal for local mines. He spent time in a saw mill for a local lumber company. He sold one or two cars a year for a Chrysler dealer a few miles from his home. The dealer said he was more of a 'customer finder' than a salesman. He couldn't handle 'paper work'. Math was not one of his strengths.

Even in his job as a car salesman, Harve's propensity for

evading the truth came through. The dealer had a rule designed to keep salesmen from making a deal with a customer who was already the customer of another salesman. Every morning each salesman had to give the name of their new potential customers to the office manager. Harve's penchant for stretching the truth was put into play immediately. He walked into the dealership each morning and turned in the name of every man or woman he had as much as said 'good morning' to or waved at on his way to the dealership that morning. Within months, according to Harve's account, 90% of the people living along Garden Creek were his customers.

People who did approach the dealer or another salesman about a new Chrysler were astonished when told they were already Harve's customer. Especially when they hadn't spoken to Harve for over a year. Normally, after Harve turned in his list of 'customers' each morning, he would drift back and forth through the area loafing, doing odd jobs, telling lies, and wind up back home to work in his garden.

As he did most summers, Harve had picked several gallons of black berries. He went door to door selling the berries. One morning he ambled into one of the company stores owned by Page Pocahontas Coal Co. with a two gallon bucket of berries in his hand. As luck would have it, he caught the General Mngr., Joe Whitley, passing through the store.

Harve walked up to Joe, set a bucket of berries up on the

counter, and began his spiel.

"Joe, these here are the biggest and sweetest berries in this whole county", said Harve. "I got this special place where I pick these berries. Nobody else knows where it is. You ain't gonna' find berries like this anywhere else. They's some people that won't buy berries from anybody but me. But, I tell you what. I like you. If your wife would like to have these berries to make some jam or jelly for the winter—why, I'd rather let you have them than anybody else I know."

Joe looked at the berries and smiled. They weren't out of ordinary, but they did look good.

"Tell you what, Harve", said Joe, as he reached for the phone hanging on the wall. "I'll ask my wife if she wants them. She's already canned some, but I'll ask her."

As Joe dialed the phone, Harve looked at him. He was puzzled. Joe's home had to be a good two miles away. When Joe's wife, Julia, answered the phone and Joe began to talk to her through the black hand-set of the phone, Harve stared at Joe intensely.

"Hey, it's me. Listen, I'm at the No. 2 store. Harve Vencil has two gallons of black berries here and wants to sell them. Do you need any more berries to can?"

Joe listened as his wife told him she had already canned so many jars of berries she would go crazy if she had to can one more jar of berries.

"Okay", responded Joe, "I'll see you this evening. Yeah, I'll be home about 5:30. Okay, see you later. Bye."

Joe hung up the phone and turned to face Harve. He thought Harve had a strange expression on his face. He studied Harve's face for a couple of seconds before speaking to him.

"Harve, my wife she says doesn't need any more berries. She's already canned all the jelly she intends to this year. But, she thanks you for offering to let her have the berries."

With disbelief and anger in his face, Harve said, "Joe, if you didn't want my berries why didn't you just say so—right to my face. You didn't have to lie to me like you just did."

Joe took a long look at Harve's face and saw that he was serious. Joe wasn't used to people talking to him in that tone of voice. And few people dared call him a liar—to his face.

"Harve, what the hell are you talking about? What's the matter with you? You saw me ask my wife if she wanted the berries. She said she didn't want them. So, where do you get off calling me a liar?"

Harve glared at Joe as he grabbed his bucket of berries off the counter.

"You must think I'm a dam fool. You ain't foolin' me one little bit. I know you ain't got your wife in that there little black box you was a-talkin' into on your store wall! Your wife is home, and that's a good two miles from here. Ain't no way in hell your wife could be in that little tiny black box—so she ain't heard one word you was a sayin' 'bout my berries!"

Joe looked at the old black rotary phone on the wall, then back at Harve as he stomped out of the store. Then—it dawned on him. Harve didn't know much, if anything, about phones. He didn't have a phone in his own home. Actually, Harve only got electricity in his home 7-8 years ago.

There were probably less than a half dozen residential phones in a 5 mile radius of where Joe was standing. Harve, by accident of birth, was born and living in the 20th century. But that didn't mean he had joined it. Most of his life was spent within a few miles of where he was born. His limited knowledge of things didn't include phones.

No, Harve really believed what he said. And he didn't believe, not on a bet, that any man kept his wife in a little box—no bigger than a small shoe box—hanging on the wall of a grocery store. It was physically impossible for any woman alive, no matter how small, to fit in that damn little 'phone box'—and it offended him that any man would believe he was so stupid he would believe such a thing.

Joe had to laugh as he watched Harve angrily stomp off the front porch of the store. He knew not everyone had a phone. But—this was the 19th century—everybody understood how a telephone worked—didn't they?

He couldn't wait to tell his wife. He told the story for years. Funny thing was, most people believed it was a story he made up.

Joe always said it was the height of irony. The biggest liar in the county becoming outraged— because he believed he was being <u>lied</u> to.

THE PREACHER

Thurman Cornell was a preacher. There were other preachers up and down Garden Creek, up Page hollow, along the highway in Oakwood, and in other coal mining communities that dotted the landscape in Buchanan County. Methodist, Baptist, Presbyterian, Pentecostal— just about all faiths were represented, except for Episcopalian, Catholic, and Jewish. The latter were not excluded by design. Folks explained their absence by saying 'It's just that there aren't any in these parts'.

Of all the preachers leading their flocks, Thurman stood out. He reached that rarified status of needing only his first name called—'Reverend Thurman'—for people to know who you were talking about. To his face, people called him 'Brother' or 'Reverend Cornell'. His people were clear on that. Thurman was firm believer in using his 'revered' title to remind his flock that he was not just their 'best bud'. He was their intercessor—their link to the Almighty. As such, he was to be addressed reverently and with respect—if not with a little fear of his awesome power. Too much familiarity breeds contempt, he felt.

Thurman was a tall, ruggedly handsome man. His smile, confidence, and booming, deep, baritone voice made him a natural speaker. His charisma made him irresistible to most. He had tons of it. He could not only command your attention—he was a true 'spellbinder'. Most folks within hearing distance of ol' Thurman when he spoke were captivated. To top it off, he had a good working knowledge of the scriptures and preached their message with a fiery passion.

Thurman was also a man with a personal life and past that were unclear. He called Russell County home. Where in Russell County was vague. Russell County covered a lot of territory.

When asked when and where he was ordained, Thurman said he was ordained by God when God called him to spread the gospel. Inquire about which church he led before availing his services to the Holiness Church at Dugout, Va., he would tell you he had been at labor in a church of God—as should every true minister of the gospel. Ol' Thurman knew you weren't likely to dispute God as the true head of all churches.

Thurman made frequent references to his loving wife and delightful children, but no one ever saw them at any of his services in Dugout. He carried some pictures in his wallet, but no one in Dugout ever met his family in person. The pictures could have been of anyone.

These vague or 'hazy' parts of Thurman's life and past divided people into two camps—those that loved him— and those who believed him to be nothing more than a charlatan, a liar of the first degree, just another man looking to make a quick dollar.

Wily old Flem VanDyke spoke for the latter group when he contemptuously spat on the ground said, "Jes' sayin' somethin' is true don't make it true! I'd sooner b'leve' a dam Republican than ol' Thurman." Flem was a life-long 'yellow-dog' Democrat.

The other camp—Thurman's faithful followers, his growing conversion of former sinners, felt these 'vague background details' hardly worth quibbling over. After all, didn't Brother Thurman constantly pack the pews with believers? How could he fool all those people? And—had he not preached several fiery sermons on the frightening devastation awaiting those trafficking in the sins of lies and deceit? Surely, a man of God wouldn't guarantee his own eternity in the 'Lake of Fire' by lying to his flock.

Thurman used, as a base, a little Pentecostal Holiness church alongside Garden Creek in a community called Dugout. He didn't limit his ministry, exclusively, to this church. In the summer Thurman would erect a big tent, which he bought at an Army surplus store, in different areas of the county and hold evening revivals in it.

These revivals included snake handling, from time to time. Brother Thurman had an almost unerring instinct about what it would take to bring folks out to his tent revivals. He was convinced that *entertainment* was a key part of bringing a big crowd to any religious service—be it a regular church or a tent revival. He also had a feel for what it would take to keep them entertained, in their seats, and in a 'giving mood' once he got them there. Sometimes it was his emotional delivery of a fiery sermon laced with promises of hell and damnation for unrepentant sinners. Sometimes, a box of snakes would do the trick—making certain the box *he* reached into was carefully cleared of all poisonous snakes before the service started. Thurman was a showman and a businessman—not a fool.

Thurman complimented his preaching and performing skills by wearing custom tailored suits. Some said he had to go all the way to Bristol to get them made. He also drove a big, shiny, black Buick RoadMaster—never more than two years old.

After Labor Day, he always dressed in an all-black outfit— except for a white shirt. From his hat, right down to his shiny, black, wingtip shoes. Summer time brought out his stunning all-white ensemble. He decked out in a white straw hat, white linen suit, white silk shirt and matching tie, and white buck shoes. Indeed, Reverend Thurman was always in black or white, top to bottom—with a fresh suit for every day of the week. Add his custom cut clothes to his height, smile, voice, and he cut quite a figure. Yessiree, you mention the name 'Reverend Thurman'—folks knew who you were talking about.

No discussion of Thurman would be complete without mentioning his insistence on generous financial support. Tithing, stewardship, whatever name you wanted to give it—dropping ten percent of your income in the collection plate when it passed in front of you was a non-negotiable matter in Brother Thurman's church.

After all, the work of a Preacher was not without expenses. Especially the part requiring tailored suits and a Buick *RoadMaster* sedan. With that dazzling smile, but with a firm voice, the good Reverend made it clear he couldn't 'bring the word' without 'support'. Those collection plates had to be full after they were passed around. And he didn't want to see any money in that plate that you couldn't hang on a clothes line. Small change was only accepted from the children's Sunday-School classes.

All in all, everything considered, his followers thought the world of Brother Thurman. The ladies of the congregations loved him, and Thurman loved them. Some of them literally—so it was whispered by some folks.

Thurman got word of those 'whispered rumors'. He took to the pulpit and promised there would be a choice place in the Lake of Fire for those repeating such 'ungodly and mis-informed rumors'. His 'one-on-one ministry with the ladies', so he said, was simply God using him to free those ladies from 'their agonies'.

No 'agony' specifics were given, but three of the ladies in his congregation testified, after several months of 'personal counseling' by Reverend Thurman, they were able to discontinue, completely, their daily consumption of 'nerve pills' that Doc Moore had prescribed for them.

Actually, it was Reverend Thurman's personal visitation with one of the ladies in his church at Dugout that led to the turning point of his ministry in Dugout.

It was in the evening of a hot summer day in August. Five of my friends and I had ridden our bikes up Garden Creek to Hanging Rock—the best swimming hole on all of Garden Creek. We skinny dipped for an hour, climbed up on the big cliff overhanging the creek, and watched the sun set while smoking 'rabbit tobacco' rolled up in *LIFE* magazine pages. As the sun sat on that soft, summer evening—life was good.

All of us had 15-20 cents we had saved for this moment. We rode another half mile up Garden Creek to Dugout. Located there was the crown-jewel of upper Garden Creek—Bascomb's General Merchandise Store. The wealth in our pockets bought us RC Colas, candy, or moon pies. All of us plopped down on the front porch of the store with our sweets. Bascomb had, thoughtfully, provided seating arrangements on the front porch—old seats taken from Jeeps and nailed to short wooden stumps. We were going to need these seats. While we gorged ourselves with sweets and watched the 'Thurman Cornell Show' in his church across the road.

Reverend Thurman was holding his biggest revival of the summer in the Dugout Church that night. The church was packed—not a vacant seat in the house. Most of us boys were Methodist. Our church services didn't involve anything near the level of emotion Thurman's congregation displayed. The passage of over a half century has not dimmed my memory of that service—or the events that followed it. I can't say for sure, but I'd bet the last nickel I have that Reverend Thurman remembers that particular evening too.

We settled in on that old store porch and watched as things got under way. The few paper fans fluttering in the church pews did little to relief the 85 degree summer heat—even with every window and door in the church open.

Prior to the actual service, folks in the pews began verbalizing their prayers—each trying to do so a little louder than the person next to them. Some men marched around the isles of the church playing guitars, mandolins, fiddles, and singing while the people in the pews prayed and shouted pleas to the Almighty for relief and deliverance from worries, illness, etc.

Once Brother Thurman *formally* started the service, the musicians took their place beside him at the podium. Then we saw the significance of music in the service at Dugout Church. By the last verse of every song played, the whole sanctuary was in a complete uproar. Men, standing before the altar, were dancing and kicking their feet so fast their feet barely touched the floor. Those in the pews were jumping up and down, clapping, waving their arms and singing. We had seen a few fairly rowdy church services before, but the music and participation by the congregation at Dugout that evening was chaotic by comparison. By the time they sang I'LL FLY AWAY, Thurman had the entire congregation in pandemonium.

When they finished that song it took Thurman a full minute to get the congregation seated and quiet so he could begin his sermon.

Brother Thurman's preaching style was rooted in the 'fire and brimstone' approach. It complimented his stated intention of leading sinners to repentance. In fact, repentance was the focal point of his lengthy sermon that evening. He started with a low voice and slow cadence to his words. With the passing of each minute, his delivery became louder and faster

The crimson flush and sheen of perspiration on Thurman's face by the mid-point of his sermon gave proof of his passionate desire to witness repentance among those present. To their credit, the congregation openly endorsed Brother Thurman's message. Adamant shouts of 'Amen', 'Oh yes', 'Praise God' rang out repeatedly from the congregation. At times the shouts of affirmation from the congregation were so loud and frequent it was difficult to hear what Thurman was saying.

After an hour of preaching, Thurman was fairly exhausted and had pretty well worn out the entire congregation. A master showman, Thurman knew when 'enough was enough'. He drew the service to a close with a prayer and altar call that drew 10 sinners to the altar for confession of sins.

With the service over, most of the faithful drifted off into the night to their homes. Reverend Thurman offered to walk Stacey Sutter to her nearby home, in a section of Dugout, known as 'Sawmill Bottom'. It was a community of 15-20 homes. Stacey's home was near the end of the rutty, dirt road that ran between the homes and ended at a saw mill located at the road's end. Her husband, Lyle, owned and operated this sawmill, about 200 feet past their home.

Lyle, not a devout man, had gone 20 miles to Fox Creek to hunt coons. He was expected to be gone, as he usually was, until dawn—and falling-down drunk when he did get home.

When Thurman walked Stacey to the front porch of her home he agreed to her plea for a continuation of the 'personal counseling' he had been giving her for some months. Thurman and Stacey proceeded straight from the porch to her bedroom. They had been in bed just long enough to begin the 'counseling' session when there was a noise on the front porch.

Lyle was back early! When Stacey heard Lyle's voice, the look on her face must have gone from puzzlement, to realization, to fear—in about two seconds flat.

With Stacey's low, shrill cries of 'Hurry—Hurry' ringing in his ears, Thurman, kicked the window screen out of the bedroom window , half way across the back yard, and bolted out of her bedroom window in his nothing but his undershorts, and shoes. His white suit, shirt, and hat were under his arm.

We were slowly riding our bicycles back down Garden Creek when we heard Lyle's yell of rage. He had come into his bedroom just in time to see Reverend Thurman jumping out the window.

 Lyle had heard Stacey squealing for Thurman to 'hurry' and staggered down the hallway to their bedroom to see who she was talking to. When he saw Thurman go out the bedroom window, he sized the situation up real quick.

He began bellowing profanities and threats of giving Thurman "a 'dirt nap' for 'pokin' my wife". He grabbed his pistol from a chest of drawers in the bedroom and staggered back outside to his truck where he grabbed his hunting rifle. It sounded like the fat was in the fire for ol' Thurman, so we stopped along-side the road to watch the 'showdown' taking place on the other side of the creek.

From the porch lights of neighboring houses we could see Thurman running toward the saw mill. He knew he had to get out of the open ground between Lyle's house and his sawmill—in a hurry. He had to find cover, if he was going to avoid being shot and escape into the night.
Lyle was about 100 feet behind Thurman, running down that old rutty, dirt road after him—a rifle in one hand and a pistol in the other. He fired shots from both as he bellowed curses and threats.

"C'mere, you SOB! You better run—ya' dam' yeller dog!

I'm gonna' shoot your ass off! Ya' think you can tamper with my wife? I get through with you, you won't be stickin' your pecker where it don't belong!"

As he ran, Thurman shouted pleas to the Almighty to deliver him from Lyle—to forgive him—to save him from death at Lyle's hands. He alternated these pleas to his Maker by shouting pleas, over his shoulder, to Lyle as he ran. He begged Lyle to forgive him—to show a little forgiveness and mercy. Lyle would answer with another round of bullets from his pistol and rifle.

Fate and the Lord were on ol' Thurman's side that night. Lyle was so drunk he pitched and staggered as he ran. The blasts from his rifle and pistol hit the ground, sailed off into the night sky, or plowed into the big pile of sawdust beside his sawmill. Thurman finally reached that big pile of sawdust without any bullets in him. That sawdust pile had to be 15 feet high and a good 30 feet in diameter.

Thurman began running around and around the sawdust pile to keep it between him and Lyle. The whole time Thurman ran around that pile of sawdust, his clothes were still under his arm. He managed to keep the mountain of sawdust between him and Lyle for a while—but he knew he couldn't keep this up indefinitely. As we boys watched him run, it was evident that he was getting tired. Lyle was too full of liquor and rage to feel tired. His pace didn't seem to be slowing—but, neither did his drunken staggering.

Beyond that pile of sawdust, it was pretty dark. The tons of sawdust blocked the lights from nearby houses. Finally, between the darkness, Lyle's drunken condition, a half dozen running trips around that sawdust pile, Thurman was able to veer off into the night, wade across Garden Creek, race across the road and clamber up the mountain side where he hid in the trees.

Lyle, thinking Thurman was still circling the sawdust pile, just out of his sight, continued to race around the sawdust pile. After a half hour of chasing, staggering, falling, shouting curses, and shooting bullets into the empty darkness, Lyle gave up. He staggered back to his house, took off his belt, and 'whupped' Stacey for 'diddlin' that Preacher-man'.

Wasn't much of beating—three or four half-hearted licks. We could hear Stacey screaming—like she was being skinned alive. Stacey was a shrewd little cookie. She knew the louder she screamed, the sooner Lyle would stop swinging the belt.

It wasn't the first time Lyle and Stacey had been through this routine. For whatever reason, Stacey, from time to time, 'forgot' the part of her matrimonial vows about 'forsaking all others'. Despite her chronic indiscretions, Lyle always forgave her. Stacey never truly considered leaving Lyle. In their own way, they loved each other. Or—maybe they loved what each other brought to the marriage. Stacey—her bedroom 'skills'. Lyle—his ownership of a saw mill that put him in the top of the 'wealthy group' in that area. Her taste for variety in men didn't blind Stacey to financial realities of life—nor Lyle to her expertise in the bedroom.

As we rode on home, recounting the events of the evening, all of us knew this was a summer night that would linger in our memories—long after we were old men.

Thurman never preached at any church in the area again. Word got around quickly to church members throughout the area. No one in the Dugout was quite sure where Thurman had gone—just that he was gone.

Twenty years later a mainstream TV station broadcasted a documentary on churches that practiced snake handling. The focus of the broadcast was a church in a town on the Virginia-West Virginia border. Who was leading the flock in that packed church?
Brother Thurman Cornell—all decked out in a white linen suit.

THE MOVIE

Hobart VanDorn was born and raised in the Prater community of Buchanan County. Hobart's parents provided a clean home, food, clothing, and necessary medical attention. They insisted on weekly attendance at a local church, and completion of high school for their 3 children. Beyond this, they could, financially, do little. The family's economic status played a major role in the reason Hobart reached adulthood without leaving the rural county boundaries more than 5-6 times in his early life.

Lois Radford was born and raised along one of the numerous 'dirt road hollows' that trailed off Jewel Ridge. Lois's Father was a self-ordained Holiness Preacher, her mother was a homemaker. Having given birth to 6 of good Reverend's children in 10 years, she hardly had time to leave the home. She was a homemaker by default. Their means were modest. Lois's parents provided a clean home, food, clothing, and necessary medical attention. They insisted on completion of high school by all of their children. Rev. And Mrs. Radford were not content with mere weekly attendance of Sunday services at their local church. Since Reverend Radford was the pastor of that church, attendance at any religious function was expected of Lois and her siblings—every time the church door was open.

Rev. Radford insisted on strict adherence to his

fundamentalist interpretation of the scriptures. For Lois that included abstinence from dancing, movies, TV, suggestive clothing, cosmetics, tobacco, alcohol, riding alone in cars with boys, having a date without a chaperone, and a long list of other practices that were designed to see that Lois avoided temptations that might lead her to un-Godly sins and temptations. Except for school, Lois was almost never out of the sight of her parents. Lois reached adulthood without leaving the mountains of the county, period.

Hobart reached 18 years of age in April of 1942. He graduated from high school in the last week of May 1942. He was drafted and inducted into the U.S. Army in the first week of June 1942. He was transported to an army fort in Georgia, given basic training, assigned to the infantry, and shipped overseas to fight in World War II.

Hobart slogged through military battles and campaigns from September 1942 until the surrender of the German army nearly three years later. He received several citations for bravery and rose to the rank of Master Sergeant. During these years, he got his introduction to the world outside his rural county by walking across Europe, from one battle to another, and infrequent 2-3 day passes for rest and recreation. The periods of rest and recreation were spent somewhere to the rear of the front lines. Whenever possible, in some town that had wine, dancing, and women willing to exchange a few hours of their companionship for money, food, or clothing. Infrequently, men on furlough could see a movie shown in an old temporary army building or tent located safely behind the front lines. Hobart embraced these fleeting pleasures as a welcome addition to the limited social life he had known in a rural county.

In August of 1945 Japan surrendered. In the spring of 1946 Hobart was honorably discharged from the army without receiving a battle wound during his entire time in the Army. Well, he did burn his hands on a gun barrel during the heat of one battle, and he suffered frost bite on one ear. Those, according to the Army, did not count as wounds.

When the army discharged Hobart they provided him with mustering out money and a bus ticket back to Granby, the county seat and home to some five thousand souls. In Granby, Hobart hired a taxi to take him home. Within a mile of his parent's home, Hobart had the cab driver stop at a tavern for a beer. He hoped he might run into some of his buddies from high school days in the tavern. Five minutes after his arrival at the tavern a fist fight broke out between two of the bar's customers. Hobart knew neither of the people involved in the fight, took no part in the melee, and watched the fracas from his seat on a stool at the end of the bar. The fist fight escalated into a gun fight. Several shots were fired, and an errant shot grazed Hobart in the left forearm.

The wound was minor. Hobart would later say he considered this to be the point in life where his luck began to go downhill. Years in raging military gun battles without a scratch, and then get shot within a mile of his home because of a fight in which he had no part—it just, by-gosh, had to be some kind of bad omen.

Hobart got a job driving a truck for the highway department in the county. His job took him up and down most of the roads in the county. One day he took his lunch break in the shade of a tree along the road in front of Lois Radford's house. Lois was hanging wash-day laundry on a clothes line in their yard. By now she was an attractive 21- year-old woman. Hobart was handsome, had the gift of gab, and endowed with a charisma that attracted a lot of women. Lois was no exception.

Hobart struck up a conversation with Lois across the fence of her front yard. Her parents walked onto the front porch, and Hobart charmed them too. Toward the end of that summer, Hobart asked Rev. Radford for Lois's hand in marriage. Rev. & Mrs. Radford, delighted by the prospect of Hobart as a son- in- law, gave their approval. On the Sunday before Labor Day, Rev. Radford married Hobart and Lois in his church.

Hobart and Lois rented a small house on the western edge of the town of Granby and near his work headquarters. Life was good, as far as Hobart was concerned. Lois—well, she wasn't sure if life was good—or just more sinful.

Lois's life had been extremely sheltered before her marriage. Hobie, as she called Hobart, over the first 3 months of their marriage, had steadily introduced her to a life style of which she knew little—and tread with misgivings. Wearing Bermuda walking shorts—outside the house, mind you—in broad daylight; cutting her hair short; shaving her legs; using lipstick and putting rouge on her face—(oh God, what was it the Bible said God did to punish a 'painted' woman); allowing Hobie to keep beer in the refrigerator—surely God would remember she didn't drink any of it; walking around in front of Hobie without a stitch of clothes on—with the lights still on.

Trying to bring all these things to an 'it's okay' point in her mind had just been overwhelming. She wrestled daily with her conscience to get past the life-long admonitions of her father that such 'doings' would open the floodgates to pain and punishment in the after-life. To beat it all, she actually *liked* some of these 'new things' Hobie had her doing. Especially some of those things they did in bed. Still there was just no way something that felt that good could be anything but a sin, she worried. The list of sins for which she daily begged forgiveness was getting longer by the day.

One Saturday Hobie announced they were going to see a movie in Granby. The Lynnwood theatre was showing the latest Roy Rogers western movie. Hobie was a big Roy Rogers fan. Lois didn't want to go. She pleaded with Hobie not to go and spoke passionately of the sin involved in seeing movies. "God knows I'm already doing way too many sinful things", she pleaded. Hobie waved off her fears and promised she would love seeing Roy Rogers in action. The discussion went on all morning. Finally, Hobie put his foot down.

"You're married to me now, not your Daddy! We're going

to live like normal people and enjoy ourselves. Normal people go to the movies once in a while. Just because you enjoy something— have fun doin' something—don't make it no sin! We're going to the movies this evening, and that's the end of it!" said Hobie.

With deep concern and reservations, Lois yielded. She agreed to see her first movie. She really didn't know what 'movie' were. Having never seen a movie and hearing her father's life-long damnation of all graven images as tools from the Devil's workshop—movies had to be wrong.

In her mind, *any* interaction she *saw* between people was <u>real</u>. In Lois's limited frame of reference on life, she believed 'movies' were a sort of real, live, <u>stage</u> play, involving <u>real</u> people—telling out a story of their daily lives. Lois wasn't exactly sure what people in this 'movie' did, but she was pretty certain it was sinful. She couldn't recall which particular scripture forbade watching movies—but what difference did that make? Sin was sin. She had heard her Father say so, in countless sermons. On the other hand, Hobie was her husband. He said they were going to the movies, so she would go. She found some relief in her Father's oft quoted admonition that a good wife should obey her husband.

Hobie and Lois found good seats in the balcony of the Lynnwood theatre. They were enjoying popcorn and an R. C. Cola when the movie started. A curtain in the front of the theatre spread open, and, seemingly out of nowhere, there were people standing at the front of the theatre talking to each other. The opening moments of the conversations between those people seemed harmless enough to Lois. Roy Rogers, a man with a nice smile, even played a guitar sang a song. Lois was beginning to relax.

Fifteen minutes into the movie, the film showed the 'crooks' scheming to rob the town bank of all its money. Then, with guns in hand, the 'bad' guys robbed the local bank at gun point. Brutally clubbing the bank teller in the head with the butt of a pistol, they they grabbed up every last bag of money in the bank and raced out of town on their horses with guns blazing. Ray and a posse of local people quickly rode after the bad guys, with the intention of doing whatever it took to capture the thieves and recover the money stolen from the bank.

True to the script followed by most western movies, Ray and the posse, riding their horses at break-neck speed, over-took the thieves not far out of town. Certain she was seeing real robbery in action, Lois became so nervous she stopped eating her popcorn and gripped the arms of her seat. As the distance between them closed, Ray and his posse exchanged gun fire with the thieves from horseback. As of this moment, no one had been hit by a bullet in the exchange of gunfire. The thieves saw the futility of trying to outrun Ray and his men, dismounted, and took refuge behind some boulders and trees. Ray and friends did the same. Then, an all-out gun battle with pistols took place between Ray & his men—and the bad guys.

The gun fight was in full fury when one of the bad guys,

fleetingly, stood up from behind a boulder and exposed himself. Ray got off a shot from his trusty chrome-plated six-shooter that hit the exposed bad guy in the chest. The bad guy dropped his gun and fell to the ground, apparently dead. The death of the bad guy was the last straw for Lois. Screaming loudly and slinging her bag of popcorn across 3 rows of seats, Lois jumped to her feet.

"Lord, have mercy! Hobie, I told you we ought'n to come in here! Now look—we've done witnessed a murder! Let's get out of here before the police come and we get accused of being involved in it! Name of God! A man shot down like a dog—right in front of me! I knew it! I told you coming in this sinful 'movie house' would come to no good end! Don't sit there lookin' at me—run for it—before we get shot and killed too", screamed Lois hysterically as she kicked Hobie's legs aside to reach the isle.

With other people seated nearby turning to stare at Lois, Hobie grabbed her by the arm and pulled her back into her seat.

"What th' hell's got into you, woman? Daggonit, it's just a movie! It's just a make-believe story! Ain't nobody been murdered! Do you see anybody else runnin' out of here? Huh? Do you see anybody else in here duckin' to keep from getting' hit by a bullet? Do you see anybody else in here a-squallin' and a-screamin'? No, you don't! Because, bygod, they ain't nothin' you see on that movie screen <u>really</u> happ'nin! Now—you straight'n up, be quiet, sit still, and watch the movie. I'll explain things to you when the movie is over!" hissed Hobie through clinched teeth as he pulled her back into her seat.

Lois, unconvinced, braced herself for what might happen next. She burrowed so low in her seat she could barely see over the back of the seat in front of her. Her hands gripped the arms of her seat so hard her knuckles were white. Her eyes swung wildly as she looked back and forth across the theatre. For all she knew, some poor soul sitting right next to her might also have been hit by a stray bullet in that gunfight. She didn't give a hoot what Hobie said, if she saw a dead person laying in a seat near her—she was running out of that theatre and straight to the Sheriff's office.

By the time Lois returned her attention to the movie, the gunfight was over. It was followed by another 15 minutes of relatively peaceful dialogue and action between the characters in the movie. But, this was not to last. The bad guys broke out of jail and made a second effort to fill their pockets with stolen gold before leaving town.

This led to another raging gun battle between Ray and the bad guys. This time the fight took place right in the town. One of the bad guys, stealthily, worked his way around a building and appeared to have the 'drop' on Ray. He was lining up a pistol shot at Ray's back. Truly, it appeared ol' Ray was about to take a life ending bullet in the back. Once again, Lois lost control of her emotions. Arms flailing and fingers pointing, she jumped to her feet.

"Look out, Ray! Turn around! There he is—hidin' 'hind the

corner of that grocery store, Ray! He's a-gonna' shoot you right in the back if you don't turn around! Lord have mercy Hobie, he's a-gonna' kill Ray!" bellowed Lois as she pointed at the movie screen while jumping up and down in the isle.

Once again, Hobie pulled Lois back into her seat. He put one hand over her mouth, and used the other hand to pin her waving arms to her sides.

"Lois, if you don't sit still and keep your mouth shut, I swear I'm gonna' take you outside and leave you on the street by yourself 'til this movie is over!" whispered Hobie angrily.

Lois resumed her death grip on the arms of her seat and watched the remainder of the movie in a silence that belied her near panic. When the movie was over, Hobie went to the theatre manager, Roger Irvin, and got permission to take Lois up to the projection room. He showed her the film being re-wound on the projector and explained that what she saw on the screen was only images of people. Lois wasn't mollified.

"I don't care if it wasn't real people we saw in that theatre! For them to make that movie they had to get some folks to kill other folks so they could take a picture them doing it! So we are still witnesses to a murder! If we don't go across the street, right now, and report what we done seen to Sheriff Watson--we are gonna' get in trouble. Hobie, you know the law says you're supposed to report any wrong-doings. If we don't, then the police might lock us up! So we ought to go over there right now—and just give it up—tell what we saw happen in this here building" Lois insisted.

Hobie shook his head and took Lois home. He gave up on the idea of taking Lois to the movies for a few weeks. Eventually, he tried again with a comedy movie starring Bud Abbott & Lou Costello. Lois found that movie a little easier to take, but still sat through it with a sense of dread.

Sadly, some years later, Hobie and Lois divorced. Their views of life, what was right or wrong, and what was 'okay' and 'fun' were just too far apart to be bridged. Hobie and Lois remarried other people and had families. Ironically, with the passage of years, Hobie began living a more conservative life and Lois' way of life became rather worldly—even a bit profane at times. But—that's just people and life. Both of them change with time.

THE PREACHER AND THE BEAR

Iaeger (pronounced Yay-ger) was a little town of some 2500 souls hidden away in the mountains of West Virginia. It was supported by coal mining and a repair yard for the Norfolk & Western railway. There were stores, banks, a movie theatre, Vinnie Francisco's Chevvy dealership, several cafes, a Town Hall, a jail, an elementary & high school, and enough churches to represent most of the mainstream religions.

Oh, there was also a hotel. It was owned by Bessie Bowman. It was called *Iaeger Hotel*. It was three floors high, with six rooms on each floor.

Iaeger was built along the banks of Tug River. Tug ran north to south between two fairly steep mountains. There was relatively little flat land between the two mountains, and Tug River took up a portion of the available flat land. The layout of the town of Iaeger was driven by this rather unique terrain and river. The majority of the businesses in Iaeger were built on the west side of Tug River. The majority of the residential area of town was on the east side of Tug, along with schools and churches. This way there was enough flat land available to accommodate the commercial and personal needs of the citizens of Iaeger.

The only means of crossing Tug River between the east and west sides of Iaeger was the H. Wyatt Sage Memorial

Bridge on the south end of town. Well—there was a narrow foot bridge on the far north end of Iaeger. It was suspended from each side of the 50 foot wide river by means of wire cables. Hence, the reason for calling it a 'swinging' bridge. Walking on the bridge was much like walking on a trampoline. It wasn't real stable. Some who used it were unsure they would reach the opposite side of Tug River without having to finish the crossing by *swimming*.

No one <u>knew</u> the exact details, but it was believed H. Wyatt traded his vote in the state legislature for a state allocation of enough money to build this main bridge over Tug River. Regardless of how H. Wyatt got the money to build the bridge, the grateful people of Iaeger named the bridge after ol' H. Wyatt. It crossed Tug River just past Bessie Bowman's' hotel.

Primarily, the bridge was built for cars and trucks. However, a lot more people walked across that bridge than rode across it. Especially during the depression of the 30s—when no one had money for gas, and in the early years of the 1940s—when gas was rationed due to WW II.

Shorty Echols was a small man. He was, maybe, five feet-four inches tall. He couldn't tip the scales at more than one hundred and thirty five pounds, even with rocks in his pockets. Shorty lived most of his life in and around Iaeger. He graduated from Iaeger High School with a diploma in Automotive & Mechanical Technical Studies.

Shorty went to work for the town's Chevvy dealership right out of high school. Arguably, he became the best mechanic in town. The owner of the dealership paid Shorty well, and he was happy in his work. He married his high school sweetheart. They had two children and a modest home in the southeast corner of Iaeger. On balance, life was good for Shorty in the early '40s.

Shorty was not without a few weaknesses. A low tolerance for alcohol was one of them. He liked to join a group of friends at Martin's Café & Bar every Friday after work for a few 'restoratives'. The word 'Café' was a gross misnomer in Martin's case. No one with any concern for their health ate the food in Martin's Cafe. His Café was nothing but a down-and-dirty bar located in the north end of Iaeger. After 9 p.m. on Friday or Saturday nights, you had to fight your way *in* and *out* of Martin's. The gathering of Shorty & friends on Friday evenings was a celebration of the end of the work week. The celebration was fueled with cheap bourbon liquor.

Whether it was Shorty's slight physical build, or his body's unnaturally poor tolerance of alcohol, no one could say. Without fear of contradiction, they *could* say, Shorty was 'falling down drunk' after three shots of whiskey.

After several drinks, Shorty imagined he had a singing voice like Bing Crosby or Vaughn Monroe. Everyone knew when he passed the dividing line between just drinking and being drunk. He would burst forth in song—loudly. He would belt out the latest hit songs being played on the radio show 'Hit

Parade'— whether you wanted to hear them or not. The absence of any accompanying music didn't bother Shorty.

His singing signaled the end of the Friday evening celebration by Shorty and friends. His friends quickly told him goodnight and fled the bar. Then Bosko Martin tossed Shorty out of the bar.

Bosko Martin was spot-on-right when he told Shorty, 'You couldn't carry a tune in a bucket'. He had the worst singing voice in the entire town. It was a shrill, high, piercing, off-key sound—way north of an Irish tenor.

Thrown out of Martin's Bar, Shorty would stagger down the street toward the H. Wyatt Sage Bridge and home. One hot Friday evening, Shorty was barely able to walk. He staggered down the sidewalk, pitching forward, staving backwards, and tilting from side to side. His wobbly stride gave him the appearance of walking on a mattress rather than a concrete sidewalk. It took him twenty minutes to cover the six blocks from Martin's to the south end of town.

Despite his difficulty in staying on his feet, Shorty continued singing with gusto. In hopes of gaining some relief from the heat of the summer night, most people left the windows of their houses open. They all heard Shorty as he passed their houses—wailing the words to some song.

Shorty eventually found himself on the sidewalk in front of Bessie Bowman's *Iaeger Hotel*. It was the last commercial building Shorty would pass before he crossed the H. Wyatt

Bridge to the residential area of town.

Bessie ran her hotel like a drill sergeant. Except for a radio at low volume, she was intolerant of any noise in or around her hotel after nine o'clock in the evening. Bessie wasn't a woman you wanted to annoy. She had a raspy, menacing voice and a legendary temper. Her willingness to back up her verbal threats with physical action was a well-known part of town lore. Nearly anyone in town could recall the night Elwood Farley got drunk, climbed 8 ft. up a street light pole in front of the *Iaeger Hotel*, bayed at the moon like a howling dog, and wouldn't stop.

Bessie leaned out the bedroom window of her apartment on the second floor of the hotel, told Elwood to, "Shut your mouth, climb down off that pole, and go home—before I take my pistol and shoot your sorry ass off that pole".

Elwood told Bessie to 'kiss my ass' and continued to wail into night while hanging from that street-light pole. Bessie took a .22 pistol from her dresser drawer, again leaned out her second story window, shot Elwood in the leg, and watched him fall eight feet from the pole to the sidewalk. After Bessie shot Elwood off the pole she got back in bed—without bothering to go down to the sidewalk and check on his condition.

Hearing the shot, someone in a nearby home called Pat Fanning—the town Undertaker. He brought his hearse down to the hotel, loaded Elwood into the hearse, and took him to the Welch Hospital. They patched ol' Elwood up, but he walked with a limp for nearly a year.

Allegedly, Bessie worked as the 'Madam' in a house of prostitution in Bradshaw—in her earlier years. Allegedly, Bessie put several of the 'clientele' of this Bradshaw 'Gentlemen's Sporting Club' in a local hospital (baseball bat traumas/knife wounds/gunshot wounds) for violating in-house house rules concerning their conduct and treatment of her 'female resident staff '. Tales or truth, Bessie made enough money in Bradshaw to retire early from the 'entertainment industry' and pay in cash for the Iaeger Hotel. It also gave her 'bona-fides' as a 'hard' woman.

Shorty stopped in front of Bessie's hotel, wrapped his arms around the street light pole for support, and burst forth with his own rendition of a currently popular radio hit tune, *The Preacher & The Bear*. Shorty finished a verse of the song, was wailing his way into the second verse, when Bessie's head shot out of her window on the second floor of the hotel.

"Shorty—if you don't shut your mouth and get the hell across that bridge—I'm coming down there! Then—by god—me, you, the preacher, and the bear is all gonna' get into it! And when I finish with you—you ain't likely to <u>ever</u> sing again—with no damn teeth in your mouth!"

Shorty was drunk, but not stupid or deaf. He heard Bessie, loud and clear. He had heard that story about Elwood Farley, too. Oh yeah—heard it from Elwood's own lips. Yes indeed—shot the man! Right in the leg! Six inches higher up his leg—that bullet would have shot off ol' Elwood's 'bell-rope'. Likely as not, that's what Bessie intended to do anyway! The man would have spent the rest of his life seeing nothing but his toes when he looked down. Shorty had seen poor ol' Elwood hopping around town on crutches for a month after she shot him off that pole—and the police didn't even arrest her!

Shorty didn't doubt for two seconds that Bessie would make some unsolicited modifications to his face with a baseball bat—send him to work Monday morning with his teeth all broken or knocked out. Knowing her, he speculated, she might even *shoot* his teeth out. 'Gawdalmighty—who needs that kind of aggravation', he thought.

Shorty brought his singing to an immediate close, and quietly staggered across the H. Wyatt Sage Bridge to home and family on McDowell St.

"Somebody sure ought to do something about that crazy ol' woman", he mumbled to himself as stumbled up his driveway. "The law is supposed to protect innocent people— and singin' ain't against no law."

AROUND TOWN

Luxemborg was a sleepy little town of some 3000 or so people. Built on three, low, rolling hills, it didn't stretch more than a half- mile from one end to the other. It was the county seat of Robeson County. The usual mix of government buildings, businesses, schools, and residences filled out the town's geography. There was the Court House, the schools, and a police department. These were complimented by 15 or so small businesses. A *Piggly Wiggly* grocery store, a movie theatre, two clothing stores, a drug store, offices occupied by doctors, a dentist, lawyers, and two insurance Agents. There were a couple of barber shops and two small automobile dealerships. The town also boasted two small garment industry factories. Six churches filled the needs of those living there. Most of the people living there were conservative by nature and enjoyed an unhurried outlook on life. A few of the town's inhabitants stood out enough to qualify as 'characters'.

Ronnie Miller lived with his parents. He was 20 years old, had completed high school, had no known ambitions, and held a clerical job at the grocery store. He saved enough money to buy an old Chevrolet coupe, dated several local girls, and loved stock car races. He enjoyed a little beer and whiskey from time to time, but lived in denial of the fact that even moderate consumption of alcohol left him physically impaired. After a few beers, let alone whiskey, performing even simple acts became difficult for him. Ronnie was honest, and very loyal to close friends. He didn't have a high I.Q. In the words of locals, Ronnie was 'not a thinkin' man'.

J. Lee Riggins lived with his grandparents, Ma & Pa Riggins. Lee had native intelligence, charisma, ambitions, the gift of gab, and put great emphasis on his clothes and appearance. Whatever the source of his magnetism, most girls were attracted to him. He was fond of saying, 'I can get a girl where most men can't even get groceries'. Lee was frustrated by the circumstances in his life. He despaired of reaching the station in life he felt his talents merited. He had no college education, no real financial means, no 'network' with people of influence who could help him move above a 'living wage' existence in Luxemborg—or anywhere else for that matter. Lee made do with a series of menial jobs, while he waited for the 'break' that would launch his rise to wealth and power.

Hawkey Powers—well—it was hard to put a label on him. Most people in town offered one word descriptions of Hawkey—like unique, strange, nut-case, pervert. He lived in Luxemborg or several small surrounding communities his entire life. Except on infrequent visits to homes of relatives or trips to sporting events, Hawkey had seldom been out of Robeson County. He wasn't bothered by this. He found total contentment in Luxemborg. He had a job at a local gas station and never entertained the idea of any job more challenging

Hawkey had one consuming passion in life. He was a voyeur. He loved peeking through bedroom windows at women in various stages of undress. He never voiced any interest in actually having sex with women he peeked at—just 'peeking' was his game. Hawkey claimed he knew more about the women in town than their husbands or boyfriends. He was never caught enjoying his nocturnal habit. This was a miracle—considering he had been seen, some evenings, walking around town with a 20 ft. extension ladder slung across his shoulder.

Hawkey had great strenght in his arm and upper body. He could do 50 chin-ups without breaking a sweat. He could jump over two feet high in the air while standing with his feet flat on the ground. Such a jump put him within grasp of the lower, outside window ledges of some homes in town. Once he grasped the window ledges with his fingers, he would use his powerful arms to raise his face to the level of the window without making a sound. He could hang on the window ledge in this fashion for thirty seconds or so while he savored the view inside the window. If a second-story window was involved—Hawkey always seemed to have his trusty extension ladder nearby

Hawkey was not a sexual predator. He had dates with some girls in and around town. He was a gentleman on dates. He took pride in his inviolable rule of 'pleasuring a girl only when she *wants* to be pleasured'. Some might say this was a contradiction in psyche. Perhaps, but it was a rule Hawkey stuck to. While peeping didn't bother his conscience in the least, he totally adhered to the accepted rules of behavior concerning sexual *relations* with women.

Robey Barton was a tall, muscular, outspoken man, with a booming voice. His temper, too often, ran as hot as the color of his fiery, red hair. He was lacking in intelligence. He tried to cover this weakness with his loud mouth and know-it-all attitude. Robey actually believed he had a superior intellect and people could benefit by listening to what he had to say. He was convinced his mission in life was to talk while others listened and drew on his knowledge. He rarely held any job for more than a year before his employer decided his services were no longer needed.

At one time, Robey was a town policeman. His attitude and badge combined to make him the most prolific traffic-ticket writer in the long history of Luxemborg. One day Robey was writing a traffic violation ticket on a school bus driver. The bus driver was a woman. The woman, no shrinking violet herself, had stopped her bus in front of the drug Store on Main St. to pick up a prescription for her child. She wasn't in the drug store more than 2 minutes. Two minutes or not, it was long enough for Robey to spot her bus parked in an illegal parking zone and begin writing her a ticket.

The bus driver, Josie Martin, tried to explain her situation and asked Robey not to write the ticket. Robey's consideration of her request was swift—and the answer was 'No'. In the strongest terms possible, Josie told Robey what she thought of him. Robey lectured her on obeying laws—including illegal parking. Their exchange became heated. Their yelling match peaked with them calling each other vile and profane names that reflected poorly on their parental lineage. Josie told Robey he could stick the ticket up his rear and slapped his face. He responded by slapping her face. Then, with a crowd of people watching, Robey snapped his hand-cuffs on Josie. With her cursing, screaming and kicking at Robey every step of the way, he drug her across the street to the Court House and tossed her in a jail cell.

Except for slapping Josie, Robey might have legally been within his official duties. The Queen-Mother of 'No-Nos' in Luxemborg was physically abusing a woman—especially in public. Compounding his 'back-handing' Josie's face, was the reservoir of ill will he had built up with his mania for writing traffic tickets to far too many citizens of Luxemborg. The Town Council fired Robey within a month of the 'Josie' incident.

Shortly after his termination as a town policeman, Robey found his true calling. He became a Minister of the Gospel. After completing a two month mail-order correspondence course, Robey was ordained a Minister. The ordination was also done by mail. He founded his own church, called the Rock of Life Church--with an ultra-conservative orthodoxy.

After his ordination, Robey was never seen without a Bible in hand. He walked the streets of Luxemborg, stopped people on the sidewalk, whipped open his Bible, and quoted scriptures to them in a loud voice. He solicited their membership in the only *true* church in town—his. Robey made that clear. It was a membership in his church, acquired only through baptism by him, or a certain journey down the sorry road to a fiery hell. This attempt at conversion was completed when Robey laid his hand on the conscripted citizen's shoulder and offered up a prayer in a voice loud enough to be heard a half block away. All the while, you could see other people scattering for two blocks away to avoid a 'sidewalk ambush' by 'Reverend' Robey.

Judge Howard Dunn was the Circuit Judge for the County. While not a noted legal scholar, he was a staunch supporter of the Democratic Party and Harry Byrd political machine in Virginia. Judge Dunn's political ties got him an appointment to the bench early in life. He had been on the bench for over 30 years. It was said Judge Dunn, before making a legal ruling from the bench, would put his finger in the air to see which way the winds of public and political opinion were blowing. Some of his rulings had scant legal basis, but they satisfied the local electorate and political powers in the State House well enough to keep him on the bench for most of his adult life.

Sam Hudson was a teacher of history at Luxemborg high school. Sam knew his history. He was respected and liked by both students and faculty. There were a couple of other noteworthy items about Sam. He had a lisp and loved to gamble. When talking excitedly, his lisp would cause him to spray spit on those standing nearby. His gambling was confined to weekend penny-ante poker games with a quarter limit. And he would shoot dice with a fifty cent limit.

You bring people like these together in a small town like Luxemborg—you are bound to give birth to some stories—like those on the following pages.

It was the day before school started. Lee Riggins intended to take his pick of the prettiest high school girls for dates that fall. He wanted his flat-top haircut, with duck tails sweeping back on both sides of his head, trimmed to perfection. Lee swore physical appearance was a big part of success with girls. Several of boys went with Lee to Acey Francisco's barber shop to get his hair trimmed to perfection.

Acey's was not only the most popular barber shop in town, but a social gathering place for many of the men in town. Acey had three barber chairs in his shop. Often, the three chairs were full and people waiting—6 days a week.

Lee hopped in the last chair available. His friends plopped down in red, vinyl covered chairs along the wall for waiting customers. Counting the barbers, there were ten people in the shop when 'Reverend' Robey Barton walked in.

Finding few potential religious converts on the sidewalks, Robey had chosen to work the town's stores and shops. Acey's barber shop was at the top of his list. Those of us in Acey's shop that afternoon were trapped. There was no time to run and no place to hide. Robey had a captive audience, and every one there would have to hear him out. You never knew how long Robey's journey into the scriptures would last, so the barbers continued to cut hair as he spoke. Time was money to them, sermons notwithstanding.

"Brothers, I'm glad to see y'all here today. I'm here to bring the gospel to you and make your lives richer. Hear me now, while I quote from the good book", intoned Robey as he launched into his spiel. Even Robey knew Acey had limits on what he would put up with, so he brought his remarks to a close in less than 4 minutes with a call for prayer.

"On your knees, gentlemen! You don't show respect for the Lord by praying while you sit on your behinds! On your knees, every head bowed, every eye shut!" thundered Robey in his booming voice.

Wanting to get this over, every person in the barbershop, barbers included, got down on their knees at the back of the shop in front of Robey. Those receiving haircuts still had the white cloths pinned around their necks as they kneeled with their backs to the front door.

Suddenly, the front door to the shop flew open. There stood Sam Hudson. He had walked by the barber shop, looked through the window, and saw men on their knees with their heads bent toward the floor. What he didn't see was Robey standing in the corner. He *assumed* the whole gang of men were shooting dice on the floor in the rear of Acey's shop. Sam Hudson began to shout, lisp and all, before he had a chance to hear Robey in mid-prayer.

"I'll thoot any damn man in the houth for fifty thents! We'll uuth your dieth or mine! All right now, whooth got balls enough to thoot dieth with me?" roared Sam, spit flying from his mouth.

Robey stopped in mid-prayer. For the first time in all the years people had known him, words failed him. Robey was speechless. Sam Hudson's profanity laced greetings when he came through the door—right when the 'Reverend' was hitting his stride in the prayer—was more than Robey's mind could process. Those on their knees stayed there, heads bowed, stifling laughter. Sam, still not seeing Robey, yelled out again.

"What th' hell ith th' matter with you boyth? Ith fifty thents too rich for your blood? Or are you juth too chicken to thoot di'eth with me?"

Lee glanced up at Robey. The color of Robey's face was coming close to that of his hair. He stepped out of the shadows of the corner and berated Sam. Robey loudly ran through a whole litany of sins Sam was guilty of. In a voice of doom, he cited scriptures that almost certainly guaranteed Sam would pay for his transgressions in the fires of Hell. 'Reverend' Robey walked toward Sam, pounding his bible, screaming for him to prepare himself for an eternity of agony in the Lake of Fire.

Sam did the sensible thing. He ran from the shop and down the sidewalk as fast as his long legs would carry him. 'Reverend' Robey stood in the door of the shop, shouting scriptural based promises of damnation at Sam until he was out of sight. Ronnie Miller was laughing his head off at Sam's misfortune. Robey slammed the door as he came back into the shop. Ronnie quickly quieted down. Lee Riggins, always the 'quick lip', spoke up.

"Reverend Robey, Mr. Sam Hudson is an un-repented sinner! His disgraceful conduct here today is proof positive of that! His shame has no equal! On the other hand, Reverend, it appears Mr. Houston is more in need of prayers for absolution from his wretched sins than threats of condemnation. From listening to you here today, sir, I'm inclined to think you may be the only man in town equal to that task. I've no doubt the Christian charity in your heart will compel you to go over to Mr. Houston's house and counsel him. Be there no doubt about it, the man must do a penance as a show of true remorse for what he did here today. He's got to give up that money he intended to gamble with here today. It can do far more good in the treasury of your church. If he intends to mend his decadent way of life, he's got to give up those ill-gotten gains he's carrying around in his pockets!"

Whatever failings Lee had, and he had some, his vocabulary and the ability to use it was not among them. Robey stared at Lee with his eyes squinted almost shut. Robey was generally smart enough to know when someone was 'running a game' on him. But he couldn't tell if Lee was 'putting him on' or was sincere in his comments. His doubt left him unable to come up with a rebuttal to Lee's challenge.

To encourage him to leave the barber shop everyone put together an offering of three dollars to support his ministry. In 1954 it took 2 hour's work to earn three dollars. It was enough to send Reverend Robey out the door and across town to Sam Hudson's home. After Reverend Robey was out of sight there was so much laughter over the whole incident that the barbers had to ask those having their hair cut to hold still so they could cut their hair properly.

A warm, humid summer evening found Hawkey Collins with nothing to do and nowhere to go. He decided to spice up his evening by doing a little 'peeking'. Hawkey was looking for a fresh angle on peeking. There was a new Elvis Presley movie showing at the local theatre. He knew every girl in town with enough money for the price of a ticket would be there.

The theatre was elevated three feet off the ground. It was supported by variously placed concrete columns. The front of the theatre had a porch, also three feet off the ground. The floor or the old porch was nothing more than two by six boards with a quarter inch space between each board. Girls stood in line on the porch, awaiting their turn to move up the window where tickets were sold for the movie.

Hawkey slipped quietly around to the rear of the theatre building. On his hands and knees, he crawled beneath the entire length of the building until he was looking up through the cracks between the boards of the theatre's front porch. This gave him the perfect vantage point for peeking under the skirt of every female movie-goer.

Hawkey was enjoying these forbidden sights when a girl dropped several small photos from her wallet. The photos fluttered to the floor of the theatre porch. Through sheer bad luck, two of the photos fell through the cracks of the porch.

The girl and several of her friends let out wails of anguish over the loss of her treasured high school photos. They picked up the one which had fallen to the floor. Even though resigned to the loss of the photos, the girls stood there—staring at the cracks through which her pictures had disappeared. To their amazement, the two photos slid back up through one the cracks. For a second or two the girls stood there in disbelief and shock at this incredible reversal of the law of gravity.

Suddenly, the explanation dawned on them. There had to be someone under the porch! They screamed as they ran from the porch. The sanctity of the area beneath their skirts had been breached! Privacy at its highest had been violated!

The town police were called. By the time they got there and crawled beneath the theatre Hawkey was long gone. The next morning, Hawkey recounted his close call to Lee, Ronnie, and Weejee. Lee shook his head in disbelief.

"Hawkey", said Lee, "why in hell did you shove those photos back up through that crack between the porch boards? What were you thinking? Why would you do a dumb thing like that, man? You just gave yourself away.

Why would you do that?"

Hawkey's face turned red with anger. His chest swelled as he indignantly spat out a reply to Lee.

"Now you jus' listen to me, Mr. Know-it-all-Lee Riggins. I didn' do nothin' dumb, by God! Far as that goes, I did some pretty smart thinkin'—and I did it fast! You see" , said Hawkey as he tapped his forehead with his finger, "I knew if them girls crawled under that there porch to get them pitchurs'—why there was no way they would not have seen me down under that porch! They would have known I had been under that there porch a lookin' up their skirts! So I shoved their pitchurs' back up through that there crack real fast, before they could get a notion to come down under that porch to get them. My fast thinkin' was all that saved me.!"

They all looked at Hawkey, as he beamed a triumphant smile. Without saying anything to him, they turned and looked at each other. Hawkey truly believed every word he had uttered. Shaking their heads, they walked away without another word to Hawkey. If he hadn't seen the obvious idiocy in his reasoning by now, they had no chance of persuading him to re-think the matter.
As usual, the police didn't catch Hawkey. The theatre owner had a couple of sheets of plywood nailed down over the old porch boards to cover the cracks. That put an end to Hawkey's use of the theatre porch as a source of 'peeking'.

One summer Saturday Ronnie and several of us spent the afternoon listening to a stock car race on the radio while enjoying a beer. Ronnie could never get his arms around the idea of 'moderate' drinking where beer was concerned. All of us had one beer—except Ronnie. He had 4-5 beers and was real tipsy when the race ended around five o'clock that afternoon. Not more than ten minutes after the race ended the phone rang at Red Pate's Garage where we had listened to the race. It was Ronnie's mother. She was putting dinner on the table and wanted Ronnie home for the meal. She told Ronnie to invite Lee, Weejie, and me to eat dinner with them.

Weejie forced a cup of black coffee into Ronnie. Lee, despite Ronnie's cursing, made him take a cold shower in the bathroom at Red's garage. Together, those things improved Ronnie's sobriety, but not as much as we had hoped.

Ronnie's mother was putting the food on the long dining room table when we walked into the house. We took our places at the table and Mrs. Miller asked Ronnie to say Grace over the food. What came out of Ronnie's mouth was totally unexpected, and was nothing any of us had ever heard anybody say before.

"Bless the meat---damn the skin---pass the bread---and let's begin", solemnly intoned Ronnie from his bowed head.

The words hardly died on his lips before Mr. Miller's hand shot out and backhanded Ronnie so hard his chair nearly turned over. Mr. & Mrs. Miller were both devout members of the Heritage Baptist Church of Luxemborg. After some strong, direct comments from Mr. Miller, and several apologies from Ronnie Mr. Miller invited everyone to begin eating.

Even the solid whack Mr. Miller laid upside Ronnie's head did little to increase his sobriety. Everyone loaded their hotdogs with chili, mustard, onions, and began to eat. Weejie, Lee, and I were nervously watching Ronnie out of the corners of our eyes as he picked up his hotdog. We feared the worst, and it happened. Ronnie opened his mouth wide, moved his hotdog toward his face with both hands, and poked himself right in the left eye with the hotdog.

We pretended to have seen nothing out of ordinary. Mrs. Miller had clearly seen the whole thing. Chili was plastered all over the left side of Ronnie's face from his eye down to the tip of his nose. Mrs. Miller tore into ol' Ronnie.

"Ronnie! What in the world is the matter with you today? Are you going blind or just trying to act silly like you did saying Grace? You pull one more stunt like that and I'm going to excuse you from the table! I'm beginning to think you've taken leave of your senses! I better not see another trick out of you the rest of the evening!"
Lee, Weejie, and I stuffed food in our mouths so fast we were on the verge of choking. We just wanted to get out of there before Mr. Miller realized what was really wrong with Ronnie and beat the crap out of him.

It was close to Labor Day when Ronnie got himself in some real trouble. Some girl Ronnie had been dating off and on for a couple of months told Ronnie she was pregnant and he was the father of the child. Ronnie denied being the father. The girl's father demanded that Ronnie marry his daughter, at once. Ronnie refused to marry the girl. The girl's father went before the Commonwealth Attorney's officer—said his daughter was pregnant—and that Ronnie had done the dirty deed. The C.A. issued a complaint warrant against Ronnie.

A County Deputy served the warrant on Ronnie at the Miller home. Mrs. Miller nearly fainted as she collapsed in a chair. Mr. Miller used a lot of profanity in the shouting match with Ronnie that followed the service of the warrant. After the initial shock of the news, Mr. & Mrs. Miller 'circled the wagons' around Ronnie. They had little choice. Mr. Miller was one of the most respected and successful merchants in Luxemborg. He was a big-wig in the local Democratic Party. If this weren't enough, he was also a member of the Board of Deacons at Heritage Baptist. Mrs. Miller was a ranking officer of the local Ladies Garden Club.

Even if they didn't believe Ronnie's denial of being the father of the illegitimate child, Mr. Miller insisted there was far too much at stake in reputation and standing in the community to let Ronnie be forced into marrying a 'nobody from a dirt road in the ass-end of the county who has questionable morals'.
No telling who fathered that child", swore Mr. Miller. "Nobody", he thundered, "is going to make a Miller the

laughing stock of this town."

Mr. Miller retained the venerable C. Asa (Acey) Lambert, Esq. to defend Ronnie in the matter of these 'reprehensible and baseless charges'. Those were Lawyer Lambert's words. The man was a poet when it came to weaving big words and legal phrases together. The trial was set for hearing in the circuit Court of Robeson County, the Honorable J. Howard Dunn, presiding. All the lawyers in the county used their middle name with their first initial in front of the middle name. Made their name sound more important— more lawyerly—more intimidating.

Ol' J. Asa built Ronnie's defense around the allegation that this 'mere acquaintance'—not 'girl-friend' of Ronnie's—was a *liar* of the first water—a woman of *loose* morals, and, one who *preyed* on innocent young men, and, as such, lacked credibility in any and all claims and testimony. On trial day, J. Asa delivered his opening remarks in defense of Ronnie in an ominous voice, arms waving in the air, and his finger stabbing in the air to drive home a point. He let his voice rise and fall and he paced the court room floor. As the trial wore on, he verbally danced around the evidence the prosecution put forth with such skill he looked better than those professional boxers ducking punches on the Friday night TV fights.

Toward the end of the day, those of us sitting in the court room were about to conclude, despite his opening statement and denials of every claim the prosecutor made, that ol' J. Asa was about to lose this case for Ronnie. Ah, but J. Asa was a cagey rascal.

Toward the end of his defense he introduced into evidence a snap-shot photo of Ronnie's *alleged* 'girl-friend'. J. Asa insisted the candid photo of the girl was clear cut evidence she was a woman of loose morals; a woman who was no stranger to any number of men. Claiming profound regret for burdening the court with such lewd evidence, he handed the photo to Judge Dunn and asked that it be admitted into evidence.

The photo was an old black and white print of the 'girl-friend' wearing Bermuda shorts. The hem of the shorts was no more than three inches above her knees. Bermuda shorts were accepted casual summer attire for both men and women at the time. Judge Dunn stared at the photo for a full 15 seconds. He stared at the girl herself for about five seconds. With a disapproving look on his face, Judge Dunn shook his head. He handed the photo to the Prosecuting Attorney, and told him to hand the photo to Ronnie's *alleged* girl-friend. With a countenance filled with disgust, Judge Dunn spoke to the girl in stern, booming voice.

"Young lady, is that you in that picture—wearing those disgraceful bloomers?"

"Yes, it's me. So what? There's nothing wrong with Bermuda shorts", said the puzzled girl.

Judge Dunn told the girl *he* would decide what was right and wrong in *his* court. He followed this declaration with a lecture full of despair about the low state of morals prevalent among too many young women of that day and time. J. Asa Lambert, right on cue, jumped to his feet and asked for a summary dismissal of the charges against his client, one Ronnie Miller.

Judge Dunn, right on cue, said he was satisfied the photo of the plaintiff in the Bermuda shorts satisfied the burden of proof that the girl accusing Ronnie was a woman of *loose* morals. As such, anybody could have fathered the child she claimed was Ronnie's. Therefore, he found the defendant, one Ronnie Miller, innocent of all charges.

While we were happy for Ronnie, we didn't know whether to laugh or shake our heads over Judge Dunn's opinion of what evidence met the burden of proof of good or bad morals. The truth of the matter was, no one knew whose child the girl was carrying. After Ronnie's trial, a half dozen men around Luxemborg admitted to having sex with the girl. Either way, Lee, Weejie, and I agreed what we had witnessed in court that day was a real incentive to avoid 'justice' dished out in Judge Dunn's court.

A few weeks after the trial, Ronnie and his parents decided a couple of years in the Army might be good for him. It was preferable to being shot dead by the ex-girl-friend's father, who had promised to do just that. Within 30 days Ronnie had enlisted in the Army and was doing basic training in some army boot camp in Georgia.

Robey—failing to found a successful church in town—took

a job as a missionary to some island in the Pacific Ocean called Cat Island. He wrote, at least, one letter every month to editor of the local paper, detailing the progress of his mission on Cat Island. He was back in Luxemborg a year later. Folks in town said Robey must be a fast Preacher to have converted everybody on that island in one year. Those less charitable said about one year was all the people of that island could take of Robey.

Lee moved north, was later drafted into the army, and never moved back to Luxemborg. When last heard from, he was selling used cars somewhere in Tennessee. Hawkey lost his job at the gas station. His brother got him a job at a coal mines in a neighboring county. He got married and had two children. One of them became a doctor. Hawkey died of Black Lung disease a few days after his sixty third birthday.

All in all, Luxemborg was just a small, sleepy town. Probably pretty much like small towns everywhere.

THE UMPIRE & THE FUNERAL

Mase Boardwine was born Mason Elijah Boardwine. His parents called him Mase. His middle name was a tribute to his maternal uncle, Elijah 'Lij' Farley. 'Lij' had been a guest at the county jail on several occasions. Nothing serious—fights—drunk and disorderly—damage to Juney Hunt's saloon during 'chair fights', etc. But, he was Mrs. Boardwine's only brother and she loved him without reservation.

Mase was an only child. Not because Mr. & Mrs. Boardwine practiced birth control or supported planned-parenthood. They met and married late in life, and Mase was the only child they were able to conceive.

Mase was born, grew up, and lived out his life in Bartlick. This was the name posted on the official highway sign near his parent's home. There was no town. Just a few modest, white frame dwellings scattered along the road that followed the creek through the mountains of the area. No one knew where the name Battlick came from—and didn't really care.

Mase's Father was a coal miner. His Mother was a homemaker. Both were honest people and devout members of a Church. Both voted a straight Democrat ticket all their lives. They did so because both were convinced the Republicans were responsible for the legendary depression of the 1920s that left Mr. Boardwine with no regular job, and very little food—until Franklin Roosevelt was elected President. From an early age, the Boardwines taught Mase to have two central figures in his life—the Lord, and President Franklin Delano Roosevelt.

With the exception of the two years he was in the Army, Mase spent his entire life within a seventy five mile radius of Bartlick. Mr. & Mrs. Boardwine passed away not long after Mase returned home from his stint in the Army. Everything they had was left to him. Everything being a small home, 4 acres of land, a GMC pick-up truck, a hunting dog, and $3,200—their life savings.

Mase graduated from high school, but continuing higher education was not high on his list of priorities. He lived the life of a laborer and was happy with it. He had a job at a local sawmill. It provided him with enough money to meet his needs. He was content—life was good.

Mase's view of a good life leaned toward simplicity— literally. Simple food, playing baseball, minimal clothing, hunting buddies, and women he 'took pleasure' with. No doubt about it, all things that gave form to his life were reduced to simple terms. Simplicity insulated him from the baggage of 'botherations' found in a more 'involved' life.

Put up with a 'botheration'? "Naw sir! Don't need it—don't want it—can't stand the miseries it brings with it", preached Mase.

He enjoyed hunting, raising a garden, country music, having a few drinks with the boys at Juney Hunt's saloon on weekends, and 'bedding' ladies that didn't require a lot of courting. Mase considered the commonly accepted rituals of courting women to be expensive, time consuming, hard to understand, and without a guarantee of sexual favors from those courted. No, he found the women who were 'regulars' at Juney's saloon more to his liking. For a little beer, wine, food, maybe a movie—they would be 'nice' to him.

Mase had one passionate love—the game of baseball. He had been a star pitcher on his high school baseball team. He played for an army team while he was in service. After returning home from the army, he played for local amateur sandlot baseball teams for ten or twelve years. These teams were organized by small towns throughout several counties near his home. During the season—weather permitting—he spent every Saturday and Sunday afternoon playing ball for one of these teams.

As the years marched on, Mase's curve ball became history and his fast ball lost its zing. He had to give up his place on the team to younger, faster, and better players. He accepted this price of aging. Still, he didn't want baseball completely out of his life. He had never married, so baseball was the major focus in his life. He found the perfect answer to his situation—he became a baseball umpire. He had a good eye for calling balls and strikes. He was already well known and trusted in the tri-county amateur baseball league. By the time Mase was forty years old, he was the premier umpire of the tri-county sandlot baseball league.

No resume on Mase would be complete without covering his particular taste in clothing. He wore denim, bib overalls—every day of his life. He wore *no* underwear shorts—every day of his life. He didn't own any under shorts. He only wore them in the Army because they made him. 'Waste of money—under shorts', so he said. His bib overalls provided cover for his privates—so why bother with under shorts. Under *shirts*— he wore in the winter, at work, or when he went to Juney Hunt's saloon on weekends. He kept the side-vent flaps on his overalls unbuttoned, at the waist, in the summer time. The open flaps provided some additional ventilation and relief from the summer heat.

Mase's wardrobe maxed out at, four pairs of bib overalls, one winter work jacket, one suit coat—for funerals or church, one white shirt—for funerals or church, four undershirts, three work shirts, 4 pairs of socks, two caps— one for work, one for weekends, one pair of work boots, and one pair of casual shoes—for weekends or church & funerals.

He wore a pair bib overalls until they were, literally, washed, worn, or rotted to shreds before replacing them. He felt no call to spend a lot of time, or money, washing his clothes or body. A bath every 2nd or 3rd third day—not including the one he took on Friday before meeting the ladies at Juney Hunt's saloon—satisfied Mase's personal hygiene regimen.

Mase usually took one girl-friend with him when he umpired a ball game. It helped him feel like he fitted in. Most of the players and spectators had girls or wives with them. He had two girl friends he, alternately, took to most of the games. Both of them were 'regulars' at Juney's bar.

Their names were Janie 'Brew' and 'Bartlick' Pearl. Pearl's nickname came from the area where she lived. Janie's came from her love of beer. Janie and Pearl weren't mental giants. Their wretched grammar was convincing testimony of a formal education that ended in the 6th grade. Both were sorely in need of remedial dental work. Neither came from homes where manners, social skills, pre-marital virginity, or high moral standards were urged—forget demanded.

On the other hand they were friendly, likeable, voluptuous to the edge of being overweight, burdened with very few inhibitions, heavy users of cheap perfume and make-up, fond of skimpy clothing, and overjoyed with all the cheap beer, wine, and food Mase bought them. They responded to his financial generosity with sexual favors while sharing his bed on weekends. So vigorous and enthusiastic were their sexual frolics, Mase once thought they had taxed his heart to the point of a coronary. But—he didn't complain. 'If you had to go—what better way', he told his friends. Never an orator, Mase summed up his appraisal of them by saying, "Their pluses outweigh their minuses by a bit".

No one knew what Janie and Pearl's last names were. Mase didn't know and didn't care. The background and reputation of people who frequented Juney Hunt's joint discouraged anything beyond a minimal revelation of personal information. On any given night, a good part of the customers in Juney's were convicted felons, people in violation of their parole, or 'persons of interest' in on-going police investigations. In the interest of not having your teeth knocked out, being stabbed or shot, you made darn few inquiries and accepted any single name or alias offered. In that spirit, Mase found the names Janie 'Brew' and 'Bartlick' Pearl quite adequate.

The Sunday Mase umpired a baseball game between Honaker and Haysi was the hottest, stifling, and humid day the town had seen that summer. The game was attended by over two hundred people. Mase brought Janie 'Brew', and 'Bartlick' Pearl to the game with him.

When he arrived at the field, Mase sat up a couple of lawn chairs in the bed of his pick-up truck for Janie and Pearl's comfort while they watched him umpire the game. For refreshments, he gave each a brown paper bag containing a one quart bottle of Mogan-David Rose' wine (89 cents a bottle, he paid for it) and a pack of nabs. That the wine was not chilled nor glasses offered was of no consequence to these ladies. Their tastes ran more to substance than etiquette.

The August sun blazed down on the playing field. Mase squatted low behind the catcher to call each pitch. The crotch had rotted out of his bib overalls. Every time he squatted behind the catcher, his scrotum would drop through the hole in the crotch of his overalls. Mase was extraordinarily well endowed. Some men compared the size of his 'manhood' to that of a horse. When he squatted *real* low behind the catcher, his scrotum dropped so far through the hole in his overalls it appeared to rest in the sandy soil behind home plate.

Most of those seated on the bleachers behind home plate had a peek at Mase's privates nearly every time he squatted to call a pitch. Some of the ladies in the audience were discreetly amused, some shocked by his size, a few thought the sight was gross, and wanted their husbands to take Mase to task for his breach of rules on anatomical exposure in public.

Most of the men thought it was laughable. Not one of them wanted to approach Mase about the matter. They figured—even if he knew what was happening—he didn't care. And, if he did, how could he correct the situation? He had no underwear, nor needle and thread. The game continued with more attention focused on Mase's repeated bodily exposures than the game.

Janie and Pearl enjoyed their wine throughout the early part of the game. By the end of the fifth inning, each had finished off a quart of wine. The combined effects of the wine and stifling heat had a telling effect on both ladies.

Wine always made Pearl drowsy. One out into the sixth

inning, she passed out. As her body relaxed, she slid from her chair to a heap on the wooden floor of Mase's truck. A couple of people standing nearby stretched her out and left her lying on her back in the bed of the truck.

Wine always had a deafening, mouthy, and exhibitionist effect on Janie. The more she drank, the louder she talked, and the less inhibited she became. Shortly after Pearl passed out, Janie stood up in the bed of the truck. In a loud voice, she began to demand the attention of the other spectators around the truck.

"Hey! Hey, y'all! You listenin' to me? I bet I can do something ain't another one of you women can do—'cause you're too prissy and ain't got th' nerve! If you think you can do any better than me--you jus' jump up here in this truck and lemme' see you do it! Now—you jus' watch this!"

With that, Janie hiked up her skirt, dropped her panties to the floor of the truck, thrust her pelvis forward, and began to make pelvic motions that indicated she intended to abuse her vaginal cavity with the neck of her empty Mogan-David wine bottle.

Mouths dropped open among the 50 or so people whose attention she had captured with her loud mouth. At first, people were too stunned and surprised to move—let alone do anything.

"I do believe that crazy woman is really gonna' 'abuse' herself with that there wine bottle. Never seen nothin' like that before. She must be plumb drunk", said one man beside the truck.

"Well, from the looks of that low-life, tired lookin' ol' tart—I'd say she oughta' be locked up for abusing the *wine bottle*", said his friend standing nearby.

Most of the men in the crowd stared in disbelief as Janie appeared on the verge of doing the unspeakable. The women's response ran from shock to outrage. But, they didn't stand there waiting for Janie to carry out her intentions.One of the women was the wife of Mayor Hymie Atwater. She ran to get Hymie. When she returned a few seconds later with Hymie, he took one look at Janie and cursed under his breath for having this mess dumped at his door. He wanted to jerk the bottle out of Janie's hand and pop her right in the head with it. But, he reacted appropriately for a responsible town official.

"Janie, you stop that—right this minute! You hear me? What th' hell are you thinkin' about—doin' a nasty thing like that in front of all these good people! Why—there's women and children in this crowd! What you're doin' is a sin and an abomination—and it's damn sure against the law! You cover yourself up, right now! You hear me? And come down off that truck, right now—'fore I call the Sheriff and have you locked up! I don't know why Mase brought you over here! You're a damn disgrace and an embarrassment to everyone here!"

Janie was too high on the wine to be awed by Hymie, his

title of Mayor, or his threat to jail her. The quart of wine she had consumed in an hour drowned any small sense of modesty she might have had. Worse, it incited her to taunt women she was sure looked down on her—drunk or sober. It was a rare opportunity for her to tell those women that— underneath those fancy dresses they strutted around in— they didn't have a thing she didn't have. When it came to sexually satisfying a man—she was sure 90% of them couldn't even hold her bra for her, let alone prove they were her equal. And they looked down their nose at her? 'What a bunch of frauds', she thought.

While swaying and staggering in the truck bed, Janie held her dress above her waist with one hand and pointed the empty wine bottle at Hymie with her other hand. She narrowed her eyes to slits and yelled at him.

"Hymie, you want this bottle—you want my dress down? Well sir, if you think you're man enough—come up here and take this bottle from me and pull my dress down! Now, Mr. Big-Shot Mayor—wha'da you think about that?

Hymie turned, raced on to the ball field, threw up his hands for the pitcher to hold his pitch, and got in Mase's surprised face. In a loud whisper, he demanded Mase take his two women and leave the field and town—immediately. Mase, unaware of Janie's little demonstration, refused to leave the game. He thought Hymie was ticked over the girls drinking wine in public on a Sunday.

Hymie pointed to Janie—still dancing around the truck bed

with her dress held above her waist. He leaned close to Mase and told him what Janie had threatened to do with the wine bottle. He made it clear, "You will *never* umpire another game in this league if you don't immediately leave the field, the town, and take those drunk sluts with you."

The threat of expulsion from his place in the world of baseball was enough to sway Mase. He walked over to his truck, jerked the wine bottle out of Janie's hand, yanked her dress down, and told her to 'shut th' hell up and get in the dam' truck'.

Angrily, he drove away from the field with Pearl still lying unconscious in the bed of his truck and Janie hanging out the window of the truck cab, shouting insults at Hymie's wife.

The next day, Mase complained to friends that he didn't know what all the fuss was about. He felt Hymie had over-reacted. His friends told him what Janie did was wrong and if he wanted to continue Umpiring games he better not show up at another ball park with Janie or Pearl. At least not until they had cleaned up their act.

Personally, Mase felt his friends were making a mountain out of a mole hill. On the other hand, he seemed to be the <u>only</u> one that *didn't* think Janie and Pearl had done anything wrong. Well, he mused—right or wrong—neither Janie or Pearl was worth giving up his prized position as top umpire of Tri-County League baseball games. For sure and for certain, he wasn't going to ever again turn either one of them loose with a whole bottle of wine. They just didn't know their limits—and that's all there was to it.

Mase continued to spend a lot of weekends with Janie and Pearl. He told his close friends, 'we went and had us some high ol' times—me and them girls'. Still, no one ever saw either of them at another baseball game with him.

Several weeks later, Mase's maternal Aunt Endie passed away. Endicott Canfield was known and loved in the area as 'Aunt Endie'. She had been his Mothers last surviving sister. Mase had always been close to Aunt Endie. He wanted to show his last respects for her properly. So he spent a good part of one morning washing a pair of his bib overalls. To get all the dirt and grease out of them, he threw them in an old tin tub filled with boiling water and home-made lye soap. He got a hair-cut, shaved, took a bath, scrubbed the mud off his dress shoes, and strapped on his fresh washed bib overalls, his white shirt, and dress coat before setting out to Aunt Endie's house for her funeral service.

As was the custom in rural areas, in that day and time, Aunt Endie's open casket viewing and funeral service were held in the living room of her house. Her house was filled to overflowing by mourners attending her viewing and funeral service.

As her closest friends passed by her casket for a final look, they unanimously agreed--Aunt Endie just didn't look like herself. The ladies of her church group were particularly distressed over the way her hair had been 'done-up' by the

Undertaker.

"Lawd have mercy, it just don't look like Endie. Why, I've known the woman for over 60 years. In all my life, I never seen her hair 'poofed up' like the undertaker has got it done-up", lamented a friend as she gazed down at Endie in her coffin. "Ain't that the truth," echoed another friend. "She just don't look natural. I know she wouldn't want to be buried lookin' like she does. You think we could fix her hair for her?"

The ladies glanced at each other, nodded in unison, and hesitated no more than a few seconds before moving toward the casket to re-do Aunt Endie's hair. They gathered around her casket, lifted her into a sitting position, and combed her hair into the style worn by her for most of her 78 years.

Mase had been listening to the ladies. He watched their hair-dressing efforts in shock.

'God, have mercy, he mused to himself. I'm 42 years old, been half way 'round this world while I was in the Army—so I seen some thangs in my days. But the good Lord knows—I ain't never seen nothin' like this! No sir. I ain't never seen nobody raised up in their own casket. Them ol' ladies is plumb crazy—carryin' on like that. What if they can't get her back down in that there casket when they're finished foolin' around with her hair? They'll be in one hell of a fix then. Might have to bury poor ol' Aunt Endie a-sittin' up—if that there is even possible. Wish the Sheriff was here—put a *stop to them crazy ol' coots a-messing with a dead woman. Don't care what their intentions is—they sure ain't showin' her no respect.'*

Just before the ladies sat Aunt Endie up to re-do her hair, Mase, finally, found an empty chair. He had been standing for over an hour and his legs were tired. The empty chair wasn't much of a chair. It was an old cane-bottom chair with most of the webbing in the seat of the chair missing. Mase had to virtually sit on the side rungs of the seat of the old, worn chair. Still, he told himself, it was better than no chair at all—especially with his legs aching.

Mase plopped down on the old, worn, chair and continued to watch, intensely, as the church ladies went about the re-combing of Aunt Endie's hair. In truth, most of the people in the room were spellbound by the act.

Even though they were clean, Mase was wearing a pair of bib overalls with the crotch rotted out. As he sat in the chair, his mind completely occupied by the re-arrangement of Aunt Endie's hair, he was unaware that his scrotum had fallen through the rotted out crotch of his overalls <u>and</u> through the tattered bottom of the old chair he was sitting in.

As Mase watched the make-over of Aunt Endie he didn't notice that Aunt Endie's big, black, tom-cat had crept under his chair. The cat looked at Mases scrotum hanging down through the chair bottom. After a few seconds of intense staring at Mase's scrotum, and fascinated by what he saw, the big cat went into action. He did what all cats do when confronted with swinging, circular objects suspended in mid-air. He raised a forepaw and swung it swiftly against Mase's scrotum. The cat's sharp claws pierced his scrotum. A searing pain flooded his crotch. With a loud, blood curdling, scream, Mase leapt off the chair and into the air.

"OHH! GAWDDAM! What th' hell was THAT!", screamed Mase, as he grabbed his crotch and spun around to look wildly at the chair.

The church ladies were so startled by Mase's outburst they screamed and dropped Aunt Endie back into the casket with her hair in disarray.

The Rev. Calvin Hash, Aunt Endie's minister, jumped to his feet and began to yell at Mase for his conduct and language. He spoke harshly to Mase about his disrespect for his Aunt, the delicate ears of the ladies present, and blaspheming.

Mase, saw the black cat crouched under the chair. He didn't know which hurt worse—the pain or the humiliation over how he came to be in pain. He stood there—bent over, hands clenched in front of his crotch, unable to stop his body from rocking back and forth. Rev. Hash glowered at Mase while he waited for an explanation and apology.

"I'm mighty sorry, Rev. Hash—jus' as sorry as I can be. An' I 'pologize to all you good people here, payin' your respects to my Ayn't Endie. Ya'll know how much I loved her. And ya'll know I ain't never showed ya'll no disrespect. Its jus' that I sat on that ol chair over there, and, by golly, it musta' had an ol' sharp nail a-stickin' up in it. I dun' sat down on that ol' nail and it hurt me so bad I squalled out before I thought about what I was a-sayin."

Mase paused just long enough to hear the mourners murmur their acceptance of his apology and then slipped out to his truck. He needed to get home quick and get a mirror. For all he knew, that dam cat could have ripped his bag open. He might be bleedin' to death right there in his own truck.

'What th' hell am I gonna' to tell them down at the hospital if I have to go down there to get muh' bag sewn back together', he wondered. *'I know those fools down at the hospital—they'll tell this all over town. I won't be able to walk down the street without people laughing at me',* he agonized.

'Worse than that, what if I get an infection and they have to cut off my balls? That happens, I'm good as finished— walkin' around with nothing but a limp dick! I might as well be dead! Dam' whoever put that ol' busted chair in the room! Weren't Funeral Homes s'pose to provide good chairs for—and who'n hell let that dam' cat in the house? Who'n hell ever heard of lettin' a dam' cat hang around a—if I ever see that black sob a'gin—I'll cut his balls off—see how he likes it! An' that preacher, yellin' at me in front of all—oh god, my bag feels like its ripped plumb open', he moaned as he pushed his truck to speeds he had never driven before.

It only took Mase 20 minutes to get home. It felt like hours to him. He raced in the house, stepped out of his overalls as he ran to the bathroom. He took a hand mirror and stuck it between his legs.

'Oh, thank god! Thank you, thank you', he thought. *'Only three scratches—maybe an inch long. Wait a minute! Wait jus' a minute! What if that dam cat hasn't had its rabies shot! Those claw-marks could be infected—they might have to cut off my whole 'man-hood'. I might even die from infection—and me still a young man—dam' that cat to hell. Oh god, I've got to put something on my bag to kill the germs',* he wailed softly as he jerked open the medicine cabinet.

The first thing he saw was a bottle of alcohol. 'Yes— alcohol—the king of all germ killers!' Being in near panic, Mase poured some alcohol out of the bottle into the cupped palm of his hand. He quickly rubbed the alcohol all over his scrotum and penis. When the alcohol made contact with the scratches and tender skin of his scrotum and penis he felt like a blow torch was burning his crotch.

Screaming and cursing the burning pain, Mase danced around the bathroom as his eyes filled with tears. With his teeth gritted together so hard he thought they would break, he threw hands full of cold water from the wash basin up into his crotch. It didn't much. He ran cold water into the bathroom tub. Without waiting for even a quarter inch of water to collect in the tub, he jumped into the tub. For an hour he sat in the tub, lowly moaning as he rocked back and forth in six inches of cold, numbing water.

As night fell, he slowly stood up in the bath tub. He was prepared to quickly sit down in the water again if that fire in his scrotum and penis returned. With great relief, he only felt a slight heat in his groin. He stepped slowly out of the tub and dried his body with a clean towel. He laid another dry, clean towel on his couch. He couldn't risk germs that might be on his bed. He swallowed several asprin, carefully wrapped his scrotum in a clean, dry wash cloth, and gingerly eased down on his couch.

As exhausted as he was, he couldn't fall asleep. His mind was still racing—'should I leave well enough alone, or put some iodine on those claw marks on my bag', he kept asking himself. 'What if iodine burns worse than the alcohol', he thought. 'God forbid—I don't think I could stand another second of the awful experience I had with the alcohol. But—suppose I DON'T put iodine on the wound—and I get an infection. Having to go to the doctor and explain my condition—no, no way. Maybe if I was to use some of that Clover brand burn salve Mommie bought off that peddler-man years ago--. Naw, not a chance—I don't know what's in that salve—and, likely as not, I'm dam near ru'int already That greasy salve might just make things worse—if that's possible'. In the dark pre-dawn hours of the next morning he dropped off to sleep while still talking to himself about what more to do—if anything—to salvage his manhood.

Against a life-long rule, he went to Ammar Brothers

department store the next morning and bought six pairs of white undershorts. After some vague questions to the local druggist about what to put on 'a gladed crotch', he bought a jar of Vaseline. For one month he walked around with his Vaseline coated scrotum encased in a pair of white undershorts.

A month later—with no infection, no pain—Mase put the Vaseline in the medicine cabinet and stopped wearing underwear—for the second and last time in his life.

Folks who figured out the truth about what happened to Mase at Aunt Endie's funeral thought that cat's claws would provide all the motivation Mase needed to sew up the crotch of his bib overalls. Six weeks later, Mase went to Banner to umpire a ball game. As he squatted behind the catcher, the rotted out crotch of his overalls gapped open— and Mase, again and again, violated the rules on public anatomical exposure.

TRUST ME

The town of Aberdeen billed itself as the crown jewel of southwestern Virginia. The nearest town to the east was Roanoke, over one hundred miles away. Bristol, straddling the Virginia-Tennessee border and 30 miles west, did have a larger population than Aberdeen. However, the Aberdeen town fathers didn't consider Bristol a fair comparison because half of it was in Tennessee.

Aberdeen was a unique town. It had a population of five thousand people in the town proper. The town included a number of magnificent old homes, whose architecture was a testament to the wealth of the people who built them in the 19th century. The magnificent wrought iron fences surrounding the manicured lawns and gardens of some of the old mansions put an exclamation point on the status of those living there. Most of these homes were inhabited by doctors, lawyers, owners of distant coal mines, people of inherited wealth, businessmen with extensive holdings, or tobacco warehouse owners.

The remainder of the population in Aberdeen was filled with craftsmen, laborers, small merchants, nurses, truck drivers, and county or municipal employees. They lived in modest homes, worked hard, were basically honest, and made enough money to keep their bills paid. Outside the town limits, there was very little to be seen except farms. They dotted the landscape for miles through the gently, rolling hills. Tobacco was the big cash crop, with cattle and dairy farms running a close second.

Aberdeen boasted the Martha Custis Inn—said to have been over-night host to a few of the founding Fathers of our nation. Its long, genteel, front porch was adorned with rocking chairs from one end to the other. The large dining room was crowned with a huge, cut-crystal chandelier. Every bedroom included a, large four poster bed, sitting area, bathroom fixtures modern to that era, and enough pieces of expensive furniture to satisfy the ego of those who could afford to stay there. Musicians played for evening meals, and there was dancing on weekends. It was a retreat that catered to gentility, wealth, and powerful people with influence over the lives of lesser mortals. The outrageous prices at the Inn guaranteed the wealthy wouldn't have to rub elbows with the masses—those of 'modest' means and income.

A live theatre was established in Aberdeen during the 1930s. Its existence came out of the 'Great Depression' era. Actors were starving in New York because no one could afford to attend the plays being staged there. Bob Porter, a producer, writer, and director of stage plays, rented an old, vacant building in Aberdeen. Through his own labor, he converted the place into to a live theatre. Porter offered starving New York actors and actresses the opportunity to continue practicing their acting skills in Aberdeen, in exchange for food and a place to sleep. Most of the people in Aberdeen, and surrounding counties, had no more money than the rest of America during the depression.

They did have food and animals raised on their land. They bartered their way into Porter's theatre with vegetables, chickens, pork, and beef. Escaping the harsh realities of the depression for two hours, the people of Aberdeen got to see a play staged by professional actors. The actors got food and a roof over their heads. As far-fetched as this idea may seem, the Barter theatre was, at one time, home to Gregory Peck, Ned Beatty, Ernest Borgnine, Patricia Neal, and numerous other professional actors. Some, later, became legendary movie stars in Hollywood. After the depression was over, the theatre began selling tickets for cash. It is still alive and well and has operated for over eighty years.

Huge tobacco warehouses were located on the eastern outskirts of Aberdeen. Farmers, from a half dozen surrounding counties, hauled their harvested tobacco to these warehouses, where it was auctioned off to the major cigarette tobacco companies in America. Tobacco drove the economy of Aberdeen. When the wind was blowing east to west, especially on damp or humid days, the pungent odor of cured tobacco drifted across the entire town.

Jack P. Bowden was born and raised on a tobacco farm outside of Aberdeen. Jack was the oldest of six children. His Mother claimed Jack began his life by talking instead of crying. While Mrs. Bowden's remark may have been an exaggeration, Jack was always known to be a talker. Jack started his life in a hard-scrabble existence on his parents' tobacco farm. He grew up hearing his parents preach the virtues of hard, honest work. He agreed with their philosophy of working hard and being honest. On the other hand, Jack saw little nobility in working a life time from sun up till sun down with nothing to show for it—at life's end—except a worn out body and barely enough money to pay for your burial. During the early years of his life, Jack carefully observed people *with* money—and people *without* money. From his point of view, life was a lot more comfortable for people *with* money. It was also clear to him that the majority of the people *with* money didn't use *physical* labor to get it. They used their heads, their powers of persuasion, their influence, and the physical labor of *others*. These habits—Jack embraced whole heartedly.

Jack used his horse-trading ability to buy an old used car for next to nothing. He used his gift of gab to sell the car for twice what he paid for it. Jack constantly bought and sold things. He made a profit on every transaction. By the time he was twenty five years old, he paid cash for his first piece of valuable real estate. When he reached his fiftieth birthday, Jack owned a wholesale grocery business, a very profitable gas station, a retail store specializing in exquisite china dinnerware and tiffany lamps, ten pieces of rental property, a major interest in a local bank, and a farm that contained a five acre tobacco allotment and 75 head of cattle.

Jack and his wife had four children. They called home a meticulously, restored old mansion in the part of town inhabited by the wealthy. Despite his lack of a formal higher education and farm-boy background, Jack was accepted by the 'power brokers' of Aberdeen as a 'member of the club'.

Even though Jack enjoyed the comforts provided by his wealth and talent for making money, his true passion was politics. He thrived on being in the public eye and positions of power. Jack became legendary for his political speeches, tactics, strategies, and campaigns. As his Mother said, Jack loved to talk. In truth, Jack became recognized as the most charismatic public speaker in southwestern Virginia. His voice and style of delivery radiated confidence, commanded trust, and swayed voters to elect him—time and time again.

Some people said the eloquence of Jack's pleas to the voters rivaled Billy Graham's petitions to the Almighty. That may or may not have been an accurate comparison. Billy's eloquence was born of inspiration from above, belief in the scriptures, and years of practice. Jacks eloquence was born of belief in himself, years of experience in selling himself, and a 'dram' of bourbon before he addressed the voters. His defenders would say Jack's use of 'spirits' was just to clear his throat. Be that as it may, Jack could outshine just about any speaker—be they a 'Fire & Brimstone' Preacher or seasoned politician. By the time Jack finished one of his fiery homilies, he had his listeners primed to do anything, short of taking up arms, to help him defeat his political opponent. Electing Jack was their vote for the triumph of good over evil. The perpetuation of their beliefs, their way of life, and their jobs were sort of joined at the hip with Jack's election or re-election to office.

No, Jack's verbal delivery *style* wasn't a problem. It was his campaign *tactics* and *substance* of his remarks that were legendary, if not infamous, in the southwestern corner of the state. His campaign handlers worried that some of the *substance* of his remarks and speeches 'pushed the envelope'. His opponents said the lack of *any* substance in Jacks remarks was far closer to the truth. Those who didn't really care what he said as long as he 'delivered' just saw Jack as a 'B.S.-er'—who just gets a little carried away from time to time'. Jack saw himself as an orator whose skills were used only in the interest of his constituents. If he employed a poetic flair in his words, took a few liberties in his remarks—well, it was for the benefit of those whom he *served*. Just that simply, Jack legitimized whatever he said and did.

Over the years, Jack clawed and climbed his way through the political hierarchy. Starting with a minor seat on a planning commission, he worked his way through municipal councils, and Board of Supervisors. Eventually, he was elected as a state Delegate. He had aspirations of becoming a state Senator, and, eventually, a U.S. Congressman.

Occasionally, Jack felt compelled to hostage his future health, as assurance of the truth of a point he was making in a campaign speech. Jacks self-sacrificial offers included these gems. "Ladies and Gentlemen, my opponent has failed to tell you good people—*'and may lightning strike me right where I'm standing if I'm lying'*—that he was arrested for DUI--etc., etc."

"Brothers and sisters, my opponent has—*'and may I never get out of this chair* (meaning struck dead by the Almighty) *if ever blessed word of what I'm tellin' you isn't God's own truth'*— just plain outright lied about his support of better schools—blah-blah, etc.

"Friends—and you are my friends—my opponent has betrayed your sacred trust when he told you—*'and here's my hand on this'*(held up his right hand as if taking a religious oath in a court of law)—he did not vote for an increase in *your* taxes, etc."

"Friends, if you elect me, I give you my pledge—*'and may I see the man on the white horse coming straight at me if I'm lying'* (reference to the biblical verse, 'Behold a pale horse, and the rider who sits upon him is called Death')—to see that our schools are improved, etc., etc."

Jack had no qualms about borrowing a page from the campaign play book of other politicians if they were successful. He admired their creativity--especially if they were elected to an office on the national level. When he was in a tight race, he would, occasionally, find it convenient to adapt the tactics of others to his own needs.

In a campaign for a state office, Jack was involved in a neck-and-neck race with his opponent. It was less than two weeks before the election. Jack was trying, desperately, to sway votes from his opponent. He was addressing an overflow crowd that included a lot of religiously devout voters. Like most successful politicians, Jack felt perception often carried as much weight as reality. He also knew, unless it was a direct promise of personal enrichment, most people wouldn't remember ninety five percent of what a politician said for more than twenty four hours. What a man had to do, Jack reasoned, was deliver two or three verbal 'bullets' in his speech. Something that would grab their attention, give them something to talk about, and keep his name on the tip of their tongue. That's how a man got elected and re-elected! Well— verbal 'bullets' and giving away a few turkeys and hams to the right people at Thanksgiving and Christmas. Jack raised his hands to bring quiet to the crowd, gain their full attention, and prepare them for one of ol' Jack P.'s speech 'bullets'. In his most solemn and somber voice he zinged a 'bullet' at them.

"Ladies and gentlemen—Ladies and gentlemen! I hate to bring up this matter. I take no pleasure in burdening you with this troubling information. Truthfully, it just makes me sick to think about it—let alone tell you about it! But, being the God-fearing men and women I know you to be, I think you have the *RIGHT* to know this. Besides, you and I know the truth always comes out in the end. And, I feel like you would never again trust me if I kept this from you. Ladies and gentlemen, I have it on good authority that my opponent's sister is a *THESPIAN*, and his brother is *HETEROSEXUAL*!"

You could hear gasps of shock throughout the auditorium. What ol' Jack said was the truth. His opponent's sister was, indeed, a professional New York theatre thespian, which is a little known word meaning actress. His brother was, as far as anyone knew, heterosexual—which is a man who prefers sexual relations with a woman. What the crowd *heard*, or *thought* they heard, were the words 'lesbian' and 'homosexual'. Ol' Jack was counting on that. He won that election by one hundred and fifteen votes. Some said Jack's use of the misconception had little to do with his victory. Others swore it was the nail in his opponent's coffin.

Jack was scheduled to make a summer campaign speech at an outdoor political rally. Jack timed his arrival so he would be a little late, and every eye would be focused on his car when he arrived. About a mile from the rally, Jack stopped his car along the shoulder of the road. He picked up a football sized rock lying beside the road and used it to smash his windshield. Then he tossed the rock in the floor of his car and sped on down the road to the rally site. When he arrived at the rally, he raced his car right up to the speaker's platform. Jack slammed on his brakes, skidded the car to a stop, jumped out of the car, and pointed to his shattered windshield as he ran up the steps to the speaker's platform with the large rock held high in his other hand.

"Ladies and gentlemen—my friends! Hear me out now—let me speak, please! I want to go on record, right here and now, as saying I don't believe my opponent had a *thing* to do with my windshield being shattered with this rock as I drove here to speak to you! No sir! I know my opponent wants—badly, mind you—to defeat me in this election. But, ladies and gentlemen— good people, I just can't believe my opponent would stoop to such a mean and cowardly act! No sir! I can't believe my opponent would endanger my life by having someone throw this huge rock off an overpass on my car---just to keep me from speaking to you this afternoon!"

Again, Jack had not wrongly accused his opponent. His reverse psychology of defending his opponent's innocence had the desired effect. By the following day, despite Jacks benevolent defense of his opponent, the rumor of Jacks near escape from injury or death at the hands of his opponent had spread throughout the county. No one wanted to be represented by a man whose morals allowed physical attempts on the life of another. Jack won the election handily.

Jack did spend time in the state legislature. He had to take satisfaction in being a member of the state legislature— because he was never able to win a seat in Congress. When Jack passed away in his late 80s the local funeral home had to extend the hours for people to pay their respect to Jack's widow and family from two to four hours. Folks who paid their respects said Jack would have been pleased to know so many people cared for him. Some said the only thing that would have pleased him more was being able to make a speech at his own funeral.

JUNE & BRIDGETTE BARDOT

Dean Bowden worked for Jack Butler. Dean was not highly skilled, but he was dependable and honest. Jack used Dean in several jobs in various businesses he owned. Dean, over ten years in Jack's employ, supervised deliveries from Jacks wholesale grocery business, collected rents from tenants in Jacks properties, or served as manager of Jacks Esso gas station. Jack paid Dean well, and Dean was happy in his employment with Jack.

Dean's wife, June, was a nurse at the Aberdeen hospital. While their marriage was relatively stable, it wasn't a story of perpetual harmony. June suspected Dean of marital infidelity. Her suspicions spanned most of the eight years of their marriage. Dean was a man of rugged good looks and a winning personality. He had charisma coming out his ears. Be it man or woman, they liked ol' Dean. June didn't have a problem with Dean's popularity among men. The women were another matter. To June, even a simple smile from a woman to Dean signaled an extra-marital affair. As far as anyone knew, Dean had never strayed. June didn't buy that. Despite the lack of any evidence—any evidence at all— June was positive Dean was sleeping with other women. She made it her mission in life to catch him doing so.

Her first line of discovery was devoted to catching Dean in the act of audltry. Failing that, she searched for some damning circumstantial evidence. Evidence strong enough to support a scathing indictment of his conduct and force a confession from him. Pictures or testimony from an eye-witness would do nicely. Once her suspicions were supported by evidence, her punishment would be swift. Her plans for retribution ran to the physical side. What she would do to Dean and 'his woman' would necessitate an overnight stay in the hospital for both of them.

Dean and June rented the upstairs of a large, old two story house that had been converted into apartments. Dean's cousin, Lee Bingham, was visiting Dean and June for the weekend. Lee was going to work for Dean at Jack's Esso gas station on Saturday. They had plans to go see a movie, featuring Bridgette Bardot, at the Zephyr movie theatre Saturday evening after closing the gas station. Bridgette was the newest Hollywood sex goddess. Rumor had it that Bardot appeared nude from the waist up, in one movie scene.

Before they left for work Saturday morning, June overheard bits and pieces of a conversation between Lee and Dean concerning 'some woman, called Bridgette'. Just before they left for work, Dean turned to June and invited her to join Lee and him for the evening.

"Honey, Lee and I are going to see a movie at the Zephyr this evening after we close the gas station. We're going to grab a bite, and then catch the last show of the evening. You want to go with us?"

June saw a real opportunity here. She trusted Lee even less

than Dean. Word had it that Lee was a real 'swordsman'—and had bedded half the girls at his high school. She knew, for a fact, a couple of nurses at the hospital had slept with him. She had overheard Dean and Lee talking earlier that morning, about seeing the tits of some slut called Bridgette. Now they were lying to her about seeing a movie. What a load of B.S.! They were covering their tracks! She saw a real chance to catch Dean in the act. As a bonus, she would nail that fancy talking, big-mouth Lee. She had long wanted to take him down a peg. "No, honey, I don't think I'll go. It will be late when you get off work. It is so cold out, and it is supposed to snow some more tonight. I have to clean the apartment today. I'll be tired this evening. I'm going to take a bath, read a while, and go to bed. You guys enjoy the movie", said June as she smiled at Dean.

June spent the entire day putting her plans together. She even browsed through the Aberdeen telephone directory on the off chance she might find the name 'Bridgette' listed. Having no luck with the phone book, she called her eighty year old Aunt. Her Aunt had lived in Aberdeen most of her life. She was a busy-body who knew the majority of the people in town. She struck out there, too. Auntie had never heard of a soul named Bridgette. Auntie thought Bridgette didn't sound like a name a *proper* Aberdeen family would give their daughter.

'Not a PROPER name', thought June as she raged to herself. *'Not proper, my rear! Her name is perfectly PROPER for a woman who goes around showing her tits and climbing into bed with other women's husbands! Damn crazy ol' woman!*

She's yammerin' about proper names, while I'm saddled with a husband who is sleeping around on me!'

At nine that evening Dean was sweeping up inside the gas station. He was using a broom with a broken handle. It had gotten broken next door at Jack's wholesale business. Dean had taped the handle, and made the broom do for sweeping the floor of the service station. As long as too much pressure wasn't applied to the handle, it worked. Lee was outside taking the readings from the gas pumps. It was cold, snow was blowing, and the entire driveway of the gas station was slick with ice all the way from the front door to the street.

Without warning, a car sped out of the street into the service area in front of the gas station. The headlights bounced up and down as the car lunged across the the gutter in the street and the stations gas pumps. Lee, seeing the car hurtling toward him, dropped the clip board holding the recording forms, and jumped behind the gas pumps. The car slid on the icy pavement of the gas station. Standing in the gas station office, Dean saw the car skidding toward him. His eyes widened with fear. He ran and stumbled toward the rear of office. The car slid to a stop just before plowing into the plate glass window of the station office.

June leaped from the car and marched to the station. She threw open the door so hard it left the imprint of the door handle in the wall. Dean stood there, his mouth open, looking at her as if she had gone insane.

"Alright! Where is she?" screamed June.

"Where is who? And why th' hell are you driving like that on snow and ice?" said Dean, with an angry look on his face.
"Don't you dare lie to me! Don't you try to change the subject, either! Where is she? I know you've got that slut, Bridgette, in here! You think I don't know what you're up to? Huh? You think I'm stupid? Going to the movies—what a bunch of b.s.!"

"June, you're not makin' any sense. There ain't no one here but Lee and me. I don't have no slut in here. I don't have *anyone* in here—or any place else. I was just closing the place, and then going to the movies. You come in here—rantin' and ravin'—actin' crazy about somebody who ain't here—you're an embarrassment to me!"

"Acting crazy, am I? Embarrassing you, am I? By god, you haven't seen crazy yet! When I find that whore, I'll show you crazy!"

June violently shoved Dean aside and began searching every corner of the building for Bridgette. Dean, following behind, begged her to listen to him and tried to calm her.

"Where is she, you lying cheat? Huh? You got her back there in the private office? Huh? She been showing you her tits? Huh? Bridgette been giving you an eye full?" spat June as she stormed through the service area .She ripped open closets and bathroom doors. Every time she opened another door and didn't see Bridgette she vented her frustration by tearing things off the wall, or knocking glasses and bottles from shelves onto the floor. Broken glass and liquid was covering the floor.

"June—enough! Stop this—now! Jack is going to be mad as hell about all the stuff you've broken! Christ almighty! Look at this place! It'll come out of my pay! There ain't no one here. There ain't never been no one here! Can't you see that? You've opened every damn door in this place—and didn't find no one! I don't know no woman named Bridgette!" screamed Dean.

He wrapped his big arms around June, pinning hers arms to her side. He lifted her kicking feet off the floor, and carried her toward the front door of the station.

June dropped her head and bit one of Dean's arms. With a howl of pain, he let her go. She ran into the bays where they did mechanical work and washed cars. She jerked boxes and barrels away from the wall and looked behind them. The containers had been so tightly packed against the walls a mouse couldn't have found room behind them. June, frustration raging through her, had heard them call Bridgette by name earlier that morning—she had to be there somewhere.

"I'll tear this place apart until I find her—so you give her up—tell her to come out!" growled June over her shoulder as she stumbled through the mess of broken things she had created all over the station .

June could see Dean closing in on her again. She grabbed the old broken-handle broom he had put down and began swinging it at his face to keep him from getting too close. As she swung the broom, she backed toward the big bay doors. She looked over her shoulder to see how close she was to the doors. There was Lee. Standing outside with his face pressed up against the glass of the bay door. He had a grin that seemed to split his face from ear to ear.

'Of course', thought June. *'Mr. Ladies' Man, Lee, had Bridgette outside. And the little jerk is laughing at me! Laughing right in my face!'*

With one more swing of the broom at Dean, June ran outside the gas station. With the broom raised over shoulder, she ran straight at Lee. Lee was quick. He ran around the gas pumps—and kept them between him and June. To get close enough to deliver a punishing blow with the broom, she chased Lee around the gas pumps.

"C'mere, you little shit! Don't you run from me! I know you're in on this! Ill whip your ass good if you don't stop running and tell me where that whore is!"

"Now June, honey, get a grip on yourself. I don't know who you're talking about. I was just reading these gas pumps when you came on the scene", said Lee as he continued to dodge from one side of the gas pumps to the other.

"Oh, bullshit! You know exactly who I'm talking about! I'll teach you not to laugh at me, you little big-nosed S.O.B!"

June decided she was close enough to Lee to take a swing at him with the broom. She swung the broom so hard the tape on the fractured broom handle broke. The head of the broom went sailing through the air. Having nothing left in her hand but a small piece of broken broom handle caused June to lose her balance on the icy asphalt. Her feet shot out from under her. With a loud thump, she fell flat on her behind. Lee couldn't control himself. He peeked around a gas pump at her lying on the icy ground, and began to laugh so hard he could hardly get his breath. June screamed every word of profanity she knew at Lee while Dean helped her to her feet. He pinned her arms to her side, and dragged her to their car. June was cursing and kicking him every step of the way.

"By god, June, enough is enough! I'm taking you home! Lee, lock up the station! Forget the movie and come on back to our apartment", shouted Dean, as he threw June into their car.

Lee locked up the gas station and followed them to their apartment in his own car. As he entered their apartment, he could hear June still screaming at Dean. Lee chuckled and went quietly to his bedroom.

"Why are you lying to me about 'Bridgette'? I heard you and Lee making plans this morning to see her! Right out of your own mouth, I heard you say she would show you her tits!"

Slowly, it dawned on Dean. June had heard them talking about seeing Bridgette Bardot in a movie.

"June, Bridgette Bardot is an actress. Lee and I were going to see her in a movie. She does a scene in the movie where she is nude from the waist up. That's all there is to it. Now you can stay in here in the living room all night yelling about a woman that only exists in movies! I'm going to bed!"

Dean walked to the bedroom, took off his clothes, turned off the light, and crawled into the bed.

"Oh no! No, no, no! You're not going to sleep until you tell me the truth", bellowed June as she stomped into the bedroom and turned on the light . "I'm not buying this crap about 'Bridgette' being a movie actress. I wasn't born yesterday! I'm going to keep this light on and in your eyes till you tell me the truth!"

Dean, without a word, got out of the bed, walked to the wall switch, turned off the lights and crawled back in the bed. June, standing by the door, turned the lights back on. Dean got up again and turned the lights off. June turned them back on.

Dean looked up at the light bulbs. They were mounted in a ceiling fixture. This old home had a nine-foot ceiling that was too high for Dean to reach and unscrew the bulbs from the sockets with his hands. Without a word, Dean walked down the hall to the kitchen. He got a skillet from the stove, walked back to bed room, reached up, swung the skillet, and broke the two light bulbs. Now, he thought, let's see her turn the light on now.

June ran into the hall, and turned on the hall light. Dean got back out of the bed, slipped his feet into his shoes, picked up the skillet, walked to the hallway, and used the skillet to break the hall light out of its socket. June ran from the hallway to the living room, turned on the light, and turned the radio up to full volume. Following her, Dean jerked the radio cord out of the wall socket, threw the radio against the wall, where It broke into several pieces Dean used the skillet to knock out the living room light.

Still screaming accusations at Dean, June retreated to the kitchen and turned that light on. He followed and broke out the kitchen light. That left every light in the apartment broken, save the one in the guest bedroom where Lee was staying. Lee had been watching the Battle-of-the-Lights through his barely opened bedroom door. After June and Dean finished their skirmish in the kitchen Lee saw June running down the hall toward his bedroom. He quickly slammed and locked his door. June began beating his bedroom door with her fist and yelling for him to open the door.
"Hey, listen to me", said Lee. "My light is off and the radio in here doesn't play. I'll see you in the morning!" June soon gave up beating on Lee's bedroom door. He drifted off to

sleep an hour later—listening to June still accusing Dean of having an affair with 'Bridgette'.

The following morning, Lee awoke to sounds of broken glass being swept up in the hallway. Dean was cleaning up broken glass throughout the apartment. June was talking in a normal tone of voice and cooking breakfast. At some point in the night, she had decided Dean *might* be telling the truth about Bridgette Bardot being a movie actress. Her reluctant concession didn't lessen her suspicions about Dean's infidelity—with someone. She was positive she would catch him one day—it was just a matter of time.

Dean and June remained married throughout their lives. To the best of anyone's knowledge, Dean never had sex with another woman throughout their marriage. To the best of anyone's knowledge, June never stopped suspecting him of doing so.

DIRECTIONS TO THE CHURCH

Albert 'Greasy' Graham was one of those people in town who always seemed 'old'. At least to anyone younger than him by 5 years or more. Why?? It was hard to put a finger on any one thing or things specifically. With the exception of the years he spent fighting in two European wars, Greasy lived his entire life in Bluestone. Yet, one would be hard put to find a soul in town that could recall moments from Greasy's life as a teen-ager or young man. Most memories of Greasy seem to run from his late thirties to his mid-eighties. He was one of those people seen---but not seen. He materialized in the consciousness of Bluestone residents during the declining years of his life.

Greasy fought in, and survived, WW I & WW II. Most of his time in the two wars was served as an Army mechanic. On balance, that sounds like a fairly safe and secure was to pass through two wars. However, any man who fought in either war would tell you *any* soldier in the field, no matter what his assignment was, had to fight, daily, just to stay alive. A fair share of Greasy's time repairing Army vehicles took place close enough to the front lines to see the enemy soldiers and hear their bullets whistling by his head. He carried a tool sack over one shoulder, and his rifle hung over the other.

He had volunteered for the Army at the beginning of World War I. When World War II broke out, Greasy, again, volunteered for duty in Army. Initially, he was rejected for re-enlistment in the Army for World War II. The reason? He wore false teeth. Greasy appealed his rejection to the Armed Services Selective Draft Board. Greasy represented himself at the appellate hearing. Not a man of letters or eloquent expressions, his appeal to the Board relied on his use of short declarative sentences.

"I thought you wanted me to shoot the Germans. I didn't know you wanted me to bite 'em to death. I'm a damn good mechanic. There ain't a day that passes when a piece Army equipment don't break down. If you ain't got no mechanics in the Army, how 'n hell you think the Army's gonna' keep their equipment running?" said Greasy.

The logic of Greasy's petition must have been compelling. His initial rejection for re-enlistment was overruled by the entire Board. On a cold, dark, pre-dawn February morning in 1942, he was put on the bus with eighty nine other Bluefield draftees being sent to various Army basic training posts.

World War II ended in June of 1945. Greasy survived 4 years of front line battles and returned to Bluestone a few days before Christmas of 1945. Whatever he did or saw during the years of two war remained locked deep in the recesses of his memory. Throughout the remainder of his life, he never talked about his war experiences. About all that was generally known about his time in the Army was that he had been honorably discharged. In fact, he was twice wounded, awarded Bronze and Silver Star medals for bravery, and received two Purple Heart medals for being twice wounded.The latter information came, confidentially, from his sister to her closest friends—not Greasy.

One or two who fought with him were more forthcoming. According to one story told, Greasy was trying to get a truck repaired. It was carrying medical supplies and had broken down, virtually on the front lines of action. Greasy was under the hood of the truck, trying to get it re-started. The Germans kept shooting at him, despite the fact that he obviously didn't have a rifle in his hands. Eventually, a shot from the Germans ricocheted off the metal of the truck and grazed Greasy's leg. The impact knocked Greasy to the ground. Uncharacteristic of Greasy, he flew into a rage. In Greasy's mind, he was working on a truck at the time, not shooting at the Germans. Thus, he reasoned, they shouldn't have been shooting at him.

Greasy screamed profanities at the German soldiers as he lay on the ground. He used a piece of wire to fashion a tourniquet for his leg. The firing from the Germans continued. Greasy found his rifle lying on the ground near where he had fallen. He spent 3 hours crawling 150 yards around and through the no-man's land between the American and German troops. A constant stream of bullets between the opposing troops whistled above his head.

Greasy worked his way around and behind the German soldiers. With his rifle, he killed a nest of German soldiers who were using a machine gun to keep a group of American troops pinned down in fox holes or behind trees for most of that day. Greasy was certain they were the Germans who shot him. With that key pocket of Germans knocked out of action, the American troops raced forward to take the position the Germans had held and chase them from that battle field. When the U.S. soldiers reached Greasy he was still screaming and swearing at the sole living German soldier for shooting him while he was 'just trying to fix a damn truck'.

The wound he received kept Greasy in a field hospital for two weeks. Reportedly, he told the Colonel who pinned the Silver Star on him he wasn't trying to get a medal for killing the Germans--he was just 'fed up with being shot at while he was trying to fix a truck'. Further, he told the Colonel, 'with all due respect sir I'd just as soon have a bottle of *Virginia Gentleman* bourbon as the medal. The Colonel stared at him, nodded, and said he understood. Greasy wasn't sure the Colonel understood at all—especially when he was released from the field hospital the following morning and handed orders to report back to duty near the front lines.

To be sure, Greasy was the recipient of his country's gratitude for his services—in the form of two monthly disability checks from the Army for injuries sustained in both World Wars. The checks continued to come—for over to 40 years—right up to the time of his death, shortly after his 88th birthday.

When Greasy got back to Bluestone in 1945 he was forty eight years old, twice divorced, without a home of his own, and well on his way to being a full blown alcoholic. He rented a bedroom at his sister's house on Franklin St. By all accounts, he was an excellent mechanic. He had a job as a master mechanic at the Crowder-Freeman *Nash* dealership. Greasy could fix most anything—except his torment from his personal demons

It was difficult to say *exactly* what brought Greasy to this emotionally bankrupt point in life. Some opined it was the stress and horror of living, fighting, and killing through two world wars in less than a 25 year period. Still, others pointed out that not everyone who faced the daily threat of death in a war returned home a chronic alcoholic.

Perhaps it was a losing struggle with the frustrations in his life; maybe the disappointments in his life had worn him down to profound hopelessness; possibly, whatever optimism he once held had been supplanted by a resentment of the better fate dealt to others around him; perchance, the day by day grind wore away his spirit and stole the heart from his life.

Whatever the truth, Greasy leavened the burdens of his days with alcohol .He never drank to the point of being a 'fall down' drunk. He finished most days by consuming enough beer or liquor to leave him in a mellow or numb state of mind.

Drunk or sober, he never had much to say to anybody about anything. His evening conversations with others, while not rude, offered brief comments, blunt assessments of the motives and actions of others, and terse, unvarnished appraisals of some people in town.

Greasy's preference for ending each day, was to have several drinks at the mid-town Virginia Bar & Grill. After satisfying his thirst for the spirits, weather permitting, he would drift out to the sidewalk, find a utility pole or parking meter, lean up against it, and light up a cigar. From that vantage point he was perfectly content to silently observe pedestrians, traffic, and sunsets yielding to night.

One summer evening, Greasy studied some gathering storm clouds while leaning against a utility pole on the corner of College Avenue and Logan St. Two corners of this intersection were home to the Westminster Presbyterian Church and the First Methodist Church. A short distance west on Logan St, sat St. John's Episcopal Church. Easterly, on Logan St., was Memorial Baptist Church. As with nearly any church in any town, each of these churches had certain people in them who were recognized as 'Pillar' , 'Voice', or 'Power' in the church. Some said of the 'Pillar', or their families, gave so much money to the church that their voice had to be recognized as the voice of that particular church. Others claimed it was the habit of certain members of a church to publicly, and loudly, quote scriptures from memory as a proclamation of their allegiance to a pious and moral life. Whatever the true reason, the names of certain Bluefield church members were the recognized 'head-honcho' of the church they attended.

As Greasy contemplated the darkening clouds, a car pulled

along-side him. The car was full of people. While Greasy exhaled a cloud of cigar smoke, one of the passengers in the car rolled down a window and spoke to him.

"Excuse me, sir. We're from out of town. We're here to attend a church revival. We're not familiar with the streets here. We can't seem to find the church. Could you tell us where we can find the Church of God?"

Greasy looked at the man—who had his head hanging out of the open car window. Greasy slowly took his cigar out of his mouth. He thought for a few seconds, slowly shook his head, and replied.

"Well, that church right there belong to Bill Wagner", Greasy said as he pointed to First Methodist. "That church over there belongs to Bubba Tanner", declared Greasy as he motioned toward Westminster Presbyterian. "That there Episcopal church belongs to Carl Cundiff," indicated Greasy as he nodded west along Logan St. to St. John's Episcopal. "Course, Memorial Baptist, down the street there, belongs to Shep Dodson", motioned Greasy as he hooked a thumb over his shoulder.

"And you say you're lookin' for the Church of *God*? Well—if God's got a church in this town I sure don't know where it is", said Greasy as he shook his head in resignation and stuffed his cigar back in his mouth.
With a perplexed look on their faces, the people in the car mumbled 'thank you' and drove away.

CUSTOMER WITH FLAPPER & RHODY'S GAS STATION IN BACKGROUND

FLAPPER IN THE ARMY, 1942.

FLAPPER WORKING AT SERVICE STATION

RHODY WORKING AT SERVICE STATION

Chapter 19

FLAPPER & RHODY

Rhody Joe Wallace and Flapper Pancake were brothers in every sense, except biologically. Both were born, raised, lived and died in the small town of Bluestone; both lived with physical handicaps their entire lives—Rhody had a severe hearing loss—Flapper had St. Vitus Dance, better known today as Tourette's Syndrome; neither completed a high school education; both had strong survival instincts—could make money, even if tied them down to a big flat rock; an occasional 'overindulgence in the spirits' plagued both of them.

Neither entered into a venture, no matter what it was, with less than a firm belief that legendary success and untold riches would follow. While some of their ventures met with moderate success, as many were failures. They wrote off any failures to external forces beyond their control, and plowed into their next venture with the same 'can't fail' optimism.

Through notices from the Draft Board to report for induction into the Armed Services, World War II came to the young men of Bluestone. The Draft Board, by rule, was supposed to work with the four divisions of Armed Services to select only on those males 'fit to serve' in the military. The Selective Service Military Draft Board was anything but 'selective'. During World War II, they filled the need for military recruits by drafting nearly every living male—fit or unfit—between the ages of 18 and 40 years of age.

To hear conversations spoken at normal levels, Rhody Joe had to use a hearing aid the size of a small transistor radio-- which he carried in his shirt pocket. Greasy Graham had already fought in WW I—had no real teeth, and was perilously close to being an alcoholic. Loose Jaw Olinger was so learning impaired he was interesting. Puud Tabor and Punk Bowen had such poor decision making skills folks were amazed when they survived from one week to the next. And then, there was Flapper Pancake. Six feet and four inches tall, 240 lbs, not an ounce of fat on him, pearly white teeth, and a disarming smile. He was also afflicted with a flaming case of St. Vitus Dance. All of these guys were drafted into the U.S. Army for WW II.

The disease of St. Vitus Dance caused Flapper's body's muscle/nerve connection with his brain to short-circuit every 10-12 seconds. This 'short circuit' manifested itself in the form of involuntary verbal and physical actions. They ranged from a slight 'tic' or twist of the face and minor halt in speech—to a major contortion of the body (hands/arms flailing the air—legs and feet skipping-dancing) and facial grimace—(head back/eyes shut/teeth bared)—while shouting ,three times, whatever word was on his mind when the short 'seizure' wracked his body. These rapid and involuntary actions lasted no more than 1 to 4 seconds before Flapper regained normal and full control over his body/verbal actions. You never knew—if the seizure would be 1 or 4 seconds. Four seconds could feel like 4 minutes to a stranger uninitiated to Flapper's seizures.

An example might draw the best picture of what people, who did NOT know Flapper, saw when he experienced a 'tic' between his brain and nervous system. Imagine standing before a gentle giant of a man—with a warm, welcoming smile. A smile that showed perfect white teeth. A man who spoke with a gentle baritone voice. Then, as if he had been touched by an electric 'cattle prod' or police 'taser', Flapper's image—in a split second—was changed to one of a huge demon—eyes shut—teeth bared. His soft voice became a roar—his arms flailed, throwing things into the air—his feet literally skip-danced—his huge fists beat on everthing from his forehead to any object nearest him— all done while he screamed everything from profanity to words that sounded like not-open-for-discussion orders. This was what strangers saw when Flapper had one of his 'tics'.
People in town who knew him well—they paid no more attention to his antics than if he had sneezed. Those who didn't—they were terrified—convinced they were in the presence of a madman.

Flapper had no more control over shouting words during bodily contortions than he did the contortions themselves. Major contortions, sometimes, included bending his knees into a near squat, drawing his mouth into a snarl, slapping himself in the forehead with the back of his hand, beating on or squeezing the nearest object or person with his open hand or fist, and tossing whatever object he was holding straight up into the air.

His rapidly shouted words might be 'wait-wait-wait', 'Rhody-Rhody-Rhody', 'stealin'-stealin'-stealin', 'no-no-no', 'hey-hey-hey', 'dam-dam-dam'—or any other word on his mind when the physical short-circuit hit his nervous system. Flapper preferred the word 'tic' rather than seizure to describe his diability. People from in town and nearby that knew Flapper paid little or no attention to his physical gyrations. People who *didn't* know him—that's another story entirely.

Some claimed the nick-name, 'Flapper', came from his physical affliction. Others said it had to with his penchant for dancing—without music. His last name, Pancake, was real. His family and family name was very well respected. In the 1930-40-50s, there was no known cure or medicine for St. Vitus Dance that offered even moderate relief from the repetitive assaults to the human neurological system. Eventually the number of known cases of St. Vitus Dance grew to a level that brought national publicity and a new name of Tourette's Syndrome. By the time research developed drugs that offered *some* relief, Flapper had passed away.

Flapper was the only young man in Bluestone judged unfit for military service by the Draft Board. Flapper was enraged by this news from Selective Service Registrar, Dolly Purdy. He went to her office to appeal his rejection by the Board. Purdy summarily dismissed his request for re-consideration. Uncharacteristically, Flapper reacted violently. He used his huge, muscular body to turn over file cabinets, desks, throw typewriters against the wall, and scatter boxes of records across the room. He was in the process of throwing an adding machine through a window when the town police chief, Bart Brown, ran into the room.

"That's enough, by God!! If that adding machine goes through the window, you can count on me wearin' your ass out with my 'stick'!" Brit growled. He raised his big wooden 'night-stick' above his head to reinforce his threat.

Amid yells of his rights to an appeal of his rejection, Flapper put the adding machine back on a desk. Between bouts of rage and tears, Dolly began picking through the wreckage of her office. She vented her anger in words that seldom passed the lips of a lady in Bluestone. Not in public, anyway. Bart grabbed her arm to keep her from stabbing Flapper with a letter opener. He promised to put him in jail. Polly was looking for punishment that involved physical pain, not jail.

"You want to join the Army, do you, Flapper? Fine, I'll fix that for you! Damn right you'll join the Army! Think you're a tough one, do you? I'll do your paper work right this minute! The Army gets you—they'll send your crazy ass straight to the front lines! Let's see how tough you are when Germans start shooting at you", Dolly screamed as she pointed her finger at him over Bart's shoulder.

The next morning, in the cold pre-dawn darkness, amid the wails and tears of mothers, ninety two young men were crammed into an old Bluestone city bus. They were taken to the local train station, and put on a troop train carrying over 500 young men to an Army basic training camp in Mississippi. Flapper Pancake and Rhody Wallace were among the 500 Army recruits on that train.

The prevailing atmosphere on that troop train was one of fatalism. The young draftees talked tough and made poor jokes about not being afraid of a shooting war. Still, the daily news of the ever increasing number of fatalities from this war was not lost on these new recruits. Privately, they believed their chances of coming home from this war alive were no better than 50-50. Why not live 'recklessly' with whatever time left in their lives, they reasoned. One of very few forms of 'reckless living' to be found on a moving troop train was gambling.

Poker games broke out in every one of the 20 cars in the train. That meant most of the 500 men were playing or wanting to play poker. Flapper couldn't hold his body still long enough to play cards. Rhody's hearing made it difficult for him to understand the bidding of the players. He was never sure when to yell 'call' 'raise' or 'fold'. For all he knew, he may have been raising against his own bet. No, Flapper and Rhody had to get in on the 'action' as 'bankers'. They both had some money. They knew which of the men from Bluefield were excellent poker players, but had no money of their own to play with. They selected some of these guys, and offered them a percentage of the winnings for playing poker as their employees. Rhody & Flapper 'bank-rolled' 10 guys with $10 each. That was every cent Rhody & Flapper had to their names.

In four short hours, Flapper and Rhody had already made more money on their $100 poker investment than they would have earned in Bluestone in 3 months doing the menials jobs they usually had. With some of their early profits, they bank-rolled more players in three additional train cars. They monitored the games they 'bank-rolled'— day and night. The need for sleep, and most of the players being broke, closed down all the games 19 hours later. Every pocket on every piece of clothing Rhody & Flapper were wearing was crammed full of money won in poker games. Almost asleep on their feet, they looked for a place to lie down. They had been awake for 24 hours now. Every seat in every train car was filled with sleeping soldiers.

At the end of the train, they found an old mail car with numerous empty mail bags lying on the floor. They piled some of the beat-up, empty, canvas mail bags in a corner of the old train car. With their duffel bags as pillows, their pockets crammed full of money, they dropped down on the dusty old bags and instantly fell asleep—happy and totally exhausted.

For the first time in their lives, one of their ventures had actually generated thousands of dollars. More money than all their wild-eyed schemes put together had ever put in their pockets. More money than they had ever seen before—let alone had in their hands. More money than they could have earned working manual labor jobs for a year in the late 1930s and early 40s.

When they awakened, it was day light. The train car was quiet—and not moving. Rhody looked through the dirty train car window at a mile long, table-flat landscape of sparse grass, sandy soil, and distant rock formations. Five empty train passenger cars were connected to the mail car—and all of them were on a side track across from a railroad station. No soldiers were in sight, nor was the train engine and the other 15 troops cars that been a part of their troop train. Flapper and Rhody quickly hopped off the train car, and trotted across the tracks to the train station. They asked the Station Master where they were, where the other soldiers and train engine were, what day it was, and what time it was.

"Humph! You boys are in one heck of a shape—you don't know where you are, what day it is, or even what time it is. You're in Sweetwater, Texas. It's 5:05 pm—on a Friday. I don't know nuthin' 'bout no other soldiers. Maybe they left 'fore I came on duty. There's a war on—soldiers comin' n' goin' all the time. Ain' no way I can keep up with 'em. They's an army fort a few miles from here. Maybe they went there. Tell you what I <u>do</u> know. I know you boys can't be gettin' back on them train cars. Yuh' heah? They gotta' be cleaned and serviced—cause they gonna use 'em tonight to take a bunch of troops from Camp Maxie to Galveston to ship out for overseas. Now—you boys wanna' call somebody over to Camp Maxie to come pick you up—you can use the phone in my office", drawled the railroad Station Master.

Flapper and Rhody were stunned. They had apparently lost

a whole day while asleep. With the help of the station master, Rhody phoned nearby Camp Maxie. He told the duty Sergeant who answered the phone they were recruits—who had gotten lost from their assigned troop train. Explaining their presence in Sweetwater was difficult. Their last actual recollection, before sleep, was passing through a town in South Carolina. They were supposed to have changed trains during a layover in Columbus, Ga., and arrived at an army training fort in Mississippi the following day.

For fear of having their poker winnings confiscated by the Army, he left out any mention of their twenty four hour marathon gambling venture. They had more money in their pockets than they had ever seen, at one time, in their entire lives. There was no way they were giving up that money .Without hesitating one second, Rhody made up a lie. He told the Sergeant lack of sleep and confusion must have caused them to get on the wrong train in a change-over in Georgia. Being unfamiliar with any of the states in the south, and it being night time—they had no idea where they were or what train they got on after the train change, he told the Sergeant. He finished his story by claiming outrage that no one on the train awakened them before that train got to Texas.

The Sergeant didn't believe a word of the story. As far as he was concerned they were just two lying, AWOL, deadbeats trying to avoid the Army. To say he was upset with the problem they caused was putting it mildly. He assured them they would be spending the first year of their army career in the brig.

Rhody and Flapper had never seen the inside of a jail. They weren't sure what happened when you were put in jail. Common sense told them their money wouldn't be safe there. One minute after the Sergeant hung up the phone they found a Western Union station. They wired all their poker winnings to their parents' homes in Virginia. Their wire included a promise to explain the money when they 'came home from the war'.

The Sergeant sent some MPs to the train station. They arrested Flapper and Rhody, threw them into a Jeep, and hauled them to Camp Maxie. After spending several hours in the base brig, a Major on the base listened to their story. He wasn't impressed with it either. In a profanity laced tirade, he told them they were either liars or idiots. Further, he told them, he didn't want <u>two</u> idiots on <u>one</u> army base. That evening Rhody was assigned to basic training in a heavy Artillery unit right there in Camp Maxey. The next morning, Flapper was put on an army cargo plane going to an army training camp in Mississippi. They were not even allowed to say good-bye to each other. Over three years would pass before they saw each other again.

Rhody's stay in artillery, even the Army itself, lasted little more than a year. With his hearing disability, he couldn't, accurately, hear all of the orders he was given. Asking people to repeat their orders became embarrassing, and irritated his superior officers. Rhody quickly tired of being cursed by officers he asked to repeat firing orders on the big howitzers. He stopped asking anybody to repeat anything. He just yanked the trigger on those big howitzers when he <u>thought</u> he heard the order to 'fire'.

Occasionally, he misinterpreted an order for an adjustment to the big canon's aim as a 'FIRE' command—and would fire a huge shell out of the long barrel of the cannon he operated. Some of his erroneous shots of the huge shells very nearly resulted in injury to or obliteration of his own troops. He missed taking out an entire ammo storage building by just 50 yards with one of his errant shots. After several serious misfire incidents in one year, the Army decided it was in their own best interest to transfer Rhody. Trouble was, there was no other job they could think of that Rhody could handle with his severe hearing loss.

They tried him in the motor pool—for a while. Again, Rhody's hearing deficit caused problems—for him and the Army. He would be told to pick up an Officer at the train station—and he would mis-interpret that instruction as an order to take a truck to a nearby town and pick up the post mail. Often, when Rhody went on these errant journeys no one knew where he was—so they couldn't contact him without sending someone to look for him. Frequently, that meant detailing other men and vehicles to track him down and bring him back to the post. The motor pool just wasn't an option for keeping Rhody in the army.

The numerous pieces of army property he damaged with misplaced shots left his immediate officers seething. They wanted to make him the main player in a court-martial because they believed he was faking his inability to hear. On further reflection, Ft. Maxey's Commandant decided—after considering Rhody's history in artillery and the motor pool and consulting with the camp doctor—the easiest way out was to just write off the damage and chaos Rhody had caused and get him out of the Army. Rhody was given a medical discharge, a disability rating for loss of hearing, and put on a train back to Bluestone. After a year of standing three feet from thunderous canon explosions and driving trucks with incredibly loud engines, his hearing loss was worse than ever.

Flapper completed his basic training in infantry. His problem with St. Vitus Dance was ignored by the army. He was a live body—and live bodies were badly needed on the front lines of battle in Europe. He was shipped overseas and wound up in Gen. George Patton's Third Army. Despite the burden of St. Vitus Dance, he stayed alive during three years on the front lines of countless infantry battles across Africa, Sicily, France, and Belgium.

According to those who fought with him, Flapper would, sometimes, engage in hand-to-hand combat with machine guns in both hands. With both guns blazing, Flapper would be screaming, his body jerking with nervous 'seizures', dancing and skipping over the ground, a hail of bullets spewing from his guns, mowing down German troops, as he yelled for the enemy soldiers to 'come and get me'. Some Germans soldiers, who had seen him up close, actually turned and ran from him—his screams—his twisted facial contortions—his physical gyrations, and his withering gun fire. The looks on some of their faces indicated they thought he was some sort of 'Tasmanian Devil', who couldn't be killed.

Eventually, the Germans did 'come and get him'. Flapper had been involved in front line action off and on for 143 days when Patton took part of the Third Army into Bastogne to relieve the 101st Airborne, who were under siege by a German Panzer Division. Flapper was badly wounded in a fire fight at Bastogne. He was taken to a field medical tent behind the front lines. They patched him up but didn't expect him to survive. He was unconscious. The Army delivered a 'Wounded-in-Action' telegram to his mother, Mrs. Ora Pancake, right in the middle of the Sunday service at Bluestone's Antioch Baptist Church.

Flapper remained in a coma, but his body would not surrender to death. After two weeks, he was taken from the medical tent to a troop hospital behind the lines in France, where he remained in a coma for another month. To get better treatment for him, they eventually moved him to a hospital in England. After ninety days in a coma, Flapper awoke in an English hospital.

Between the burdens of St. Vitus Dance, 3 years of combat, bullet wounds, and a long coma—Flapper had seen better days. They kept him in England for another two months. The doctors gave him drugs to heal his wounds, muffle the pain, mask his nightmares, and even some experimental drugs they thought might help control the St. Vitus Dance. Time, medical care, and drugs healed most of his physical injuries in a few months. The nightmares and fatigue from years of combat took the better part of a year to fade into the shadows of his memory. Sadly, the experimental drugs didn't soften the intensity of his St Vitus Dance seizures.

In late May of 1945, they shipped Flapper back to Bluestone. It had been over 3 1/2 years since he had seen home. For his 3 1/2 years in battle he was awarded a purple heart for injuries, two Silver Star metals for bravery in battle, ribbons for battles he fought in, an honorable discharge, and a military medical disability rating. In another 3 months, the war would be over.

Back home, Rhody and Flapper were reunited. They worked at a variety of manual jobs until the war ended in August 1945. The money they won bank rolling poker games and most of their army pay was still in the local bank. Flapper paid cash for a home for his widowed Mother, bought a used Nash automobile, and still had money in the bank. He and Rhody were receiving monthly military disability checks, and would continue to do so as long as they lived.

Unhappily, Flapper's time as a licensed automobile driver was brief. The experience yielded little more than bitter fruit. Hardly 3 months after purchasing his first and only car, he stopped behind four cars at a traffic light in uptown Bluestone. As he sat in his car, engine idling, a St. Vitus 'tic' hit him. No amount of effort could still or control those 'tics' when they hit his body.

With a sudden shout of 'WAIT-WAIT-WAIT' and an

involuntary body contortion, his left foot came off the clutch and his right foot stomped the accelerator in exact timing with the three times he yelled 'wait'. With his first stomp on the accelerator, his car shot forward and slammed into the rear of the car in front of him. That pushed the car he hit into the car in front of it. This same thing happened with his second and third stomp on his accelerator. By the time the 'tic' episode had run its course, Flapper had damaged all 4 cars in front of him by ramming them one-into-the-other until all 5 cars were wedged together in one big damaged heap.

The situation deteriorated when the occupants of the other vehicles staggered from their cars—just in time to see Flapper jump from his car in the grip of another full-blown physical 'tic'—including repetitive, maniacal screams. They had intended to vent their anger on the fool who repeatedly rammed their cars. As they watched Flapper, in wide-eyed disbelief, not one of them could find the voice to utter a single word. His feet fairly flew as he danced and skipped around his car on Federal St. His fist hammered the hood of his car as he screamed "Heyyy, DAMIT-DAMIT-DAMIT". He screwed his eyes shut, bared his teeth, slapped himself in the forehead with an open hand, and, involuntarily, kicked the tire of the car in front of his.

He re-gained control of himself, got that big familiar, warm smile on his face, and spoke to the driver of the first car he hit.

"Sir, I apologize. This is all my fault. I (tic) GOT-GOT-GOT—

insurance. My insurance will pay for all the damage"—(tic) Flapper's huge hand shot out, slammed down on the shoulder of the man in front of him , squeezed hard, shook him like a rag doll, and bawled—"TO-TO-TO—fix your car, sir."

Flapper's efforts at penitence only succeeded in making the man whose shoulder he squeezed flinch in pain and slide sideways to get away from Flapper. Flapper never noticed. He was already looking at the woman who was the driver of the second car in the line of cars he had rammed together. She had an uneasy look on her face—having seen Flapper's interaction with the man who shoulder he just 'crushed'.

Flapper trotted over to her car, anxious to assure her she had no worries about payment for the damage to her car. She was standing beside the front door of her car when Flapper got to her and rested his big left hand on the rear view mirror mounted on her left front door.

"Now mam, please don't be concerned about all this damage to your nice car. I'll—". Here Flapper's assurances to the woman were interrupted by a major tic. His huge hand on her outside rear view mirror clamped down. His involuntary muscle reaction caused him to rip the mirror completely off her car door and hammer the roof of her car with it 3 times in cadence with his screams of --"TAKE-TAKE-TAKE—care of all damages—including this mirror."

As Flapper tried to hand her the destRayed mirror the woman jerked open her car door, dived inside the car, locked the door, and began screaming hysterically for people standing nearby to save her—call the police.

That was it. All the drivers of the cars he hit were dead certain they were in the presence of a mad man—who might put an exclamation point on the damage to their cars by beating them senseless—if not outright killing them.

The owner of the first car, whose shoulder was still aching, ran into Alfred Land's Jewelry store and refused to come out without a police escort. The lady—she remained barricaded in her car. By then, the other two car owners were already running up Bland St—begging the merchant of every store they passed "For God's sake—call the police."

'Pick' Zambus, a local police officer, arrived on the scene. Flapper got a ticket. Flapper satisfied 'Pick' that Shep Dodson's company insured his car. Some cars were towed away, including Flapper's.

Flapper appeared before Judge Singleton who, in the best future interest of all car owners and pedestrians, took Flapper's driving license from him.

Flapper had his car repaired. He begged friends into service as his driver when he wanted to go somewhere. Driving Flapper was a task most of his friends didn't relish. There were no air conditioners in cars in 1946. People got relief from summer heat by driving with the car windows rolled down.

Flapper, with a friend driving his car, would be cruising slowly through town, windows down, enjoying the sights and sounds of people mingling on the crowded sidewalks during a summer evening. Flapper would ride with his huge arm out the window, his ham-sized hand resting on the roof of the car. He'd spot an attractive woman walking along the sidewalk. He enjoyed his salacious thoughts about the woman in private—until a 'tic' hit him. Then his fist would begin hammering a tattoo on the roof of the car as he loudly yelled out the open window, "C'MERE WOMAN, I'M HORNY!" The driver of his car would have to go roaring off down Bland St. before the woman could see their faces or get the car's license number. As time went on, incidents like this made it increasingly difficult for Flapper to find *anyone* willing to drive his car.

After receiving his medical discharge from the army and returning to Bluefield, Rhody continued to live with his parents. He had not married. He held a series of menial jobs during the remaining years the country was at war. With so many men away at war, the single women in town outnumbered the men by 5 to 1. Rhody devoted every hour of his leisure time to helping as many women as possible satisfy their thirst for male companionship.

Connie Mack once said, "Opportunity knocks once at every man's door". Flapper and Rhody didn't believe that for one second. They knew a lot of people who had lived their entire lives in Bluestone without hearing a 'knock' from opportunity. The only 'knock' of their acquaintance was the 'school of hard knocks'—and that involved more pain than opportunity. As far as they were concerned, the successful man created his own opportunity. With the war over, a lot of soldiers were back in civilian life and taking the few available jobs. They decided it was time to invest in a venture that would secure their own future.

Rhody Joe was always frugal with his money. He had spent very little of his troop-train poker winnings and army pay. He lived from week to week on what he earned working jobs in service stations, tire recapping plants, and driving a delivery truck.

Even after buying his widowed mother a house and himself a car, Flapper still had some money in the bank. He lived in the house he bought his mother, and worked odd jobs— like being a bouncer at the local American Legion Club. Then a 'tic' hit him while he was throwing some drunk out of the Legion Hall, causing Flapper to break the guy's arm— thus ending that job. He also kept $2000 stashed in a cigar box in his attic. That represented some of his winnings from poker games he financed. He also had his army pay saved from 3+ years he was on the front lines—too busy fighting to stay alive to spend his pay.

Rhody Joe made a down payment on a Shell gasoline service station located at the west end of town on Rt. 19/460. It was a big east-west tourist route. The down payment took most of the money Rhody had. To get additional money to stock the place with tires, gas, and auto repair tools, he let Flapper buy into the service station as a minor partner.

The deed listed the formal name of the gas station as Wallace Super Shell. Even though there were 3-4 other gas stations in town, Wallace Super Shell became known as 'The Gas Station'. It had two bays for washing or working on cars, two gas pumps, equipment for mounting and balancing tires, and equipment used to diagnose/repair auto engine problems. The majority of their income came from selling tires, washing and waxing cars, road service on broken down vehicles, and routine engine repairs. Gas sales, to locals and tourists passing through town, added modest income to the till. Flapper & Rhody were known and trusted in town. Within a year the station was providing them with a steady and comfortable income.

When Rhody was medically discharged from the army he was given, as part of his disability rating, a hearing aid. The type of hearing aid the Veterans Administration hospital issued was the current 'cutting edge' in hearing aids. Specifically, the hearing aid mechanism was built into the stems of a pair of eye glasses. Wiring and batteries that amplified sound ran from the stems to small speaker molds fitted in both his ears. While this hearing aid didn't dramatically improve Rhody's hearing, it did offer *some* improvement. However, he found the clear glass lens in the frames a nuisance. Having enjoyed life-long perfect vision, he saw no need to be burdened with the chore of keeping dirt, sweat, and smudges off lens which were nothing but clear glass. He also claimed the lens distorted his vision and gave him a headache.

Rhody firmly believed the best solution to every problem was to reduce it to its simplest terms. In this case, his 'simple' solution was to press his thumbs against the glass lenses, pop them out of eye-glass frames, and wear the frames without lenses. Looking at the matter from his view, problem solved. No more dirty lenses to clean, no distortions, no headaches. It never occurred to him that people might think it a bit odd to see him wearing eye-glass frames with no lens in them. He truly believed most people wouldn't notice the absence of the lenses, and those that did would understand. Time and events at 'The Gas Station' would lay waste to Rhody Joe's sunny conclusions about his self-modified eye-glass frames.

So began the gas station partnership of Rhody and Flapper. One coping with a severe hearing loss, marginally improved by use of a government issued hearing aid housed in a pair of 'owner-modified' eye glass frames. The other a victim of a medical condition manifested by involuntary physical contortions, compounded with repeated screams of any word on his mind when the seizure hit him.
Rhody and Flapper ran a 'full service' gas station. If for no other reason, there were no self-serve gas stations in the 1940s and 1950s. When a customer's car pulled up to the gas pumps it rolled over a compression line lying on the concrete apron surrounding the gas pumps. This activated a loud bell inside the station. Rhody and Flapper had their routine down pat. At the sound of the bell, they quickly walked out to the customer's car with a big, welcoming smile on their faces.

Flapper would grab a paper towel, a squirt bottle of Windex, and begin cleaning the car's windshield. While cleaning the windshield, he would ask the car owner if he wanted his engine oil level checked. During the window cleaning, Flapper would, almost invariably, have one of his 'tics'. Some episodes were minor—hardly noticeable. Others involved physical and verbal reactions so severe they left mind bending impressions on those unsuspecting customers exposed to such an episode for the first time.

To make sure he heard the customer's answer to his question of, "Fill 'er up?", Rhody would lean down, and put his head so close to the driver's open side window that his head would almost be inside the car. Combine this 'face-in-the-window' approach with Rhody's hard-of-hearing habit of shouting every word he uttered—he created quite a compelling presence. After interacting with Rhody & Flapper, some tourist/gas customers left the station convinced they had been involved in a 'close encounter of the worst kind'.

Here are some of the stories that grew out of the 29 year partnership of Rhody and Flapper at 'The Gas Station'.

\\\\\\\\\\\\\

Summer heat was shimmering off the concrete apron in front of the gas station that afternoon. A car rolled up to the gas pumps with tourists, an elderly man and woman, in the car. Rhody and Flapper strolled out to the car. Flapper grabbed a rag and began wiping the windshield.

"Fill 'er up?", yelled Rhody, as he his stuck his head half way through the open window of the car door.

With a startled look, the car's driver found himself staring into a face barely ten inches from his own—wearing a pair of eye glasses with no lenses in the frame. Leaning away from Rhody's face, the old man nodded nervously and mumbled 'yes'. Rhody drew his head out of the window and ambled to the gas pump. The old man and lady turned to watch Flapper, who was leaning over their windshield, briskly cleaning the glass. At that precise moment, Flapper's body was struck by a 'tic'.

"WATCHIT'-WATCHIT'-WATCHIT", bellowed Flapper as his face contorted into a teeth-bared snarl just inches away from the outside of the windshield. Simultaneously, he threw the Windex bottle and cleaning towel up in the air and beat the roof of the car with his fist in perfect timing with each 'WATCHIT' he bellowed.

Within seconds of having the 'tic', Flapper returned to normal conduct, picked up the Windex bottle, and continued wiping off the windshield. The car driver and his wife sat glued to their seats, unbridled fear etched in their faces. Not a word came from their lips as the driver clamped his fingers around the steering wheel. His wife clutched her purse tightly to her chest with both arms. Actually, her lips *were* moving—but no sound came from them.

"CHECK YA' AWL?" yelled Rhody through the open window.

Flinching from unexpected scream into his left ear, the driver turned to find Rhody's face and lens-less glasses, once again, inside the open window of his car door.

"Wha— uh, no. No, the oil's fine, thank you. Just—."

Flapper was standing in front of the car ready to raise the hood to check the oil. A 'tic' hit him just as he heard the old man say 'no' to the offer to check his oil.

"NO-NO-NO, RHODY! The awl' is okay—don't need to check it", whooped Flapper, as he bared his teeth, threw back his head, slapped his forehead with one hand, while slapping the hood of the car with the other hand. Again, he regained his composure and eased back into normal behavior a few seconds after yelling and slapping the car with his hand.

The customer and his wife sat in silent panic. Any restraints they might have shown in their quiet, mental prayers to the Almighty for protection were abandoned. In a quivering voice, the wife began openly verbalizing a prayer for their protection and deliverance. Shortly into her plea for protection from above, she abandoned her mumbled prayers in favor of loud, hysterical directions to her husband.

"God above, Herman! Don't just sit there! For goodness sake—pay the bill! Let's get out of this place 'fore we get hurt or killed! One of those fools screamin' his head off, an' wearin' eye-glasses with no lens in 'em—and the other one havin' fits and beatin' our car to pieces!"

"Uh, sir? Sir! How much do I owe you? Please sir, just let me pay you", pleaded the car owner through his side window, now rolled up to the point where it was only opened to a one inch slit.

"That'll be nine dollars and fifty cents, even", roared Rhody.

"Here's ten dollars—please keep the change." The customer slipped a ten dollar bill through the narrow opening in the window while frantically starting the car's engine. Without waiting for a response from Rhody, he jerked his car into gear and tore across the station lot to the highway.

"Thank ye' kindly, sir", Rhody screamed at the retreating car. Completely oblivious to the shocking impression they had made on the fleeing customers, Rhody and Flapper waved farewell to the fleeing customers.

~~~~~~~~~~

An old, long black '47 Chrysler sedan rolled up the gas pumps. Flapper ambled out to handle the customer by himself. The customer told Flapper to 'filler-up'. Flapper stuck the gas nozzle into the car's gas filler pipe, set it on automatic, and walked to the front of the car with window cleaning fluid and paper towel in hand. The customer was an African-American, with a wife and four kids in the car. His license plate said he was from Georgia.

"'Scuse me, suh'. D'yall have a rest ru'um?" said the driver

"Sure do—right around th' corner of th' building—both open and clean", said Flapper with a big smile.

All four doors of the cars opened. As the entire family started to pile out of the car, Flapper's nervous system fell prey to a *major* 'tic'.

"WAIT-WAIT-WAIT!" screamed Flapper. His face screwed into a snarl that bared his teeth and squeezed his eyes shut. His big left hand convulsively clamped down on the squeeze-bottle of window cleaning solution, draining it completely. An entire 1/4 pint of window cleaning fluid instantly shot out of the bottle in a straight-up jet stream. It saturated the windshield, hood, and roof of the car when gravity took over and pulled it down out of the air. With his other hand balled into a fist, Flapper beat the windshield of the car in perfect cadence with his screams of 'wait'. He followed this by punching his left arm skyward, tossing the cleaner fluid bottle high in the air, while repeatedly slapping himself in the forehead with his right hand. He completed the episode by performing a show-stopping exhibition of his 'Donald-Duck' walk/dance in front of the customer's car. This whole episode played out in 3-4 seconds.

Before the screams of 'WAIT-WAIT-WAIT' had died on

Flapper's lips, the entire family jumped back in their car. As Flapper's convulsive antics continued, all four doors slammed shut, simultaneously. The white of every eye in that car seemed to measure the size of a half-dollar. The arms of four of the car's occupants frantically rolled all car windows shut and hammered door locks tightly into place.

Flapper's little display had literally frightened the wits out of the entire family. They didn't know if his screams of 'wait' were an all-out warning of a life-threatening danger, or a demand that they not exit their car without his express permission. The shock of the incident left them prepared to deny their bodies' relief in the gas station rest rooms— just pee in the floor of the car if need be. They weren't coming out of that car again.

Just as quickly as he had gone into that mind-blowing 'tic', Flapper's normal body movements and conversational tone returned. As if nothing out of ordinary had taken place, Flapper began mopping the window cleaner fluid off the car hood and said.

"How's ya' 'awl?"

"We're jus' fine. How 'ah you?" came the muffled reply from inside the tightly closed car.

"Wha---, wha'd you say?"

For the first time, Flapper noticed the scared, wide-eyed look from 6 people packed into a car with all the windows closed—on a blistering hot day.

"Hey, don't ya' wanna' use th' rest rooms? They're empty now. Y'all go ahead on. It's okay. Ya' heah' me? Hey, man---, I can't heah' ya'. How 'bout rollin' th' window down? Ya' wan' me to check ya' 'awl? Y'all c'mon outa' there, now. It's okay. Use th' rest room while I finish gasin' up ya' awtuhmobeel."

No amount of coaching from Flapper could persuade those folks to leave the locked safety of their car. As far as they were concerned, the metal skin of their car was all that stood between them and an unrestrained mad man.

"Ah—ah, no-- Thas' al'right. We're jus' fine. Don't nobody need to use no rest ru'um. I'll jus' pay you. How much do I owe you, suh'?" came the muffled voice from inside the car.

"Well--, okay. Suit ya'self. That'll be $11.75", Flapper drawled.

The customer rolled the window down an inch. He leaned to the middle of the car as he passed a ten and two one dollar bills to Flapper through the narrow opening of the window. A minor 'tic' hit Flapper as he reached for the money. As his right hand closed around the money it shot forward, and slammed into the car roof just above the driver's door with enough force to rock the entire car.

"I don' need no change!" shrieked the driver, as he started

the car in motion toward the highway.

Flapper stood by the gas pumps, shaking his head as he watched the fleeing car swerve on to the highway. He mumbled to himself and yelled at Rhody as he walked back into the building.

"That fool is crazier 'n hell, Rhody. Ridin' 'round in this heat with his windows all rolled up. Hey, RHODY-RHODY-RHODY! I got a quarter tip. Cigarette money. Won't have to steal them— STEALIN'-STEALIN'-STEALIN'—out of our cigarette machine tomorrow", laughed Flapper while he rang up the sale on the cash register.

~~~~~~

An aging, white Studebaker Lark pulled into the gas station toward the end of a warm spring day. The car was dirty and worn looking. It had an Alabama plate hanging from the bumper by one bolt.

A young woman was driving the car. Her face had an exhausted, resigned look about it. There were two small children asleep on blankets spread across luggage, clothing, and other household property, piled high on the back floor and seat of the car.

The woman told Rhody to put eight dollars of gas in the tank. Rhody pumped the gas into the car, and began cleaning the windshield. As he cleaned the window, he stared at the trash in the front floor of the car. The floor was covered with candy and food wrappers, empty cigarette packs, soda cans, and even some old lettuce leaves.

Rhody was wondering how anybody could ride in a car that filthy when the woman sitting in the car spoke to him. He believed the woman had caught him staring at the trash in the floor of her car, and asked him.

"Do you have a whisk broom?"

Now Rhody felt bad. He had embarrassed the poor woman. She had seen the disapproving look he gave the trash in the floor of her car. He felt obligated to make amends. He decided he would offer to clean the trash out of her car floor for her.

"No mam, I don't", said Rhody in answer to her question. "But, if you'll pull right over there I'll blow it out for you", said Rhody as he pointed to his air hose hanging on the side of the building.

"Go to hell, you filthy-mouth jerk!" shouted the woman.

Rhody stood there with a stunned look on his face. The woman threw a bunch of wadded up dollar bills at him, started her car, and raced across the concrete apron to the highway.

Rhody stared at the car until it was out of sight. He picked up the wadded up money from the ground, counted it, shook his head, and walked back to the gas station office with an angry look on his face. Flapper was standing in the door way with a big grin splitting his face.

"What th' hell was wrong with that crazy woman, Flapper? I offer to do her a free service and she cusses me!" said Rhody.

"Rhody, what did the woman ask you?" asked Flapper.

"She asked me if I had a whisk broom", said Rhody.

"No. No, my friend. She asked you if you had a REST ROOM. And you told her you didn't have one, but offered to 'blow it out' for her—with our AIR HOSE." replied Flapper as he collapsed in laughter.

Flapper lived into his late 60s. Rhody lived to be 88 years old, before collapsing from a massive stroke in the sanctuary of his church one morning. Flapper is buried next to his parents. Rhody is buried beside his wife, next to his parents. Both are buried in Maple Hill Cemetery, not 75 yards apart— almost in sight of the service station where they spent so many years of their lives.

MISS SALLY

Miss Sally was born to wealth, to society, given advantages withheld from those not as well born in town. She was the only child of Mr.& Mrs. Samuel Liestz, who were among the wealthiest people in Bluestone. Their huge white mansion sat on top of Blake Hill, overlooking the town of some 5000 souls. If their wealth, land holdings, and social status weren't a sufficiently clear proclamation of their place in society, the Liestz *personally* made it known they were properly 'Mayflowered'.

Even from her early years, Miss Sally was blessed with extraordinary beauty and a phenomenal soprano voice. Not even the town cynics denied her world class beauty in her late teens—absolutely stunning. When she sang, she was in a class occupied by few others. Her soaring solos could and did bring tears to the eyes of some. A few in our church would say her rendition of some spirituals left them so emotionally drained they were on the verge of begging her to 'have a little mercy'. I don't know if I would have gone that far, but I won't deny the jaw dropping effects of some songs she belted out at Antioch Baptist's Sunday morning services. Even on sweltering summer Sundays, those paper fans donated to the church by Wagner's Funeral Home stopped fluttering when she rose to sing.

Mr. Samuel Leistz used his wealth and influence to assure

Miss Sally's acceptance in one of the country's finest *Finishing Schools for Young Ladies*. Once she was properly *'finished'*, he spared no expense in having her outstanding singing skills honed to a professional level by the most sought-after voice coaches.

By the time she was twenty three years old, Miss Sally was singing with the Philharmonic Symphony Orchestra. Media critics dubbed her 'The Nightingale of the South'. Her singing voice was the first to be broadcast from North America to the European continent. She performed at World Fairs in Chicago and St. Louis. She toured Europe with a Chicago Opera Company. She was also the toast of the New York opera scene.

When she was twenty five, Miss Sally met and was lavishly courted by the dashing Walter Standish Davison, II, of the very-well-to-do Davisons of Newport, Rhode Island. It was widely rumored Walter, II was being groomed to be Rhode Island's next United States Senator.

When she was twenty six, Miss Sally and the charming Walter Standish Davison, II were united in marriage. Not only was Walter, II a handsome man, he had, according to my grandfather, 'a wood box full of money'. The town of Bluestone couldn't recall playing host to such a lavish wedding—ever. It was attended by the Who's-Who of Rhode Island society, the elite of the concert music world, politicians from the state and national level, and the 'privileged' of Bluestone—who were few in numbers. No doubt about it, Mrs. Sally Liestz Davison had joined the 'larger-than-life' club of this world.

When Miss Sally was thirty years of age, things—I mean everything—went south on her. Up to this point in age, her world had included everything she needed or wanted. In her world, for the first thirty years of her life, 'need' and 'want' meant the same thing. Then, inside 1-2 years, her world, as she knew it, evaporated.

I heard my uncle telling my Aunt Wilma about it. According to him, "One minute she was on top of the world. The next minute, damn near everything she had disappeared faster than a fart in the wind." Great guy, my uncle—but not the one to turn an eloquent phrase for the situation. His philosophical summarization of Miss Sally's bad luck ran more to the cliché, 'That's life—here today—gone tomorrow'.

First, Miss Sally's father, Mr. Samuel Liestz, lost the majority of his wealth through bad investments by stock brokers and the market crash. He came out of it with about enough money to keep his membership at the Country Club, keep his maid and yard man for his mansion, keep gas in the family Packard, take his annual vacation to Myrtle Beach, and host his annual Christmas party, and keep his checking account solvent. He lost about 85% of his vast wealth, all told.

Secondly, that scoundrel, Walter Standish Davison, II, left Miss Sally for a twenty one year old society belle of Boston, Mass. Ol' Walter II, had been having an affair with this 'younger woman' for 6 months. He broke the bad news to

Miss Sally by having divorce papers served on her the very day she returned from a one month European opera tour. Compounding his callous conduct, Walter II rubbed salt in the wound when he denied Miss Sally a financial divorce settlement that would have secured her future years and, perhaps, cushioned his betrayal of her. His politically connected and powerful Attorneys pushed a financial settlement through the divorce court which included, for the most part, only the money Miss Sally had earned during their relatively short marriage. Compared to the expense of the life style Miss Sally was accustomed to, the money she got out of the divorce was pocket change.

Thirdly, Miss Sally's ability to belt out the vocal high notes critical to opera performances faded in the change of a concert season. Opera Divas live in a highly competitive dog-eat-dog atmosphere. When her voice range slipped an octave, the Chicago Opera Company summarily replaced her with a younger star with a stronger voice.

Finally, to make her destruction total, her beauty went from stunning to just average in the two years it took ol' Walter to legally finalize their divorce. The stress of bad luck and time took a devastating toll on her face and body.

I overheard my grandparents discussing Miss Sally's divorce. The Liestzes attended our church. My grandparents had known them for years. My grandmother said she heard, at the monthly meeting of the church's Ladies Missionary Society, that those 'low-down Davidsons' tried to take back some of the more expensive pieces of jewelry Walter II had given Miss Sally in happier times—claiming they were family heirlooms. My grandfather said Mr. Samuel confided, at a meeting of the church Board of Deacons, that Walter II gave Miss Sally next to no money in the divorce settlement. My grandfather was a man who spoke bluntly. He told my grandmother, "If what Sam Liestz says is true, Sally didn't get enough money out of that divorce to buy a pair of bloomers for a hummingbird."

Further, he said her ex-husband's adulterous conduct during the marriage and divorce, "Has aged that young woman beyond her years and torn her nerves all to pieces". "Of course," he bellowed, "what else would you expect from a Yankee Episcopalian". My grandfather was frugal with his trust of anyone not of the Baptist faith or born north of the Mason-Dixon Line.

Regardless of how you looked at it, the whole mess took its toll on Miss Sally. Mentally, physically, and financially—she was a somewhere between 'bad' and 'worse'. Mr. Samuel Liestz was outraged. But, he was too old and frail to give Walter, II the 'damn good thrashing he has coming to him'.

My Uncle said the pitiful balance in Mr. Samuel's bank account after the market crash left him financially unable to hire high-dollar lawyers who could go 'toe to toe' with the well-heeled Davisons' lawyers. Mr. Samuel and Miss Sally were both in a rage over their inability to do much of anything about the 'legal horse-whipping' that Walter's lawyers were giving her.

It was pretty evident Miss Sally was right on the edge of a full-blown nervous breakdown. She had to let her hair down to someone—or wind up in a padded room over at the Marion Insane Asylum. That 'someone' turned out to be Essie Graham. In their earlier years, Miss Essie and Miss Sally had been friends. Miss Essie, a strong personality and sharp businesswoman, had built up three thriving dance school/studios in and around Bluestone while Miss Sally was working her way up through the concert world. Miss Essie had already divorced one husband and was having serious thoughts about sending the second one packing. This gave her something in common with Miss Sally's recent marital woes.

Before and between marriages, Miss Essie lived with her parents for as long as I can remember. The Grahams had been next door neighbors to my grandparents long before I was even born. The Graham's big backyard adjoined my grandparent's one acre vegetable garden. I was out of sight as I hoed the tall rows of corn in our garden that afternoon, listening quietly as Essie took Miss Sally into her backyard, poured both of them a strong bourbon highball, and said "Okay honey, tell me all about it". That invitation, and the three bourbon highballs Miss Sally belted down, was all it took. Crying, screaming, and cussing, Miss Sally detailed the nightmare her life had become.

"Having a setback is <u>one</u> thing", she said as he pounded the chair arm with her fist. "Being stabbed in the back by a lying, cheating husband is <u>one</u> thing! Being fired from my job without warning is <u>one</u> thing! Having my father's entire fortune squandered by a bunch of thieving, lying stock brokers is <u>one</u> thing! But, damn it all" she sobbed to Miss Essie, "having <u>every one</u> of these things dumped on you at <u>once</u> —that's <u>NOT</u> one thing. That's <u>EVERY damn thing</u> at <u>ONE damn time</u>! Do you know one other living soul who had this much crap dumped on them at once? Hell no! So, why me? Essie, I'm sick and tired of being kicked around by everybody—and then told I can't kick <u>back</u>! I feel like I've been whipped through hell with a soot bag!"

Miss Essie did a lot of listening that afternoon. As a rule, Miss Essie was an impatient listener. She didn't take time to hear much of anything that didn't put money in her pocket. Small talk—shooting the breeze—it didn't fit in with her barn-burner personality Still, three bourbon highballs under her belt mellowed her enough to make her 'listener'. After two hours of listening to Miss Sally vent while they knocked off a fifth of bourbon, Miss Essie leaned close to Miss Sally, looked her in the eye, and did some talking of her own. I leaned on my hoe and listened to her.

"Sally, listen to me." said Miss Essie as she cupped Miss Sally's chin in her hand. "I agree with you. A lot of people you trusted—yeah, they dumped on you. Okay, that's over and done—not going to change. And all your pleas to God to take your side, and bring down a hairy hell on the people who stuck it to you--? Forget it sweetheart. I can tell you from personal experience—God doesn't get personally involved in marital disputes, the theft of family fortunes, and abuses of ungrateful employers. So—he isn't going to 'smite 'em dead for you'."

"Face reality, sweetheart. You cannot sit around feeling sorry for yourself—waiting for some 'White Knight in Shining Armor' to come along and make things right for you. The important thing now is, what are <u>you</u> going to do about it? <u>You</u>—Sally—not someone else—must pull <u>you</u> out of the hole you're in! If you want out of this mess, make <u>your</u> plans for getting out of it."

"Honey", Miss Essie went on, "let me be real clear. Your plans better include getting your hands on some *serious* money. Well-meaning people are going to hand you a line about 'money isn't everything'. And they are right—it isn't *everything*. But, by-golly, honey, its way th' hell ahead of whatever's in second place. I don't care what you do to get money—as long as *how* you get it doesn't get you thrown in jail."

"Money is power! With power in your hands—most of your problems will disappear overnight! With money and power, you get what you 'want'. Without them, you get what you 'need'—maybe. So your #1 prioity is to get yourself some money—real money. Now—I don't care what anybody says or thinks—you make that plan work! Plans that don't work—they're worthless! You want to be back on top— that's the way back to the top!

One more thing, Sally. If you run out of money, to live on, before you get your hands on some *real* money—don't pull this 'I've-got- my-pride' stuff on me. You come to me. I've got some money—I'll loan you enough to hold you for a few months until you figure out some way to put yourself back in the game."

Maybe it was the confidence Miss Essie exuded when she talked to Miss Sally. Maybe it was the fire in her voice. Maybe it was those three highballs Miss Sally drank in two hours. Either way, she was laughing and in a much better mood when she staggered out of Miss Essie's back yard late that afternoon. Floating on the warmth of that reservoir of bourbon inside her, she found new courage and resolve.

"I'm going back to Chicago—I'm going to call in some favors—I'll head-line some musical shows in the downtown theatres. My name will sell tickets. By the time the fall season for shows rolls around—I'll have my name back in the marquee lights. I'll be making big bucks again", Miss Sally declared as Miss Esther walked her out to her car. Miss Sally had a sassy air about her as she fired up the old family Packard and drove away from a waving Miss Essie.

Back in Chicago, Miss Sally found she had overestimated the drawing power of her name and her pull with producers who were her 'best buds' when she had top billing with the Chicago Opera. Opera Divas and stars of theatre musicals were two different breeds. Besides—singers in theatre musicals were most always good dancers. Miss Sally just didn't have the rhythm and balance that are second nature to good dancers. She could hold her own in a waltz or fox trot—outside of those two dances, she didn't have it and never would. So that limited her chances for major roles in most theatre musicals.

Out of the 'big leagues' of music, no substantial money from her divorce settlement, burdened with a fading beauty and declining voice, Miss Sally found she didn't have too many options open to her in Chicago. She utilized her name, experience, and reputation of past years to get a role in whatever low-budget theatre musicals she could. Without the role of a current Diva in the Chicago Symphony, her name just didn't command the respect and money it used to. For two years she gave voice lessons in Chicago to aspiring singers, appeared in several mid-tier musical shows in mid-western states, and put together some solo singing gigs doing pop or blues songs with local night club bands. Even working days, evenings and weekends, there were some months when her income did little more than cover her expenses. She was slowly draining her bank account cover anything above the essentials.

After two years of hard work and little financial success, Miss Sally gave up on Chicago and came home to Bluestone. At least, she could live rent free in her parent's home. With reduced expenses, she felt her income from a musical profession in Bluestone and surrounding towns would afford her a comfortable living. Upon his death a year later, Mr. Samuel Liestz left her an inheritance of the aging family mansion, a worn Packard automobile, and enough cash in the bank to cover a modest existence— for 4-5 years, at best.

Miss Sally had truly fallen to the depths feared by all those born to wealth and a life of ease. She was going to have to *work* for money—possibly working day after day at a job she didn't like. Restraint would have to replace indulgence in her life—maybe forever. As revolting at the thought was, Miss Sally knew it was a sacrifice she would have to make—until she came up with some*one* or some*thing* to put some *real* money in her pocket. The last few years of existing on 'paydays' had convinced her of the undeniable truth in Miss Essie's advice, "—honey—money is power—your plan better include getting your hands on some *real money*—".

While alive and wealthy, Mr.& Mrs. Samuel Liestz paid for most of the stained glass in the sanctuary of Antioch Baptist. They dropped more money in the collection plate on Sunday than any other ten members. So the church felt bound to hire Miss Sally when she applied for their open position for a Music-Choir Director. For a modest salary, she became the church's all-in-one pianist/organist/choir director/ soprano Diva—'*modest*' salary being the operative word. Still, it allowed Miss Sally to retain the title of 'Professional Musician' and pay her bills. Better that than working in Metcalf's mattress factory or standing behind a Teller's cage at the Flat Top National Bank for $35 a week.

A job that offered the latitude of a minor professional musician's title at a meager salary did little to wipe away her financial fragility, nor her seething frustration over no longer being a society lion in Bluestone. No doubt about it—Miss Sally was well and truly pissed. Put down by a martini swilling playboy-husband for some little slut;

booted from a major concert orchestra like an unwashed dog; her father's fortune ill-invested and lost by stock brokers who offered nothing but hypocritical apologies; and stuck with a church choir whose members included a stroke victim— and two others with voices so wretched they sounded worse than the stroke victim.

Well, none of this changed the fact that '*she* was Sally Liestz, Nightingale-of-The-South, she proudly reflected. A former star in major orchestras all over the country—heard in most European countries before she was'—oh let it go, she told herself. Dwelling on the past wouldn't bring it back. On the other hand, she vowed, she wasn't going to become another of the nameless rabble who were satisfied to exist from one paycheck to the next. She had had money, position, power—and she had *not* had it. From her viewpoint, life was a lot better when she *had* it—and she would find a way to get it again, she swore to herself.

'Don't let anybody or anything stand in the way of your plan—', so said Miss Essie. 'Okay, I know what I need to do—I'll jolly well do it—and woe-be-unto the person who gets in my way'.

To set about becoming one of '*THE*' people in town, Miss Sally (1)ingratiated herself with the 'right' people in town— the movers and shakers (2) used her connections to become an officer of The Ladies Lodge, (3) staked out the moral high-ground by becoming the self-appointed town sobriety/morals police, (4) dedicated herself to whipping that gaggle of misfits in the church choir into the premier choir in town, (5) launched a 'no holds barred' campaign to become the wife of my friend Norm Roberts' widowed dad, Frank.

She knew Frank Roberts wasn't all that much to look at—and he was a mite too fond of liquor for her taste. On the other hand, he was a kind and decent man. His house and car were paid for, he lived in the right part of town, was educated, and had a good income. Of critical importance, Ol' Frank had some *real* money in the bank. He was a member of the bank's Board of Directors. His children were grown and out of the house, he had social connections with the right people, and he could fit in comfortably at upper-crust social affairs. All things considered, tying the knot with Frank Roberts was the perfect answer to her *real* money needs.

Since Sally's return to Bluestone, Mrs. Grat McElRay had become a trusted mentor and confidant to her. Mrs. McElRay had been her Mother's close friend for years. It was Mrs. McElRay's support that got Miss Sally elected to an office in The Ladies Lodge. Her devotion to and admiration for Mrs. McElRay was exceeded only by her contempt for Mrs. McElRay's husband, Grat.

Ol' Grat was going to be her ticket to recognition as the town's primo 'Morals Police'. Grat, is years past, was the town's legendary 'ladies-man'. The men had called Grat 'the town's #1 'Swordsman'. If Miss Sally could 'take down' Grat—and get married to Frank—she was sure she would be 'back on top'. At least, in the town of Bluestone.

Swearing a few trusted Lodge Sisters to secrecy, Miss Sally shared Mrs. McElRay's revelation of ol' Grat's ravenous sexual appetite. Miss Sally said Mrs. McElRay confided—and her in her late 70s, mind you—that Grat still expected frequent and vigorous sexual intercourse with her. Even worse, his foreplay was limited to "Brace yourself, Colleen, I'm comin' in". Miss Sally claimed Grat's sexual pillaging of Mrs. McElRay's body left the poor woman mentally distracted and physically exhausted. Worse still, the frequency of Grat's sexual liberties with Mrs. McElRay seldom allowed the poor soul the welfare of more than 2 straight nights of uninterrupted sleep.

To supplement his frequent use and abuse of Mrs. McElRay's body, Miss Sally swore ol' Grat was having a flaming affair with John Arville's 50 year old widowed sister, Agnes. If this testimony wasn't sufficiently damning, an eye witness—Sally couldn't dare say who—told her Grat carried a 'rubber' in his wallet, at all times—in case a gratuitous and unexpected offer of sex popped up. All of this, claimed Miss Sally, could leave no doubt that Grat McElRay was a sexually depraved 'white slaver'.

Phenomenal claims, all—when you consider ol' Grat was 84 years old when Miss Sally claimed he was an insatiable sexual dynamo. Actually, Grat had a fatal heart attack in the summer of his 84th year—relieving Miss Sally of the burden of building a case that would support his indictment for spousal abuse, adultery, and fornication. She put out the word that Grat's heart attack was the end result of sexual excess— what with him being a sex fiend and all.

Most people didn't believe this, since he had his heart attack while driving down Logan Hill at mid-day—when he passed out and ran into that fire hydrant in front of the Episcopal Church. Ol' Grat was dead before the first person got to him in his car—setting atop that broken fire hydrant, while water slowly filled the interior of his car.

Regardless of the true cause of Grat's untimely demise, Miss Sally celebrated his transition to the ranks of the 'dear departed' with a 'good riddance' benediction, and praised the Almighty for delivering Mrs. McElRay from a life of sexual servitude.

Greasy Graham was drifting to the end of another day. Having spent the earlier part of Friday evening drinking a pint of Four Roses bourbon, he was leaning against a street-light pole on the sidewalk outside the Virginia Bar & Grill. My buddy, J. Hudson Hudnall, III, and I were sitting on the sidewalk near Greasy, licking ice cream cones—waiting for our grandmothers to come out of their monthly Lodge meeting.

We knew Greasy well and were comfortable with him. He lit a cigar and fell into small talk with us while we all watched the summer sun drop below the horizon. We could hear the drone of voices through the open window in the Lodge Hall above Harmon's Dry Goods store. One voice stood out above the others. It was more assertive and louder than any other voice in the Lodge Hall. Greasy slowly shook his head and rolled his eyes in resignation. He knew he was listening to the voice of the town's self-appointed 'morals minder/sobriety police', Miss Sally.

'God put Miss Sally on this earth to give folks a real live example of what the pain of hell was going to be like', so said Greasy. Bad-Eye Pierce (pronounced Piercey) seconded that notion—with enthusiasm. 'Miss Sally ain't really a 'thorn' in anyone's side—she's the whole damn thorn bush wrapped around you', claimed Bad-Eye.

For her part, Miss Sally swore Greasy and Bad-Eye's very existence in town was the Almighty's supreme test of her obedience to the commandment 'Thou Shalt Not Kill'. Their personalities, attitudes, habits, beliefs could not possibly have been more opposed to hers. She found them to be without redeeming values—period. Their cavalier attitude about life, work, and rules of social conduct was irritating. Their habit of drinking outrageous quantities of liquor made her want to scream. Their dismissive attitude toward her counsel on the evils of drink got both of them dumped into her verbal 'condemned to a fiery hell' category.

In her opinion, the drunken sots spent more time in the Virginia Bar & Grill than they did at work and home, combined. The failure of police Chief, Brit Bronson, to arrest those two for chronic, public drunkenness made him a disgrace to his office, so she told anyone who would listen. She campaigned tirelessly to have Greasy and Bad-Eye sentenced to a year in the Bland Prison Farm, 'to stop their drinking and teach them a good lesson'.

The Lodge meeting adjourned. The ladies drifted out of the Lodge Hall and walked home in the gathering dusk of the evening. Miss Sally stepped out of the Lodge Hall and saw Greasy leaning against the utility pole, talking to Hudson and I while we ate our ice cream. Hell flew through her a mile wide. Here was that ne'er-do-well town drunk, talking to impressionable boys—too young to know better than to talk to him. She marched across the sidewalk and glowered at Greasy.

"Greasy! Are you drunk again?" demanded Miss Sally. Although it was unlikely, she hoped for an immediate confession of guilt from Greasy. It would make it so much easier to demand that Brit arrest him on the spot.

"Naw. I ain't drunk. Not that it's any of your business. Wish I was tho'—might make it a lil' easier to lis'n to an ol' busy-body like you", Greasy drawled while exhaling cigar smoke in her face.

Miss Sally let the slight pass, waved the cigar smoke aside, and pressed on with her questioning.

"If you aren't drunk, then why are you leaning against that light pole? You look to me like you're about ready to fall flat on your face!"

"Why, Miss Sally—I'm holding this pole up! The power company is paying me to hold up this here light pole. You're a woman of some education. I woulda' thought you coulda' seen what I'm doing."

Greasy's flippant reply pushed her beyond control. The thought of a reprobate like Greasy showing disrespect to a Liestz was just too much. Her face twisted in rage, she drew back her big, black purse and swung it at Greasy's head with every ounce of strength she possessed. Greasy anticipated her action. He quickly slid off the pole and dodged her purse as it arced through the air. The force of her swing left Miss Sally unable to stop the flight of her purse when it missed Greasy's head. Momentum and gravity carried the purse downward until it struck the arm of my buddy, J. Hudson. The blow knocked his ice cream cone out of his hand and into the gutter.

Miss Sally grabbed a nearby parking meter to regain her balance. Hudson let out a wail. More for the loss of his ice cream cone than pain from the purse bouncing off his arm. Ol' J. Hudson happened to be the favorite grandson of the wealthiest man in town, Mr. J. Hudson Hudnall, Sr. His charity always included the donation of a sizable wad of money to Miss Sally for her work in organizing and directing the big Choral Group in the town's annual Christmas concert staged at City Hall auditorium.

"Uhh-oh, Miss Sally! Now look what you've gone an' done. Law'd have mercy! Ol' man Hudnall will cut off your Chris'mas concert money for sure! I mean—gawd a'mighty, woman—you done gone and hit his prize gran' child! Me bein' a witness to it, I'll be bound to tell him that it was you what went and done it. I prob'ly oughta' stop by his place tonight—set him straight on what done happened here. You might wanna' head on home, start thinking 'bout some other way to replace all that money he's been a'givin' you. Ol' Pappy Hudnall ain't gonna' be happy with you a'tall."

"You shut your filthy mouth, you illiterate trash! The Devil's got you by the tail on a downhill pull, and I hope you burn in—", bawled Miss Sally at Greasy until Hudson's wail grew too loud to ignore. "Oh—here honey, don't you cry. I'm so sorry about that. I didn't mean to hit you—you know that. I love all you children and—you aren't hurt are you?"

"You're the cause of this whole thing—you good-for-nothing, drunken, sot---" hissed Miss Sally at Greasy as she dug frantically in her purse for coins. "Here, sweetheart, you just take this money and go buy yourself another ice cream cone. And here, here's a nickel for your little friend too", she cooed as she handed nickels to Hudson and me.

J.Hudson and I hurried off the drug store for more ice cream. Miss Sally turned back to unleash another dose of 'Ol' Billie Hell' on Greasy—only to see him ambling slowly down the street, a half block away. Her jaw locked, she seethed in frustration as Greasy reached the corner, turned, smiled, and waved to her.

She clenched her fingers into a white knuckled fist to keep from answering Greasy's wave with her extended middle finger. It was beyond her why the rules of good conduct forbade a woman of breeding to publicly scream curses at a low-life like Greasy Graham. The same went for Bad-Eye

Pierce— a lazy, ignorant, deadbeat, wino who hadn't had bath in a week or a job in years. 'Damn Walter Davison', she muttered under her breath, 'for his part in putting her back here with the likes of Greasy and Bad-Eye'.

In a way, Greasy and Bad-Eye turned out to be minor problems for Miss Sally. Things got worse for her. Less than two months before she and Mr. Frank Roberts were to be married, he had a heart attack, collapsed, and died on his front porch one summer Saturday morning.

From her kitchen window, Mrs. Grat McElRay saw the crowd gathering around Mr. Roberts' porch. When Brit Bronson's police cruiser showed up she knew he wasn't there for a social call. She telephoned Miss Sally right away. Miss Sally was on the scene in less than five minutes—just as I walked up to Frank Robert's front yard with my grandparents. She was inconsolable.

"This can't be happening", she screamed—"not to me!" The Gods of Fate had had dragged her through misery for three and a half years—and now this. Marriage to Frank Roberts was the linch-pin of her plans for a return to a happy, secure, and comfortable life. With no marriage license in hand, she was pretty certain she wouldn't get a dime of Frank's estate. His kids had never liked her. They made no bones about it either.

Worse still, she had no back-up candidate for marriage. It was a relatively small town. Bad-Eye Pierce's choice of words might have been harsh, but his opinion of Miss

Sally's prospects for marriage was pretty much on point when he said, "It ain't like that woman's got a buncha' men lined up to tie the knot with her. It's gotta' be Frank Roberts—or nobody."

Rage temporarily displaced her grief. Miss Sally laid into Mr. Patterson, Mr. Roberts' next door neighbor. The Roberts and Pattersons were both long-time neighbors of my grandparents. It was to my grandparents, and several other neighbors, that Miss Sally vented her feelings about Patterson.

"If Patterson—the mean, stingy, old hermit—had been any kind of neighbor to Frank a'tall, he would have seen him fall. He could have gone to help him—get him some medical aid—saved his life", she wailed to my grandmother. Miss Sally saw her plans for a better life sliding right out from under her as Wagner's hearse hauled Mr. Roberts' body away. With no marriage license to use as a lever, she knew Mr. Roberts' kids would leave her high and dry—just like that lout Walter Davison and his thieving lawyers did.

Well—she had learned her lesson with Walter. And the 'who-gets-what' game would be played out in Bluestone this time—in her back yard, she told herself. The Liestz name meant something in this town. Frank's snot-nosed kids weren't going to throw her in the ditch, she promised herself.

Miss Sally called on the venerable J. Crockett Howard, Sr. Esq. He would see that her interests in Frank Roberts' estate were protected—so she told her close 'buds'. Actually, J. Crockett and Claude Smyth were the only lawyers in town who did much work in *WILLS*. Both had reputations as honest men, but their legal specialties were pretty much limited to real estate, municipal matters, wills, and small criminal misdemeanors. Neither had the quick mind or oratorical skills of a top trial lawyer. Matter of fact, they went out of their way to avoid appearing on a trial floor. Just the rigors of a day spent searching through land titles and municipal codes compelled them to seek relief at the end of the day with a nip or two of bourbon, so I once heard my Uncle say. Nothing excessive, he said, just a little something to 'smooth off the edges' of their professional burdens.

Miss Sally laid out her problem of potential exclusion from the late Frank Roberts' estate. Ol' J. Crockett listened to her, sympathized with her, agreed life had, of late, dealt harshly with her—*but*—.Then, the <u>real</u> truth that usually follows the word '*but*' in <u>any</u> conversation came out of his mouth. "Absent possession of written documents attesting to Mr. Roberts' intent to share his estate with you," said J. Crockett, "you have no <u>legally</u> enforceable claim to any part of his estate. By law, the entire estate would pass to his children—especially if his legal will so states."

Miss Sally felt the blood draining from her face. The air in her lungs left so quickly she couldn't speak. J. Crockett's legal opinion of her chances of getting even one dime of Frank's estate left her floating between paralysis and passing out. As she fought to regain her self-control, she decided to reveal her 'ace in the hole'. She had hoped, in the interest of good taste, not to have to use it.

After some squirming in her chair, she asked J. Crockett for his solemn promise he would never divulge the basis, which she was about to reveal, for her claim to a share of Frank Roberts' estate. After his solemn promise to never breach her confidence, she leaned forward and whispered to J. Crockett.

"Frank and I had 'relations'—'*intimate* relations'—once every week or so—over the past year. I only agreed to this because Frank *personally* told me he loved me, *already* considered me his *wife*—and *everything* he had belonged to *me* too. So—the formality of our coming marriage ceremony—just weeks away, really—would have been nothing more than a confirmation of what he and I *already* considered our relationship to be."

J. Crockett slowly shook his head. He quoted case law as he explained that *unwitnessed* verbal promises and alleged pre-marital sex carried no legal weight as proof of legal marriage—intent to marry—nor intent to legally convey property between two people. No court would seriously consider her claim on those grounds, he told her.

Miss Sally thrust her left hand, with her engagement ring on it, in J. Crockett's face and said, "Don't tell me an engagement ring from a man means *nothing!* Why would Frank give me this ring if he had no intentions of making me his wife?"

J. Crockett looked at the ring, nodded slowly, and replied, "Yes—but, don't you see, that ring only speaks of his *intent* to marry you—at some point in the future. It does not make you his wife—which is what you need to be if you wish to legally claim ownership of his estate."

Miss Sally swallowed her anger and humiliation and tried one last time. She asked about bringing a civil suit against Mr. Patterson for his failure to 'do the right thing'—look out for his neighbor—letting Frank die right on his own porch—less than a hundred feet from 'that evil old man's' own front door. Everybody, she whispered to J. Crockett, knew the old miser had a lot of money. Surely his failure to get timely help for Frank was worth some monetary court award against Patton—to cushion her loss of Frank and his property. Again, J. Crockett explained the rules of legal evidence to her. There was no law to support a legal action against Mr. Patterson for some 'social' failure she 'believed' he was guilty of.

Miss Sally was devastated. She had no 'fall back' plan. Frank Roberts had been her only real chance at a life she wanted—no, a life she *needed*. And this 'joke' of a lawyer sitting in front of her was letting her needs evaporate like smoke in the wind.

She glared at J. Crockett—a glare that said, 'Did you pick up your law license along with a hammer and pair of pliers downs at *Sears*. She wasn't buying J. Crockett's opinion. She had been screwed by her ex-husbands' lawyers' misapplication of *'the law'*. It wasn't going to happen again. There had to be something—somewhere in all of those law books—that protected *HER* rights. She had given up her 'virtue', on a regular basis, mind you—to a man who had the bad the bad taste to up and die before he went through the formal marriage vows that guaranteed his promises for the pre-marital 'favors' she performed in his bed! No way— what's right is right! What th' hell is the law for if not to make things right, she fumed. She was mad as hell, and she wasn't going to take it anymore! She left J Crockett's office, loudly questioning his possession of a set of gonads, telling him he was a disgrace to his profession—and slamming the door to his office so hard the glass rattled.

She marched down the street, into Attorney Claude Smyth's office and got a second opinion from him. He told her the much same thing J. Crockett did. 'What a bunch of malarkey', she told herself as she walked away from Mr. Claude's office. 'Bunch of incompetent hacks', she brooded. She was sure there was collusion between the two of them. 'Telling me going to bed with Frank to seal promises he made didn't carry any weight! Everybody knows that's a breach of promise', she told herself through gritted teeth. 'Why did they think I went to bed with him—because I enjoyed it? Not on your life', she mumbled. 'They didn't know the law, didn't want to take a case against Frank's kids—or were afraid of that little weasel, Angus Patterson'.

At that week's Lodge meeting, Miss Sally shared her view of lawyers in Bluestone. In her opinion, she said, the ladies should look elsewhere—anywhere else—before extending their trust for legal advice to Attorneys Howard or Smyth. They both, she opined, were incompetent, spineless drunks. Although she omitted the details of her intimate life with Frank, her tearful account of being cut out of Frank Roberts' will touched the hearts of her Lodge sisters.

A few of the Lodge sisters assumed Miss Sally was sharing Frank's bed before he died. Considering Frank and Miss Sally had been 'seeing' each other for a year before his untimely death, it wasn't an unreasonable assumption that their 'seeing' included the privacy of Frank's bedroom. Being realists, they felt it naïve to believe two adults passed through a lengthy engagement period without 'sampling the fruits'. While not openly condoning the sin of fornication, the wedding ceremony, in the mind of the Lodge sisters, was just a formality that legalized a relationship already consummated in a bedroom. They felt Miss Sally had already suffered entirely too much in her relationship with men, thanks to that Yankee Walter Davison, II. Legalities be damned, they agreed, she was jolly well entitled to *something* for letting Frank 'have his way' with her.

Even with the sisters closing ranks around Miss Sally, all that meeting boiled down to was just a bunch of talk. *Morally*, Miss Sally had a point. *Legally*, J. Crockett and Clarence Smith were right. *Legally* and *morally*, as Miss Sally learned for the second time in her relationship with a man, were not the same things. She got nothing from Frank Roberts' estate. His kids didn't give her as much as a photograph of their dad.

Adding it all up, the collision of events in Miss Sally's life carried her into her sunset years as a disappointed woman. Looking at things from her viewpoint, some of us figured had *we* been stuck under that black cloud that seemed to hang over her—we too would have felt that cloud had an unending dose of Castor Oil pumped into it.

She spent the remainder of her life working as Musical Director of our church—and giving voice and music lessons to boys and girls around town. Actually, some of her former voice/music students became quite wealthy and successful in adult life. Some were professional singers/musicians—some became doctors, dentists, and lawyers. To their credit, their generous financial gifts to Miss Sally, over her later years, made their gratitude for what she had done for them very clear. These gifts also made her declining years quite comfortable and financially secure.

Despite the fact that my grandfather took me down to the church boiler room one Sunday and spanked my back side good for chuckling out loud at her pronunciation of the word 'happy' as 'hoppy' (her opera training coming through) as she offered up a soaring rendition of the old Baptist hymn, *I Sing Because I'm Happy*, I eventually came to understand and appreciate the gifts Miss Sally brought to the town of Bluestone.

Even when Miss Sally was 65 years old, her voice was still so powerful and clear she could literally vibrate the windows of the church sanctuary. She lived alone, stayed busy, and sang through the years until she died of a heart attack in her late 80s.

The line of cars to her graveside service stretched for over a half mile down Tazewell Avenue. She was buried in the family plot at Maple Hills Cemetery— close to many friends, Mr.& Mrs. Grat McElRay, Greasy Graham, Bad-Eye Piercy, etc.

Ironic— some of them adversaries in life, neighbors in their final place of rest. Maybe their close resting places in Maple Hills is a reminder of the Biblical promises that that our life in eternity won't be encumbered by the things that make it a challenge to be at peace with each other in this life. I hope so. In their own way, they were all good people.

THE ROOMING HOUSE

Noni Potter was a sharp business woman. She was also a visionary. She saw a large, two-story white frame house with a 60 foot deep front yard, nestled between a theatre and an apartment building. She didn't see it as an old house by-passed by progress. No—she saw it as the doorway to a money-making investment.

Noni bought the two-story house, used the front yard to build a furniture store, and connected the rear of the new store to the front of the old house. By cutting a couple of doorways, she created easy access between the new store and two story house.

Noni's store was called *NONI'S CLASSIC FURNITURE*. She sold high-dollar solid wood furniture, reproductions of Colonial American and Federalist period pieces—made only by manufacturers with respected names in hand crafted furniture. With her store located in a six block commercial area, called Arlandria, on the Alexandria City/Arlington County border, she had a market of hundreds of thousands of people who earned incomes in the mid to high six figures.

Never one to ignore an opportunity, Noni converted the former old two story home, now connected to the rear of her store, into a rooming house. She had 4 bedrooms, a bath, and a TV room upstairs. Down stairs, she converted all rooms into 4 bedrooms and a bath. The house had a separate entrance on the ground-floor rear of the house for tenants.

I was one of the tenants who rented a bedroom from Noni. LeRay, Joe Bill, and I had bedrooms upstairs. Noni reserved the 4th, and best, upstairs bedroom for her personal use—when the need arose.

Weegee, Swede, and a couple of other guys had the bedrooms on the first floor. At $15 per tenant per week, all utilities and a TV room included, it wasn't a bad deal in 1960. Especially if you didn't like cooking your own meals. There were restaurants nearby with good food and cheap prices, a couple of good bars, and a short walk or ride to our work places. There were also drug stores, two grocery stores, dry cleaners, a clothing store, and a theatre with first run movies within 1-4 blocks of Noni's rooming house. There was free parking in the rear of the old house. An alley-way separated Noni's store/rooming house from the movie theatre next door.

Noni was also a woman of large sexual appetites. She was 35 years old, had a stunning face surrounded by a wall of thick auburn hair, a voluptuous figure, and an insatiable libido. Her tastes ran to married men. She once told Joe Bill and I that married men were the logical choice for her because, one—they were more experienced in matters sexual; two—they would keep their mouths shut about private matters; three—their marriage and professional positions would keep them from creating problems when she wanted to end their affair.

You see, Noni's affairs with men rarely last more than 2 months. No—there were no fights—no big disagreements with her paramours. She just grew tired of them—wanted the excitement of a new lover.

Her attitude seemed a bit cold, but, you had to consider that Noni wasn't looking for romance and a happily-ever-after story.Noni already had a husband. He owned and operated a very successful commercial sign designing and erection company. His work kept him on the road and out of town 50% of most weeks. This suited Noni's life style to a 'T'. In her own way, she loved the guy and had no intention of divorcing him. She never uttered an unkind word about him. Simply put, she just felt an overwhelming need to satisfy her need for variety in men.

When it suited, Noni would use the bedroom across the hall from mine to bed down her lovers. Things went on this way for the better part of 8-9 months without incident. Then Noni found a new love interest in the Sales Manager for a local Lincoln-Mercury dealership. Tony Scarboni was a tall, good looking, charismatic, guy. He fairly exuded confidence. He had that rare ability to make any woman feel she had his undivided attention—that his only mission in life was to make her happy.

Tony and Noni were about a month into their relationship. Noni was wild for Tony. Tony kept one or two suits of clothes in the closet of Noni's bedroom in the rooming house. They were spending the entire night in the bedroom often enough for Tony to keep a change of clothing there.

Did I mention that Tony was married—to woman who strongly suspected he was 'running around' on her? A woman who had no intention of giving up Tony as her husband? A woman with a notoriously short temper and lack of impulse control? A woman who was doing her own detective work to 'get the goods' on whomever Tony was 'seeing'? A woman who carried a .38 snub-nosed pistol in her purse? A woman with no reservations about taking the law into her own hands—appointing herself as judge, jury, and executioner? No?? Well, be advised—Mrs. Scarboni was *all* of the above, and more.

Tony dropped off one of his $500 tailor-made suits and two $75 dress shirts at the Empire Dry Cleaners, across the street from Noni's store as he left for work one Friday morning. Around 5:30 that afternoon, as Joe Bill, Ray, Nate, and I were getting ready for a weekend night out in Washington, D.C., Tony called Noni and asked her to pick up his dry cleaning. We had drifted to the sidewalk in front of Noni's store when she breezed out the front door with a big smile on her face.

"Hi, guys. Gotta' pick up Tony's dry cleaning. We're going dancing this evening", she said as she darted across Mt. Vernon Ave between oncoming cars.

In less than a minute, Noni came bouncing back out of the dry cleaners carrying Tony's suit and shirts on hangers. She stepped out into Mt. Vernon Ave—hadn't quite cleared one lane of traffic when a black sports car raced up Mt. Vernon Ave toward her at high speed. We were sure it would hit Noni. With a terrified look on her face, Noni froze in the middle of the street with her hand held out in a protective gesture in front of her.

At the last second the brakes on the black car were locked up and all four tires laid down rubber with loud squeals. A bare two feet from Noni, the car came to a stop. The car door flew open, and Mrs. Tony Scarboni jumped from the car. Shouting curses and accusations about Noni being a slut and home-breaker, Mrs. Scarboni charged straight at Noni. Noni was standing stock still in surprise and shock when Mrs. Scarboni got within arm's reach of her.

"Are those are my husband's clothes you're carrying, you slut? Going to use those clothes for a good time out tonight with my husband? Huh? Here—I'll show you what you can give him to wear—you whore!"

Mrs. Scarboni jerked the dry cleaned suit and laundered shirts out of Noni's hand. She tore them from the plastic covers and began, literally, to rip the shirts to pieces and throw them to the pavement. Then she took the $500 suit, threw it to the pavement, stomped it, and tried to rip the sleeves off the jacket while she stood on it. While she tore Tony's clothes to tatters, she screamed endless profanities at Noni.

Joe Bill, Nate, and I began to quietly walk backwards from the sidewalk into Noni's store. We wanted no part of this disagreement. We were satisfied to watch things unfold through one of the big display windows in her show room.

Suddenly, Noni blinked her eyes and snapped out of the trance which had paralyzed her throughout Mrs. Scarboni's tirade and destruction of ol' Tony's expensive clothing. Without a word, Noni aggressively walked up behind Mrs. Scarboni, who was totally absorbed in turning Tony's clothes into a pile of rags. Mrs. Scarboni didn't see Noni cock her fist and swing a knockout punch that caught her squarely in the temple of her head. Mrs. Scarboni 's body twisted from the force of Noni's punch—and then she fell, face down, on the hood of her own car.

For a few seconds, Noni stood over Mrs. Scarboni as she lay prone on her car hood—not moving a muscle. It appeared she had been knocked senseless—unconscious—or worse.

With tears of anger in her eyes, Noni picked up the ragged remains of Tony's suit and shirts from the street—cursing the motionless Mrs. Scarboni the entire time. Noni appeared to be carrying a bundle of rags as she strode angrily toward her store.

We didn't want to feel the heat of Noni's anger or get involved—so we did what any devout cowards would do. We turned tail and fled up the back steps of the store and into our bedrooms in the upstairs of the old house.

Joe Bill, Nate, LeRay, and I huddled behind my locked bedroom door with our ears to the door. We had hoped

Noni would take refuge downstairs, in her office at the rear of the store. No such luck. We heard her stomp up the stairs, trod heavily down the hallway, go in her reserved bedroom across from mine, and slam the door. She was still mumbling curses in her bedroom when we heard a pistol shot from down stairs in the store.

It was Mrs. Scarboni. She had regained consciousness and come in search of Noni—to finish their fight. She announced her presence in the store with that pistol shot we heard. Amid hysterical screams and pleas for her life from Mrs. Perkins, Noni's office manager, we heard Mrs. Scarboni demand that Mrs. Perkins tell her where Noni was hiding.

"Where is that bitch? I know you know—and I want to know where she is, right now!"

Not one to play the role of the sacrificial heroine—not with a gun pointed at her face— Mrs. Perkins gave up Noni without a second's hesitation.

"She upstairs somewhere—oh god—I'm not involved in this—I'm a single mother—I just work here".

Seeing Mrs. Scarboni cock her gun and disappear up the stairs at the rear of the store, Mrs. Perkins fled through the front door of the store and down the sidewalk—screaming for help and wailing for someone to call the police.

Noni, always a thinking woman, had heard the gun shot and

shouts from down stairs. She knew Mrs. Scraboni would check every bedroom upstairs until she found her. The bedroom door locks weren't that secure. Noni quickly left her bedroom and barricaded herself in the upstairs bathroom. It had an additional bolt lock on it. More importantly, the tub in the bathroom was made of thick, cast iron. Noni laid down in the tub, counting on it to deflect stray bullets from Mrs. Scarboni's pistol if she tried to shoot the bolt lock off the bathroom door.

Noni wasn't the only one thinking ahead. To a man, the sound of that pistol shot served as all the encouragement we needed to stop talking about doing it and physically bail out of my bedroom window. We began desperately pushing and shoving on the window to get it open. The bathroom Noni was hiding in was right next to my bedroom. That made it even more imperative that we get out of my bedroom—immediately. After several seconds of grunting and shoving, the big double-hung window slid open.

It was a 10 foot drop from the window to the pavement in the alley. To avoid breaking bones in our efforts to save our lives, our plan for going out the window was to go out legs first, hang to the window sash by our fingers—and drop through the air for the remaining 5 feet to the ground in the alleyway between the house and the theatre next door. One after another, we quickly dropped from my bedroom window to the alley—without injuries.

We didn't have to wait long for action in the upstairs of the house. As our feet were landing in the alley, we heard Mrs. Scarboni come stomping down the hall—screaming for Noni to come out of hiding. Mrs. Scarboni's promise to 'stick my gun up your ass and blow your brains out' wasn't much of an incentive for Noni to reveal herself. For those of us standing in that alley, hearing Mrs. Scarboni scream death-threats to Noni was one hell of an impetus to stop standing there and run from that alley as fast as our legs would carry us.

As we were running down the alley, we heard Mrs. Scarboni's gun go off several times. Finding Noni's bedroom empty and the bathroom door locked, she rightly assumed Noni's had locked herself in the bathroom. As she was trying to blow the bathroom door off its hinges with bullets, Mrs. Scarboni heard the sound of police sirens getting close to Noni's store.

From the safety of the Fireside Grill across the street we watched Mrs. Scarboni race from Noni's store, dive into her car, and lay down rubber on the street as she peeled away from the scene as fast as her car would take her.

Mrs. Scarboni's car was almost out of sight when Noni came running out of her store. Siren wailing, Officer Joe Logwood came to a tire-screeching halt in front of Noni's store. Noni was already in the middle of Mt. Vernon Ave—screaming, jumping up and down, and pointing at Mrs. Scarboni's fast disappearing car.

The scene that followed was chaotic. Officer Logwood was

trying to get some basic information about what-who-when-why. Noni was screaming at him to go after Mrs. Scarboni before she got away—screaming about attempted murder. Other police cars converged on the scene with more sirens blaring. Some of the police jumped from their cars with guns drawn—their heads swiveling—trying desperately to locate an assailant at whom they could point their guns.

Not wishing to be any more involved in the fiasco than we already were, we discreetly hustled a block down the street to a booth in the rear of Bertolli's and ordered a pitcher of beer. We decided to let things cool off while we drank cheap beer and gave thanks that none of our bodies had stopped one of Mrs. Scarboni's stray bullets.

Later that evening, after Noni and the police were gone, we wandered back to our rooming house. I walked into the bathroom and sat down on the john. It was then that I realized I was watching traffic outside—moving along Mt. Vernon Ave. One of Mrs. Scarboni's bullets had not only passed through the bathroom door—it had traversed the length of the bathroom—and passed completely through the exterior wall of the bathroom. It left a hole big enough for me to poke two fingers through.

During the remainder of the summer, the hole was a matter of humor for those of us that used that bathroom. Actually, people visited us just to see the only bathroom in town that provided a view of traffic on Mt. Vernon Ave while 'taking their ease' on our 'john'. When winter came, we used toilet paper to plug the hole—in the interest of staying warm while we showered and shaved.

To our surprise, the local papers carried no stories about the 'shoot out'. Noni curtly dismissed any questions we asked about what happened to Mrs. Scarboni. She said the whole thing was just a misunderstanding—and she didn't want to talk about it—ever again. Obviously, it was one of those situations that could call attention to too many people caught in embarrassing positions. Everyone involved wanted the whole thing to 'go away'.

And, except when we were watching Mt. Vernon Ave traffic from the john in our bathroom—the whole thing did just 'go away'.

LOOKING WEST TOWARD WALLACE HOME PLACE and BENNY ALLEN'S HOME—40 years after childhood.

VENCIL STREET

Calling all the Bluestone residents of Vencil Street 'close' neighbors may be a bit generous. Granted, they lived side-by-side in relative harmony. With two notable exceptions, the modest homes on the street signaled working class people. The inhabitants were 95% Caucasian. Most of them were first generation descendants of immigrants. A few were immigrants, here maybe 10-15 years—from Scotland,

Ireland, Wales, England, France, and Germany. The year was 1943. From east to west, the street was a little less than 1/2 mile long.

Vencil Street was an oddity. The street was located on the north side of town. It was within the town limits. The street was paved and there were street lights.

On the other hand, 150'-200' past the back yards of the homes on either side of Vencil St. the land was open or wooded. Some was used for gardening, pasturing livestock, fruit trees and vines. A small portion of it was just wooded area, choked with underbrush. The street ended on its eastern end 200 yards past the home of my grandfather.

My grandfather immigrated to this country with his parents from Glasgow, Scotland. For 46 years, 1909--1955, he built those old steam locomotives the N & W Railway used for many years to pull coal and freight across their tracks. Despite a formal education that ended in the fifth grade, my grandfather's native intelligence and natural inclination for math gave him the skills to build anything made of metal or wood. And he could grow any kind of fruit or vegetable known to mankind.

The Wallaces, Grahams, Yosts, Hankins, Allens, Lawlesses, Pierces, Colemans, Fowlers, Bargers, and Matthews were all white, working class people. They were railroad workers, bookkeepers, merchants, carpenters, and auto mechanics. The large majority were hard workers, honest, and Portestant. Most of the residents of the street had children or grandchildren living in their homes during the 1930s-40s. Some had both at the same time. Out of common interests and needs, these people got along with each other and could be counted on for friendship and support when it was needed.

Then—we had the Riesters and DuValls. They were more residents than 'neighbors' of Vencil St. A few folks living on Vencil insisted the use of cuss words was the only way to adequately express the intensity of their feelings about those two families.

Before the turn of 19th Century, most of the land on the north side of Vencil St. was owned by Abner Riester and his wife, Mame. The majority of the land on the south side of the street was owned by Josiah DuVall and his wife, Maude. Abner and Josiah were both wealthy. As a rule, these families spoke only to each other, family members by marriage, others in town of with 'proper' family names/breeding, and God. Lesser mortals were tolerated. Conversation with the 'masses' was usually limited to minimal salutations like 'good morning' or 'good evening', and then only because the rules of business or civility required it.

By the time Abner and Josiah died in the late 1920s, circumstances, the Great Depression, and bad investments had wiped out most of their wealth. Their surviving family heirs, had to sell off most of their land along Vencil St.—to keep the family home, 3 ½ acres of land surrounding it, and have some money to live on. The land they sold was eventually divided into residential lots—the working class families bought these lots—built modest homes—moved in and raised families beside each other. At the time of their deaths, all of Josiah's and one of Abner's children were well educated. They had had jobs, businesses, or marriages that took them to others towns and states. Abner and Josiah's deaths left behind two disappointed, frustrated, and embittered widows—who struggled to live modestly comfortable in their sunset years.

The people who purchased the lots the Reister and DuVall families sold off along Vencil looked at Mame and Maudie as people much like themselves—trying to maintain homes, feed themselves and their families, and put a few dollars in their savings accounts each month. For the most part, they felt Mame & Maudie had no more—or less—day to day challenges than they did. Most of the Vencil residents accepted the abrasive attitude Mame & Maudie exhibited over having lives of financial ease deteriorate into a lives of frugality in their later years. Most of the residents—except Grandpa Lawless, Bad-Eye Pierce, and next-door neighbors—cut them 'some slack' and left them alone.

Maudie's children were financially secure enough to send her enough money each month to help meet expenses and keep her modestly comfortable. Still—Maudie's bitterness over having 'working class' people treat her as an 'equal' did not set well with her. With little to do and no close friends living nearby, Maudie spent most of her days looking for offensive actions—real or imagined—by Vencil St. residents. Weather permitting, she constantly prowled the grounds surrounding her old mansion—looking for trespassers, thieves—anyone uninvited. At one time or another, she had threatened many of her nearby residents with legal action by her Attorney, the formidable K. Wayland Newland, Esq.

If 'Way-Lay', as K. Wayland was called behind his back, told Maudie she had no legal grounds for some imagined 'wrong' by a neighbor, she would seek justice through 'other means'. 'Other means' meant spraying a load of buckshot in the direction of offenders, from her ever-present .410 gauge shot gun she cradled under her arm as she wandered around her meager acreage.

She would shoot a load of buckshot from that old gun about once every 2-3 weeks— <u>mostly,</u> straight up in the air. Sometimes, her shotgun was discharged at an angle above the heads of people—mostly people using the alley beside her property—who swore they heard the buckshot cutting through tree leaves 8-10 feet over their heads. In general, Grandpa George Lawless <u>not</u> included, the Vencil St. residents didn't believe Maudie meant them physical <u>harm</u>. She was just a bitter old woman who vented her bitterness and frustration by trying to scare people—to let them know her 'will' still 'ruled the day' on Vencil St.

Mame Riester's children were John, Elizabeth, and Penelope. Penelope was educated, well thought of in the community, and a real beauty. She married a lawyer in Carolina, seldom came home, and rarely communicated with Mame or her siblings. John and Elizabeth graduated from high school, never married, and remained in the family home on Vencil St. until their death.

Mame, John, and Elizabeth were said to be 'eccentric', by the more charitable neighbors on Vencil. A few neighbors, less inclined to charity, labeled all three as 'crazier n' hell'. That label was a figurative one. Had to be. While Mame, John, and Liz did some things that pushed the limits of eccentricity, John and Liz both held jobs. Liz sold tickets at the local movie theatre. John worked at J.C. Penny's department store in the shoe department. Despite being, 'odd', John could think 'tactically'.

If someone came into the store's shoe department, no matter how crowded the customer traffic in the shoe department was at that moment, John was determined they would not leave the shoe department before he had a chance to sell them some shoes. He had a habit that is still talked about to this day. If you came into the shoe department and John was busy helping another customer, he would pause for a few seconds in his sales pitch to the customer he was waiting on—walk over to you—look down at your shoes, and say.

"Let's see one of those shoes you have on—what size is it—let me have a look at it."

You would surrender one of your shoes to John. He would tuck it under his arm, and walk back to the customer he had been serving when he walked over to you and took one of your shoes.. Fifteen minutes later you would find you were still sitting there in a chair, with only one shoe on—unable to get up and walk away. Glance around the shoe department, and you'd see 5-6 other people sitting in chairs—all of them wearing only one shoe. A peek at John would show him still waiting on the original customer—with 5-6 odd shoes under his arms. You and the other 5-6 souls were stuck in your chairs until John could get around to you. He was not moved by your pleas of 'I have to leave', or, 'I'll come back tomorrow'.

"I'm going to be right with you. I've got a shoe on the shelf that's just made for *you*. Just sit back, relax, and I'll be right with you", John would say, as he hustled off to tell another 'captive customer' the very same thing.

Eccentric—probably. Maybe even a little paranoid on some days. But, I don't think there is any way you could say anybody crafty enough tie up 5-6 potential shoe customers for 30 minutes was flat out crazy—as some people claimed John was. Not in his younger years, at least.
When John and Liz were in their early 60s—their mental grasp of reality was almost assuredly diminished. One incident, in particular, highlighted the frailty of their mental state in their later years.

Mame had passed away—in her 87th year. Neighbors ignored years of unstable behavior by Mame and did the right thing by trying to ease the family's burden during her wake. There must have been 35-40 people on the street who fixed some food and took it to Mame's home so John and Liz would have food for any out-of-town family or friends who might attend Mame's wake or funeral.

All morning and into the afternoon people came to the front door of the Riester home with prepared food. John or Liz answered each knock on the front door. People, who had <u>never seen</u> the inside of Mame's house, knocked on her door— offeing a dish or pan of food. They weren't going to <u>see</u> the interior of Mame's house on this occasion either—forget be <u>invited</u> in.

John or Liz would, step out on their front porch, take the food from them, hear their condolences, thank them, and close the door in their faces. In their sunset years, John and Liz were obviously sinking into the mental sickness of paranoia. People bringing food to their door—when they didn't recognize them as friends—or weren't sure they knew them at all---?? As far as John and Liz were concerned, there was something wrong with this picture— it made no sense. People parading to their door with free food? There had to be a motive—and it couldn't be good. Liz verbalized her thoughts on the matter first.

"My God—if one more person comes to that door with food in their hands—I think I'm going to scream!" said Liz.

"Don't touch it! They're trying to kill us! Throw it out! Throw it <u>all</u> out—in the back yard!" bellowed John.

Liz and John went to the kitchen. John opened the back door. Liz began handing dishes, pan, and pots of food to him. As she handed the food to him he threw it into their back yard—dishes and pans included. By nightfall, there were bread, vegetables, meat, desserts and assorted dishes or pans scattered over most of their back yard. John and Liz were both certain they had avoided poisoning by people who bore them ill tidings.

In the last months her life, Liz was placed in a state mental hospital. While delusional and paranoid in his last year of life, John managed to live alone in the family home until his death at the age of 70.

Some long-time acquaintances swore lunacy ran in the family of Mame Riester. They said, 'Abner losing his money didn't have squat to do with Mame goin' crazy. She was that way when he married her'. Ol' man, George Lawless, voiced his usual blunt opinion when he said, "Mame ain't never been right in the head from day-one, and she done handed it down to ol' John and Liz. Like as not, all three of them will wind up in the state 'nut-house' over at Marion".

Mame's home and land were bounded on the east side by the home and property of Bad-Eye Pierce and his mother. Their last name was pronounced Peer-See. Bad-Eye claimed French ancestry—said the French always put the emphasis on the last syllable of a name. My cousin, Beulah, who was a school teacher, said Bad-Eye was just repeating something someone told him—that he was too illiterate to know what a 'syllable' was. My grandmother once told my grandfather, "If Bad-Eye is descended from anyone, it has to be some lazy, ne'er-do-well, drunk from Ireland."

The Pierce home was little more than a wooden shack wrapped in tarpaper manufactured to look like red brick siding. The *'Big Bad Wolf'*, of the *'Three Little Pigs'* nursery story, could have blown down the rickety Pierce house. Setting on three acres of land, it looked like a hovel right out of an Erskine Caldwell novel.

Pierce's house the last one on the east end of Vencil Street. The entry to it was a 90 ft narrow, rutty, dirt road—that barely held back nature's efforts to reclaim it with overhanging trees, thick brush, and wild vines. The Pierce home included an outdoor toilet, a wood shed, and a leaning, sagging, barn. They had a cow, a horse, a hog, and a red-bone hound named Major. Their fences were little more than rusty, broken, strands of barbed wire drooping between rotting, leaning fence posts—which often let their animals roam the neighborhood at will.

'Bad-Eye' was so named due to a disfiguring eye injury received in a brawl at a local bar. Specifically, the injury to his eye was the end result of his ill-considered decision to get in a fight with a man who had a metal beer-can opener in his hand. Bad-Eye, by nature, was an easy-going, likeable, person. While not confrontational, he wouldn't back down from a fight—especially when he was drinking. He knew—if he wanted to hang out in the Virginia Bar & Grill on weekends—he was going to have to fight from time to time. Either that or get bullied and pushed around by every loud mouth who walked through the door of the bar. He won his fair share of the fights—drunk or sober. However, the injury to his eye-lid and cheek-bone were permanent reminders that he came out of *that* fight in 'second place'.

Bad-Eye had his habits. They ran from colorful, to distasteful, to repugnant, to shocking. He drank cheap beer, wine, and liquor to the excess; he belched or farted loudly—regardless of the time, place, or people present; he refused to hold a steady job; he bought worn out cars that seldom ran more 60 days after purchase; he played the guitar poorly and sang worse; he cut his own hair—badly; and his personal hygiene didn't involve a timely change of clothes or the frequent use of soap, water, and toothpaste.

On the other hand—, Bad-Eye had a skill for making money by buying, selling, and trading things of little or no value. For years, he survived by doing odd jobs and 'tradin' thangs'. Having no steady job matched Bad-Eye's vision of an ideal life. Holding a regular 9-to-5 job, for more than 30 days, was 'like bein' in jail' to Bad-Eye.

The Pierce home was surrounded by 3 acres—2 acres of which was packed solid with junk. These two acres ran from the Pierce house to the eastern edge of Mame's property. The front of Bad Eye's house faced Mame's house—unlike all other houses on the street that faced Vencil St. The Pierce property was down-hill from Mame's place—so her view from the front porch of her big white mansion was an unimpeded view of the Pierce property—including the junk Bad-Eye had for sale and his ramshackle, tar-paper covered house.

The two acres of junk between Bad-Eye's house and Mame's yard included; old cars—all of which needed some sort of repair before they would start or run; old wringer washing machines; worn kitchen cook stoves; odd pieces of wooden furniture; metal signs advertising gasoline or other commercial products; rusty & worn farm implements; used and abused hand tools; car wheels, worn car tires/tubes, hub caps; horse-drawn farm wagons; scrap iron; galvanized wash tubs; glass canning jars & bottles; and a vast array of other odds & ends. The entire collection of worn metal, glass, rubber, and wood was an intriguing sight. It strained the bounds of imagination to believe so many items of so little value could be accumulated on two acres of a residential setting.

Bad-Eye constantly traded or sold the junk on the Pierce land. My grandfather once told me Bad-Eye would climb a greasy pole to trade something, rather than stand on the ground and hold a regular job that paid the same amount of money.

Bad-Eye swore 'tradin' thangs' put more money in his pocket than a regular job. In his case, this was possible-- considering Bad-Eye kept no records, nor paid taxes— ever—on any profit he made on his trades or sales.

Malcolm Allen, Benny's daddy, swore Bad-Eye didn't make a sum total of a dollar's profit on all the junk he traded from one year to the next—so the government would never be able to convict him of income tax evasion. My grandfather said that couldn't possibly be true, because Bad-Eye spent a total of, at the very least, $1.77 a week for 59-cents-a-bottle rot-gut wine—not to mention what he paid Leck Thompson for moonshine whiskey or paid for beer at the Virginia Bar & Grill every weekend.

Bad-Eye's father died in a work related accident on the railroad. Bad-Eye and his Mom lived, for majority of their lives, on monthly disability checks she received from the railroad and the 'guvmint'. It kept them in food, snuff, a table radio perpetually tuned to country music, a steady supply of .59 a bottle wine, a new piece of clothing once or twice a year for Bad-Eye or herself, paid for the utilities, and bought a dump truck load of coal every fall to heat the house during the winter. Bad-Eye and his mother had never had much in their entire lives—so they didn't miss something they never had. A roof over their head, food, snuff, wine—they were happy with their place in life.

These souls who called Vencil Street home were, in a way, individual stories in themselves. But, it was their interaction with each other that created the better stories of Vencil St. Here are some stories the 'collsions' of their lives gave birth to.

MAME & BAD-EYE

Mame Richardson became more reclusive, paranoid, confrontational, and dictatorial with the passing years. By the time she reached her 60s, paranoia and confrontation became a dominant part of her personality. She wanted no one on or near any portion of her property. Keeping every living person and creature out of her yard and the sloping, one acre broom sage field that tied her front yard to the edge of Vencil St and the Pierce property consumed many of her waking hours. Insofar as possible, she preferred having no one within sight or sound of her perennial post behind the huge 6 foot high windows of the Richardson home, or her perch on the high, big, wrap-around front porch of the family manse.

She also became obsessed with seeking out and publicizing the sins and perceived ill will of others. She was the self-appointed arbiter of 'rules to live by'. Mame, bless her heart, lived in a fantasy that included a personal mandate from God to point out to others their failures, offenses—and demand an *immediate* penance, correction of the offending act, and blood oath to never do it again. Living next door to Bad-Eye Pierce, with her attitude and his habits, guaranteed a busy and tortured life for Mame. The situation created some interesting moments for Bad-Eye, as well.

Bad-Eye's happy-go-lucky, attitude, coupled with his daily consumption of wine/moonshine—well, it all led him to handle Mame's tirades in his own unique, mellowed-out way. That and years of learning how useless it was to waste his time answering Mame's antagonistic tirades with angry rebuttals.

Over the years, Bad-Eye's 2 acre junk-yard—including the 12-15 old junk cars that were a perpetual part of his inventory; his free roaming livestock; the poor condition of his fences; his chronic bouts of public drunkenness; 'mooning' Mame from his front porch; using his side yard as a dump for empty wine bottles; the near-collapse condition of his house;—had all been the cause of repeated tirades, complaints, and threats by Mame. From the vantage point of her front porch, she shouted or screeched every negative adjective (i.e., shiftless, worthless, filthy, ignorant, no-good, liar, thief, drunken-sot, etc) in her vocabulary to be sure Bad-Eye fully grasped the intensity of her ill feelings for him.

She called Sheriff Bart Brown, at least once a week, to report offensive acts and violations of municipal ordnances or criminal laws by Bad-Eye. From time to time he would, personally, show up on Vencil Street to half-heartedly investigate Mame's complaints. He never arrested Bad-Eye, nor did he have any intention of doing so. He knew (1) Bad-Eye had no money to pay a fine (2) Judge Sexton would give Bad-Eye 10 days in his jail in lieu of a fine (3) he would have to feed Bad-Eye for 10 days, launder his clothes, and force him to bath every two days. Bart wasn't about to bring that misery on himself.

Most of Bart's investigations of Mame's complaints ended with him telling her he couldn't arrest Bad-Eye because (1) there were no collaborating witnesses (2) Bad-Eye denied her accusations (3) it was one person's word against another person's (4) Bay-Eye claimed to be 'collecting' junk—not selling it—and 'collecting' on residential property was not against the law.

On this particular day, Bad-Eye's addition of a 1932 Ford Coupe brought the inventory of broken down cars in his junk yard to an even 12 cars. Mame stormed out of her house on to the huge wrap-around front porch that served as her bully-pulpit for most of her tirades against Bad-Eye and other neighbors. In her shrill and abrasive voice, Mame screamed a scathing indictment at Bad-Eye—compounded with a battery of threats.

"Bad-Eye Pierce! You good for nothing piece of trash! I see you! Oh yes! I see you putting another broken down, rusty, old car in with that bunch of good-for-nothing cars you already have on that hill side! Don't you think for one moment I don't know what you're doing! You're trying to make me live in your wretched pile of junk! You can't sell *any* of those cars, or any of that junk, because it's useless— *do you hear me*—useless junk! And you're a dishonest, shiftless, drunk! No one wants to buy *anything* from you! If you put that car on that hill I'm going to call the law! I'll have Bart Brown arrest you and throw you in jail where you belong! Do you hear—DON'T YOU TURN YOUR BACK ON ME WHEN I'M TALKING TO YOU! That's the ultimate height of ill manners! Well—answer me, you rude dog!" bawled

Mame as she angrily stomped her foot on her porch.

"Mame—", said Bad-Eye with a smile as he shaded his eyes with his hand and squinted toward Mame's front porch. "Is that you Mame—honey? I declare, I can't rightfully see you darlin'—what with the mornin' sun in my eyes, n' all. Or is it th' radiance of your smile that's done blinded me this fine mornin'? Well—don' make no never-mind. I'm just glad to see you still got your health, darlin'—up and out on your porch, takin' the air before the sun gets too hot. 'Scuse me, Sweetheart. I got to set the brakes on this car I traded for this very mornin—".

"How dare you talk to me like that!" shrilled Mame as she pounded the porch banister with her clenched fist. "You have no respect for---DON'T YOU DARE WALK AWAY FROM ME WHEN I'M ADDRESSING YOU! May God give me strength— you're a disgrace, Bad-Eye Pierce! A disgrace to this entire street! Why aren't you in the army? Fighting in the war—like so many of the brave young men in this town? Just answer me that—if you have an ounce of truth in you! I pray you will be drafted, sent to the front lines, and shot on your very first day there! Lord knows I'm not one to wish ill to others—but being rid of you would be a blessing to this entire street! If I have to put up with you much longer, I won't wait for the Army to get you shot! I'll do it my—NO—no-no—STOP! Don't you dare put that old rattle-trap car in that field!"

"Ahhh—I see the 1932 Ford I jus' traded for has done caught your eye, darlin'. It is a beauty—ain't it? Tell you what, Mame—us bein' neighbors n' all—I can let you have this here Ford for—well—you can have it for what I got in it. I'm robbin' myself blind—but you can buy this here car for next to nothin'—give your boy, John, somethin' to ride to work in. Then he won't have to be standin' around in the weather—waiting for them city buses to come by. Why—I'd let you have this here '32 Ford for—."

"The day has yet to dawn when I would buy even <u>one</u> piece of your useless junk, Bad-Eye Pierce! Let alone a car that doesn't run! Even if it did run—you half-wit—the war has caused gas and tires to be rationed! Why would anyone buy a car when they can't get gas or tires for it? And the rest of that junk you have piled up over there—".

"Oh—I see. You got your eye on some of my other tradin' goods over here. Well now—you come on over here—take a close look at what I got. You find somethin' you need—I'll treat you right give you a good deal on it. You jus' ask anybody in town 'bout ol' H.B. Pierce. They'll tell he never took a dime he didn't earn. You mentioned the war and rationin'. I'm doin' my bit to supply folks with these hard-to-get items they need to keep their homes and farms a-runnin'. You jus' slip your sun bonnet on—delicate lady like you won't want too much sun on your skin—and come on over here for a close look-see at some of these treasures I got. Listen—honey, I got to go now. I'll look forward to talkin' to you agin'—sometime real soon."

Bad-Eye turned, walked toward his wood shed, mumbling under his breath, "G'wan back in your hidey-hole—crazy ol' wart—leave me alone for a while. Talk about *me* drivin' *you* crazy—! Honey, you was gone-'round-the-bend crazy way before I set up my business over here. Hard to say who's a-gonna' wind up locked up over Marion first—you or Mad-Maudie DuVall. Likely as not, you'll both end up room-mates in that hell-hole of an asylum. It's a mystery why you ain't locked up already. By-George—this is my land. I got a right to make a living any dam way I want—whether you like it or not. Ol' bat—on me about drinkin'—you 'spect me to put up with you sober?"

"Bad-Eye, so help me God", shrilled Mame at his retreating back, "You take the liberty of calling me 'honey' or 'darlin' one more time—I'll have you arrested for taking un-due liberties with me! We aren't friends—and you don't know me well enough to use 'familiarities' when you address me! And another thing—you park that car in that junk lot of yours, I *will* call Bart Brown and have you arrested for transacting commercial enterprise on a lot zoned strictly for residential purposes! You have abused my patience for the last time! I'll have Bart Brown put you in jail where your kind belongs! You don't deserve to live among civilized people!"

Bad-Eye shook his head and dismissed Mame with a wave of his hand. 'No point 'n trying to talk to the batty ol' wretch', he thought. 'She's is so daft anything I say to her goes in one ear and out the other 'n—without ever passin' thru her brain—if she had one that worked'.
Bad-Eye hooked up his horse to the '32 Ford and pulled it into line with his other junk cars, while he pondered on

what made some people like Mame talk and act so crazy. It seemed like she was purely possessed by one of them demons Preacher Cummins used to talk about in his tent revivals, mused Bad-Eye. He wished he could remember what Bible verse Preacher Cummins said would drive them demons out of a person— 'cause it sure looked like one of 'em demons had a hold on Mame's head—.

By the time Bad-Eye finished placing the old '32 Ford on the hillside beside the other junk cars Mame's shrieks of protest had become so hysterical she lost her breath. Her words ran together, spittle ran from the corners of her mouth, and she became incoherent.

After he finished dragging the old Ford in line, he put his horse back in the pasture. Then he shuffled to his wood shed and pulled a bottle of cheap wine from under the eaves of the shed. He acknowledged Mame's hysterical rant by raising the bottle toward her, then finishing off the wine in two big swallows.

"Oh yes! I see you—you don't need to wave your bottle at me! I've told you before Bad-Eye Pierce, the wages of sin is *death!* Your drinking is a sin! You'll pay for it, you God-less heathen!"

In her fervor to forewarn Bad-Eye of his impending doom, Mame forgot the liberal leanings of the Episcopalian faith in which she was raised and embraced the Baptist ideology of total abstinence from alcohol.

"Drink ye neither strong wine nor liquor", ranted Mame. "That's what the Bible says, Bad-Eye! You think you're not being watched, don't you? Well—*HE* knows! Yes indeedy! You may not believe that on *this* side of the grave, you drunken sot—but you surely will one second on the *other* side of the grave! And you'll have other low-life sinners, like that bootlegger Leck Thompson, to keep you company—IN THE LAKE OF FIRE!"

Bad-Eye shook his head in resignation, wiped his mouth on his shirt sleeve, and slung the empty wine bottle to the far end of his side yard. As he turned and ambled slowly toward the porch of his ramshackle house, he could hear Mame screaming scriptures that underwrote his damnation for drinking.

Bad-Eye slowly swung back and forth on his porch swing, letting the warmth of the wine spread through his body. He pondered Mame's promise of a fiery hell as the price for drinking wine. 'That can't be true', he reasoned. 'Wine is the 'tonic of life'—one of the things that makes a man's weary journey on this earth tolerable. 'Nah', he said as he dismissed the idea, 'that's just a crazy idea from a crazy ol' woman.'`

THE GREAT ALLEY BATTLE

It was a summer day! It was Saturday morning on Vencil St.! A glorious Saturday morning. Saturdays on Vencil St. were best day of the entire week for kids. It was a day without the usual chores. A morning of complete freedom—to play Cowboys & Indians—hunt for hidden treasure—catch 'craw-dabs' in the creek—whatever we felt like doing.

Mondays through Fridays were a lot more structured. There were chores to be done, routines and rituals to be followed Oh, we played during the week, but not with the abandon of Saturdays. Actually, Benny Allen, my best friend, and I spent some of every week-day doing chores assigned by our parents or grandparents.

I lived in the Vencil St. home of my grandparents— a 'mini-farm' of 5 acres. My grandfather, who built railroad steam locomotives for the N&W railway, was a good man. My grandmother was an angel on this earth—and, I loved both of them. My grandfather was a 'straight and narrow tee-totaler'—meaning no drinking, no smoking, no cussing, no dancing—but plenty of week-day work—especially for me. My grandfather was unwavering in his belief that hard work 'built a good work ethic' in all young boys.

Grandpa Lawless, Benny's maternal grandfather, on the other hand, embraced cussing, fighting, and drinking liquor with a passion—especially on weekends. To his credit,

Grandpa Lawless was mostly sober on week days and favored days filled with work—especially for Benny. While Grandpa Lawless didn't allow anyone else to verbally or physically abuse Benny, he felt it was his duty to teach 'the value of hard work' to Benny—whom he called a 'lazy little cuss'.

Bless God in his heaven for setting up Saturdays with few, if any at all, chores for young boys. After a morning of unbridled playing, it was a quick wash-up on the back porch, diving into a secret hiding place in our bedroom closet for our allowance, and fairly running to the Lee Theatre in town for the Saturday afternoon matinees. A whole afternoon of movies, that depicted the daring-do of Batman and Robin in their unrelenting pursuit of evil-doers; the dead-eye shots of Roy Rogers as he pursued cattle rustlers and restored law and order in western towns; and serials that always left us hanging on the apparent death of the heroes until the next week. While lost in our revelry as side-kicks to our movie heroes, we washed down boxes of pop-corn with big cups of RC Cola.

The tightest buddies of the Vencil St. kids were Bennie Allen, J. Hudson Hudnall, III (aka 'Hud'), Jim Harvey, Bub Bailey, and I. Bennie Allen lived next door to my grandparents, with his parents, Malcolm & Belle Allen, his sister Biddie, and Grandpa Lawless.

The Allens had a big two-story house on a 2 acre lot. A dirt-road alley ran between their house and that of the 'Wicked Witch of the North Side', Maudie DuVall. Maudie and

Grandpa Lawless were arch enemies. Finding ways to torment and wreak vengeance on each other occupied a good part of the days of their sunset years.

Grandpa Lawless celebrated most weekends by dressing in his best black suit, a white shirt starched so stiff it was bullet proof, his one and only neck tie—and consuming a fifth of *Old Crow* or *Four Roses* bourbon. Grandpa Lawless was strictly a bourbon man. Repeatedly, he told Bennie and me he would drink water out of a mud-hole before he would drink scotch whiskey, wine, or beer.

Maudie spent most Saturdays wandering about the acres of over-grown land surrounding her big, old, brick mansion. She maintained a constant vigil for any sign of trespass on her property—especially by her arch-enemy, 'Devil George' Lawless.

Her property, so Maudie believed, included the dirt-road alley that ran between her home and that of Malcolm Allen. In truth, the alley road belonged to the town. It was an access road to the N&W railroad. The railroad maintenance crews used that alley to service railroad spur lines to businesses in the area. Maudie's one-track mind held *her* property claim to that alley to be superior to any town claim. As far as Maudie was concerned, it was her alley, and no trespasses of any kind would be tolerated.

"The Town Fathers (Town Council) of Bluestone", snorted Maudie to her neighbor, Mrs. Flora Graham. "are nothing but a bunch of lazy bums, who live on *my* tax dollars.

People, whose salary is paid by *you,* sure as hell don't tell *you* what *you* own and don't own, nor what to do with what *you* do own! This alley is, always has been, and always will be DuVall property! It's all that stands between me and that devil, George Lawless—curse his black soul!"

Bennie, Bub, and I were playing 'Cowboys & Indians' that Saturday morning. Our dogs, Mickey and Mose—two playful half-breed collies—were playing the role of the 'Indians'. Although, they didn't know they had been dubbed Indians. As usual, our dogs ran 10-20 ft. ahead of us—exploring land on either side of the road. Our chase of the 'Indians' led us 'Cowboys' down that dirt alley. We were yelling, running, and firing our cap pistols as we chased our 'dog-Indians' down the dusty alley.

Hearing us yelling and galloping down the alley, Maudie hustled around the corner of her house—her worn Remington .410 gauge shot-gun in hand.

"Hey! What did I tell you boys about playing in *my* alley? What did I tell you I was gonna' do if I caught you in *my* alley again?" she barked at us.

The heat of our battle with the Indians was so intense, the sounds of our cap-buster pistols so loud—we didn't really hear or listen to what Maudie said. She was always yelling at us for something. She usually limited her tantrums to yells and threats—but not that morning. I don't know— maybe we had gotten on her nerves one time too many. Without warning, she fired a load of buck shot from her shot gun. *That* got our attention—real fast.

Frightened by the nearby blast from her rifle, we instinctively dropped flat on our stomachs in the alley. Then we quickly crawled in the dirt to the side of the alley and rolled down the slight hill to the safety of Bennie's back yard.

In truth, Maudie aimed her rifle up into the air when she pulled the trigger. As ornery as Maudie could be, she would never have deliberately at shot one of us kids. She just wanted to scare the daylights out of us. At the time, we were too young to realize that. We thought Maudie had just made a real effort to fill our hides full of buck shot. As we lay in Benny's back yard, breathing hard and scared for our lives, Bub Bailey whispered, "Hoo-ee—that was close! Ol' Maudie's mind ain't screwed together jus' right. My Momma done tol' me Maudie would jus' as soon kill yuh' as look at yuh'."

The sound of Maudie's shotgun blast and her shrill, loud voice was a call-to-arms for Grandpa Lawless. The sound from Maudie's shotgun had hardly died in the air when Grandpa George Lawless lunged out the back door of the Allen house. It was still an hour till noontime, and Grandpa Lawless was already knee-walking drunk. He screamed obscenities and threats of a painful death at Maudie as he pitched and staggered across the backyard to his car.

Most of us 'Vencil Street Boys' heard many of our 'cuss' words for the first time by listening to Grandpa Lawless verbally abuse Maudie—and she him. When it came to cussing, Maudie gave as well as she got. More than that, listening to Grandpa Lawless and Maudie rage at each other taught us boys how to weave a verbal tapestry out of a string of profanities. Just one minute of their verbal exchanges included enough cursing to inspire a raging condemnation from any minister in town.

Grandpa Lawless crawled into his used and abused, black, 1940 Chevrolet *FleetMaster* sedan. Grandpa Lawless didn't own a gun. His weapon of choice for most of his battles with Maudie was that big, 4 dr sedan. The fact that he was 70 years old and too often soaked in bourbon to chase Maudie on foot may have played a major role in that choice.

Grandpa Lawless started his car, gunned the motor, and roared across the Allen's back yard to the alley. Bennie, Bub, and I scattered across the yard to avoid being accidentally run down by Grandpa Lawless as he barreled toward the alley and Maudie.

Shotgun in hand, the venerable Maudie, responded passionately to Grandpa Lawless' shouted curses, threats, and actions. She screamed her contempt for Grandpa Lawless' threats with her usual retort of "Kiss my ass, you devil." She stood her ground in the alley and pointed her shotgun at Grandpa Lawless' car as it sped across the Allen's yard toward her. "You dirty, miserable, rotten, blankety-blank son of a so and so", she screamed.

Grandpa Lawless, his car gaining speed with his head hanging out the car window, bellowed his intentions to "Teach you a dam good lesson when I run over you—you ugly old turd". Maudie was surly, maybe even a little 'mental' at times—but not stupid. She knew Grandpa Lawless, liquored up on bourbon to the max, would not hesitate to run over her with his car. She fired a load of buckshot straight at Grandpa Lawless' rocketing car before jumping behind a big oak tree—not 2 seconds before Grandpa Lawless' car roared over the exact spot in the alley where she had been standing. "You mean ol' so-and-so of a mangy hag" he screamed at her.

Grandpa Lawless missed Maudie's body by little more than 5-6 feet as he sped by. Not a shrinking violet, Maudie lunged back into alley after his car flashed past her—shouting, "Here's something for you, you mean devil". Then she let go with another round of buckshot into the rear of Grandpa Lawless' car as it sped on down the alley. This time Maudie's gun was aimed straight at the rear of his car when she pulled the trigger. Grandpa Lawless's car was already 50-60 feet away by then. Still—most of her buckshot pellets peppered the rear of his car. The dings the buckshot pellets added to the car's paint were lost in the numerous dents and scratches already on the car.

Bennie's father came running out of their house, yelling at Grandpa Lawless and Maudie. He took the car keys from Grandpa Lawless, put his old Chevvy back in the yard, locked it, and put the keys in his pocket. He drug Grandpa Lawless into the house by his arm, and dared him to come out of it before supper time. Bennie's dad tore into Maudie—told her the next time she fired her gun in the direction of his house he would take it from her. From her front yard, Maudie dared him to try and take her gun.

Tommie Yost's mother marched across Vencil Street to Maudie's front yard. She shook her finger in Maudie's face and gave her a tongue lashing we could hear half-way down the alley. Mrs. Yost swore some of the pellets Maudie fired at Grandpa Lawless hit her house. Mrs. Yost told Maudie, "That is the last straw—if you as much as point that gun at my house again I will swear out a warrant for your arrest!"

Maudie knew she had pushed matters a little too far this time. Sulking, she mumbled under her breath as she walked across the yard to her house. With one long look at the Allen yard to be sure 'Devil George' Lawless was not in sight, she turned and shuffled into her house.

That rang down the curtain on another—but not the last—battle between 'Devil George' Lawless and 'Mad-Maudie' DuVall.

THE MILK BOTTLE RAID

It was another Saturday morning. Benny, Bub, and I looked for some place to play besides 'the alley'. We didn't want Maudie shooting at us again—especially before we went to the movies. As we sat on the fence of our barn yard staring at our cow and horse in the barnyard, an idea hit me.

With Benny and Bub's help, I put a bridle on my Uncle's horse, Pinto. We didn't bother to saddle him. All of us climbed aboard Pinto's back and rode him out of the barn yard to the site of another game of 'Cowboys & Indians'.

Benny and Bub agreed to be the Indians for the first go-round of the game. I sat on Pinto, in Vencil St., to give them a couple of minutes to 'hide out and set up an ambush site'. Then, riding Pinto, I was to hunt them down and blast them to glory with my deadly, chrome plated, six-shot, cap-buster pistol—before they did the same to me.

Benny and Bub decided to make Mame Riester's one acre broom-sage field their hide-out. The broom-sage on that sloping field had to be 3 feet tall and thick as the hair on a dog's back. A finer place for an ambush, you couldn't imagine. On foot, it was difficult to see more than four feet ahead of your face.

I was pretty sure Benny and Bub would hide in Mame's broom-sage field or in Bad-Eye Pierce's junk yard. Bad-Eye had some customers in his junk yard—so I figured they had to be in Mame's field. After giving them two minutes to hide, I dug my heels into Pinto's flanks and cautiously rode him into Mame's broom sage field. If those 'Indians' weren't hiding in that broom sage, I would press on to Bad-Eye's junk yard. This was going to be tricky. Roy Rogers and Gene Autry, in their movie gunfights, always seemed to have boulders and trees to duck behind during a gunfight. Unable to see squat in that thick broom-sage made me wonder if I wasn't about to be mowed down in a flurry of 'hot lead' from my hidden companions.

Benny and Bub sprang out of hiding in the broom sage and opened fire on me. I leaned low over Pinto's neck, and prodded him into a gallop around Benny and Bub. I blazed away with my lethal six-shooter as I guided Pinto with my free hand. All three of us were ducking bullets, yelling, shooting, and claiming to have 'drilled' each other first.

The noise of this 'shoot-out' was bound to be heard. Mame's front door flew open so fast it bounced off the wall. She trotted to the edge of her front porch overlooking the broom sage field. Mame's strident, preachy, voice joined our fun-filled shouts.

"You there! I see you! I know every one of you! You have no business being on my property! How many times have I told you rude little imps to stay away from my place? You get off my property! Right now! You are tearing up my grass! Do you hear me? Don't you act like you don't hear me! I know where every one of you live! Maybe you'd like me to call Bart Brown and have you sent to a Reform

School! Maybe that would teach you some manners! You're nothing but limbs of Satan—every last one of you! This is my property—now, get off it! "

"Miz Riester, we ain't hurtin' nothin'. We jus' playin' Cowboys & Indians", pleaded Bub.

"I don't care what you are playing. You can't do it on my land. Now—I don't want to hear another word from you. I do want to see you leaving— right now!"

I wasn't real sure Bub and Benny had given up on our battle, so I continued to ride back and forth across Mame's field, through her entire lecture, pouring 'hot lead' from my cap buster at them. Benny and Bub had continued to run and duck behind clumps of broom sage as Bub conversed with Mame. Mame's loud demands and threats had little impact on any of us as we continued our shoot-out. By now, I had ridden Pinto on so many charges around Benny and Bub that his hooves had trampled down a good bit of the tall grass. This, along with our reluctance to leave her property, pushed Mame's patience beyond the breaking point.

"I'll teach to listen to me, you little ill-mannered urchins", shrilled Mame. With that, she began throwing glass milk bottles at us. Big shiny, goose-neck, milk bottles—with 'Clover Dew Dairy' proudly emblazoned in orange letters across the middle of every bottle Some of them hit the ground close enough to us to get our attention. We began dodging the one-quart milk bottles. I got the message and was urging Pinto out of Mame's field when I noticed Bub picking up some of the milk bottles she had thrown at us. Bub could run like a jack-rabbit. He zig-zagged across the field, picking up milk bottles as he ran.

"C'mon, Bub. What are you doing? Mame's so worked up she's running hot. Let's get out of here before she hits us with one of those big bottles", I said.

"No way", yelled Bub as he continued to fly around the field picking up empty milk bottles. "These here bottles each have a 3 cent deposit on each one. We can turn them in at Doke Matthews' store in town and he'll give us 3 cents for each bottle. We can buy tickets for the movies with the money he gives us", shouted Bub

Bub's arms would only hold four bottles. When his arms were full he would hand them to Benny, who would hand them up to me. When each of us had four bottles under our arms we high-tailed it out of Mame's field with the sound of her voice following us.

"Don't you dare take my milk bottles! Those are my bottles! I'll have you arrested for stealing! I'm going to tell your parents. You think you can steal from me and get away with it, do you? We'll just see about that! You hear me—I'm calling the police—right this minute!"

We ignored Mame. She had thrown the bottles away—we found them in the grass—now they were our bottles. We put Pinto back in the pasture and headed for Doke

Matthrews' grocery store in town. Just like Bub said, Doke gave us 3 cents for each bottle. Our total wealth was increased by 36 cents. A ticket to the Saturday matinees at the local movie theatre cost 11 cents. We had enough money to buy all our tickets, with three cents left over to buy each of us a piece of 'blow gum' to chew on during the movie. Life was good.

Actually, life lost some 'good' by the end of the day. Mame, true to her word, called our parents or grandparents. We confessed to taking Mame's bottles and converting them to show tickets. Our parents or grandparents spanked the living daylights out of us. That day we learned taking property of others was at or near the top of the list of offenses that would be dealt with harshly on Vencil Street. After our spanking, with tears still in our eyes, we were each given 12 cents and marched across the street to give the money to Mame—along with our apologies. If we were expecting smiles or forgiveness from Mame, we were badly mistaken. Mame met us at her front door, listened to our apologies, took the money from us, said she hoped we had learned a good lesson, and slammed the door in our faces.

Our families took the 12 cents out of our weekly allowance of 15 cents over the rest of the month. I think this is the place in a story where the writer usually says something like 'the spanking and loss of allowance served as a reminder to never again set foot on Mame's property'. Pretty sure I remember similar 'lessons learned' in children's story books I read over the years. Thing is—those were fairy tales. You and I, we're talking real life here.

About a year after the 'milk bottle' thing, Jim Harvey, Benny, and I were playing when Hud Hudnall, III dropped by with a box of matches. On Vencil Street, most kids were not allowed to even strike a match, let alone have a whole box of them in their possession. Hud was the grandson of the wealthiest man in town—Mr. J. Hudson Hudnall, Sr. A lot of rules that governed most kids' lives didn't apply to Hud.

Hud wanted to show us what you could do with a box of matches—besides light a fire in the kitchen stove. The most flammable thing accessible to us was Mame's broom sage field. You guessed it. We sneaked into her field. Hud struck a match, lighted a large stalk of that dry broom sage—and the whole one acre field seemed to turn into one big orange ball of flames in the blink of an eye. My Grandmother saw the fire about the same time Bennie's Dad and George Graham did. They came running with hoes, rakes, and old, wet burlap animal-feed sacks. Bad-Eye Piercey joined others in fighting the fire. The best they could do was keep the fire from spreading beyond Mame's broom-sage field. By the time the last spark of that fire was out the entire broom-sage field was burned to charred, black stubble.

Hud took his matches and ran for home—about two seconds after he saw the fire spreading out of control. The Vencil Street boys, including your truly, were grilled by our families on the cause of the fire. Didn't take them long to get the truth out of us. We were scared—and old enough to realize how close we came to burning down Mame's house—with her in it.

We ratted out Hud. We were quick to point out that we had only been witnesses to Hud's demonstration of an alternative use of kitchen matches. Our parents and grandparents felt no personal responsibility for any loss Mame might have suffered—if the absence of that raggedy broom-sage was any loss at all.

Mame showed no sense of restraint in her anger over the loss of her broom-sage grass. Within 24 hours she had a warrant served against Mr. J. Hudson Hudnall, Jr (Hud's father), guardian of J. Hudson (Hud) Hudnall, III. She wanted $100 for the loss of the broom sage in her field.

 Mr. J. Hudson Hudnall, Sr., Hud's grandfather, retained the services of the town's primo trial lawyer, 'Way-Lay' Newton. 'Way-Lay' filed a defensive motion with the court that said (1) J.Hud, III had no knowledge of the origin of the fire, (2) he was of such a tender age he was not, legally, capable of knowing right from wrong and (3) the removal of the broom sage was an *improvement* of the grounds— hence, Mame suffered no monetary loss.

Ol' Way-Lay had a silver tongue—especially when he was being paid to use it. Judge Standish ruled in favor of 'Way-Lay's motion to drop all charges against Hud. Mame left the court room with nothing but her disdain for Judge Standish.

Other than our parents/grandparents talking to me, Benny, and Bub like unwashed dogs for watching Hud set fire to that field, nothing much ever came of the matter. It was made crystal clear to all of us what punishment would be meted out to all of us if we were even *seen* with a match in our hands—for *any* reason.

Mame wasn't through with the incident. She called Sheriff Bart Brown. She wanted him to arrest Hud for criminal trespass. Bart—he basically did nothing. Like any small town Sheriff, he understood politics and the power of money very well He wasn't going to irritate Mr. J. Hudson Hudnall, Sr.— the most powerful man in town. He knew he would never get the County's Commonwealth Attorney to bring criminal charges over an acre of wild, worthless, grass. The whole matter just kind of 'went-away' with time.

As I think back on the whole thing now, it seems incredible a one acre field of tall, wild grass could give birth to a lasting memory about a few small boys and a match.

THE RUNAWAY CAR

My youngest uncle, who also lived with my grandparents, owned an A-Model Ford. This was a time when only two in five families owned a car. Many folks walked or relied on a bus, train, or horse for transportation. So my uncle was extremely proud to be the owner of that A-Model Ford.

He bought it used. Hard to say if he was the second, third, or fourth owner of the car. Wasn't hard at all to say the car was 'well used' by the time he took ownership of it. The car seated two people—with room in the outside rear 'rumble' seat for two more people—if weather permitted. He paid for it out of his weekly salary, earned by driving a delivery truck for Doke Matthews' grocery store in down town Bluestone.

While that little, black, A-Model Ford may have been better than no car at all, it was mighty close to it. The gas flowed from the gas tank to the engine by gravity. This required turning off the gas flow valve when the car wasn't running or, literally, have gasoline flood the engine. You started the car's engine with a hand crank inserted through the grill. Before you cranked the engine, you had to adjust the engine 'spark' or timing, with a mechanism on the steering wheel. Every soul who started one of those A-Models by hand crank risked a broken hand or arm if the engine compression blew backwards and forced the crank in reverse motion—with no warning.

The windshield wipers were operated by vacuum pressure. Put simply, there was insufficient vacuum pressure generated by the car's motor to operate the wipers when the car was *traveling* on an *uphill* grade. All available vacuum power produced by the engine was used to help get the car to the top of the hill. During rain, on an uphill grade, someone inside the car had to operate the windshield wipers by hand so the driver could see through the windshield well enough to keep the car in the road. Most roads of that day were challenging on a dry, clear day. Driving an A-Model Ford on a rainy day—God forbid at night—was a virtual invitation to a wreck. Rainy night trips—they were sheer *survival* adventures.

Finally, the A-Model's brakes were mechanical, as opposed to the hydraulic brakes used on the cars of today. In plain terms, having mechanical brakes meant foot pressure applied to the brake pedal inside the car transferred the downward motion of the brake pedal to the four car wheels through a series of inter-connecting rods. The mechanical brakes on those old cars were out of adjustment more than they were in adjustment. Manually re-adjusting the brakes, to apply an equal application of braking pressure on each of the four wheels, had to be done every week—if not more often. The only way to do this was to have one person sit in the car with a foot on the brake pedal while another person crawled beneath the car with a wrench and manually adjusted the brakes to the correct setting for each of the four wheels.

It was a pain in the back, literally, crawling around under the car to adjust those brakes. Pain or not, it was better than the alternative of colliding with something or somebody when the car failed to stop because those lousy mechanical brakes were operating properly on only one or two wheels.

It was late in the morning on a nice summer day when my uncle collared me to help adjust the brakes on his A-Model. He had me sit in the car with my foot pressing down on the brake pedal. As you had to do, to adjust the *foot* brakes, my uncle reached through the passenger door and released the *hand-parking* brake. He kept the parking brake engaged at all times when the car was parked on the street because Vencil Street was sloped downhill on a slight grade in front of our house. So—my foot on the brake pedal was all that held the car in a 'stopped' position that morning.

With me pressing down hard on the car's foot brake, my uncle crawled under the car and began adjusting the brakes on each wheel. It wasn't hard to crawl beneath an A-Model Ford because the floors of those old cars stood a good 20 inches off the ground.

My uncle worked steadily at adjusting the brakes. I was no more than 8 years old—I was bored—and growing tired of pressing my foot against the brake pedal. My leg was beginning to ache, I wanted to go play with my friends, and I was getting hungry. Relief arrived for me in an unexpected form. My grandmother came to the door of our house and cried out to say lunch was ready. How could I be expected to sit there in that old car, pressing on a brake pedal, when my grandmother—a respected authority figure—said it was time for me to eat lunch??

The door of the car was already open. I took my foot off the brake pedal, quietly slid off the seat of the car to the street, walked around the back of the car, and skipped across the street to my grandmother's house. Just as I reached the gate to the front yard I heard my uncle yell.

"Hey! What—Reese—are you pressing on the brake pedal? Press hard on that pedal—now!"

I looked back across the street at the old car. To my surprise, it was beginning to roll slowly down Vencil St.—with no one at the steering wheel. My Uncle was still lying under the car, trying hopelessly to stop it from rolling down the street. He was holding onto the rear-axel while desperately digging his shoe heels into the asphalt of the street. It was a losing battle. The weight of the car and the downhill slope of the street were too much for my uncle to overcome. The A-Model was rolling right on down the street, and dragging my Uncle along for the trip.

My uncle let the car drag him down the street for 5-10 feet before he gave up and let go of the axel. There was very little danger of injury to him, since his body was positioned between the left and right wheels. As soon as the rear of the car had passed over his body, my uncle jumped to his feet and began chasing his car down Vencil St. After a chase of 30 ft. or so, he caught up with the car, jumped on the running board, dived inside the car, and stomped on the brake pedal. The brakes held and the car came to a stop.

My uncle set the parking brake, used the old hand crank to get the car started, and backed the car up to its usual parking place on the street. Once he had the car safely parked and the motor off, he trotted across the street to our house to have 'a good talk' with me. In short, he was 'spitting' mad over the near loss of his car.

I had my 'short-comings'. Being slow to recognize trouble coming my way was not one of them. Living on Vencil Street taught you to be quick on the up-take. When I saw that old car rolling down Vencil St. with my uncle chasing it, I didn't waste a second in looking for safer ground. I ran through the house, grabbed a biscuit from the kitchen table, stiff-armed the back screen door open, raced across the back porch, and virtually flew through the back yard. My grandmother yelled for me to come back and finish my lunch, I sped through the barn and pasture while yelling over my shoulder that I wasn't hungry. I was across the creek and halfway to Tabor's house before I stopped running. I figured I would kill the afternoon playing with Pug Tabor.

Better to give my uncle a little time to calm down. I would amble on home in the late afternoon. Then make sure my grandmother was there to stand between me and my uncle—just in case he still harbored ill feelings over his car running away.

After all, an eight year old boy can't be held responsible for Henry Ford's flawed decision to use mechanical brakes in his A-Model Fords. Right?

JOSIE & ALCIE

Had they never met, Joe Dodson and Alcie Perkins would have been part of the masses that pass through life known only to family, neighbors, and a few friends. Not bad people. Not exceptional people. Just two people, too average to stand out from other ordinary individuals.

But they did meet. They married. That union was the wellspring of stories about the two of them for years to come.

Joe was the formal first name given by the Dodsons to their son. Almost from birth he was called by the nickname of 'Josie'. The name stuck.—In time, only a few of Josie's family knew his real first name was Joe.

Josie and Alcie both came from poor, but honest, large, mountain families. Their families made a living through manual labor for the most part, and often discontinued their formal education before entering high school. It wasn't a matter of the parents of Josie & Alcie's generation being 'anti-education'. Their paucity of formal education stemmed more from (a) living an inconvenient distance from schools, (b) family incomes that provided little beyond food, shelter, clothing, (c) an overwhelming need for the children to take a paying job early in life to help meet the cost of basic subsistence in their home.

Even with formal education often getting a lower priority

than a paying job, *most* of these families stressed the need for *some* basic education, a good work ethic, religion, cleanliness. From an early age, *most* of these families taught their children that respect must be *earned*. Near the top of the list of ways to earn respect was to *earn* a living through honest work or trade. Those who would not work—those who shunned work in favor of a handout or welfare—those who failed to acquire enough education to enable them to, at least, perform manual tasks—they were held in low respect, or even contempt. More than a few people who knew Josie's family said they fell in the 'low-respect' category.

Alcie was the last of 11 children. Her father died when she was a child. Life was filled with hardships. It made Alcie a survivor. She wanted more than the hard-scrabble life she saw around her. She joined the Womens Army Corp soon after WW II began. This didn't sit well with her family. Some people, especially her family, were of the opinion that women of 'low morals' populated the WACs. The family didn't feel her membership in such a group was a good reflection on the family name. This was of little concern to Alcie. She saw the WAC as her way out of a life which offered her little beyond back-breaking work and deprivation.

Josie was a simple, laid back, humble man. Those who knew Josie best differed on what 'simple' meant. Some described Josie as one without the benefit of a proper upbringing and too few years of formal education. Others called him a half-wit and lazy.

It was salt in the wound when Alcie finished her hitch in the WACs and announced, to her family, that she was marrying Josie. Alcie's mother and siblings had little use for Josie before the wedding. They had even less afterwards. They were down-right angry with Alcie for marrying 'that piece of trash'. After the wedding several of Alcie's brothers and sisters approached their mother. They asked for her opinion of the marriage. The family matriarch was brief.

"Nothing + Nothing = Nothing", she said. That was her total and final summation of Alcie & Josie's marriage. She never altered her opinion as the decades passed.

Right or wrong, the majority of Alcie's siblings' life-long attitude toward Josie, Alcie, and their family varied from barely tolerant to open disdain. Despite the lack of a close relationship between all of Aclie & Josie's siblings, some humorous stories came out of their lives and marriage. Some, like those that follow, even reached a 'ledgendary' status and continue to be shared.

THE BIKE RIDE

Josie and Alcie lived in a house at the 'head of 8 hollow'. That is to say, they lived in one of the last houses along the row of company owned houses that stretched from the town center of Jenkinjones to a point a mile away—where the road started over the mountain to Abbs Valley. In short, they were a mile away from town.

It was the middle of summer. It was still 85 degrees at 7:30 in the evening, and not a breeze was stirring. Alcie was trying desperately to come up with an idea to relieve the heat and boredom of another summer evening in Jenkinjones. She was not a woman to make frivolous demands—but the heat and humidity of this JenkinJones summer was absolutely making her crazy. Even worse, any idea she came up with was inconvenient or impractical—because she and Josie (1) had no car (2) very little money (3) the JenkinJones stores were a half-mile away

Alcie was sure of two things. She wasn't going to spend another evening sitting on her front porch until mid-night while their lone window fan replaced the hot air inside the house with hot air from outside. Secondly, she wasn't spending another evening sipping tea with no ice—because the ice melted in 10 minutes.

'My god'—she thought—'by the time it gets any cooler at all it will be mid-night. It will take me a half hour to drift off to sleep in my own sweat. I'll would have to be back on my feet at 5 am to make breakfast for Josie before he goes to work in the mines. Hmmph! What was the point in going to bed at all, for 4 and ½ hours of sleep—just to face another day and night of unending 90+ degree heat'.

'An ice cream cone—that's what she wanted. Wanted?—hell, she *needed* it'! she told herself. 'It would be cool—it would be sweet—it didn't cost much—and it would be real break from the crushing heat and boredom of being stuck up an asphalt road a half-mile from everything', she decided with finality.

"Josie, I want a double scoop of maple nut ice cream from down at the ice cream Parlor", said Alcie—with a big grin.

"Yeah, I bet you do. And I'd purely love for you to have one, Owsie (Josie's pronunciation of Alcie). But, they ain't no way that I can think of to git you one—not 'fore it melted", drawled Josie as he scuffed the porch floor with his shoe.

"Josie, surprise me—use your head. What if I was to walk down to JenkinJones *with* you?"

Josie's head snapped back. A look of sheer disbelief filled his eyes. He looked at Alcie as if she had, in the blink of an eye, gone completely crazy.

"What th' hell—you talkin' bout'—walking down '8 hollow' for a mile to get an ice cream cone? You done lost your mind? I done already worked 8 hours in the mines—and you want me to walk a mile for ice cream? Sides—by the time we got there th' place would be closed. And even if it wasn't, we'd be so wore out from this heat we'd puke if we tried to eat ice cream—or anything else! Walk clear out of '8 hollow' for an ice cream cone? Uh-uh, not me!"

"Josie, I guess I didn't make it clear to you. I wanna' to get away from this house—even if it's only for an hour. I wanna' taste a cool ice cream cone. An' I wanna' do it now! I don't care how durn far away the ice cream store is. I don't care if it just makes me *think* I'm cooler. An' lemme' make it real *plain* for you—I AM gonna' have some ice cream from th' ice cream parlor! If you can't think of a way to get us there without goin' all 'faint' on me—then I will. If I have to go by m'self, Josie, I just might not make it back home tonight! I might just find some place else to spend the night! So—you can get y'self up in the morning, fix your own breakfast, pack your own dinner bucket, and get breakfast for the kids! Now—how's that sound to you? Huh? I don't hear you sayin' nothin', Josie."

Josie knew the discussion was over. Even as he mumbled his displeasure under his breath, he was searching his mind for a way to get to JenkinJones—that didn't involve walking. As he gazed around their yard, his eyes fell on their daughter's bicycle.

"OK, you wanna' go for some ice cream. Alright, I'll take you! C'mon, let's go. It's gettin' dark", said Josie as he rolled the bike into the street.

"Josie, that's a girl's bicycle. There ain't no cross-bar for me to sit on. Where'd you think I was gonna' sit?"

"Jus' sit up here on the handle bars, unless you done decided you don't want no ice cream so bad after all."

"Okay—I'm gettin' on the handle bars. You jus' make sure you watch what you're doin'. Don't mess this bike ride up— like you do most things."

With Alcie perched precariously on the handle bars, Josie started down the old pot-hole filled black top road. There were houses and parked cars on the right side of the road. On the left side was a creek, four feet below the road. Josie hadn't counted on Alcie blocking his view of the road. She was a 'full-figured' woman. She had his view of the road blocked—almost completely. Josie kept leaning his head to the left and right of Alcie's generous body to see where he was going—and keep the bike in the road. That road was narrow, it sloped downhill, and the bike was picking up speed with every foot it rolled.

"Josie—Josie! Watch where you're goin'! You almost hit one of them parked cars. Watch—now you're headin' toward th' creek! Are you blind—or jus' not payin' attention?"

"Owsie, you think I'm not trying? Huh? You think drivin' this bike is so easy—you get back here and try it! I can't see 'round you worth a hoot. And hold still! You wigglin' makes th' handle bars turn and I can't hold the bike in a straight line!"

"Josie—jus' pull over and stop this bi—. Oh god—car's a-comin'—car's a-comin! Stop this thing!"

Josie ducked his head to the left of Alcie's body—just in time to see the car coming toward him—not 30 feet away from the bike. He jerked the bikes handle bars to the left and stood on the brake pedals. With the bike's back tire sliding and the front wheel pointed toward the creek, the inevitable was already set in motion.

"Oh god—stop this thing, Josie! We're headin' toward th' creek!"

It was desperation time. Things were happening fast—and none of them were good.

"Owsie, drag your feet on the road! Quick now! Hep' me stop this bike!"

From Elsie's view on the handle bars, the situation had progressed way beyond dragging her feet. It looked like 'bail out' time to her. She planted her hands on the handle bars, lifted her rump into the air, and jumped off the bike. If she had had more time, she may have given some thought to the fact that the bike was moving at a speed of 10-12 mph before she jumped off it—and stopping her body's 10 mph forward motion in a short distance wasn't going to be an easy task. She was close to the edge of the creek when she jumped from the bike. Josie saw Alcie jumping off the bike and decided to follow suit. He lifted his butt off the bike seat and let his feet drop to the asphalt road.

When their feet touched the road their legs couldn't keep up with the 10 mph speed of their bodies. Their forward momentum catapulted them forward, over the creek bank, and through the air—as if they had launched from a canon. Their bodies flew through the air—for one long second— before gravity took over, and they dropped 4 feet into a foot of cold water flowing over the rocky bed of the creek.

When their bodies hit the creek bed there were two loud 'WHUMMPP' sounds. This was followed, a split second later, with the sounds of splashing water and rocks rattling as the flight of their bodies displaced water and re-arranged the rocks strewn across the rocky creek bed.

For the next several seconds the water tumbling over rocks in the bed of the creek was the only thing that broke the absolute silence. The silence was soon broken by moans and cries of pain. Josie's voice was the first to come out of the closing darkness of the evening.

"Owsie! Owsie, honey, are ya' alright? Ooohh, Gawd! I think I done broke my knee—maybe my arm too. Gawdalmighty, it hurts. Owsie! Where are ya'?"

Alcie's head felt like it had split open. She was sure she heard it crack when her head landed on that big rock in the creek. Her legs were skinned and bleeding. Two of her fingers were already so stiff and sore she couldn't bend them. She could hear a sound—like ringing—or rattling—

strange sounds. The sound was getting closer—or maybe louder. What *was* that sound? She put her hand down to raise her body from where it lay. 'Lord, have mercy—now my hand has gone cold—and what was that bubbly sound?' she thought. Her vision began to clear. She looked down— and realized she was half sitting and half lying in water— running water. Then her memory returned—she was in th' creek. That fool, Josie, had wrecked and caused both of them to end up in that filthy, cold creek!

As Alcie looked around her— she saw that half-wit, Josie, crawling and stumbling through the creek water and rocks as he moved toward her. He was screamin' her name—like she was deaf or somethin'. Why was the fool screamin'? He was only 8 feet away from her. 'God—this creek water is freezin' me', she moaned to herself. She had to get up and out of that creek. Every movement she made to get up caused a new pain to shoot through her body—pain so bad it made her scream out loud.

Josie could see her moving and looking at him. He felt so relieved to find her alive. They were both too young to be dead. And who would look after their kids if they had died?

As Alcie regained full consciousness, the pains from her injuries washed over her. Her momentary happiness over being alive was replaced with rage over what Josie had done. As she watched Josie get closer she was consumed with desire to beat him senseless. She managed to get to her feet. She tried to pick up a big rock in the creek water. She wanted to use it bash in Josie's thick head—so he would know just how angry she was. She stared at her hand on the big rock—but her fingers were too swollen and painful to close around it. As she twisted her body to use her other hand to pick up the rock, her painfully injured knee collapsed. Once again, she was lying in the creek— face down this time.

Alcie was trying to raise her face out of the water before she drowned when Josie got to her and lifted her to her feet. Alcie glared at Josie—silently begging the Lord to give her the strength to hit Josie; strength enough to knock every tooth in his head out; break his nose with her fist.

It seemed to Alcie the answer to most of her prayers in the past few years had been 'No'—with a capitol 'N'. This time, it looked like the Lord was coming down on her side. Right in front of her face was a tree limb, hanging from a scrub-oak that grew along the creek bank. She grasped the tree limb and tried to break it off. If she could just break that limb off, she would use it to put Josie in the hospital—for weeks.

Josie saw Alcie struggling with the tree limb. He patted her on the shoulder as he spoke.

"That's a good idea, honey. You pull on that tree limb. I'll get behind you and push, and we'll get you up out of this old creek in no time. You ain't hurt too much to pull yo'sef' up the creek bank are you, Owsie? Considerin' ever thing we went thru' when we hit that there creek bed—why you don't hardly look hurt a'tall. Naw sir—you look okay to me."

Alcie stopped twisting and tearing at the tree limb. With not an ounce of energy left; her entire body throbbing with pain; half blind from a bloody, swollen eye; her voice quivering with pain and rage—she turned to face Josie

"HURT? OKAY? Is that what you're askin'? You're honest to God lookin' RIGHT AT ME—and askin' me if I'm HURT? Huh? What th' hell—are you blind, or just plain stupid? You wreck that bike—throw me through th' air—into the middle of a pile of rocks and cold, dirty water—I'm layin' there, almost knocked out—my head is split open—my fingers are broke—my left ankle couldn't hold up a feather—I got blood comin' out of me in a half dozen places—and you got the gall to ask if I'm HURT?", screamed Alcie.

So much anger and adrenaline shot through Alcie that she grabbed the tree limb again—twisting and jerking on it. Realizing the limb wasn't going to yield, she decided to use her fist to pulverize Josie's face. She took one step toward him and felt a sharp pain shoot through her foot. For the first time she realized she had lost both her shoes and couldn't walk on the sharp rocks under her feet. Besides, her ankle was so swollen and painful any real weight on it would cause her leg to collapse—and she would be lying face down in the creek again. Holding on to the tree limb to steady herself, she bellowed at Josie.

"I'm gonna' make ya' pay for this, Josie! As God is my

witness—you're gonna' pay! What th' hell were you thinkin'—. Listen to me—askin' you what you were *thinkin'* — and you without a brain in your head!"

"Ooh—have mercy—my ankle has got to be broken—I can't even stand on it. You lookin' to do a good deed, are ya'? Gonna' push me up the creek bank, are ya'? I tell ya' what. You wanna' do a good deed? Do one for yourself. Get the police to lock you up—cause if they don't—and I can get my hands on ya'—I'm gonna' put ya' in the hospital for the next 30 days. So don't you go makin' no plans for the next 30 days. One way or th' other—if you ain't locked up where I can't get to ya'—I'm gonna' put you in the hospital!"

"Now Owsie, I'm downright sorry 'bout all o' this. If you want to blame me, you go right ahead. But, it wasn't my fault. That car crowded me out of the road—here, let me hep' you up the creek bank to the road."

"You couldn' hep' it? You're sorry? Oh—well, that just takes care of everythi—get away from me! I'll get myself up the bank. Last thing I want is more of your hep'. You come within an inch of killin' me and you want to—Josie, you come one step closer to me and I'll whup' you with my bare hands!"

Josie looked at Elsie's hands—all bloody and swollen. They didn't look like she could do anything with them—let alone give him a good whuppin'. But, she was really mad at him right now. Yeah, he thought, better just let her crawl up the creek bank on her own. He would hang back behind her—in case she lost her balance and fell backwards. Yeah, he thought, that's a good plan. Besides—he had to get Gilly's bike out of the creek. That bike was bent up so bad it couldn't be fixed. Gilly was going to be really mad at him. She only had that bike 6 months. Alcie was mad at him—and now Gilly was gonna' be mad. How come everything was his fault, he wondered.

By then, people from nearby houses had gathered around the creek bank. They helped Alcie up the bank, amid her curses and cries of pain. She was one sight to behold. No shoes on—half the buttons on her dress torn off. One of the neighbors spread a blanket in the bed of his pick-up truck and eased Alcie on to it for a quick trip to Dr. Murray's office.

The man who owned the truck tried to lay Josie beside Alcie on the truck bed. Alcie raised up on one elbow, shouted a string of curses at Josie, and tried to take a swing at him. The truck owner moved Josie up in the cab of the truck with him.

Josie missed 3 days of work while nursing his injuries. Alcie took a little longer to recover. She had a slight concussion, two fractured fingers, a sprained ankle and knee, and a ton of scrapes and bruises. Josie told the neighbors Alcie had more black and blue skin than white for a week. Alcie was able to see out of her swollen eye 3 days after the accident.

Josie slept on the sofa for the next two weeks. He claimed Alcie was moaning so much he couldn't sleep at night. Alcie had another story about their sleeping arrangements. She said her pain pills let her sleep just fine—felt relatively little pain. Josie, she said, was sleeping on the sofa because it was difficult to get out of bed with her injuries—and her hands wouldn't reach from her 'sick' bed to Josie's neck on that sofa.

Hard to say which version of those stories was closer to the truth. One thing was true about the bike wreck. It became a chronological 'dating' point for the neighbors. For years after it happened, when neighbors were trying to pinpoint the date for some other incident in the neighborhood—they would say something like.

"Oh, it was about a week after Josie and Alcie ran in the creek on that bike"—or—"well, it was the summer Josie and Alcie wrecked that bike in the creek—".

Actually, there was one other thing you could say was true concerning the 'bike ride'. It was the last time Josie took Alcie for a bike ride.

THE CAB RIDE

Tony sat in his taxi staring through the film of dirt and dust on the windshield—at nothing. There was nothing to stare at in the town of Anawalt. Just a few buildings past their prime, and a creek. Some of the buildings were still in use—others empty. The creek was littered with bottles and cans. The low hanging limbs of scrubby trees lining the banks of the creek had odd looking pieces of used toilet tissue paper hanging here and there—courtesy of a recent, heavy, rain.

Tony mulled over his choices. He could stare—or doze off. It was so hot he didn't think he could doze. Besides—never knew when a fare might come along. He had a better chance of getting a customer if he had his eyes open. God, it was hot. It would be nice to feel a breeze, he thought. Tony's big, long, Dodge cab didn't have a fan in it. He didn't have a working radio in his cab either. He thought about having the radio fixed, but he was hardly making enough in fares to buy gas and live on. Still—it beat working in the coal mines. The mine bosses just worked a man until he dropped. And it was dark in there. Cold, wet, and dark. He hated the coal mines.

Tony reached under the seat for the pint of John Paul Jones bourbon he kept there. For the second time that morning, he felt himself in need of relief that John Paul Jones gave him. He took a long swallow. He wondered if he would have any more customers today. He only had two this morning—

and it was already past noon. He was considering calling it quits for the day. He could go home—sit on the porch—catch a breeze—take a nap until dinner. He was reaching for the starter button of his cab when he saw Alcie Perkins and Myrtle Switzer turn the corner and walk toward his cab.

Alcie and Myrtle were old friends. Myrtle had lived her entire life in Anawalt. Alcie, on reaching 18 years of age, found nothing in Anawalt that held any promise for what she wanted from life. Alcie had started her life with nothing. After 18 years she still had close to nothing. She had no intentions of having nothing after the next 18 years. She joined the Women's Army Corp. It wasn't a dream life—but it was a way out of depending on coal mining related work for a subsistence wage.

Now, she was home on furlough. Her first stop was the home of her long time 'running buddy', Myrtle Switzer. A bottle of bourbon was brought out. Myrtle and Alcie toasted their reunion—several times. Alcie wanted to visit her sister in JenkinJones—show off her new uniform. She hadn't seen her sister for almost a year. Actually, she thought, she hadn't seen any of her family for a year—or longer. She was close to her sister, Bessie. She hoped Bessie would be proud of her new uniform and what she was making of her life.

Bessie lived in JenkinJones. That was 8 miles from Anawalt. Too far to walk, and neither Myrtle nor Alcie had a car. Alcie was flush with her furlough pay. They would take a cab.

Taking a cab meant hiring Tony's cab—the only one in Anawalt. Alcie and Myrtle greeted Tony like the old friends they were. Hugs were exchanged, and they climbed in the back of the cab. Alcie told Tony to take them up to her sister's place in JenkinJones. Tony knew where her sister lived and rolled off up the narrow asphalt road.

The road rose and fell. The curves were so numerous in the road they seemed to be joined—one to another. Tony became engrossed in the conversation between Myrtle and Alcie in the back seat. The two women were a sight more interesting than the pot-hole filled road he had been over a thousand times. Tony watched Alcie and Myrtle through his rear view mirror as he drove along the road. He joined in their conversation, watching their faces in the mirror for their reaction to his comments.

As Tony passed the O'Toole neighborhood the road rose sharply up the side of a hill for 75-80 feet and leveled off. The whiskey Tony had drunk earlier was kicking in. He felt better than he had all day. Aahh, forget about watching the women through the mirror, he thought. As he crested the O'Toole hill he turned in his seat and faced the women— still steering his car along the old narrow road.

With Tony looking at Alcie and Myrtle, chatting with them, still clutching the steering wheel, and the cab moving forward at 35 mph—the car drifted slowly to the right side of the road. No one noticed the car was running off the road. Only when both right wheels of the big, old Dodge dropped over the edge of the hill and the car leaned heavily to the right with a sudden jolt did anyone realize there was trouble.

Tony's head whipped around as the car tilted sharply to the right. His eyes wide with panic, his hands clamped down on the steering wheel while he slammed both feet down on the brake and clutch. Alcie and Myrtle had already begun to scream, even before Tony's foot touched the brake pedal.

"For Christ sake Tony—watch out", screamed Myrtle.

Alcie, ever the more direct and outspoken one, yelled at Tony.

Put the brakes on! Why th' hell are you just sittin' there? Do it—put the brakes on! Oh no—watch—it's gonna' roll!"

"I got it—I got it", yelled Tony. "Just hang on now—I got— oh Lord—she's sliding—she sliding! Oh Lord—she's gonna' roll! Grab somethin'—hang on!"

Nothing Tony did slowed down the inevitable. The downhill slope of the bank was, at least 70 degrees. Darn close to a straight down drop. Once the center of the floor of the old car had dropped over the edge of the road, gravity took over. The car made a slow tilt that turned into a slow roll. After the first roll of the car, the roll picked up speed. It rolled completely over—once—twice—three times.

Through the open or broken windows of the tumbling car came screams, wails, and hysterical pleas to God for protection from injury or death. The answer was 'no' on injuries—'yes' on death. There were no seat belts in cars of that day, so the three occupants were tossed around inside the car like marbles in an empty can. Their bodies bounced off the seats, floor, roof, and doors. By the time the car was in its third roll Tony, Alcie, and Myrtle could no longer tell which side of the car was in the air and which side was against the ground.

Various pieces broke off the car and flew through the air as the car rolled down the steep embankment. One hub cap broke away from the car's wheel and sailed through the air like a Frisbee until it struck a tree over 40 feet from the bottom of the embankment.

The rumbling sound caused by the tumbling car grew louder with each roll of the car. Small trees and brush broke with loud snapping and cracking sounds as the car rolled over them. The big turret-top car flattened everything in its path without slowing at all.

Suddenly, the car stopped rolling. Whether it was Divine intervention or luck, that old Dodge came to rest on its wheels at the bottom of the steep hill. Miraculously, not one of the car doors had opened during the numerous rolls down the hill. Against all odds, when Tony opened the car's door he found himself looking down at remains of an old asphalt road that had been out of use for some years. In years past, the old road had traveled along the bottom of this hill before being replaced the present road much higher on the side of the hill. In fact, some soul had built a house on a flat area adjoining the old road—and were using the old road as their driveway out to the presently used highway. The same highway Tony would have been on—had he not rolled down that hill.

Tony, Alcie, and Myrtle and slowly crawled out of the cab and collapsed on the old road bed. They were a motley sight.

Most of Alcie's shiny, brass uniform buttons were ripped off her crisp, tan, uniform—or left hanging by a thread. Her arms and legs were covered with bloody scrapes and scratches. Her hair was drooping over her face, one eye was already swelling shut, her hat was missing, and her hose were torn and sagging around her ankles.

Myrtle had a trickle of blood running out of her nose, her eyes were unfocused, one knee was scraped, the other knee badly bruised, she had only one shoe on, one sleeve on her dress was torn loose at the shoulder, and black oil ran her bare shoulder.

Tony came out of the wreck with minor injuries. He had a small cut on one hand, a scratch on his leg, and pain in his groin because his crotch got hung on the gear shift handle during the rolls down the hill. Generally, he just looked dirty and disheveled.

The people who lived in the nearby house ran to car when

it came to a stop, virtually in their front yard. They had heard the noise—the car rolling—the screams of those inside it as it tumbled. As Alcie, Myrtle, and Tony crawled from the car the people's eyes grew wide. They had expected everyone in that car to be dead—or too hurt to move.

The good people virtually carried them to nearby lawn chairs under a shady tree. Alcie and Myrtle barely made it to the lawn chairs before collapsing in them. Limping, Tony made it on his own power. The people living there brought out soap, water, antiseptics, and helped all three clean off their wounds and bodies.

After their injuries were cleaned it was apparent to Alcie and Myrtle that they had no serious injuries. They ached—all over their bodies. Their fear of serious injuries or death behind them, they turned their wrath on Tony.

"You almost got us killed", screamed Myrtle. "Where th' hell did you learn to drive? Huh? Don't you know better'n to drive a movin' car while you're lookin' at people in the back seat?"

"Tony, you fool—look at me", growled Alcie as she slowly got to her feet and staggered toward Tony. "Listen to me, you imbecile! If my injuries cause the Army to discharge me—just throw me out of the Army—you can count on me whippin' you till you can't walk or drive! And another thing—I'll sue your ass off! I'll take ever ever last thing you own! Hey--*look* at me when I'm talkin' to you—stop starin' at the ground! Nobody drives a car while they're staring up somebody's dress in the back seat! Oh—Lord—the pain in my leg! If my knee wasn't dam near broke I'd kick your teeth out—right here and now!"

Tony could think of nothing to say. At least nothing that would satisfy Myrtle and Alcie. To him, they appeared barely able to muster any self-restraint at all—with him saying nothing.

Myrtle looked around her. Not another house was in sight of the one where they were sitting. Not a one. The people living in this house had no phone. Even if they had one, she didn't know anybody in Anawalt that had a phone—so she wouldn't know who to call. Her knee hurt too bad to walk—even out of the yard she was sitting in. If that wasn't enough, she only had one shoe on—didn't have a hair of a notion where the other one was. 'What'm I gonna' to do now', she wondered. 'Can't sit here forever', she told herself. She wondered if the people who owned this house had a gun she could use to shoot Tony. That might make her feel better.

As Myrtle looked around her gaze fell on Tony, digging at the ground with the toe of his shoe.

"Alright, Mr. Cab-Driver, you got us in this fix—you jolly well better get us out of it. And don't even think about suggestin' we walk out of here. Stop standin' there, diggin' in th' dirt with your shoe! Do somethin'—'fore I 'brain' you with a rock!"

Tony had no idea what to do, but he wasn't going to tell Myrtle that. To gain a little time and make it appear he was trying to do something positive, he shuffled back to the cab. He made a big show of looking under the car—raising the hood to examine the engine. He didn't know why he was looking at on the engine. He wasn't a mechanic. He closed the hood of the car.

Tony climbed in the car and sat down under the steering wheel. The ignition key was still in the 'On' position. He pushed the clutch out and pressed the starter button. The engine turned over, but the engine didn't start. He tried again. On his second attempt, the big engine came to life and ran smoothly. Tony couldn't have been more surprised if he had just been named head of the State Liquor Commission. He covered his surprise well.

"Well—you said you wanted to go someplace. You gonna' get in, or what?" he said smugly. "Come on, I ain't got all day."

Myrtle and Alcie sat there, speechless. Not in their wildest dreams did they think that old cab would run again—ever. They looked at each other. Did they dare get back in the cab with that fool Tony under the wheel? If not, what were they going to do, stuck out here in the middle of nowhere— with no other way out? They knew they couldn't trust Tony to send help. At that moment, neither of them would have trusted Tony—not even with 25 lbs of cow dung. There was no real *choice*. They got in the cab.

Fifteen minutes later, Tony stopped in front of Alcie's sister's house. Family members and church friends were gathered there for a big Sunday dinner. As the cab slid to a stop, every eye in and around the house was on it. Every voice stopped. None of them had seen anything like it. A car without a single piece of metal on it that didn't have dents, scratches, or holes in it. The roof was flattened, the windshield was missing, both headlights were broken, not one hub cap on the car, and every wheel on the car was bent and wobbling.

The stares turned to Myrtle and Alcie as the rear door opened and they slowly crawled from the back seat. Both were bloody and bruised. Their clothes were filthy, torn, and their nylons were hanging around their ankles. Their hair hung in disarray about their faces. One of them was wearing only one shoe.

Alcie slammed the car door shut. She stood unsteadily on the sidewalk as she and Myrtle muttered a few last curses at Tony. They leaned on each other for support as they made their way up the walk to the front porch of her sister's house. People standing in the yard saw the menacing looks on the faces and in the eyes of Alcie and Myrtle—and decided not to ask any questions.

Alcie's sister was more of a commanding presence. When Alcie saw the questioning look in her sister's eyes she spoke quietly to her.

"Bessie—don't say a word. Please—not one question—not yet. Just give Myrtle and me some coffee and aspirin. It's a long story and I'm not going to be able to talk until I first get some aspirin in me for the pain. I will say this. Don't ever call that fool Tony to take you anywhere, unless you are just plain tired of living.

Word gets around quickly in small communities. For weeks people drove down to O'Toole Hill to see where Tony rolled Alcie and Myrtle down the hill in his cab. The story became legendary.

THE FRIDAY NIGHT BATH

Joe and Edna Falkey called JenkinJones home. Joe worked in the No. 8 coal mines at JenkinJones Coal Co. It was a typical coal mining town. There was a coal loading tipple, a company owned general merchandise store, a post office, an ice cream parlor, a small movie theatre, a church, an elementary school, and 140-150 residential homes.

The houses were built and owned by JenkinJones Coal Co. They were rented to men who worked in their mines. Most all homes were built from one of 3 or 4 patterns, and were modest no-frills homes. All had water piped into the kitchen of the house, but not all included indoor bathrooms. Water was heated by a coal burning stove.

In those homes without a bathroom, bathing was done by placing a galvanized tub—normally used for laundering clothes—in the kitchen floor and filling it with hot water heated on the kitchen's coal burning stove. The routine for bathing in this tub was simple. You removed your clothes, knelt on your knees on the floor, leaned over the tub to wash your face and hair, then climbed, bodily, into the tub to bathe the rest of your body. This routine for bathing was a part of the daily life of Joe and Edna Falkey in their JenkinJones company owned home..

Payday for employees of JenkinJones was at the end of the

work day on Fridays. Joe collected his wages at the company office's 'pay window'. As he often did, Joe moved directly from the pay-window to a car parked nearby where he bought a pint of cheap whiskey from a bootlegger. Without hesitation, Joe celebrated Friday and payday by swallowing a half-pint of whiskey. Whiskey did two things to Joe. It made him feel warm inside, and it brought out the mouthy, ill-tempered side of him.

When Joe came through the kitchen door of his house Edna was pouring his bath water in a wash tub on the kitchen floor. The tub wasn't completely filled with water, it wasn't as hot as Joe liked the water to be, and the air in the kitchen felt cold to him. As Joe stripped for his bath he got in a bad mood real quick. Between all these aggravations and the whiskey's effects on him—it was too much for him to bear quietly.

"You know, I work all day long in a cold, dark, hole in the ground. I come home lookin' for a warm room and a hot bath. That ain't a lot to ask. If you'd get off your lazy butt and do somethin' for change, I'd be bathin' now instead of standin' here freezin' my balls off", snarled Joe.

Not one to accept verbal abuse quietly, Edna gave 'lip' about as good as she got it.

"If you don't like the way I'm doin' things you can just kiss my ass and do it yourself, you sorry drunk!" yelled Edna. Joe's answer to Edna's remark was swift. His arm shot out in an arc that backhanded Edna against the kitchen table and sent her tumbling over a chair. Edna and the chair both came to rest lying in the kitchen floor. Edna was stunned for a moment. Her vision, blurred at first, came into focus as she saw Joe standing over her.

"Now—by god! Don't you say another word! Not one word! You get over to that stove, put some more coal on that far', and get more heat in this dam room—right now", bellowed Joe.

Without a word, Edna stood up. She went to the stove and poured more coal on the top of the bed of red hot coals already glowing in the stove. Then she stuck the iron stove poker, about 2 feet along, in the stove and began stirring the red hot coals with it.

Joe, satisfied Edna had gotten his message, knelt on the floor, tore the wrapper of a new bar of *Sweetheart* bath soap—about 8 ounces and shaped like a football—and dropped his entire head into the tub of water. He pulled his head out of the water and, with his eyes squeezed tightly shut, worked up a good lather of soap over his hair and face. He scrubbed vigorously to clean the black coal dust off his face.

Defeat did not come easily to Edna. The whole time Joe was lathering soap over his face and head, Edna left the iron stove poker among the red hot coals in the stove. When she was satisfied Joe's face was full of soap and his eyes shut tightly, Edna pulled the fiery hot poker from the stove. Timing was everything for what she had in mind for Joe.

Just as Joe bent over the tub of water to rinse the soap off his face, Edna stepped up behind him and slapped the red hot poker against his bare butt.

"There—take that! How do *you* like it? Huh? Wanna' hit me again? I got some more of this poker for you—right here! I'll stick it up your mean ass!"

The scream from Joe could be heard for a distance of 2 houses in every direction from his house. His eyes bulged open. Soap ran into his eyes, stinging so bad he was forced to shut them again. He sprang to his feet. One hand gripping a painfully burned butt cheek—the other still locked around the bar of *Sweetheart* soap. He took his hand off his throbbing butt long enough to take a towel and wipe the soap out of his eyes. The first thing he saw when he got the soap out of his eyes was a defiant Edna—standing with the poker still in her hand.

"Edna—bygod—I'm gonna' teach you a lesson you won't forget! I'm gonna' whup you good and proper! And I'm gonna' use that there poker to do it!"

Edna's bravado faded quickly—and reality hit home even quicker. She realized she had gone too far to satisfy her anger. She knew Joe was angry and drunk enough to actually beat her with the poker.

Without hesitation, Edna threw the poker at Joe, jerked open the door leading to their back yard, dived through the door, jumped from their back porch into the yard, and began running around their house. Joe dodged the thrown poker and raced, butt naked, into the yard after Edna. He was so angry and in such pain that his nakedness was of no concern to him at the moment.

Edna had a small advantage in this foot race over the cold grass, dirt, and rocks that made up the yard around their house. She had a 15 foot lead on Joe, and shoes on her feet. The only thing Joe had was that new football-shaped bar of *Sweetheart* soap, still tightly clenched in his right hand. Both raced around the house—three or four times.

"Hep'! Somebody hep' me, please! Joe's trying to kill me! He's a-gonna' kill me", screamed Edna as she raced around the house. "Joe—oh god—please, Joe! I didn't mean to do that to you! I'm sorry—swear to god— sorry as I can be! I don't know what come over me—you hittin' me like that just made me crazy", pleaded Edna over her shoulder as she continued to race around the house.

Joe ignored her pleas as he raced after her. He was oblivious to the neighbors, standing in their yards, listening to Edna scream, and watch a stark naked Joe chase after her. Some of them shouted encouragement to Joe or Edna, depending on where their loyalties lay.

"Edna, you better stop runnin' from me! You better stop right now—c'mere and take your whuppin'! You make me run you down—I'll *really* whup your ass—till you can't get out of bed for a week! You hear me? I mean it—you better stop—right now!"

Edna strongly suspected Joe wasn't going to show her any restraint or mercy—whether she stopped running or not. On the other hand, she reasoned, so long as she could outrun Joe—the whuppin' was, at the very least, delayed. Maybe he would get so tired he couldn't give her a whuppin'—if she could just keep him runnin' til she wore him down. She kept on running.

After the fifth or sixth trip around the house Joe realized he wasn't closing the distance between Edna and him that much. The rocks in the yard were hurting his feet, something awful. He just couldn't run fast enough to catch her.

When Joe turned the corner of the house he had Edna in sight for about 4-5 steps before she turned the next corner and went out of his sight. Joe decided to use a desperation tactic. With Edna in sight, Joe still running at full speed, he drew back his right hand and threw the bar of *Sweetheart* soap at her as hard as he could.

The Gods were on Joe's side. The bar of football shaped soap flew through the air like a guided missile. It caught Edna in the back of the head just before she turned the next corner of the house. Edna's body dropped like a rock. Unconscious before she hit the ground.

"He done cold-cocked her", said the neighbor nearest Edna's unconscious form. Edna lay where she fell—on her back, face up, eyes closed.

Joe raced to where Edna lay and gave her a swift kick in her tail with his bare foot. Joe cursed Edna and yelled what he intended to do to her for burning him with the poker. After a minute had passed, with no response from Edna, it occurred to Joe that Edna was not pleading for mercy. In fact, she hadn't said a word or moved a muscle since she fell to the ground. Not even when he gave her a kick in the behind.

'What th' hell's a-goin' on here', mumbled Joe as he knelt over her body. He looked closely at her closed eyes. He shook her body—twice, with no response from Edna. Not a sound—not a movement.

Fear gripped Joe. Lord—suppose he had killed her. Panic raced through him. He thought of having to go to jail— maybe even get the electric chair—for killing his wife. His neighbors had been witnesses to it.

"Edna, honey—get on up now, honey. You alright, honey?" pleaded Joe as he began to stroke and pat her face. "I didn't mean to hurt you, sweetheart. You know 'ol Joe was just upset. I didn't mean none of them things I said. You know that. C'mon now, lemme' hep' you back in the house."

While Joe was trying to coach some sign of life from Edna he noticed hovering neighbors staring at his nakedness. Hardly any of them were looking at Edna. A few looked concerned for Edna, but most of them were grinning at the naked Joe and about the 'show' they had just witnessed. A few didn't give a hoot, one way or the other—about Joe or Edna.

"What th' hell you lookin' at? Huh? This ain't none of your business. Git' th' hell back in your own houses! Mind your own dam business!" yelled Joe

"Why don't you and that crazy wife of yours act like you got some sense? Then nobody would be lookin' at you", replied one of the men as they drifted back to their houses.

Joe was ready to go across the fence after the man when he heard a moan from Edna.

Joe dropped to ground, raised her to a sitting position, wrapped his arms around her, and began telling her how much he loved her. He was so relieved Edna hadn't 'gone 'n died' on him that he forgave her for burning him with the poker.

Edna was so elated to find she wasn't going to get a whuppin' with a poker she forgave Joe for knocking her out with the bar of soap—even if she did have a splitting headache.

The neighbors watched a naked Joe, supporting an unsteady Edna, cross their yard and disappear into the house. Both of them were laughing when they closed the door behind them.

THE CHASE

Josie was smiling. He stood in the kitchen of his house. He felt good when he got up that morning. It was going to be a good day. He could just feel it in his bones. The air was cool and crisp. The sun was shining. Not a cloud in the sky. Yes sir, if there was ever a day for hunting this was it. Josie loved being in the woods with his rifle and dog. Just sitting, watching, listening—hoping for that one good shot at game. BLAM! Just that one shot and he could have meat on his table. Squirrel, rabbit, maybe even a deer. Why, his family could eat for a week if he could bag a good size buck.

Josie heard the 'work' whistle blowing at the mine tipple. His head dropped. A scowl crossed his face. That whistle meant he should be 'signing in' for his job at the mines— right now. Josie had been working in the mines for a year. He didn't like it. It wasn't natural, he told himself. A man just wasn't meant to be working in a dark, cold, wet, dirty hole in the ground.

Some of the men in the neighborhood who worked with Josie said it wasn't the dark or the dirty part of the mines that bothered him. It was the idea that he was expected to work, every day, for the money he was being paid by the coal company. It was the opinion of his fellow miners that Josie didn't dislike the coal mining in particular. He just didn't like WORK period.
Josie knew the men thought he was lazy. It didn't bother

him. They were just wrong in their thinking. He didn't mind work—didn't mind it at all. Why, he had worked all his life. He left school early to go to work and help his family. And the hitch he pulled in the Army—that was purely hard work. No sir, he didn't mind work. What he minded was working ALL the time.

Matter of fact, Josie wasn't sure he liked the idea of working five days a week—sometimes six—for weeks and months on end. He recalled hearing a Preacher say that a man should rest on Sunday. Just because he didn't mention those other days of the week didn't mean the Lord didn't want a man to take a break on week days—now and then. No sir. When Josie got up on a beautiful day like this, it was clear to him that the Lord was inviting him—no—*telling* him to spend time in the woods. God was offering to let him have, maybe with only one bullet, meat on his table for a week. He would have to work in the mines for a week to earn enough money to buy the meat he could get from one deer. Josie listened to reason—the Lord's reason. He walked in his house picked up his rifle, and yelled to Alcie that he was going hunting. With his dogs at his heels, he walked into the woods—a happy man.

When Josie didn't show up for work it meant his work crew was one man short. It also meant others crew members would have to work a little harder to cover Josie's absence and keep up with the company's schedule for moving coal out of the mountain and on to coal cars.

One of Josie's work crew was his brother in law, Burt. Burt

had never liked Josie. However, to help his sister, Alcie, keep a roof over her head and food on the table—he used his influence in the miners' union to get Josie a job the company's number 8 mines. It paid good money and qualified Josie for tenancy in a company house near the mines. There were close to 200 such houses near the mines. Burt rented one of the houses himself—about 200 feet down the road from Josie's house.

The day passed—with Josie lounging in the woods and having no luck in catching any game at all. The day passed for Burt too—working hard with the rest of Josie's work crew to cover Josie's absence and keep coal flowing out of the mine at the usual pace.

When Burt got home from work he was tired and angry. He sat on his front porch, sipping ice tea and wondering where th' hell Josie was and what his lame excuse for not showing up at work would be this time. The more he thought about it the angrier he became.
Burt heard whistling coming from his left, on the road in front of his house. He leaned forward on the porch banister and looked down to the road—to see Josie strolling up the road with a rifle over his shoulder.

Burt was livid. Here he was, sitting on his porch with his back aching from a hard day in the mines—and that sorry-assed Josie was walking up the road without a care in the world. Well—Burt was going to speak his mind to Josie about it.
"Hey—if you had come to work today, instead of fartin'

around in the woods—without a thing to show for it—the rest of the crew wouldn't have had to work our asses off to cover for you—you lazy SOB!", shouted Burt from his porch.

Josie was upset with Burt—for running the end of a good day for him—and shaming him in front of all the other neighbors, who heard every word Burt said. Josie wasn't going to let that pass.

"You're not the boss of me! If you don't like me missing work you can just kiss my ass!" Josie yelled defiantly.

Josie's reply to Burt was the last straw. First Josie skipped worked—and then he taunted Burt for calling his hand on it. Burt decided the time had come to teach Josie a lesson.

Burt's porch banister railing was supported by closely spaced 2" x 2" wooden palings about 30 inches long nailed to the banister. Without hesitating, Louie reached down, grabbed one of the wooden palings, physically ripped it away from the banister, ran down the steps of his porch— paling raised above his head—and shouted to Josie.

"You tell me to kiss your ass? I tell you what I *am* a-gonna' do—I'm a-gonna take this here paling and whup your ass till you can't walk! C'mere!" yelled Burt as he ran toward Josie.

Josie didn't hesitate. He began running up the narrow asphalt road toward his own home—as fast as his legs would carry him. Josie didn't know exactly how fast he could run, but with Louie no more than 30 feet behind him, screaming threats while he waved a big piece of wood in his hand—he was about to find out what his top speed was.

Josie reached the front yard of his house still 15 feet in front of Burt. Trouble was, 15 feet of distance between him and Burt wouldn't give him enough to open his front door, dive through it, shut and lock the door before Burt got within reach of his body with that paling in his hand.

Without slowing one step, Josie began to run through his yard, around the rear corner of his house, and back to the front of his house. Josie continued to run around and around his house while he tried to think of some way to get in his house before Burt could reach him with that paling. Suddenly, the answer appeared to him—right before his eyes—ALCIE! Hearing all the shouting from the two men as they raced around the house, she came out on the front porch and began screaming at Burt not to hit Josie. Burt paid no attention to her. He continued to chase Josie— gaining a step on him in every trip around the house.

The whole time he had been racing around his house Josie had been screaming 'OW-SIE—OW-SIE—H'EP ME, OW-SIE'!

As Josie raced passed his front porch—for the 5th time—he shouted to Alcie.

"Hold that dam' door open, Owsie—I'm goin' round one more time!"
On the next trip past the front of the house Josie leaped up

on the front porch in a single bound, dived inside the front door Alcie was holding open, Alcie slammed the door shut, and rammed the dead bolt lock into place one second before Burt's hand twisted the front door knob.

For a few minutes Burt stood on the porch, cursing Josie, challenging him to be man enough to come out of the house and face him like a man. Josie didn't come out of the house. In truth, he wouldn't have come out of that house with a gun at his back. Not with Burt beating on his front door with that wooden paling.

After a few minutes, when it was obvious Josie wasn't coming out of the house, Burt gave the front door of Josie's house one more, good round-house slam with that wooden paling and walked off down the road to his own home. Every few feet Burt would look over his shoulder at Josie house and shout a promise of vengeance the next time he laid eyes on Josie.

The only thing that kept Burt from keeping his word about giving Josie a good going over was the company Mine Boss interceding. He got Josie to apologize to Burt, told them both he wanted that to be the end of it, and made them shake hands. Burt still held a grudge over the matter for many years.

Josie was eventually laid off from his job at the mines—for excessive absenteeism and unacceptable work habits.

GET ME TO THE CHURCH ON TIME

During the mid-1970s, there was a guy in our neighborhood who was Director of Sales for a local firm that made church furniture and stained glass windows. His name was Ray. He was a good man and a good neighbor. Like most of us, he had some habits which caused him a bit of distress from time to time. Ray's 'problem' habit was being late for appointments. The major cause of his being late was taking on too many tasks to perform in too little time.

Ray was Vice President of Eschbach Church Furniture's sales division for their entire territory—which was the entire Atlantic Seaboard, from New England to Florida—and west to a line that ran from Arkansas to Iowa. Sounds like too much geography for one man. In fact, Ray had salesmen that covered the various states. There weren't that many makers of church furniture—even less of stained glass. His salesmen got word of churches building or re-modeling , visited the churches, took careful measurements of the area involved, listened what the church members desired in terms of pews, altars, stained glass, carpeting, and submitted all of this to the Eschbach factory.

Eschbach completed the design and drawing details, had a Commercial Artist do scale model color pictures of what the church sanctuary would look like if Eschbach was given the job, and computed a bid-price on the job. The salesman returned to the 'customer-church'—exhibited the proposed drawings and design of pews, altars, carpet, and stained glass, quoted a the bid price—got the job—or didn't.

Ray had a hard time trusting his sales people to make a winning sales 'pitch' of Eschbach's proposed design and price for a job—especially when a lot of money was at stake. Ray felt no one could sell Eschbach's design, proposal and price with the impact, enthusiasm, and success he could. He was *positive* he could sell their proposals at the bid price, if *he* could *personally* speak to any church's Building Committee.

In truth, Ray *was* a dynamic and charismatic speaker. Problem was, he already had plenty to do at the factory— overseeing the design and pricing, of various proposals and jobs that came in and went out daily from and to the vast territory covered by Eschbach. He didn't have enough free time left in his work day to personally run around to every state east of the Mississippi giving *personal* 'closing' presentations to church building committees.

Did I mention that Ray was also very determined? He attended a lot of sale 'closing' presentations around the country—whether he had the time or not.

Ray made room in his schedule to make these personal presentations by cutting down on the travel time normally required to get from his factory to whatever town in whatever state the 'customer church' was located. Let me clarify the last sentence. Ray exceeded the posted highway speed limit—flagrantly. A trip to, say, Atlanta from his factory—averaging 50-55 mph—normally took 8 hours, by car. Ray would do the trip it in 6 ½ hours—which included a last minute tire-squealing stop in front of the church.

Ray had a big Buick *RoadMaster* Station Wagon. On the day of a trip to some distant church, he would come tearing into his driveway, pick up his clothes and shaving kit, throw them in the car, and roar off down the street. His entire car, from the back of the front seat to the rear window, would be filled with easels, charts, color drawings of pews, stained glass windows—even a 3 foot square poster-board panoramic, color rendering of what the entire church sanctuary would look like if Eschbach were awarded the contract to furnish this church. These drawings were beautiful—captivated your attention—whether or not you were a Church Building Committee that was considering making these breath-taking drawings a reality in your next church sanctuary.

When Ray roared out of his driveway at noon-time on this particular day, he was already an hour behind schedule for covering the 8 hour drive to an Atlanta suburb in time for the 7 pm meeting with the Board of Deacons and the Building Committee. Undaunted, he hit the road—with his car's accelerator mashed to the floor and the engine howling. Amazingly, Ray had only received one speeding ticket in 8 years of rocketing up and down the East Coast at speeds of 85-90 mph. He assumed, since he was doing so in the interest of furnishing 'God's Houses', he would enjoy the same 'Divine Immunity' from police interference on this day.

Ray cruised down the street in the sprawling Georgia town where the church was located at 7:15 pm. He was only 15 minutes late. He would use 'traffic' as his excuse if the church members raised the issue of his tardiness for the appointment. He hustled down the street as fast as he could while still looking right and left for the church. He saw a church ahead—built on a small hill eight feet above the street. Yes—there was a man standing at the church's front door, peering up and down the street, as if looking for him..

Ray pulled to a stop on the street close to the church, hopped out, and waved to the man standing in front of the church. The man waved back, smiled, and trotted down the steps to meet Ray. Ray was pulling his visual aids out of the back of his Buick when the man from the church walked up to him, with his hand extended.

"Good evening, sir. Are you the man we have been waiting for?" said the man.

"Yes indeed—I certainly am", said Ray as he gave the man a big smile and firm hand shake. "I apologize for being late—the traffic was just awful this evening. But, I'm delighted to be here. I've been looking forward to talking to the good people of your church for some time. I'm excited about it. I think I can do some wonderful things for your church. I truly believe you are going to be very happy with the message and good news I bring you and your church."

"That's wonderful! We're looking forward to hearing your

message. It's a blessing to have you in our church this evening. Your things—do you need help in carrying some things inside the church? You seem to have your arms full."

"Thank you—and yes, I certainly can use your help. I brought some color renderings—drawings if you will—that I feel will help the people of the church understand what I've got to say and why."

"Praise God! I can see you're a man who wants his message to enter every heart! Let me help you and we'll get right into the church."

The man helped Ray carry all his boards, easels, pictures, and color drawings up the steep steps from the sidewalk and into the church sanctuary. As they entered the sanctuary Ray was surprised to see 40-45 people sitting in the pews near the front of the church. Wow, he thought, not only is this a big building committee, but every last one of them must be here. That's mean's they are interested in what I have to offer. I'll give them a primo presentation— lay it all out for them. I'll have a signed contract for this proposal before I leave town, he told himself.

Ray quickly set up three easels, on which he mounted large, professionally done color renderings of every stained glass window Eschbach proposed to install in a sanctuary. He had two different sets of color drawings that offered a stunning, panoramic, view of what Eschbach could do for them in the way of comfortable pews and an inspiring altar. The lighting on the color picture of the stained glass behind the altar and minister's podium offered a dramatic and moving appearance of Christ with his arms outstretched—in a welcoming appearance. When Ray had his pictures set up along the entire front of the sanctuary he nodded to the Minister to signal his readiness to speak.

The Minister gave a short prayer of gratitude for Ray's presence, and asked for blessings upon Ray, his message, and the Brethren there to hear his message.

Ray began by thanking all those present for being there, for coming out after a day of work to hear what he had to say, and for joining him in his attempt to make their church one that would be a testament of the church members' love of the Lord.

"Amen, brother!", cried out one of the church members. Ray was a bit surprised by the man's outcry. He was used to silence, questions, and a nod or two when he did a presentation. Man, he thought, they're getting into this thing—and I haven't gotten warmed up yet.

Ray called the church member's attention to the beautiful and large color drawing he had paid a professional artist to do of the huge stained glass window that would cover almost the entire wall behind the pulpit. It was a picture of Christ—looking down—with his hands open, palms upturned, and arms extended. It was, truly, a beautiful thing to behold—especially in its 3' x3' size.

"This drawing of Christ symbolizes one of the central

messages of his ministry—'Come to Me—with your troubles—your worries—for refuge—for—", said Ray, before he was cut off by a shout from another of the people sitting in the pews.

"Word of the Lord!", cried out another man sitting in the pews.

"Indeed", nodded Ray. "These windows are not just windows. They depict and memorialize the greatness, goodness, and work of God and his son—as they healed—fed thousands—saved those lost and—".

"Amen! Tell it like it is!" shouted another church member, as he jumped to his feet.

"Uh—yes. I certainly will—and thank you", agreed Ray. "These beautiful stained glass side-windows you see here—they depict the ministry of Jesus during his performance of miracles. Here we have him healing the blind—in this window we see him feed the multitudes from a meager ration of bread and fish—and here we see him raising the dead—."

"Jee-sus!" cried out another man. His declaration was followed by a loud chorus of 'Amens' from half the congregation.

Ray continued speaking for the next 10 minutes, trying to explain the meaning and symbolism of the side windows—the huge 10' X 12' central stained glass—the proposed

bow-shaped seating arrangement of the sanctuary pews—
the deep maroon carpeting throughout the sanctuary.

The next five minutes of his remarks were constantly
interrupted by shouts of affirmations and declarations—as
the loud cries from the church members rolled across the
sanctuary with increasing frequency and volume. The
verbal enthusiasm of the congregation reached the point
where Ray hardly got out a dozen words of a sentence
before his comments were lost in the vigorous cries of
"Hallelujah", "Praise God", "Jee-sus", 'Amen", from the
excited parishioners. To compound Ray's problems, the
church members began to joyously clap their hands and
wave their arms over their heads. One church member
finished his verbal outburst with a short dance-step in the
isle of the church. One soul began bouncing about in the
pew with a jerking motion that suggested he was fully
engaged in an epileptic seizure.

During the last five minutes of his presentation Ray stopped
speaking completely at times—to let the church members
reign in their emotions and quiet down enough to hear his
remarks. At the twenty minute mark in his presentation he
gave up trying to talk. Too many of the church member
were constantly yelling, clapping their hands, jumping up
and down, dancing, and loudly petitioning the spirit of the
Deity to be with them.

Ray saw no need to continue. A good salesman knew when
to stop—avoid 'overkill' in a presentation. The church
members showed incredible enthusiasm for the color

drawings of the pews, the stained glass windows, and well—everything he shown them and talked about. More than that, the verbal and physical involvement of the church members in the meeting made it impossible for him to even hear himself talk. Ray stood nodding and smiling at those in the pews—waiting for them to quiet down. After a couple of minutes, Ray took advantage of a brief lull in the congregational demonstrations to speak once more.

"Folks—folks! I believe I have said everything I came here to say to you tonight. I appreciate the warm welcome and hospitality you have shown me this evening. I'm going to invite your minister to offer a closing prayer—then I'm going to clear out of here, go to my hotel, and let you good people think about, talk about, and pray about all the information I have shared with you this evening. I trust you understood everything I said, but if there are any questions you can contact me at the Holiday Inn here in town. I'll be there overnight, before returning to my home tomorrow. I hope to hear from you real soon. Thank you, and God bless all in this room."

The minister's closing prayer was stirring. It included the entire church body's gratitude for Ray's message. He implored the Lord to bless Ray and see to his safe keeping.

Ray loaded all of his visual aids and material in his Buick, and drove the 6-7 miles to the Holiday Inn. When he checked in, the man at the desk said, "Oh, you're Mr. Burton. I sure am glad to see you. I've got a bunch of messages here for you. Some Preacher has been calling for you every 2-3 minutes for the past 30 minutes. Here's his phone number."

Ray was ecstatic. All these messages from the Preacher—those guys must have taken a vote and come up with a 'yes' to my proposal before I was out of sight of the church, thought Ray. I knew they were enthusiastic about my presentation, but, Lord, I didn't think the vote would be that quick, he mused.

Ray dialed the number from the message slip and the phone was answered on the first ring.

"Yes, hello?"

"Reverend Pitsinger? Ray Burton here—returning your calls from earlier this evening. What can I do for you, sir?"

"Well—I'd say it's what you *could* have done, Mr. Burton. I don't know that you can do much of *anything*, now—after skipping your appointment with our Board of Deacons and church Building Committee this evening. Frankly, I'm very disappointed with your conduct in this matter."

"Wait a minute—if you please, Reverend. I can tell from the tone of your voice that you are upset. What don't understand is 'why'. I kept my appointment with you. I spoke to your people, outlined my proposal—right in your own church—not 35 minutes ago."

"Oh—come now, Mr. Burton! Your failure to keep

appointment is one thing. Denying your failure is another. Especially when you tell me you spoke to me and our church officials earlier this evening. Sir, how can you expect me to believe such an obvious and blatant falsehood? I had 17 people in church tonight—who waited for 45 minutes past the appointed time you had set to present your company's proposal for selling our church some furniture, carpet, and stained glass windows. Are you telling me you were there—on time—you spoke to us, when *not a one of us* saw or heard you?"

"Reverend Pitsinger—I don't know what to say to you. I am not losing my mind and I'm not trying to cover a missed appointment with a lie. I was in your church—you met me at the front door—you helped carry my equipment up those steep steps, you helped set up my drawings of our proposal for furniture and stained glass for your church. You offered a beautiful opening prayer, and I've never had a presentation received more enthusiastically by 35-40 church members in all my years of making presentations to churches. I—"

"Wait—wait just a minute, Mr. Burton! We don't have any *steep* steps in front of our church. There were only 17 people in our church to hear you tonight—not 35-40. Something—something is not right here. What street do you have as the address for our church?"

"Uh—yes, here it is— 326 Bollinger Street—and I was on Bollinger Street—I looked at the street sign when I turned onto Bollinger."

"What did our church look like, Mr. Burton? Can you describe the outside of the church you went to?"

"Yes sir. Your church is built on a hill about 8 feet above the street, it is made of a light colored brick, the door and windows are trimmed in white paint---"

"Mr. Burton, my church, *THE CHURCH OF GOD*, is made of limestone. The church and parking lot are at street level. The parking lot, alone, covers two acres. My church is located at 826 Bollinger Street. From your description of the church you were in this evening—I'd almost guarantee you were in the CHURCH OF GOD *OF* **PROPHECY**, which is located at 326 Bollinger Street. I know that church and the minister fairly well, and I'd say that is who you spoke to."

"Reverend Pitsinger—I don't know what to say. You certainly ought to know the churches and ministers in the area. But—my gosh—the minister said his people were waiting to hear *me* speak. They listened to my presentation—which I had to close after 20 minutes because the church members were yelling and clapping so loudly to demonstrate their enthusiasm for what I said. I could hardly hear myself talk over all the shouting. How could they sit there and not realize---"

"Mr. Burton, this is Wednesday night—a traditional night for Prayer Meetings in most Protestant churches. Actually, we moved our own Prayer Meeting up an hour so we would be done by the time you arrived to make your presentation.

It is just a guess, but I expect the Church of God of *Prophecy* was waiting for a guest speaker for their prayer meeting when you showed up at their church. As for the shouting and enthusiasm exhibited at your presentation—well, the Church of God of *Prophecy members* are what we call 'charismatic'. That is, they believe in verbally and physically venting their feelings <u>during</u> a service. In the Church of God, the congregation doesn't exhibit such verbal or physical displays during the services."

"You mean those people thought I was delivering a religious message—a sermon—, even when I was showing them big color pictures of stained glass windows and sanctuary furniture? Not one soul realized it was a sales presentation, not a sermon?"

"Maybe you are a good speaker. Maybe your visual pictures, not usually included in a minister's sermon, were enough to bring the good people of that church to a height of emotion a bit out of the ordinary—even for them. Maybe they thought your visuals were to buttress a sermon you were giving. Look, I understand what happened now— even as unbelievable as it sounds. If you want to stay in town for an extra day, I'll try to get my people back together for a meeting tomorrow evening. When I tell them what happened, I may not have any trouble at all getting them here again. I suspect every last one of them will want to see and hear a man who delivered a prayer meeting sermon to the Church of God of Prophecy and didn't even realize he was doing it."

Ray did stay in town and made his presentation to the *correct* church the following evening. He could do little but laugh along with the members of that church's Board of Deacons when they ribbed him about 'preaching without a license'. The story does have a good ending. The Church of God did buy their church furniture and stained glass windows from Ray.

This story should have a 'lesson learned' message for Ray. It doesn't. Ray left late for an appointment in Kentucky two weeks later. He said he would make up the time on the highway.

Mutter

The highway sign said the name of the village was Rock Branch. It was located on a curvy, narrow road 9 miles off the nearest major highway, about 20 miles from, well—everything. It's only industry, and, in truth, its sole reason for existence, was mining a type of rock called slate or 'soapstone'. A vein of slate ran just below the surface of the ground for a depth of 400 feet, in a quarter mile width, by a half mile length.

The slate was used for laboratory tables and wash basins in high school science class rooms, hospitals, mortician's preparation rooms, research and development labs, and bathroom shower walls across most of the entire United States and a good many foreign countries. Some of the more elaborately designed office buildings in major cities chose large, milled, highly polished, slabs of the slate for exterior wall finishing on the lower floors. Many municipal buildings chose it for the surface of their lobby floors and stairs.

There was enough slate in the ground at Rock Branch and enough demand for it to entice the Green Stone Slate Co to build 50-60 frame homes, called 'company houses', to lure employees to the rather isolated and uninviting terrain where the slate deposit was located. They also built a large building in the center of the village that housed the Green Stone Slate Co. General Store.

They had little choice. There were few cars in that area during the 1920-30s. The roads suitable for automobiles were few in number. Those that existed were composed of dirt or gravel and were poorly maintained. Also—there wasn't another General Merchandise store within 20 miles of Rock Branch. Coincidentally, selling their employees food to live on and clothes to wear allowed Green Stone Slate Company to fatten their profits by taking back a good portion of the salaries paid to employees working in their slate quarry.

As is true of the site of most rock deposits, Rock Branch was located in a hilly area. The trees were clear cut from close, 'bowl' shaped hills surrounding the slate quarry. Houses were built on one end of the 'bowl'…the quarry was located on the opposite end. Living in Rock Branch was akin to living in a giant coliseum. Every one living there could see each other's closely spaced houses, the store, and most activity that took place. Sound carried clearly as it caromed off the hills and houses in the 'bowl'. The 300 or so souls living in Rock Branch often ended summer days by sitting on their own front porches and conversing with each other—without having to raise their voices.

Like most small towns, Rock Branch had a 'unique' or 'character' citizen. In Rock Branch's case, it was the colorful Mrs. Roxie White, aka, 'Mutter'.
No one could say exactly when, where, how, or why Roxie's Christian name was displaced by the nick-name of 'Mutter'. Everyone just called her Mutter. This included her husband and six children. Her husband died early—in his 58th year.

Shortly after the untimely death of her late husband, Mutter received a letter from Green Stone Slate Co informing her of (1) Its intent to cease operations due to decreasing profits and demand for their product (2) Their offer to sell her the house she was renting from them.

Rock Branch was Mutter's chosen home—where she raised her children. She had more friends, relatives, and acquaintances around Rock Branch than elsewhere. Upon his death, Mutter's husband had left her the proceeds of a small Life Insurance policy. It was enough to bury him, buy her house in Rock Branch, and put a little aside for future 'hard times'. Mutters became the sole owner of her house in Rock Branch 60 days after the company's offer.

Green Stone Slate Co. sold the 'Company Store' to someone who continued to operate it, albeit on a cash basis. Muddlers had a roof over her head, heat and water in the house, a TV, a grocery store 75 yards from her front door, and a modest income from Social Security. A small world in 1962, but it satisfied Mutter's needs.

Thirty eight years slid by and the year 2000 arrived in Rock Branch so quickly Muddlers couldn't rightfully recall how it all happened. Except for some impact events, like deaths, winter storms, the death of her beloved dog, and neighbor, Abner Collins, catching a wicked dose of the clapp at 66 years of age—she couldn't recollect a lot of events since she bought the 'home place' in '62.

Her kids moved away when they grew up, but came to see her from time to time. She had a bunch of grand- children couldn't remember all their names—or how many there were. Mutter supposed most Grandparents didn't know the names of all their Grandchildren. Didn't see them all that much anyway—so how could she be expected you to remember all those names?

Mutter's children got their first notice of Mutter's 'memory problems' in the spring of 2000. Her youngest son and his wife came all the way from Florida to visit Mutter. He brought his three month old son for his very first visit with 'Granny Mutter'.

Mutter's son and wife walked through her front yard, his son under one arm, a play-pen under the other. Mutter eyes narrowed as she watched them walk into her yard. She rose from her porch rocker, walked to the edge of the porch, held out an upturned hand at the end of a stiff right arm.

"Now sir—you just hold it right there! No—no you don't! You just turn right around and take that baby and play-pen away from here! I don't know who you think you are, but I done raised my kids. I ain't taking care of that baby! No sir! I ain't taking care of no more kids! Now you turn yourself right around and git' away from here."

"Mutter—what's wrong with you? It's Marcellus. I'm your baby boy. I just came to visit you and brought my new baby son for you to meet. I came all the way from Florida for you to see him."

"Marcellus? Don't know no Marcellus. Don't bring that baby and play-pen in here! Take that baby and get on away from here—right now—'fore I call the Sheriff on you." Crushed, Marcellus and his wife retreated to their car. They went to the home of his older brother, Alvin, in Lynchburg, and spent several days with him before returning to Florida. After listening to Marcellus' story, Alvin called his sister, Dolores, who lived in a town near Rock Branch. They decided a personal visit with Mutter, to look into her memory problem, was a must—sooner rather than later.

Basically, Mutter was a God-fearing woman. Pius nature notwithstanding, she had small use for diplomacy. While generally charitable to the truly needy, she could also be a determined and unyielding woman. She would, without hesitation, tell you exactly what she thought, and let the chips fall where they may. Still, running Marcellus, his wife, and new baby off without even letting them come up on the front porch was –well—that was a bit much. And claiming not to know Marcellus—what was that all about? Say what you would about Mutter, she never turned her back on her own.

Alvin gave it some thought. He knew Mutter was not close to any of her grandchildren. His own daughter, Dawn, and Mutter never had a warm relationship. Saying they were 'civil' to each other was being generous. Dawn always addressed Mutter as 'Mrs. White'. Mutter called her 'Dawn Durbin'. It was believed she got the name from a song or poem, but Mutter never offered an explanation. Dawn's Mother once told her the reason she and Mutter didn't get along well was because they were so much alike. Both of them were too likely to respond to an antagonist with a rebuttal of 'kiss my butt'.

A week later Alvin and Dolores visited Mutter. It was mid-morning when they got there. There was no response to knocks on the front or back door. Both doors were unlocked so they went in. They searched the house completely—not a sign of Mutter. Yelling her name brought no response. Her neighbors hadn't seen her for a day or so. A search party was formed with the neighbors.

For want of a better place to start, Dolores looked in the old woodshed located at the far end of Mutter's back yard. She found Mutter in the woodshed, curled up in a fetal position on the dirt floor of the old shed. All she was wearing was an old, thin night gown. She was dirty, cold, frightened, and confused. She told her daughter she had gone to the woodshed to get wood for her kitchen stove and forgot how to get back to her house. So she spent the night on the cold, dirt floor of the drafty old shed.
Dolores helped Mutter back to the house, cleaned her, fed her, and put her to bed. Then Alvin and Dolores talked. Mutter was 92 years old. Stick whatever label you want on it—they were pretty sure she was suffering from Alzhiemers, dementia, or some sort of memory-loss condition.
Regardless, being left alone was no longer practical. They were going to have to talk to her about living in a nursing

home. Alvin didn't envy bringing up the subject of a nursing home to Mutter. He didn't say it out loud, but he would rather wrestle a Wildcat, bare-handed, than tell Mutter she had to move out of her house. Maybe, they thought, they could get some doctor to examine her—get him on their side—and let him suggest the nursing home to her.

Toward the end of the day, Mutter awoke. Oddly enough, her mind seemed clear. Nonetheless, Alvin and Dolores pressed Mutter to let them make an appointment for her complete medical exam at the University hospital. As with most elderly people, especially those slipping into the early stages of senility, Mutter became agitated at the suggestion she wasn't well, or that she undergo a medical exam to pinpoint her illness. She was unaware the disease was slowly carrying her to a life that only existed in the moment, with no memories of the past and no thoughts of the future.

Mutter, secretly, was afraid an examination of her aged body would bring about a forced change of the lifestyle she had known for most of her life. She dismissed the night spent in the woodshed as "just something I just decided to do—and I ain't goin' to see no dam doctor! I'm fine. This is my house and I'm stayin' right here".

Mutter's use of profanity was puzzling and another cause for unease. A crusty old woman—yes. A profane woman— no. Mutter had never used profanity to lend 'force' to her conversations with others. After they suggested a medical exam, they heard Mutter mumble cuss words, several times. Still, she appeared to be in her 'right mind'—for the moment.

Alvin wasn't sure they could legally force the old lady to submit to a medical exam. Suppose they did make her go— and the exam revealed no mental or physical problems? They would look like fools, and Mutter would throw it up to them forever—if she even let them in the house again. Alvin and Dolores decided to 'let things ride' for a while. They carried in wood for her stove and stocked her cupboard with groceries. After asking the neighbors to keep an eye out for her, they went home.

Three months passed without problems involving Mutter. Then Dolores got a call from the neighbors. Mutter, they said, was walking around the neighborhood calling for her dog, Boss, who had died several years ago. Despite pleas from the neighbors, Mutter wouldn't call off the search for the dog. She continued to knock on doors in the neighborhood and inquire after her lost dog. She had let her dog out, Mutter told them, to 'do his business', and he had wandered off somewhere. Every neighbor in Rock Branch knew Mutter's dog had been dead for close to three years. They told her so, but Mutter wasn't buying it.

Dolores, drove from her nearby home, apologized to the neighbors, put Mutter in her car, and took her home. Dolores spoke directly and firmly to Mutter. She told Mutter her dog had been dead for three years. If she continued to wander through the neighborhood looking for a dead dog, Dolores told her, the family would be forced to 'have her put some place' where she couldn't go wandering around looking for a dead dog. The threat sobered Mutter. Once again, her mind grasped reality.

Dolores, again, seriously considered forcing mental tests and enrollment in an Assisted Living Facility on Mutter. She knew Mutter would fight it every step of the way. Until she could talk with Alvin, she settled for writing a note on a large piece of brown paper she tore out of a big grocery bag. She taped the note to the kitchen door at face level. The note said, 'Momma- The dog is dead!! He has been dead for three years. Don't go outside looking for the dog'.

Mutter's children, living within a moderate driving distance, agreed to take turns driving to Mutter's house and spending the day with her. There were 4 of them—which was enough to see that most weeks passed without trouble. They kept her house clean, warm in the winter, and food prepared. To offer stories of Mutter' gratitude for their concern and help would be nice—but untrue. In fact, she found their company an annoyance, an intrusion, and told them so—frequently. She also drove her irritation home with verbal outbursts rich in profanity. Mutter's use of profanity seemed to increase with time, as did her frustration over forgetting how to do things and the presence of others in her home. Her children's gentle, verbal, efforts to fill in her memory lapses only increased her irritation.

With her children spending days with her, a year passed without unmanageable problems. Still, it was a make-shift arrangement. Something had to go awry sooner or later—and it did. A Friday came along when it was just impossible for anyone to be with Mutter. With no other options, it was decided to leave Mutter alone for a day and hope for the best. After all, what could she do wrong in 1 day? As events proved—plenty.

Mutter's neighbor, on an opposing hillside, sold his house and moved away. He came by and said goodbye to Mutter'—but his 'farewell' escaped Mutter' short term memory the moment he was out of sight. The old neighbor left a week before the Friday Mutter was left alone.

The new owners moved in on a Saturday. As the new owners moved furniture and personal belongings into their newly purchased home, Mutter watched them from her living room window. Rage flew through Mutter a mile wide. A bunch of strangers going in her neighbor's house, she fumed. Looked like they were stealing the furniture! Damned thieves are everywhere, she thought. Well, she was a good neighbor. She wasn't going to stand by and see the meager possessions of her hard working neighbors ransacked by a bunch of thieves! Mutter stormed on to her front porch— an iron stove poker in hand—waving it angrily in front of her as she bellowed at the newcomers.

"Hey---! What are you doin' in that house? That ain't your house! You better get out of that house—and right now! Get out of there! You buncha' damn thieves! And take them snotty-nosed little kids with you!"

"Excuse me—excuse me, Mam. This is our house. We bought it last week from Mr. Joe Farley. We ain't no thieves—and don't you be yelling at our kids. You're a-scarin' them."

Mutter didn't believe the newcomers—or forgot what they said two minutes after they said it. She retreated to her house—but only for a minute or two. Once again, she ran out on her porch, waving her poker menacingly, and shouting threats laced with profanity.

Other neighbors assured the newcomers, 'Mutter gets a little confused from time to time, but she's harmless'. The children of the new family retreated inside their new home. The new owners ignored Mutter as they continued to move their possessions into their new home. This tactic was short lived.

Mutter burst out of her house again, poker in hand, and trotted toward the home of the new neighbors. She had never gone any further than her own front porch until now. As she crossed the road between the houses she swung her poker in the air and screamed threats that included bodily harm.

"I'll run you outta' that there house—I'll crack your thieving heads with this here poker--!" bellowed Mutter as she charged at the new owners on their own front porch.

Ignoring the shrill ranting of a senile old woman from a distance of 200 feet was one thing. Barricading themselves in their own home to avoid assault by a crazy old woman wielding an iron poker was another. It was a concession they weren't prepared to make. The young couple went inside their new home, locked the doors, and placed a 911 call to the police.

As Mutter charged the home of the new neighbors, one of her long-time neighbors called her son and daughter to inform them of the possibility of having to bail Mutter out of the county jail. They hated to bring news like that to her children's door. On the other hand—given Mutter's last up-close 'greetings' to the new neighbors— they just didn't feature the Sheriff just letting her little escapade slide. Especially if the deputy came on the scene to find Mutter walking the street, cursing, brandishing an iron poker as a weapon, and threatening people in their own home. The old soul, they reasoned, had 'just flat out lost her mind' this time.

Some of the long-time inhabitants of Rock Branch gathered in knots, from a safe distance, and watched Mutter' as she strode menacingly back and forth in the street. She shouted threats and mumbled curses, while swinging her poker wildly. A neighbor proposed that one of them approach Mutter—try to calm her down and get her to go inside her house—or, at least, to her own porch. However, none of them were certain Mutter would show any sense of restraint if they got too close to her. It might even be their head that had an unsolicited meeting with her poker. The idea of one of *them* being a mediator was abandoned almost as quickly as it had been brought up. Mutter, in times past, was a fairly reasonable woman. At the moment, she was being down-right 'hos-tile'. She was in a frame of mind to 'take somebody upside the head' with that poker.

Shame to this world that it was, something *drastic* needed to be done with Mutter. Not by them, of course—that's what the Po-leese are for.

Dolores and Alvin pulled their car to a stop in front of Mutter's house to find a County Sherriff's Deputy sitting on her front porch. He had arrived on the scene to find Mutter' in full 'rant'. A few questions of the newcomers and old neighbors satisfied him Mutter hadn't gone beyond threats at that point. The Deputy convinced Mutter to let him handle the thing with the 'thieves'. He patiently listened to her rage about thieves in the neighborhood as he gently took the poker from her and guided her back to the warmth of her house.

After assuring the new neighbors they were safe, he learned from others that Mutter's son and daughter were on their way to her home 'to do something with the poor ol' soul'. The Deputy's promise to take up a post on her front porch to be sure the 'strangers' didn't take anything from her old neighbor's house won a promise from Mutter to stay in her house. That's where Alvin and Dolores found the Deputy and Mutter when they arrived an hour later.

Alvin and Dolores, with the help of the Deputy, made arrangements for Mutter to be taken to the Psychiatric ward of a University hospital for observation and examination. Mutter fought the move to the hospital tooth and nail—every step of the way. Promises of admitting her to the hospital for a 'routine medical examination' didn't fly. Mutter didn't buy a word of it. Every one of her kids, she informed anyone who would listen, were involved in a conspiracy to lock her up and take her home from her.

"I don't need to see no doctor! I ain't sick! You think I don't know what you're a-doin'? You're puttin' me in that hospital so you can take my house! You ain't foolin' me one bit! You think I don't know you think I'm crazy? Well—I ain't goin' to no hospital—and you can't make me! Get outa' my house—right now!"

Letting Mutter have a voice in her care was suspended for the time being. Backed by the County Deputy, Alvin made arrangements to have her involuntarily committed to the University Hospital Psych Ward until a proper diagnosis could be made of her problem and what, in her own interests, should be done with her.

Mutter's stay in the hospital Psych ward was short—and eventful. Mutter was generous with her verbal abuse of the entire Psych medical staff. She accused everyone in earshot of being involved in a conspiracy to hold her there against her will, and take her home in the bargain. The staff of the Pscyh ward dismissed her tirades as just those of another aged and demented soul, tormented by demons created by a brain which was dying faster than her body.

Mutter's conversations with the resident Psychiatrist, a

battery of diagnostic tests, and an MRI confirmed Mutter was fully in the grip of Alzheimer's Disease. The family was told there was no cure for the disease and the damage already done to her brain was irreversible. Her mental decline, the doctor said, was inevitable—for the remainder of her life. Mentally, some of her days might be better than others—she would recognize them off and on for a while— but even the 'good' days would disappear with passing time. The best they could do was find a combination of drugs to slow her mental deterioration and 'keep her comfortable' for the remainder of her life. They also advised the family that Mutter could no longer live by herself. Constant care and supervision was now a necessity.

The family wondered about Mutter' life span, knowing the disease was laying waste to her brain. The doctors were reluctant to offer any specifics. It almost sounded like a recorded speech when the doctor pointed out, given her age of 94—almost 95, she had had lived 'a good long life'— and the family should just 'keep her comfortable' and 'enjoy her company' for whatever life she had left.

Recalling Mutter's attitude over the past two years, the family was dubious about 'enjoying' Mutter's company' in her current state of mind. Enjoying Mutter's company when she was 'in her *right* mind' took some effort—of late. The strain of living through the 'late unpleasantness', of the past two years, had taken a toll on the family. Mutter's idea of being 'kept comfortable' meant, "take me back to my own house and leave me alone".

After her diagnosis in the Psych ward, Mutter still had about 45 days of hospitalization left that Medicare would pay for. She was transferred out of the Psych ward into a semi-private room on a floor of the general hospital population. The Med Staff figured her for an easy billing of Medicare covered hospital fees for another 45 days while they 'regulated her meds'. Then they would transfer her to a nursing home. That was their plan—not Mutter's.

Within a week, the entire Medical staff recognized their severe under-estimation of Mutter. She verbally abused every member of the Med Staff who came within earshot or eyesight.

"What are you doin' in my house?" she railed as the doctor entered her room. "Who asked you to come in here? Whadda' *you* want? You think I don't know what's goin' on here? Huh?"

"Good morning, Mrs. White. I'm Dr. Bailey. I'm just going to check your blood pressure and your heart, and see how you're doing on your new medication. You look better today. Let's listen to your heart first and make sure—."

"Hey—watch where you're putting your hands! I know what you're up to, sonny! You think I'm an old woman—think I don't know you're tryin' to do? Huh? Gonna' feel me up, are you? You just slip your hand under *my* bed sheet and you'll draw back a—hey, hey,--back off! Leave my gown closed—you pervert! Get out of my house! I'll call the Sheriff—have you put in jail!"

"Mrs. White—I'm just going to check your heart rate. I can do it through your gown if that is more comfortable for—."

"Check my heart rate? More like lookin' at my boobs—ain't it?"

"Mrs. White—would you be more comfortable if I had one of the nurses in the room while I checked your vital signs?"

"Nurses? Is that what you call them whores runnin' in and out of *my* house all day and night? No sir! I don't want them in my house—or you either. So get outta'here!"

In one week, the doctors severely regretted admitting her to the floor. The floor nurses all but refused to enter her room. Probably because Mutter's rebuttal to everything they asked her to do was "No—I'm not doin' it! Get outa' my house!" At the beginning of the second week the Med Staff told the family (1) they had done all they could for Mutter (2) she needed to be transferred to a nursing home—immediately.

Not far from Mutter' own home, Alvin found a Nursing Home that would accept her. He tried to buy her cooperation by telling her how close to her own home the Nursing Home was—how nice the people would be to her at this Nursing home—how it would feel just like home to her. Despite her threats, accusations, and refusal to cooperate in any way, Alvin got her moved into the Lordstown Nursing Home.

Mutter had hardly settled in her room at the nursing home when she began using a good portion of the time and energy of the nursing staff to control her movements and actions. Within days of moving into the nursing home, she came to believe the entire nursing home was her home back in Rock Branch. She would spend her days rolling up and down the hallways in her wheel chair--approaching and threatening staff, patients, and visitors at the nursing home.

"Hey there! You—! Yes—I'm talkin' to *you*! What are you doin' in my house? Who let you in here? What's your name? Where do you live? You tryin' to steal from me? Who you lookin' at? Huh? You lookin' at *me*? What are you lookin' at me for? Huh? Get outta' my house!"

The nurses would, gently, take her back to her room and explain that other people lived there too.

"What—live here too? This is my house! I didn't say they could come in here? Didn't invite you in either! Who are you? I see you and them other whores runnin' around here—I want every last one of you out of my house!"

Some months passed. The family visited her when they could. Sometimes she recognized them—sometimes not. The time she spent there did nothing to convince Mutter that she wasn't in her own home. She assumed the right to question the presence of every soul she met in the nursing home—and demand the expulsion of any soul she encountered. Actually, things got worse.

Mutter began getting out of her bed at night. She mounted her trusty wheel chair, grabbed her ever present flashlight, rolled her chair down the hallway—stopping at each room along the way. She entered each room with authority, shined her flash light in the occupants eyes—awakened them—and began her interrogation and tongue lashing.

"Who are *you*? What are you doin' in *my* house? Who let you in here? What's your name? What are you lookin' at me for? Get your clothes on and get out of my house! I don't have any room for you here—and I ain't feedin' you either!"

After several weeks of returning Mutter to her bed, two and three times each night, the nurses' patience was exhausted. When they put Mutter to bed for the night, they took the batteries out of her flashlight, and took her wheel chair out of her room. She could still walk for short distances. But, the nurses told her, if she came out of her room before morning they would have to use 'restraints' to keep her in bed. Mutter' understood restraints. She didn't want that. On the other hand, she wasn't ready to trust the safe-keeping of 'my house' to those she saw walking in 'her' hallways and sleeping in her bedrooms.

Her paranoia forced her to work out a compromise. She got out of her bed each night, pulled a chair close to the door leading from her room to the hallway, sat down, cracked the door a half inch, and spent a good part of the night

observing the night time/early morning routine of a nursing home. For a good part of every night she watched the nurses going in and out of rooms, checking on patients.
A week later, Alvin and his family visited Mutter. His family made the usual inquiry of 'how're you doing'. They had asked Mutter the wrong question.

"How'm I *doin'*? You wanna' know how I'm *doin'*? I'll tell you how I'm doin'. I'm livin' in a whorehouse! That's how I'm doin'!" She pointed an accusing finger at Alvin as her voice rose.
"My own son—done made me live in a whore house! Nothing but a bunch of whores—and I'm stuck right in the middle of 'em."

"You think I don' know what's goin' on here, Alvin? You think I don' know I'm not in my own house? Huh? That what you think? Think I'm some crazy ol' woman--who don' know what's a-goin' on 'round here? Well, you're badly mistaken! This is nothing but a whorehouse! I sat at my door all night last night and I saw them whores that work here goin' in and out of them ol' men's rooms all night long! Yes sir! They didn't even take a break. No sir! In and out of them ol' fools' rooms—doin' 'em—one right after th' other!"

Alvin tried to calm Mutter—assured her the women she saw were nurses—attending to patients, not whores. Mutter gave Alvin a withering look and then turned to his wife, Madeline.

"Madeline, did you ever know any whores? You can tell 'em by just lookin' at 'em—can't you? When you go out of here, you take a look at them wenches. You tell me they ain't whores."

Mutter had a stroke a few months later. It left her paralyzed on one side. This stroke was followed by a fatal stroke, one week later. Mutter was laid to rest beside her husband near Rock Branch, just a few days before her 96th birthday.

Mutter body left this life—not her spirit, nor the memories and the stories she spawned. There are those who say you are never truly 'departed' from this earth until the last person who knew you leaves this earth too. If that's true, the memory and spirit Mutter will rattle around this earth for a good while after she went to 'live in my own house' in the sky.

In-Home delivery made here. Resident was seated on Porch swing behind hedge. Fateful glass storm door is seen at end of walk-way.

Note—road drops out of sight just as it
Passes home of customer where milk-man
stopped his truck to make a delivery.

Milk truck left parked at top of hill while milk-man ran
up drive way to right

View looking up—Milk truck ran away down this hill—note sharp curve at bottom of hill—and utility pole

RUN-AWAY MILK TRUCK

HIT POLE AT BOTTOM OF HILL

THE MILK MAN

Bob Collins wanted to be the *best* milk-man at Westover Dairy. His delivery route was in a good area of town, with potential for growth. With the right kind of work record, he could be looking at a promotion to Route Supervisor. From there he hoped to work his way into a management position in the Dairy plant itself. First he had to gain recognition for outstanding door-to-door delivery of milk to customer's homes along his route.

The town, for the most part, was built on seven hills. That meant the streets and homes of his customers were, mostly, on hills. On the other hand, the streets were well paved, and nearly every home had a paved walk leading from the street to the front porch, where he left their fresh milk in pristine glass bottles during the predawn hours. All in all, not a bad situation for a man trying to work his way up the promotion ladder in the commercial world of dairy products.

Bob was focused. His knew his key to success depended on: (1) Speed – be certain deliveries on his route were made before his customers took their morning shuffle to the front porch to look for their milk. (2) Be certain his deliveries were exactly what his customers ordered. (3) Increase the kind and amount of dairy products purchased by each customer. The ability to sell more dairy products reflected well on a route 'Milkman'.

Bob had the 'speed of delivery' part of his job down pat. He was never late for work. He had the correct amount of products on his milk truck to fill orders from his customers. His truck always rolled away from the Dairy bottling plant no later than 2 a.m. in the morning. Bob was in good physical shape. He had to be. Jumping off and on a truck over a 150 times in pre-dawn hours; moving at a run-trot up walkways to front porches with a metal carrier holding bottles of milk for that customer; hurrying to the next house on the route, and doing the same thing all over again. You had to have *great* physical stamina, to be a successful milk-man.

It was warm, humid August morning when Bob pulled his truck to a quick stop on Sandy Blvd. The high temperature the previous day had set a record. It was still in the 90s after the sun went down. It was now 4 a.m. of the next day, pitch dark, and Bob thought it didn't feel like the temperature had dropped all that much from the unbearable 90s of the previous day. His shirt was already soaked with perspiration as he set the truck's hand brake and grabbed his bottle carrier.

His metal carrier held six one-quart, glass bottles of milk. He used the carrier to carry milk from the truck to the homes of his customers, and ferry the empty bottles he picked up on their porch back to his truck. Six empty glass bottles were heavy enough. Fill them with milk—they were a load in that metal carrier.

To offset the weight of the loaded carrier in his right hand,

Bob leaned a little to his left and swung the loaded carrier to and fro as he loped up the walk to each house. If I hustle, he thought, maybe I can complete my deliveries before the sun comes up. Yeah, deliver my milk, get the truck back to the plant, unload the empties, and head on home before the heat of the sun starts sucking the very life out of me.

Bob wasn't the only one whose mind was pre-occupied by the discomfort of the pre-dawn summer heat. The home-owner to whom he was about to deliver milk had been unable to sleep. He had no home air-conditioner and the heat in his home made sleep impossible for him. The old man had given up on sleep, toddled out to his front porch, and sat down in his front porch swing. Maybe he could catch a breeze on the porch, he thought. He left the porch light off so it wouldn't attract insects to compound the discomfort of the heat. He just sat there quietly, swaying slowly in the swing, waiting for dawn.

He heard Bob's truck grind to a halt in front of his house. He could see the reflection of his truck lights. He could hear Bob trotting up his front walk. He couldn't actually see him because of the privacy hedge growing along his front porch. It afforded 'porch sitting' privacy for him and his wife. The old man decided to be neighborly. He would give Bob a hearty greeting when he stepped up on the porch with his milk.

Bob was in full trot as he crossed the front lawn to the front porch. He swung his milk carrier forward, in a high arc in front of him, to give him balance as he jumped up the steps from the walk to the front porch. The porch wasn't wide. Six or seven feet from the steps to the front door. The thick, evergreen privacy hedge made it impossible to see anyone on the porch before you were actually standing on the porch—even in broad daylight—and it was pitch dark when Bob's feet hit that porch.

Just as Bob's feet hit the front porch the old man's deep, gravely, voice boomed out of the inky darkness and washed over Bob.

"HEY—what you doin' there, boy?"

The fright of a totally unexpected, growly, voice coming from the black corner of the porch at 4 a.m. was an overload on Bob's nervous system. His reflexes kicked in without waiting for his brain to analyze the situation.

"WHA--NO!!" yelled Bob. As Bob screamed, he physically reacted to the fright of an unexpected voice from the dark by letting his metal milk carrier go flying out of his hand. The loaded milk carrier was already swinging forward when Bob, in mid-stride, let go of it. The forward momentum of Bob's swinging arm, combined with the speed of his trot up on to the porch, propelled the milk loaded carrier in a forward arc through the air, across the width of the porch, through the glass of the old man's front storm-door, and three feet into the house's interior foyer before gravity brought it crashing to the floor.

Some of the six 1-quart bottles of milk broke when they,

and the metal carrier, hit the hard oak floor. The remaining 3 bottles flew out of the carrier and broke as they bounced off each other while skidding down the wooden hallway floor to the kitchen.

If anyone in that house *had* been asleep, they weren't after the last of those 6 bottles of milk and the glass storm door had shattered. The noise sounded like a glass factory under siege from an earthquake. There was broken glass and milk scattered from the front door to a point ten feet down the interior hallway of the old man's home. Not one glass bottle or pane of storm door glass remained unbroken. Bob recovered his composure and tried to think of some appropriate explanation and apology. As he surveyed the damage to the door and inside the house he wasn't sure *any* apology would sufficiently cover this mess.

Then anger gripped him. He fought the urge to get in the old man's face and say, "For God's sake, ol' man! What are you doing sitting out here in the dark—at 4a.m in the morning? You scared th' life out of me! Darn it all, I feel like throwing *you* through that storm-door, too!"

Restraint and passionate apologies, coupled with promises that all damage would be paid for, seemed to be the better course of action—and that's what Bob offered.

Actually, the old man was rather unperturbed by the whole thing. He scratched his head as he peered through the shattered storm-door, from the porch, and surveyed the debris of glass and spilled milk littering the interior of his home. While Bob began picking up glass, the old man went in search of a broom, mop, rags, buckets, and soapy water to use in cleaning up the mess.

Bob spent 30 minutes picking up glass, sweeping, mopping—and re-mopping—four times. He promised to have the Dairy's insurance company contact the old man about his ruined door and floor. The floor was so cut up it looked like someone had tried to ice skate on it with razor sharp skate blades

After what seemed like an eternity, Bob was finally able to drive away from the customer's house. He didn't know how the rest of his day would go. What he *did know* was—it couldn't get any worse than it started. That was worth something, he guessed.

'Well', he told himself, 'things happen. What can I say'? In a manner of speaking, it was his first 'IN-home' delivery. He hoped it would be his last. He didn't look forward to reporting the incident when he got back to the plant. Bob sighed, shook his head, and hustled to the home of his next customer.

THE MISSING MILK TRUCK

Bob was off to a good start on his milk delivery route. It was a Friday—3 a.m. on a pitch-black but pleasant pre-dawn morning—and he was ahead of schedule. He would finish with his Friday deliveries in another two hours, drop off his truck and empties at the plant, and be ready for a fun-filled weekend.

Bob was in the Ford Hill neighborhood, which had its share of hills. Some of them were darn steep. According to history buffs, a big Civil War battle had taken place up and down these same cascading hills almost a hundred years ago.

Bob's attention snapped back to business. He braked his truck to a quick stop in front of a customer's house. The street, at that particular point, was on a slight, downhill slope. Fifty feet beyond the customer's house the street became a long, straight, steep, downhill grade. The steep part of the street always reminded Bob of the long ski-slope used in the Olympic Games by skiers attempting to launch themselves farthermost through the air before they touched the ground again.

He set the truck's hand brake, grabbed a couple of quarts of milk, and trotted through the darkness, to the customer's back door. As he put the milk in the milk box, he saw a note from the customer requesting a quart of orange juice. He picked up the empty milk bottles, hurried back up the driveway to his truck, jumped through the truck's rear door, and grabbed a bottle of orange juice. Juice in hand, he slammed the rear door shut. Another quick trip to the customer's house to leave the juice on their door step, and he trotted back up the driveway.

Bob was within 10 feet of the street when he stopped dead in his tracks. His milk truck wasn't there! Gone! Completely! Without a sound! He felt the bottom of his stomach drop out. In shock and disbelief, Bob began talking out loud.

"What th' devil--. I—I was just in that truck—not 10 seconds ago! Jesus Christ! How can a truck that big just up and vanish—that fast—without a sound! The brake was on, for cryin' out loud!"

He hadn't heard a sound or seen anyone—so nobody could have driven off with the truck—or he would have seen or heard the truck being stolen and driven off. He would have heard the engine. Besides, he wondered, who would steal a big white milk truck—right out of the middle of the street?

Bob wondered if his eyes were playing tricks with him in the darkness of the pre-dawn hours. He ran up the last 6 ft of the customer's driveway to the curb where he had left his truck. With his hands extended in front of him, he half expected to bump into his truck as he walked into the pitch black darkness of the street. After all, trucks just don't up and disappear into thin air—like they do on that weird TV show, *Twilight Zone*. 'Awww—what am I thinking—I left the truck lights on—how can I not see it', he mumbled in frustration.

As Bob turned 360 degrees in the middle of the street he wondered how he was going to explain losing a truck to his boss. In the absolute stillness of the dark, early morning hours he heard a soft, rumbling noise to his right. He turned, raced down the street until he was looking down the 300 foot long, steep, downhill run of the street. To his horror, he saw the tail lights on his truck—rolling down the hill and gathering speed.

For a split second, Bob's mind and body were paralyzed with shock. He quickly got a grip on himself and began chasing the truck down the hill. He had driven down that hill hundreds of times, and never realized the hill was *that* steep. Bob was a fast runner, but it was no contest. The truck had started its runaway too long before he discovered it missing, and was gaining speed with every turn of the wheels.

Bob, in his mind, already had that truck 'colored' wrecked. If he had wings he couldn't get to that truck before it crashed into—. 'Crashed!' he said to himself. 'Crashed into what? Oh God! What if there is a car coming the other way on the street, he agonized. That truck is big enough to run right through a car! Somebody could be killed! No telling what the police would charge me with if someone gets killed!'

The fear of the truck running over some soul shot

adrenaline into Bob's system. It spurred him to run even faster. Maybe he could get to the truck before it got to somebody else. As he flew down that hill, he tried to look for head lights coming toward the runaway truck. He couldn't see beyond the bottom of the hill because the street turned to the right and—.

"Oh my God!", he murmured. "The street had to turn to the *right* at the foot of the hill because there is a *parking lot* at the foot of the hill for two apartment buildings on the *left* side of the street!", he mumbled in horror.

"God almighty!" he moaned aloud. "What if some person is coming out of one of those apartment buildings to go to work—and doesn't see or hear that truck flying down the hill toward them. The truck could run over them before they knew they were hit. They could be killed! Even worse, suppose the truck runs straight into the apartment building and kills someone right in their own bed!"

Despite running faster than he had run in his whole life, Bob didn't reduce the distance between him and the truck. He knew he wasn't going to reach that truck before something or someone had an unexpected meeting with it. He saw the truck reach the bottom of that steep hill and continue straight toward the parking lot of the apartment building.

Bob had run half way down the hill when the quiet, dark, still morning air was broken with a loud 'WHUMP' sound of metal slamming into wood. The dark sky lit up as a bright ball of fire and shower of sparks arced through the air. The display of lights, sparks, and sounds were over in seconds. Darkness closed in again.

After what seemed an eternity, Bob reached the bottom of the hill to find his truck setting against a broken, wooden, utility pole. Of all the things or persons that truck could have hit with tragic results, it found a lone utility pole to stop its runaway journey.

'Alright, so the utility pole was history, and the front end of the milk truck would wind up in a junkyard. Also, the good citizens who lived around there would find they had no electricity when they crawled out of their beds that morning. A small price to pay, considering how much worse the end results *could* have been', reasoned Bob.

Bob found a phone booth nearby. He called the police, and his boss at the plant. It was daylight before the police allowed his truck to be pulled off the utility pole and towed from the scene. An hour later the electric company had power restored to the area.

Bob just knew, between his boss and the police, he would probably be hung right on the spot. Mercifully, the police discovered a defective and ruptured brake hose on the truck. This was the cause of the truck 'running away'. Much to Bob's relief, the police found the hand brake still on and properly set when they arrived at the scene of the crash.

Bob caught a ride back to the dairy bottling plant with the

tow truck driver. He filled out paper work on the accident, being careful to add that the police had not charged him with fault in the accident.

It was late in the day when he left the plant. But, it was payday, so he had some money in his pocket. Maybe the weekend would get better, he thought, as he looked at the setting sun.

THE MILK BANDITS

One of Bob's customers complained, on several occasions, about Bob's failure to leave her a quart of chocolate milk. Even though Bob knew he had left the chocolate milk, the Dairy always agreed to deduct it from her bill.

After her third complaint, Bob and his supervisor decided it was time to investigate the matter of the missing chocolate milk. The Dairy felt it was odd the customer agreed Bob never failed to deliver her *white* milk. No other customers on the street were complaining of a milk order being 'shorted'.

The customer missing the chocolate milk lived in a nice neighborhood. The homes were all nice homes built on a level street that stretched for an entire block. There were no fences between the houses, and all had nice lawns that adjoined each other. There were street lights on either end of the street that afforded a modest amount of light in front of the houses at night.

Bob's supervisor rode with him on the morning he was scheduled to make a delivery of chocolate milk to the complaining customer. Bob placed chocolate and white milk on the customer's front porch around 3 a.m. on a summer morning. It was dark, but the street lamps afforded some visibility.

After the delivery was made, Bob completed other deliveries on the street, turned the corner, and drove out of sight. Instead of following his usual routine of making deliveries on other streets, he drove back down the adjacent street, cut his truck headlights off, and coasted around the corner to the upper end of the street on which he had just delivered the chocolate milk. He cut the truck engine. He and his supervisor sat quietly in the truck, peering through the darkness at the house where the chocolate milk had been left on the porch.

They didn't have long to wait. Fifteen minutes later, three boys came out of the shadows of one of the other homes. Without hesitation they walked to the porch where the chocolate milk was left. They took turns drinking the milk, while standing right on the customer's front door step. Bob and his Supervisor quietly climbed out of the truck and made their way up the street toward the boys. They were within thirty feet of the boys when the boys heard their footsteps and began to run. Bob and his supervisor gave chase, yelling for the boys to stop. The boys cut between two of the homes into the back yard. It was dark in the back yards. The only light of any kind to reach the backyards was indirect reflections from the street lights in front of the houses—which was almost no light at all.

Bob lost sight of his supervisor. He could hear the running footsteps of the boys ahead of him. He couldn't see them, but he could hear them ahead of him. Bob could flat out run. There were no fences between the back yards of those houses. He dug in and was fairly flying toward the sound of the running feet close in front of him.

While running at full tilt, and with no warning at all, something grabbed Bob across his face, neck, and chest. It instantly stopped the forward motion of his upper body. The momentum of his legs continued forward for just one more step before he legs flew up in the air until they were higher than his head. His whole body hung suspended, upside down, in the air for just a split second. Then his whole body completed a 360 degree turn in the air and was was slammed to the ground with a loud 'WHOMP'.

Bob felt as if he was being choked. There wasn't enough light to see who or what was doing it. Whatever was wound around his head, neck, and arms was not yielding. He fought like a wild man to break loose from the bindings that held him so tightly. 'If I just had enough light to see— maybe I could get out of whatever trap has me tied up and is choking the very breath out of me', he thought.

The more he fought and twisted, the tighter the bindings wrapped around him. Every time he managed to get to his feet, he became even more entangled, and fell back to the ground. Every time he fell back to the ground, the 'bindings' just got tighter. Bob began to panic. He was sure he was going to choke to death—by himself—all alone-- in the darkness of someone's back yard.

By now he was convinced that the boys who stole the milk had deliberately led him to the back yard of one of the homes where they had a trap set for him. Chasing a thief was one thing—getting killed doing it was another. He didn't want to choke to death over a quart of chocolate milk.

Bob began screaming for his supervisor to come to him—to get him out of the trap he was caught in—before he choked to death. It wasn't a time for modesty. He was yelling loudly enough to be heard along the entire block of houses. He heard his supervisor yelling back to him—asking where he was—but he couldn't see him. His efforts to twist his face toward the sound of his Supervisor's voice only bound him more tightly in 'the trap'. Bob's supervisor continued yelling, asking him where he was. In the darkness, his supervisor just couldn't find him. Bob continued to yell,

"I'm over here! Get me out of this thing—before I die! Hurry, I'm choking to death!"

The people living in the houses had been awakened by Bob's screams and the yelling between him and his supervisor. Some of them turned on their back porch lights to find out where the screams were coming from and what they were about. From the sound of the shouts and screams, they feared someone was being hurt or killed right in their own back yard. Judging from the faces peeping from behind window curtains, it appeared half the people on the street were awake and looking into their back yards.

The exterior lights of the house behind which Bob lay bound up and screaming came on. His supervisor could see him now. He ran to where Bob was lying on the ground. He was still yelling at his Supervisor to cut him loose before he choked to death. The man, in whose backyard Bob was 'trapped', came out on his back porch and demanded to know what Bob and his Supervisor were doing on his property.

Bob's supervisor tried to get him on his feet while explaining to the owner of the house that Bob had fallen into a 'trap' while chasing some boys they caught stealing milk. His supervisor was trying to untangle the ropes and netting wound around Bob's head and body. He couldn't decide what to do first to get him out of all the 'strange' netting wrapped around him. He was wondering what kind of hellish 'trap' Bob's had fallen into and who would build a 'trap' like that when he owner of the house yelled down to them.

"Hey, that's my son's brand new badminton net you have torn down and are rolling around in. If you break one piece of it, you'll be buying him a new one! Another thing---, if you don't put it back just like it was before you ran into it, I'm calling the cops!"

For the first time since Bob hit that badminton net, he knew what happened to him. He hit that net running at full force after the boys who had stolen the milk. When the top part of his body made contact with the net some of the net anchor posts had pulled loose, some hadn't. It all combined to jerk his legs from under him, swing his body completely around in the air, and bind him in the netting and anchor ropes. In the total darkness, trying desperately to get loose, every move he made only served to cause him to become more twisted and entangled in the net and anchor ropes. What felt like a terrible trap—deliberately choking the life out of his body—was nothing more than a child's badminton net wrapped around him.

With the help of his Supervisor and the man who owned the net, Bob was slowly untangled from the net and anchor ropes. With what light they had, Bob, his supervisor, and the net owner worked until they had the badminton net back in its proper position.

Bob couldn't decide what angered him the most about the whole affair. Was it letting the thieving boys get away, running into the badminton net, the embarrassment of waking up half the neighborhood, or having to spend 20 minutes setting that badminton net back up—using the meager light bulb 80 ft. away.

As he pulled into the Dairy plant, Bob decided to look on the bright side. His boss now knew he had told the truth about delivering that chocolate milk. Plus—it was likely those boys had stolen their last bottle of milk on his route. His unsolicited meeting with that badminton net and waking up the neighborhood had served to alert every family on the street to the presence of a milk-thief in the neighborhood. The whole neighborhood would be watching now to see whose kids were stealing milk.

Note the long, steep, back yard. Looking closely—
you may be able to see the wire fence/posts at the bottom of hill/yard.

WOODIE & RITA

Logan Woodrow Watson and Irita Cearson Watson, better
known as Woodie and Rita, were as *unalike* as two humans
could be. Possibly, when they first met, they found enough
in common to believe they were in love with each other.
Possibly, their marriage was based on the 'Equity Theory'.
This theory suggests certain people choose to marry
because neither could have done any better in terms of

persuading someone to become their spouse. Some wondered if the marriage resulted from a 'have to' situation brought on by pregnancy. Whatever--, they did marry and produced two daughters.

In their mid-life and declining years, some said the only things they had in common were their two daughters. Much of their lives together revolved around conflicts, quarrels, and uneasy truces.

Woodie was 6" 2" tall, a no-nonsense authoritative type. He was notoriously tight with a dollar, could do with a minimum of social life, held courtesy and consideration for others in high regard, believed deeply in right and wrong, saw life in black and white—never shades of gray. Once made, his decisions were pretty much unalterable.

Rita was short, barely 5' tall, a social gadfly, outspoken to the edge of rudeness, loved good bourbon, never saw a dollar she couldn't spend, and was happiest in group settings or parties. You had a better chance of giving a Wildcat an enema than you did of getting her to embrace courtesy and social graces. She saw no black and white in life—only shades of gray. To her, an answer of 'no' only meant the issue was open to negotiation. Rita's mouth constantly wrote checks her butt couldn't cash. This didn't stop her from presenting herself as the savviest woman who ever strapped on shoe leather.

Woodie spent a hitch in the Army and rose to the rank of Sergeant. When his military obligation ended, he became a

Trooper with the Virginia State Police. After an unrewarding 8 year police career—mostly spent in high speed car chases after moonshine whiskey haulers in Henry and Franklin counties—he accepted a job as an Insurance Adjuster for National Insurance Company. He worked his way up to an entry level management position in claims. He worked more than 25 years for National.

Rita was a professional photographer. She worked a few years for a newspaper, where her assertive nature served her well. After their children came along, Rita got part-time jobs with local department stores—taking family portrait pictures. She combined this with free-lance work as a photographer of weddings and other celebratory occasions. As the years passed, Rita's consumption of bourbon increased from occasional to a daily habit. This diminished her demand as a photographer to a level close to non-existent.

Woodie and Rita's life became more of coexistence than cohabitation. Their daughters left home right out of high school because— well, who knows *exactly* why. Perhaps to escape the stress of Rita and Woodie's home—possibly, to find love—or to try their hand at creating an idyllic home life. One guess would be a good as another. The daughters' lives, as emancipated women, produced results that were not models of happiness or success.

The younger daughter married a high school sweetheart the day after high school graduation. Neither was very mature. Both had emotional and impulse control issues. A little more than a year after their marriage, the younger daughter's husband took his life with a pistol. He was a few days past his nineteenth birthday.

After the graveside rites for her late husband, this younger daughter of Woodie & Rita asked a close friend to take her to a rural spot on a grassy hillside where she and her late husband used to have picnics. She had the friend wait in the car while she walked up the side of the hill to the picnic spot. She turned to face the friend in the car, took a pistol out of her purse, and took her life with the pistol as the friend watched in horror. A few days after the daughter's funeral, it was discovered that the daughter had a written suicide pact with her late husband. If one of them took their life—the other would follow suit—and they would be happily reunited in their afterlife.

The older daughter married a man twenty two years her senior. The man was a successful local banker. There was little pretense of passion between them. The husband provided a good income, an impressive home in a well-to-do part of town, and security. Woodie's daughter acquitted herself well at social and business functions with her husband, volunteered her time for charitable causes, and traveled frequently with her husband. They had no children. Woodie and Rita were neither advised of nor invited to the daughter's wedding. She never returned to Woodie and Rita's home. Even though the daughter's new home was less than seven miles from the home of Woodie & Rita, her contact with them was limited to rare phone calls.

Some philosophers suggest much of humor is based on adversity, misfortune, or ignorance. This may be true. Despite a marriage filled with conflict and unhappiness, Woodie and Rita's years together created some humorous, and poignant, stories. Many of the incidents which gave birth to humorous stories weren't all that humorous when they happened. Time, which gives things a different perspective, brought out the humor in some of the incidents. I worked for Woodie for the better part of 5 years. Below are a few memories.

THE OIL TANK

Woodie and Rita purchased a ranch style home on a half-acre lot on Graves Avenue, west of the city. The homes were one story ranch style or modest 1 1/2 story colonials. The lots sloped downhill, steeply, off both sides of Graves Avenue. Most of the homes were set back about fifty feet from the street. The lots were limited to a frontage of about 90 feet wide, but were deep. Woodie's lot fell away, steeply, behind his house for a distance of 150 feet. It ended at a wire and split rail fence he had constructed. There wasn't a tree or shrub in his back yard.

Woodie had sown grass seed over his new back yard when they moved into the house, but he sowed the seed too late in the fall for the grass seed to germinate and mature into a good stand of grass before winter. For the most part, his backyard was bare of grass. The soil on his lot was fiery-red, clay. Early spring, with its alternate days of freezing and warm temperatures, created a soil in Woodie's yard that was slick, gooey, fire-engine-red clay. Walking in his back yard was like walking on a hillside sprayed with grease.

Woodie was on temporary medical disability. A deteriorating disc problem in his back had necessitated back surgery. After a couple of weeks in the hospital for recuperation and rehab, he was placed in a hard plaster body-cast that ran from his neck to his pelvic area. The body cast, in addition to immobilizing his upper torso, bound his arms to his upper torso from his shoulders to his elbows.
Woodie was able to walk—in an awkward, robotic manner. He could perform some minimal tasks with the lower parts of his arms. Partially immobilized in this body cast, Woodie was released from the hospital to complete his final weeks of recuperation at his new home.

Woodie, never one to spend a penny he didn't have to, had elected to heat his home with an oil furnace—because he it was cheaper than electric heat. He had an 85 gallon heating-oil tank mounted on metal legs, standing two feet off the ground against the rear of his house. Gravity fed oil from the tank to the furnace in his basement.

Woodie had been home for a couple of weeks when Rita yelled out one morning to say the heat in the house had gone off. It was in the early part of spring, and much too cool to be without heat. In her usual profane and snarling manner, Rita described their situation to Woodie.

"The heat has gone off! The damn furnace has quit running. This house isn't even a year old—and the furnace is breaking down already? What th' hell are we supposed to do now? Freeze to death? You're the one that wanted an oil furnace. I begged you to get electric heat—but, no—not you. You were too smart to pay for electric heat when you could get oil cheaper. Alright, Mr. 'Tightwad'—here we sit, with no heat. What're you gonna' do now?"

"Rita, did you check the oil tank? It was full when we turned on the furnace late in the fall. That was 4 months ago. Maybe we are out of oil. Did you check it?"

"What—you're asking *me* if *I* checked the oil tank? Hell no, I didn't check it! That's not my job! You're the one who wanted that big, ugly, oil tank stacked up against the back of the house! Why th' hell didn't *you* check it?"

"Rita, let's just solve the problem. Take the measuring rod, go out to the tank, and see if it has any oil in it?"

"Hell no— I'm not checking any oil tank. Climb up on that damn tank in the freezing cold wind—to stick some stupid little wooden measuring rod in it? You must think I'm as crazy as you are! I'll call a repairman. Let him fix the thing."

"No, Rita. I don't want to pay a repairman to come out here, just to tell me we are out of oil when we can determine that ourselves—at no cost."

"You want th' oil tank checked? All right, Mr. Tightwad, check it yourself. I don't know how th' hell you're going to do it in that body cast. How do you think you're going to get up those rickety, cinder blocks you stacked on top of each other and call 'steps'? Huh? You can hardly walk across the floor without falling on your ass. Call the repairman!"

"Rita, I'll check the oil tank myself. How difficult can it be to stick a measuring rod in an oil tank?"

Woodie picked up a slender wooden rod with gallon measurement marks on it. He put his hat and house slippers on and, with Rita yelling and swearing at him every step of the way, shuffled out of the house. He slowly inched his way across the slippery, red clay at the top of his back yard. Once he reached the oil tank he laboriously climbed a group of stacked cinder block steps to the top of the oil tank. Wearing nothing but his cast, a pair of undershorts, his hat, and a pair of cloth house slippers, he could feel the bite of the cold air. The brisk March wind was causing his body to sway back and forth as he stuck the measuring rod in the tank—all four feet of it. Getting the rod back *out* of the tank proved to be more difficult—with the long cast binding his upper arms to his body.

Awkward as it was, he finally withdrew the last few inches of the measuring rod from the tank. He peered closely, at the measuring rod—not one drop of oil on it. Muttering curses, Woodie was climbing backwards down the make-shift steps when a strong gust of wind knocked him off balance. With his arms bound to his sides by the heavy body cast, he didn't have a prayer of recovering his balance. He fell to the ground and began to roll down his steep back yard through the thawing red, clay mud.

With his arms bound so close to his ribs in the body cast, he rolled down his backyard as if he was a barrel. His body picked up speed as he rolled. After rolling 150 feet to the bottom of his yard, Woodie came to a halt when his body cast hit a fence post with a soft 'thud'.

 As nearly as Woodie could tell, he wasn't hurt. He felt no pain, but the wind and wet mud felt so cold on his bare legs and head. He was lying on his side, looking up the steep yard to his house. With that body cast on, there wasn't a chance of him standing up by himself. It just wasn't going to happen. He saw Rita standing on their carport, arms crossed, not saying a word, looking down the hill at him lying there.

"Rita, since you are just standing there, would you mind coming down here and helping me up to my feet? If I can stand up, perhaps I can walk back up the yard."

"Hell no—I'm not coming down there in that mud! I told you not to go near that oil tank! But no, you didn't listen! I told you to call a repairman! But no--, you didn't listen!

Now look at you! Lying flat on your back, way th' hell down that steep, muddy hill! And you want *me* to come down there too? Hell no! I could end up lying on my ass beside you! Besides, that cast you got wrapped around you must weigh twenty pounds. How th' hell you think I'm going to lift you *and* that cast without breaking my own back? No sir, Mr. Hardhead—you got yourself in this mess, so you lie right there until you figure some *other* way out of it!"

"Rita, for God's sake! You're going to have to do something! I can't continue to lie here in this cold and I can't get up."

"I'll call somebody! See if I can get somebody to come out here and drag you back up here. I don't know who to call—I don't know anyone that stupid—but *I'm* sure as hell not coming down there! You just lie there until I call somebody. You're not going to freeze to death in 10 minutes."

At the time, Les Calfee had worked for Woodie for 5 years. Woodie didn't really have any friends or employees who thought of him as a 'close' friend. Les got along well with well enough. They had hammered out a good working relationship over the years and respected each other—but they weren't *close*. Les had learned to deal with the 'adversarial' nature of Woodie's marriage—when he *did* have to deal with Rita. Rita and he got along—on the rare occasions they were forced into a one-on-one situation. For the most part, Les—as did all of us— absorbed her verbal abuse without comment or defense. That left her with little reason to *really* empty her guns into him.

Still, I was never absolutely certain why Rita called Les on the fateful day Woodie was marooned at the bottom of his backyard. There were 8 of us working in that office. Any one of us would have been reluctant to refuse a plea for help from 'the boss'. Possibly, she decided Les could be trusted to keep his mouth shut about this delicate situation. Maybe she just told the lady on the telephone switchboard to connect her with *anybody* in the office. Regardless of the reason, Rita's call was put through to Les's desk.

"Les, this is Rita. Woodie needs you! Come out to our house, right now! Bye!"

That was vintage Rita. No preamble. No explanation. No 'would you please'. No amenities or small talk. Just staccato, assertive, comments or orders—barked at you.

Les jumped in his car and hustled out to Woodie's house. It was 7-8 minutes from the office. Rita came barreling out of the house as Les pulled into their driveway. Les didn't see Woodie.

"Rita, where's Woodie? What's the problem?" Without a word, Rita walked across their carport. Still looking around for Woodie, Les followed.

"There he is! Way th' hell down that hill —all covered in that damn red mud!" she snarled as she pointed down their back yard.

Appalled, Les stared down the hill at Woodie. He was lying on the ground, a good 150 feet away. Except for his undershorts, he had no clothes on. Covered from head to toe in sticky, red, mud, he was rocking back and forth in his body cast, trying to get to his feet. The only things on him not colored red were his eyes, a few patches of skin, and some of his dark hair. As Les took off his overcoat, jacket, and tie, Woodie saw him.

"Thanks for coming, Les", he yelled, "I apologize for intruding on your work day. That said, would you please come down here and get me on my feet? I must get back to the house. I'm really cold and in some pain now."

"Hang on, Woodie! I'm coming right now! Don't try to move! You might re-injure your back. Rita, give me a blanket to wrap around him. He could catch pneumonia" said Les

Rita looked in the carport storage locker and found a ragged and torn old blanket they used to carry tree leaves out of their front lawn in the fall.

"Here! I'm not giving you a good blanket to ruin with that damn red mud."

Les hadn't taken a dozen steps down that steep muddy yard before he felt his feet sliding from under him. He caught his balance, crab-walked to the side of the yard, and grabbed the fence. It became his life line down the long hill to Woodie. It took Les the better part of three minutes to slip-slide down that hill. Probably felt like 30 minutes to Woodie, lying there in the cold, wet, mud.

When Les reached Woodie, he had three goals in mind. One, find a way to get Woodie on his feet—without worsening the damage to his already crippled back. Two, get Woodie back up that steep, slippery, muddy hill without re-injuring his spine. Three—although it held a lower priority—try not to soil his own clothing with that mud. Les could barely maintain his footing coming *down* the hill—by himself.

As Les struggled to wrap the blanket around Woody, he took a chance and asked, "Woodie, this may not be best time to ask—but what on earth put you down here and in this condition?"

Woodie could do little to help Les as he covered him with the blanket and considered the safest possible way to get him on his feet. So Woodie busied himself telling Les what happened—including a word by word recollection of the verbal exchanges between he and Rita, including her taunts bellowed down the yard from their carport 150 feet away. He trusted Les not to repeat anything he told him—or figured no one would believe such an outrageous story if he did repeat it to a third party.

Les decided the only way to get Woodie on his feet and not destRay his spinal recuperation was by grabbing him in a bear hug around his body cast. Les' goal of protecting his own clothing was lost right off the bat. With Woodie unable to help Les, his dead weight just hung in Les' arms. As Les lifted Woodie his own back hurt and his groin burned. He felt like he was getting the mother of all hernias.

'Probably won't be able to lift my legs to get my trousers on in the morning', he thought. He thought of an uncle, who got a hernia from lifting sacks of grain. Testicles swelled up big as duck eggs before they operated on him. He hoped he wasn't in for the same nightmare.

As Les struggled to bring Woodie to a standing position he pondered the irony of the whole situation. He was trying to get a man over six feet tall, weighing almost 200 lbs on his feet. He was covered with another 3-4 lbs of wet mud. He should not, and would not, have been in this ridiculous situation but for the want of a wife who could have, and should have, climbed those damn rickety, homemade, cinder block steps to check the oil level in the freakin' oil tank. Rita, in his opinion, was far more deserving of an accidental roll down that ski-slope yard than Woodie. And—he could have picked up her bantam weight so much easier.

Les snapped back to reality as Woodie began pleading with Les not to drop him. The strain of getting Woodie safely on his feet had beads of sweat standing on Les' forehead.

"Make sure your arms are locked around my cast, Les! If you drop me it may cause my spinal discs to rupture again. I don't think I can survive another operation on my back."

"I've got you, Woodie! Just concentrate on getting your feet under your body when I lift you upright. If your feet don't take your weight off me the minute I have you upright, I don't know how much longer I'll be able to support your weight."

Les' arms and legs were shaking when Woodie announced that he had both feet firmly on the ground. While Les caught his breath, Woodie held on to the fence. His body swayed a little as his blood flow got used to his upright position again.

"Les, I know how hard that was on you. I'm so grateful to you. I hate to follow a statement of gratitude with a plea—but my feet are freezing in this mud. I'm never going to be able to get back up that hill if my feet are numb. I need some shoes or you'll never get me back up that yard."

'Another problem—what next?' thought Les. Then, out of nowhere, the solution hit him.

"Rita, could you bring Woodie's's golf shoes down here—please. The cleats in those golf shoes will help him keep his feet under him while we climb the hill."

"*Me* bring his shoes down there? Hell no! I told Woodie I wasn't coming down there in that damn mud. Why do you think I called *you* out here?"

Rita walked out of sight with Woodie shouting curses of damnation at her. He screamed promises of a painful and harsh 'payback' when he did get back to the house.

Between mumbled curses and threats to throw Rita out of the house, he told Les his golf shoes were in the hall closet. Les left Woodie holding on to the fence with both hands and began climbing up the hill by himself. He hoped he would be able to find Woodie's golf shoes. Given Rita's attitude, he wouldn't have been surprised to find all doors to the house locked when he got to it. Les hadn't climbed more than 20 feet up the hill when Rita re-appeared on the carport.

"Here's your golf shoes, Woodie! The damn things are all stiff and dirty! Didn't I tell you to clean these things up last fall? Didn't I? Didn't I tell you to clean them with saddle soap before you put them away? But no--, not Mr. 'Hardhead' Watson! Got to do everything his way! Alright, let's see you get these stiff, dirty, things on your feet and walk in them!"

With that scathing indictment, Rita drew back her arm to throw Woodie's shoes down the back yard. Les knew that wasn't going to work. The muscles in Rita's arm were only developed enough to support the weight of a glass of bourbon from a table to her face. Woodie wore a size 11 ½ shoe. With the metal cleats in them, the shoes had to weigh 3 lbs.

"Rita! Wait! Wait! You can't throw the shoes all the way down here! You might throw them into the *middle* of the yard and I can't get out__", pleaded Les in vain.

Rita's respect for what Les said ranked no higher than

Woodie's comments to her. She didn't give a rat's rear end what Les was begging her not to do. She drew back her arm. Spun around like an Olympic Discus thrower, and sent the shoes flying through the air.

Just what Les was afraid of—they landed half way down the hill, in the *middle* of the yard. One of the shoes hit the ground, cleats down, and stopped right where it landed. The other one landed on its side and rolled 3 feet further down the hill. The shoes were a good 50 feet up the hill from Les, and 30 feet to the right—with not one single thing for Les to hold on to while he climbed across and up that treacherous, slick, muddy hill to get them.

Les abandoned any remaining hopes of salvaging his own clothing or shoes. He had paid $60 for his Bostonian loafers at a time when he was working for $150 a week—before taxes. His worsted wool trousers had come from the store of S.H. Franklin—*Clothier of Finer Dressed Gentlemen* in town. For the privilege of being among the '*finer dressed gentlemen*' in town, he paid $75 for those trousers. It took him four months to save the money for those trousers. His wife was living in sweat shirts at home so he could work in clothing that spoke well of him as a representative of his company. And to what end—wallowing in a mud pit?

Bitter as he was, Les saw no point in delaying the inevitable. He began climbing across and up the middle of the yard to get Woodie's shoes. To gain footing, he splayed his feet and walked on the insides of the soles of his shoes. He 'duck-walked' unsteadily— like a duck with his legs shot full of novocaine. He felt that gooey clay oozing down inside of his shoes. He also used his bare hands, to claw his way across and up the yard. Even these efforts were not equal to the challenge of the climb. Every third step or so, his loafers would slip in the mud, and Les would drop down to one knee of his worsted wool clad legs. Between the mud and the red iron-ore in the soil, Les knew those trousers and shoes had seen their last day of use in public.

Les consoled himself as he slipped and clawed his way up the hill by quietly petitioning the Almighty to reserve the hottest corner of Hell for Rita. Feeling only marginally more charitable towards Woodie, he silently begged God to let Woodie taste nothing but ashes and iron for the rest of his life. Had they worked a little harder to find some common ground in their marriage, he might be back in his office instead of ruining his clothes on this slope from hell they call a back yard, Les fumed to himself.

Though it seemed twice as long, Les got Woodie's golf shoes and was back at Woodie's side within 4 minutes. He cleaned the mud off Woodie's feet, wedged them into the old golf shoes, and tied them tightly. Throughout the chore of Les putting shoes on his feet, Woodie was mumbling something to himself. Finally, he cleared his throat and spoke hesitantly to Les.

"Les, I'm just wondering how safe it will be for you to walk me up my back yard. You were having trouble navigating the hill—by yourself. If you lose your footing and let me to fall, I may have more back problems than I already do. I'm wondering if we ought to consider an alternative method of getting me up the hill to my house."

"Woodie, I'm open to any ideas— that don't take <u>too</u> long to implement. You've been in this cold air with no clothes on too long. The temperature is dropping. You get pneumonia in your condition, recovery may not be guaranteed for you. What would you like to do?"

"What do you think about calling the rescue squad?"

"What do I think? Not much, sir. In truth, not much at all."

"Why not?"

"First, they are going to have to confront the same conditions facing me. This muddy hill will be no less slippery for them. At best, they might bring 1-2 people assist you up the slope. They could all fall as easily as I— and re-injure your back. Secondly, I'm really not sure we can get Rita to call them—or anyone. Third, they would have to come all the way from the city, meaning a waiting period of, at least, 12-15 minutes. Finally, they will need a rope 150 feet long to pull you up the hill on a sled. I doubt any of the local rescue squads have a rope that long on their vehicles."

"What you say is all true. Still—watching you try to negotiate my back yard in this mud, by yourself, makes me question if you and I have any chance at all of getting me to the top of my yard without injuring me further. Can you think of anything else we can do in a short time."

"At the risk of sounding facetious, Woodie, I can think of one possibility. If you are willing to pay for it, we can call one of those big tow trucks used to pull wrecked trucks back onto the highway from long distances down highway embankments. They'll have plenty of long cables. There is such a truck at Glen Trent's garage, not 8 miles from here. Of course, there will be a substantial charge for using Trent's equipment. Are you prepared to pay whatever he wants to come out here?"

Les knew Woodie's reluctance to spend a dime he didn't have to would cause him to nix his 'wrecker' suggestion, right out of the box. Les had to do something to get him in a notion of trying to get himself up the hill in short order— before he caught pneumonia. He couldn't think of any other viable alternative. He knew, realistically, additional bodies to help get Woodie up the hill would certainly enhance their chances of success without further injuries to him. However, he knew the chances of 2 men and a 150 foot rope appearing, in short order was sheer fantasy.

"No—no. I don't think I want to call a tow truck. Not only would it be costly, but it would look ridiculous. Let's you and I see how well we do climbing the first 20-30 feet up the yard."

Holding to the fence, moving slowly, Woodie and Les began the climb up the yard. After each step, Les made sure the cleats on Woodie's golf shoes were firmly planted in the ground and his hands firmly griping the fence. Les would lock the soles of his shoes sideways in the mud, hold to the fence with one hand, and push Woodie another step up the yard.

With over 100 feet still ahead of them before they reached Woodie's house, Les anticipated a hard and solitary climb. He was wrong. Hard—yes. Solitary—not even close. Between periodic trips inside the house to escape the cold wind, Rita stood on the carport to watch them climb. Leaning over the carport wall, she shouted mockery, taunts, derision, and assurances of failure at Woodie and Les.

"Look at the two of you! Can't tell who's helping who. Both of you look like cripples in one of those damn convalescent homes! No way in hell you're going to make it up that hill without falling, Woodie! You two claim be men of some education—and this pushing-crawling crap is the best you could come up with to get a cripple up his yard? Pitiful! You look like those two dwarves in the Snow White movie— Dopey and Goofy. Hell, if this is how you perform at work— you're just damn lucky you haven't been fired already!"

Rita would, occasionally, scoot back in the house to capture what little heat remained in the house. Once she was out of earshot, Woodie would tell Les to pay no attention to her and mutter curses at her retreating body. Les, silently, agreed with some of his curses and comments about 'that mouthy bitch'. On a personal level, Les had to admit their appearance and slow progress were not fodder for inspiration. Actually, the irritation of Rita's negative commentary took his mind off the numbing, cold wind. Rita popped out the kitchen door again, resumed her perch at the back of the carport, and continued her tirade.

"All you had to do was listen to me—just get the oil deliveries put on automatic refill. But no—not Mr. Know-It-All Woodie Watson! Not going to get his money one day ahead of time! Well, look at you now! Look at all that damn mud on you! Who do you think is going to clean all that shit off you? Huh? Not me! I can tell you that right now! That stinking red mud is going to infect your incision—if pneumonia doesn't get you first! Either way—you'll end up back in the hospital—and, by God, you deserve it! When they get through ramming a hypodermic needle in your ass three times a day for a week—maybe you'll listen to me!"

With luck, the Grace of God, and most of the strength both of them had, Woodie and Les finally made it back to the level surface of Woodie's carport. Both had so much red mud on them it was hard to see a clean patch of skin, clothing, or white body cast on either of them. Rita did <u>not</u> bring out blankets for warmth or chairs for them to rest in. She did continue her string of profanity laced negative comments. Woodie, repeatedly, told her to 'shut the hell up'. Rita, repeatedly, ignored him. Surprisingly, she agreed to call the heating oil company to come out and refill their oil tank while Les cleaned the mud off Woodie.

Even without Rita's declaration that neither man was coming inside the house with that mud on them, Les knew he had to get most of the mud off Woodie's body cast and body while they were still outside. Rita did bring them rags, water, soap and a scrub brush.

Les found an old rubber squeegee, used to clean off auto windshields, in the trunk of his car. He scraped the heaviest part of the mud off Woodie and his cast with the squeegee. He couldn't put much water on his plaster cast. He had horrible visions of the cast dissolving off Woodie's body right before his eyes. He used a dry scrub brush to get even more of the mud off the cast, and wiped off the remainder with damp and dry rags. Even at that, the entire cast was now a pinkish-orange color. Les cleaned the remainder of mud off his Woodie's body with water and rags. It was just impossible to get all the mud out of his hair, but Les combed and brushed until the majority of it was gone.

When both of them were satisfied he was as clean as practical, Woodie did two things. He thanked Les for his help. Then, with a tone of voice that left no doubt he meant what he said, Woodie told Les he didn't want one word of this episode to reach the office. Les nodded and draped an old, ragged blanket around Woodie's shoulders. He shuffled into the house, and closed the door behind him.

Les knew he couldn't get in his car with his muddy clothing on—not without ruining the fabric of the seats. He threw modesty to the wind. Standing on Woodie's carport, possibly visible to his neighbors, Les stripped down to his underwear. He threw his ruined clothes and shoes in the trunk of his car and drove to his home in nothing but his skivvies. He never gave a moment's thought to trying to clean or launder any of his mud soaked clothing or shoes. As much as those things cost him, he threw every piece into the trash can.

Les needed his job. He had a family to feed and bills to pay. So, he did as Woodie instructed. He never mentioned the events of that day to anyone in or out of his office. He saw Woodie and Rita together on infrequent social occasions over the next few years. They never said word one about that day, and neither did he. Except to his wife, he never spoke of the matter until Woodie passed away and he had been promoted to a job 500 miles away.
In all fairness, it should mention that Woodie gave Les a 10% increase in salary a few months after that incident, which was 2% more than anybody else in the office got that year.

THE CHRISTMAS PARTY

The company's annual Christmas party for the regional employees and their spouses was under way on a December evening at a local social club. It was the season of good cheer--, made even more so by the generous amounts of whiskey consumed by the guests from the open bar the company had set up for the pre-dinner social hour.

Management and employees used the social hour to mingle and converse. About forty five minutes into the social hour my wife and I were standing with a group that included

Woodie, Rita, Hobie Honaker, his wife Katie, Wade Kenville, and his wife, Evelyn.

Wade had recently been transferred from our Northern Virginia office to the company's Regional Office in central Virginia, where he was promoted to a management staff job. Wade's job with the company in Northern Virginia had been a field job—which included the full time use of a company car, at no expense to Wade. Per company policy, any employee *promoted* to an 'inside' administrative job—which caused the loss of an expense free company car—was given six hundred dollars, minus one hundred and twenty dollars for taxes, to purchase a personal car.

All company employees knew this six hundred dollar cash allowance for a personal car was a joke. At the time, new Fords or Chevvys were selling for close to $3800. Neither the *net* $480 personal car cash allowance, nor the salary of the entry level management position Wade had been given would support the purchase of a <u>new</u> car without a real financial strain. All promoted employees, Wade included, looked around for a good buy in a <u>used</u> car. One good enough to make the short daily run from home to office and back.

Woodie and Rita had just purchased a new 1967 Plymouth sedan. Woodie was trying to sell his worn, 11 year old, 1956, 6 cylinder Chevvy Bel Air sedan—with no power steering or air conditioning. He offered this gem of a car to Wade for the low, low price of $600. Woodie was 'giving it away' by letting it go for that price, he assured Wade. He could have gotten more for it from a neighbor—on a blood oath, he swore. *But*—he would rather help out a young employee, like Wade, who had been cast upon the shoals of the company's ludicrous $600 allowance for a dependable car.

On his word as a gentleman and fellow Lodge Brother, Woodie promised Wade this '56 Chevvy had no mechanical or body problems. Never burned a drop of oil—never spent a day in the shop for anything but ordinary maintenance. Woodie had owned the car since it was new—never abused a day in its life—used for little more than shuttling back and forth to work. Never failed to start—even on the coldest days; never overheated—even in the cauldron of a central Virginia summer. Good rubber on it, oil just changed, state inspection done last month.

Whether any or all of this was true, Wade needed a car. He had only $480 cash in hand. He would have to get the rest of the money out of his meager savings. He bought Woodie's '56 Chevvy for $600 two months before the company's annual Christmas party.

Our group was just making small talk, waiting for the mellowing effect of the free liquor to set in and dinner to be called.

"Rita, are you still working as a photographer for the Miller & Rhoads department store down town?" asked Katie.

Rita, as always, had had taken advantage of the open bar to fortify herself with 2-3 glasses of bourbon by the time the half-way mark of the Social Hour was reached. As always, the bluntness of her comments and the volume of her voice increased in direct proportion to the amount of liquor she had consumed.

"Oh yeah--, I'm still down there. Don't know how much longer I'll be there, though. They don't want to pay you anything for your work! That bunch that runs Miller & Rhoads-- nothing but a buncha' damn Jews—ever one of them! Steal the gold right out of your teeth if you don't watch them! Can't trust a one of them!"

Woodie shook his head and pointed at me, as he replied to Rita. "Rita, for Christ sake! The General Manager of the entire Miller & Rhoads department store is R. J.'s Uncle! His mother's brother! You may not have noticed, but R.J. isn't a Jew. So that makes it pretty clear that every manager at Miller & Rhoads isn't a Jew."

"Well, his uncle may not be Jew by blood. But—bygod—a bunch of Jews own the store. His uncle has been around them so long now he acts just like a Jew! You hang around a buncha' Jews long enough—rubs off on ya'—ya' become just as big a thief as they are!"

What rebuttal do you offer to a comment like that from your boss's wife? The obvious answer is, none. I just smiled, nodded, and offered no comment.

Quickly changing the subject, Katie nervously said, "Well, tell me Rita, were you and Woodie able to sell your old

Chevvy when you bought your new Plymouth?"

"What—oh, that ol' junker? Oh yeah, Woodie got rid of it—
finally. He sold it to some horse's ass down at the
company's Regional Office. Got $600 for the damn thing.
Can you believe that?"

Standing beside me, it was Wade's turn to sport a neutral
smile—and say nothing. His wife, Evelyn, looked like she
had just been hit by lightning. Her face turned so red I
thought smoke would start rolling off her head. If scathing
looks could have done it, Evelyn's glare would have burned
Rita down to a small pile of ashes—right on the spot.

Woodie's face reddened, his chin dropped, and he fought
to keep control of his emotions. He spoke in slow,
measured, tones as he pointed to Wade—standing less
than three feet away from them—and said.
"Rita--, this is the 'horse's ass' who bought our Chevvy."

If Wade or Evelyn were anticipating a quick retraction,
apology, or a 'just joking' disclaimer from Rita—their
anticipation was sorely misplaced. Rita didn't do apologies.

"Here—get me another drink, Woodie, before those damn
company tightwads close the bar", said Rita, as she waved
dismissively at Wade and Evelyn. For months after this
party, Wade was, in private, referred to as 'Horse's Ass' and
I was called 'Jew Boy'—thanks to Rita.

THE ATTORNEY'S OFFICE

A fellow employee and close friend worked in our local office. Both of us worked for Woodie. As noon approached one day, this friend, Wiley, suggested we drive into down town Lynchburg, pick up his wife, and go to lunch together. I agreed.

Wiley's wife, Abbie, worked in a hi-rise office building down town. For the most part, this tall building contained suites of offices occupied by the more successful Attorneys and doctors in Lynchburg. Wiley and I were sauntering down the hallway of the 10th floor of the building, toward his wife's office. We were passing the entrance to the legal offices of the formidable Marshall Darrington, Esquire. The door to Marshall's suite of offices popped open and Rita stepped into the hallway—directly in front of Wiley and I.

Rita looked like she had just come out of a Chinese hatchet fight—and finished in <u>last</u> place. Her face was covered with bruises, she had a world class black eye, and numerous other facial contusions left no doubt her head had stopped some serious blows.

Rita knew Wiley and I worked for Woodie. We knew Woodie and Rita had differences, but were, almost never, settled physically. As *employees* of Woodie, Wiley and I were <u>not</u> supposed to be privy to the *details* of their relationship. Nor did we *wish* to know any of the details. In the 60s it was a dangerous thing to have personal knowledge of embarrassing details about any company manager's personal life—let alone your *own* manager. In years past, having possession of such knowledge was known to have created a 'situation' that led to the 'involuntary' re-assignment of more than one company underling. In stunned silence, Wiley and I stood there looking at Rita. Neither Wiley nor I wanted to be the company's next 'involuntary' re-assignment.

"Look at me! Just look at me", shouted Rita. Her tone of voice and comments made it clear she was expecting some kind of verbal response from us. Me—I stood there—in a state of silent paralysis.

"Oh—you've had your hair done! Looks good!" said Wiley with a big, toothy smile. I nodded enthusiastically. I would have applauded had I thought it would help sell Wiley's compliment.

"No—dammit! Woodie beat me up! Look at this!" Rita reached down, grabbed the hem of her dress and pulled it up around her neck. Her bony little legs were covered with bruises from her knees all the way up her legs until her thighs disappeared under her panties.

After Rita's anatomical revelations—Wiley and I would have openly welcomed a strike by lightning as a merciful solution to the mess Rita had dropped us into.

"I'm not taking it anymore! I'm gonna' divorce Woodie! I'll

sue his ass off! Marshall Darrington is gonna' represent me in court. He won't have a shirt on his back when Marshall gets through with him! When Marshall tells the court how Woodie beat me like a damn dog—well—he'll get his then! The company will fire his ass!"

Wiley and I stood there—mute. I didn't know whether to pray (1) for death by lightning or (2) to be struck deaf/blind—so I could invoke the old '*I don't know nothin' 'bout nothin'* defense.

Again, Wiley recovered his wits first. Forgetting about lunch with his wife, his thoughts turned to job-preservation. He leaned close to Rita and whispered.

"Rita—I'm not going to tell anybody I saw you or spoke to you. And don't you tell anybody you saw me either."

Having given Rita his position of her marital problems, he turned and began running, full speed, down the hallway. With only a second's hesitation, I said, "Uh—yeah, Rita— that goes for me too!" I waved goodbye to Rita over my shoulder and followed Wiley down the hall. When I turned the corner at the end of the hall, I was running so fast I banked off the wall of the intersecting hallway. I ran straight to the stairway. No way was I going to stand there waiting for the elevator on the 10th floor—risk letting Rita catch up with me and offer additional details about the 'going over' Woodie gave her.

Wiley and I skipped our planned restaurant lunch that day.

We drove to Mr. Turner's General Merchandise store on the outskirts of town—where we bought a 6-pack of beer and had him cut us a pound of cheese out of that big wheel of 'rat' cheese he kept in the cooler. I'm sure that cheese had some formal 'name-type'—but I didn't know what it was—and never asked. That cheese was popularly known as 'rat' cheese—because it was the favored cheese with which to bait rat traps. It also complimented the taste of cheap beer—which was all Wiley and I could afford.

We walked under the shade of a big oak tree in the store parking lot. We drank the beer, ate the cheese, and made up a plausible lie about not seeing Rita that day—in case she tried to call us as witnesses. Neither of us wanted to lose our jobs—especially for being in possession of info we didn't need, didn't want—and couldn't afford it if we did. Personally, we opined that Rita had finally driven Woodie over the edge with her drinking and verbal abuse—he just lost control of himself and broke bad on her. Speculation aside, we had no interest in admitting we *knew* anything about anything concerning him or her—period.

EPILOGUE

Eventually, Woodie and Rita did get a divorce. The judge gave Rita a generous portion of the property and money they had accumulated over the years. Woodie gave her the house on Graves Ave. He moved into an apartment in town.

Rita didn't let something like the final divorce decree stand in her way of calling Woodie after the divorce. Sometimes, she was sober, lonely, and just wanted to chat. Sometimes she was drunk and wanted to vent her rage on the person she felt was responsible for her rage—Woodie.

Eventually, Woodie tired of her repeated calls. He changed his phone number to an unlisted status. This only incited Rita to show up, personally, on his door step—where the neighbors could witness her giving Woodie another verbal 'dose'—delivered <u>through</u> his front door.

Woodie appealed to a fellow Manager to switch territories with him. The manager agreed and Woodie moved to an office an hour west of the city. This was enough distance to gain some peace and quiet from Rita.

Woodie found a new girl-friend. A lady about his age. Things were progressing nicely between them. He took her to a dance at the Elk Lodge one Friday night—and had a fatal heart attack on the dance floor.

The girl friend was too new to *know* any of Woodie's

friends or co-workers. She *knew* Woodie didn't want Rita around. She *knew* his only daughter refused to have any kind of relationship with him. She *knew* he had recently purchased a plot in a local cemetery and had pre-arranged his burial details with a local funeral home. She felt she had to do something. In accordance with his wishes, she made arrangements to bury him, locally, at the earliest date— which was Monday following his death on Friday night.

No one in our company knew any of this. Not even the employees in Woodie's current office. The girl friend knew no employees to call. She did have his Obituary put in the Monday morning edition of the city paper. One of the people in our office, scanning the Monday morning newspaper Obits, saw Woodie's name among those of the recently departed.

Eight of us, Managers and employees, piled into two cars and hustled 45 miles from the office to the graveside service. We got there just in time to hear a Minister say some final words over Woodie and implore God to take him into his safekeeping.

Rita died some 4-5 years later, alone, with a body destRayed by alcohol. Neither Woodie nor Rita's funeral was attended by their surviving daughter, nor did she make any claims on their estates. The daughter's own husband died of cancer 3 years later. She sold their home, took their money and investments, moved to south Florida where she lived very comfortably. Very few people in town ever heard from her again.

While <u>some</u> interesting—perhaps even entertaining—stories came out of the relationship of Woodie and Rita, the end of their lives is a sad commentary on a way of life that witnesses some people living and dying on this earth with no compelling evidence they were ever here—beyond the memory of stories involving them.

Chapter 41

BENT FENDERS AND RUSTY BUMPERS

Monday morning was past its mid-point and Hal was a no-show for his first two appointments. The profane complaint calls to Hal's manager, Hobie Honaker, made his failure to keep the appointments a fact. These weren't the first appointments Hal had failed to keep. They were far enough down the long list of Hal's tardiness and no-shows that Hobie decided immediate action—possibly firing him—was something he could no longer put off.

Hal Snyder lived in a modest, attached, two story duplex on the west side of town with his wife and two children. He was 34 years old, an avid reader, had a high I.Q, and a college degree in Mathematics. Hal could read, in one evening, a thick novel that would take 98% of people 3-4 evenings to wade through. In fact, he took, on approval, 3-4 books a week from a national book club. He would read them all in 3-4 evenings, return them as 'unwanted', and order another 3-4 books—on approval. Hal never paid for more than one book a month—to keep the club from canceling his 'on approval' privilege.

All in all, he was a good guy. He cared for his family, paid his bills, and was a devout Catholic. Like most people of superior intellect, he had nothing but contempt for the mundane routines and requirements of his job. Most people, even if grudgingly, accept these repetitive and unchallenging parts of their jobs as just a part of life dealt to us all. His personality was that of an intellectual introvert—prickly. His people handling skills were somewhere south of poor.

After the second complaint of the morning on Hal, Hobie called his home. Hal's wife, Lettie, answered.

"Lettie, a good morning to you. This is Hobie Honaker, at Hal's office. I apologize for calling your home, but I need to talk to Hal. Do you know where he went this morning and when?"

"Oh Hobie, I'd be glad to let you speak to him—but Hal is in his room—and he won't come out."

"I don't understand. What do you mean in 'his room'? And why won't he come out of—whatever 'his room' is?"

"I mean he is upstairs in our bedroom. He has the door locked. He won't talk to me and he won't open the door."

"Uh-huh, well—tell you what. I'm coming down to your home. You tell Hal I'll be there in about 20 minutes and will want to talk to him when I get there."

"I'll tell him, Hobie."

Hobie was still putting his coat on and mumbling curses under his breath when he strode out of his office. He looked around our office, pointed his finger at me and said,

"Get your car and take me down to Hal Snyder's house—now."

On the way to Hal's house I drove, said nothing, and listened to Hobie mumble angrily down his shirt collar. This wasn't the first time Hal had created a problem that forced ol' Hobie to become involved in his work assignments. It was, however, the first time Hal's screw-ups had caused a personal visit to his home by the boss. There was nothing I could say that would help—so I just looked straight ahead, drove the car, and kept my mouth shut. Hobie told me to go into Hal's house with him—as a witness. When we got to Hal's home Lettie met us at the door.

"Hobie, I'm real sorry about this. I told Hal you were coming to see him. He still won't answer me or open the bedroom door. If you like, you can go upstairs and try to talk to him through the bedroom door. Maybe he will talk to you and open the door."

I stood in the small foyer of the home and watched Hobie reluctantly climb the stairs. Their bedroom was at the top of the stairs. Hobie knocked on the door, cleared his throat, and loudly said, "Hal —this is Hobart Honaker. Hal, you and I need to talk. You've created a serious work situation, and it has to be resolved—now."

There was no reply from inside the bedroom. There was a sound of foot-steps from inside the bedroom, but no answer.

"Hal, do you hear me? Did you hear what I just said?"

Hobie waited for 5 seconds but got no reply from Hal. Hobie had been staring at the floor while he waited for a reply. He noticed the bedroom door had a small gap between the bottom of the door and the floor. Hobie got down on his knees and put his face close to the small space between the door and floor. As he crouched there, he began speaking to Hal, again.

"Hal —now I know you can hear me. What you are doing is wrong and you know it. You are creating a problem for yourself, for me, and the company. Your refusal to talk to me isn't going to solve the problem. If you won't do your job, you leave me with no choice but to ask for your resignation. I'm going to leave now. I'll be back here at 5 o'clock this evening. You just leave your company car keys, the tire gauge the company issued you, any company manuals or documents you have, and your written resignation on the table in your entrance foyer downstairs. If I don't find your resignation among those things on the table I will have to fire you, and it will be on your Personnel Record. If you don't give me the keys to your car, along with any other company property you might have in your possession, I'll have to swear out a warrant for your arrest. I'm leaving now."

With his ear pressed closely to the bottom of the bedroom door, Hobie remained crouched on the floor for another 4-5 seconds. Not a sound came from the bedroom.

Hobie got up, looked at the bedroom door, shook his head, and walked slowly down the stairs.

"Lettie, I'll be back here at 5 o'clock to get Hal's car and company issued equipment. If he doesn't want to talk to me—okay. But, I want his car keys and equipment on this table right here—or I'll go from here down to the County Clerk's office and get a warrant for his arrest. I'm truly sorry about this, but he leaves me no choice."

As we drove away I waved to Lettie—standing on the porch, tears in her eyes, waving back to me. I drove quietly, lost in my thoughts. Hal's lackadaisical approach to customer service had gotten him in trouble before, but he had never let it go this far. He had a nice family. I wondered how he would take care of them with no money coming in. Given our salary range, he didn't make enough money to have much of a savings account.

True to his word, Hobie had me take him back to Hal's house that evening. He was prepared to pick up Hal's car had and drive away without another attempt to coach Hal out of his bedroom. Hobie was a reasonable man and a good boss. On the other hand, if you created problems that landed on his desk—he wouldn't hesitate to dip your butt into the proverbial 'lake of fire'. And one 'dipping' was usually enough to send a message that found a permanent place in your memory. I truly thought he was about to give Ol' Hal his final and terminal taste of 'the lake'.

Surprisingly, Hal was sitting in the swing on his front porch when we pulled into his driveway. His eyes and posture conveyed a tired, defeated look. He was courteous, asked us to sit down, and told Hobie he would like to talk. Hobie hesitated, looked at Hal for a long second, and nodded.

"Hobie, I'm sorry about not talking to you this morning—I just couldn't face anyone when you came by. And—I'm sorry about not keeping my appointments this morning. I know that created a problem for you, the customers, and the auto body shops waiting for me to make estimates of repairs for the customer's cars. I don't blame you for being angry with me."

"Hal —if you are aware of all this now, you must have known it this morning before you locked yourself in your bedroom and missed those appointments without as much as a phone call to anybody to explain yourself. The question that concerns me right now is—why on earth did you do it?" asked Hobie .

Hal hesitated, looked down at the floor of the porch, searching for words to explain himself. He finally looked up at Hobie with a pained look on his face while he spoke slowly and deliberately.

"I'll tell you why, Hobie. When I got up this morning to go to work, I knew if I had to argue with one more 'red-neck' or 'nigra' about a bent fender or a rusty bumper—I would, literally, lose my mind. I just could not take one more hour, let alone another day or week, of arguing with policyholders and claimants over damn dirty, damaged, cars and car parts—most of which were nothing but junk before they were wrecked—usually by some friggin' drunk!"

Hal's outburst described the effects of prolonged work in the field of auto and property insurance claims. Work in insurance claims is, too often, a life filled with conflict and controversy. Most Claims Reps realize this about 30 days into the job, and start planning a way out of claims work within 1-2 years—through a transfer, a promotion, or failing that, just plain quitting the job. Hal's problem was, he couldn't see a happier future in either insurance underwriting or sales positions. Even worse, he couldn't think of any other line of work he would enjoy that paid wages he could live comfortably on.

"Hal, I'm sorry your job has gotten you down. It's hard to do a good job when you don't even *want* to come to work. All of us, if we are to succeed in our jobs, have to *want* to do them—and *want* to do them well. Unfortunately, you— ".

"Hell Hobie, you think I don't *want* to do my job well? I *want* to do my job well—just as much as you and or anybody working for you. I know my work product isn't satisfactory. My trouble isn't that I don't *want* to do well. My problem is—I <u>don't</u> <u>like</u> my job! Each day on my job is like a trip around the inside of a silo. I have to *push* myself to make the trip around the silo. *But,* I <u>don't</u> see *anything motivating* in the trip around the silo. The *worst* part of it all is this. I complete the trip around the silo—knowing tomorrow's trip will be *no* better—that I'm going *nowhere*—just *stuck* in a damn miserable circle!"

Hobie saw the pain and misery in Hal's eyes. He came here to fire Hal. He would have taken no joy in it. Hal's poor work aside, Hobie liked him. He admired Hal's keen analytical ability. After listening to him bare his soul, Hobie couldn't bring himself to end Hal's career on the hot, dusty, little front porch of his home. At that moment, Hobie couldn't come up with a logical alternative to firing Hal. On the other hand, he didn't want to add to Hal's depression and troubles by summarily firing him.

"Hal, you've got two weeks of vacation coming. You're on vacation, effective today. Take that time to think about what you want to do with your life. At the end of that time, I'll give you an opportunity to convince me you are capable of handling your job satisfactorily. No promises. Frankly, after listening to your comments this evening, I don't think you should continue in this line of work. However, I'll give you an opportunity, two weeks from now, to convince me otherwise. I'll let you keep your company car. If you want to use it to look for another job, it's okay with me. In the meantime, I'm going to think about what you said, think about your work skills and strengths—see if I can come with an idea of some other job you might do well. Frankly, right now, I don't have one idea of what work or job that might be. Then again, you just never know what fate and two weeks will bring to your door. See you in two weeks."

Riding back to the office, Hobie and I said very little about

Hal. Being my boss, as well as Hal's, I didn't expect him to discuss the matter with me. Personally, I didn't think Hobie believed he had any chance of finding a job Hal would enjoy and do well. However, waiting two weeks would make it appear Hobie had considered alternatives—as opposed to just arbitrarily firing Hal on his own front porch.

Hobie knew Hal was in a weak state of mind right now. Had Hobie fired him on the spot, and Hal, God forbid, took his own life—well, the publicity fall-out would have been hard for Hobie's family or the company to handle, regardless of who was responsible.

No, I featured Hobie letting the two weeks pass while he prepared Hal's termination paper work. When Hal came around after his two week vacation, I figured Hobie would hand him his final check, collect his company equipment, and wish him well in any other future job he found.

During the week following his 'sit-down' with Hal, Hobie got a call from a long-time friend in the company's Home Office. During their conversation, Hobie unloaded on the friend about his plight with Hal —how he wished there was an alternative to firing him. On learning Hal was schooled as a Mathematician, the friend suggested Hobie send him to Home Office to interview for an opening the company had for an Actuary.

Hal interviewed for the Actuary job and got it. He moved to Home Office, and flourished in the job of converting statistics into rate tables that would produce a profit for the company's insurance policies. He passed the test for his Actuarial License on his first try. Not many people pass the Actuarial licensing exam on their first try. Most people take two or three tries to pass that difficult exam. Hal was in his element now. He considered the job of an Actuarial worthy of his abilities. He was truly contributing and his abilities were recognized. Within 3 years of his arrival at Home Office, Hal, single handedly, designed the rate tables and contract language for what became known as the company's Comprehensive Family Liability Insurance Policy.

From that launching pad, Hal refined that contract language and rate tables so family liability coverage could become a standard part of every Home Owner policy sold by the company. The company had hundreds of thousands of Home Owner policies in force. The company was the first insurance company to write, rate, and sell such a policy successfully. They made millions of dollars in profit from Hal's efforts. Every major insurance company in the country eventually adopted Hal's model for Home Owner liability coverage.

Hal was promoted and given a salary in the six figure range. This was quite a feat in the early 1970s. He was happy, but wanted more. He had ground breaking ideas on how much more profit could be made on other policies the company sold. But to make his ideas a reality, he needed a title that gave him some control over the company's Underwriting Division.

About this time Doug Murphy came to the southwest. He,

too, was transferred there from Virginia. Doug and his wife had a son born deaf at birth. They needed to be near schools that could fill their son's special needs. The Coventry School for the Deaf & Blind was the leading school in the country for children with severe hearing defects. To help Doug, the company agreed to transfer him to Home Office under the Employee Family Hardship Provisions.

Doug had potential beyond the mundane job of Claims Examiner they assigned him to when he came to Home Office. The job had little opportunity for advancement. Doug had no one above him he could 'network' for advancement. He had no mentor and little chance for acquiring one. He chaffed in his job, but put up with it for the sake of his son. Still, he was on the lookout for a better job.

Doug had been in Home Office a year when he bumped into Hal. They had worked with each other, a little, while both were in Virginia. They renewed and expanded their friendship. They really 'clicked' when it came to 'thinking outside the box'. Radical though they seemed in the company's environment, they had some had well supported ideas on how, to whom, and under what terms insurance policies should be sold in order to maximize profit.

On their own time, they put together rate tables and policies of insurance they felt were certain winners. Trouble was, to enact these programs would mean taking over, or at least encroaching upon, the 'empires' of other entrenched officers in the company. The inevitable 'corporate infighting' began. Alliances were formed for the turf battles. It didn't take Hal and Doug long to see who was going to finish the battle in second place. And it was almost certain the second place finisher would be declared 'Personae Non Grata' on the company's career advancement list. In short, their careers at the company were about to be history.

While still appearing to push their proposals to the company officers, Hal and Doug began to seek outside investors for a new insurance company they would launch. They both hocked every asset they had to raise some money. They found some venture capital people who bought into their proposal for operating an insurance company at maximum profit. With barely enough venture capital money to start their own insurance company, they resigned from their jobs.

A month later, they had their new corporate charter. Their company was called E & E Insurance Company. Hal was President/CEO of the company and had full powers over Actuarial and Underwriting functions. Doug was Vice President of Personnel. They hired an experienced CPA from an insurance background, and made him Vice President of Finance, Treasurer, and Chief Financial Officer. From one of the leading insurance companies in Texas, they took their top Claims Manager and made him Vice President of the E&E claims department.

None of these guys were making a lot of money at E&E.

Some of them were making less money than they were before they came with E&E. But—Doug had done a great job of selling them on a future at E&E that would, eventually, double their old salaries. Though they were little more than titles in the beginning, they had titles as company officers. It would have taken them a life-time in their old jobs to rise to the jobs and titles they now held. If this thing worked, they all would be 'walking in tall clover'—on their stock options alone. If it failed, they figured they could always find another job somewhere else—and probably at a salary close to the one they had when they left to join Hal.

Hal's idea was to sell insurance policies for, Autos, Home Owners, and Life to no one but people who were either educators or corporate executives. He had spent the last ten years preparing statistical tables which supported the best way to maximize the profit from the sale of insurance policies. He *knew* the best and most profitable results in insurance came from policies sold to people who were educators or company executives.

As far as cars went—the vast majority of them didn't buy hot, muscle cars. They weren't out late at night, driving while drunk, and causing accidents. They took care of their autos and were seldom in situations that left the vehicles open to theft. Their homes were in the 'good' areas of town. They were well built and well maintained. They were reluctant to turn in small, nuisance claims and they didn't try to use their home owner policies to avoid maintaining their homes out of the own pockets.

They led healthy lives and treated their bodies well—so few early demises were expected to generate claims against their Life Insurance policies. Statistics like these allowed E&E to offer rates far lower than the insurance companies educators and executives were presently insured with. E&E took these people from other mainstream insurance companies in droves. They were the cream of the crop in any insurance company's book of business.

Within 7 years of its founding, the E & E Insurance Co. had become one of the most profitable companies in the insurance industry. Their financial reserves and low personnel turnover earned them the highest rating in the industry. Their employees were well trained, well paid, given a reasonable work load, and were happy in their jobs. In return, the company expected above average performance and work product from them—and got it. Their service led to satisfied policyholders. E & E became a model for every major insurance company in America who had any idea of rising above their present plod-along financial performance.

Fifteen years later, a chain store decided they wanted to get into the insurance business. Sort of like Sears did with Allstate. The success rate for start-up insurance companies was so low they quickly decided to skip the pain of developing a successful company by buying an existing and profitable insurance company. They made the owners of E&E an offer they couldn't refuse. With their profit from the sale of E&E to the chain, the officers of E&E counted their wealth in 8 figures. A money manager of even mediocre talent could keep them finanacially comfortable for life, on just the annual interest earned from their share of the profits from the sale of E&E.

Hal, Doug, and the other E&E officers stayed on, by agreement, with the chain store for a period of 2 years after their purchase of E&E—to make the transition successful. After that period, the buyer kept all the lower level employees—who ran the company's day-to-day operations. The officers—they fell prey to chain's corporate infighting to build their own empire and protect their own turf. After two years, the chain bade Hal, Doug, and other former E&E Executives farewell— replaced them with their own executives.

Within 10 years, the chain had run the old E&E company into the ground and were losing money at an unsustainable rate. They went out of the insurance business—for good.

Hal was too old and too prickly to convince another insurance company to take him on as a CEO or President. Doug and most of the other Officers—they really weren't looking for any serious work. They accepted some periodic work as Consultants, but spent most of their time in southern Florida or Arizona.

Hal —his story didn't have a happy ending. Like many people of superior intelligence, he didn't have a lot of friends. His social skills were on the low end of the scale. He had no outlet to feed his ego and brash attitude of 'I'm the only man who knows how to really run an insurance company'. His years of personal conduct and attitude killed what little love and respect Lettie may have had for him. She divorced him. His kids had contact with him only when they had to. Lettie got half of Hal's worth in the divorce and his kids got trusts.

Hal sought solace in a new friend—alcohol. Within 5 years, he was a hopeless alcoholic. He died from alcohol poisoning—living in a one bedroom apartment—alone. Other than his family, there were scarcely a dozen people at his funeral.

There was a eulogy—given by Doug Murphy. He said some nice things about Hal. What he said could be summarized as 'Hal was a good man, and a bad boy'.

Me—I always thought Hal's life came to a tragic and early end because he just couldn't deal with the demons in his life any longer. He just couldn't face another day of dealing with the 'bent fenders and rusty bumpers' of life.

FIRE AT THE PONCE deLEON

Joe was on the Home Office Staff of our Senior Vice-President of Claims. They gave him a title of, as best I can remember, Superintendent of Commercial Claims. Sounds like heady stuff. In fact, he answered to a company Director, who answered directly to the Senior Vice President. Joe's job, primarily, was doing Performance Evaluations on the work of employees in company claims offices in various states around the country.

One winter Joe was assigned to a team of 8 people—led by Claims Director, Ray Hanson—bound for Syracuse, New York. They were to deliver their evaluation of the work product of the New York state claims operation to the New York Regional Vice President.

Joe anticipated trouble on this trip when it was scheduled for February. No one goes to Syracuse, New York in the month of February—without a virtual gun at their head. Some people in the company opposed going to Syracuse at *any* time of the year. A few swore it was a northern ice box that had only one day of summer—the 4th of July. They insisted the other 364 days of the year were as wretched as those in the North Pole.

Be that as it may, the team was in Syracuse in February. They landed in late afternoon. Joe couldn't remember, ever, feeling a colder or more cutting wind than the one that hit him when he stepped off the company plane to the airport tarmac. He stood in snow up to his knees as he tossed his luggage into the trunk of the car taking them to their hotel.

Their arrival was too late in the day for them to begin their verbal reports and analysis to the local Vice President. They were taken to their hotel and told they would meet with the local Vice President the following morning.

The company's Travel & Accommodations office had a policy of furnishing the employees with 'economical, safe, and clean accommodations' when out-of-town overnight stays were required. Translated, that meant hotels several rungs down the ladder from those in the Five-Star range. In this particular instance, it meant the Hotel Ponce DeLeon (pronounced dilly-OWN) in downtown Syracuse. It was 12 stories high, built about 30 years earlier, was equipped with elevators that ran slowly, and had rooms with 9 foot ceilings—and were clean.

They put the team in rooms on the 9th and 10th floors. Their rooms had a large windows that offered a view of the noisy, snowy, frozen street far below. The windows were the old type. They could be raised by hand and had a flimsy, wire screen over them. This was the prevalent type of window used when the hotel was constructed many decades ago. Why the windows hadn't been replaced with something more modern in the intervening 30 years was debatable. A logical guess would be—the hotel didn't want the expense of replacing all the windows, or—the manual easy-opening windows were left in place as an accommodation to guests who could <u>not</u> face one more day of the weather in Syracuse.

Led by Ray, the team had dinner at one of the finer Italian restaurants in Syracuse. In no hurry to return to their uninspiring hotel rooms, they prolonged dinner with drinks before and after dinner. For most of them, that meant 1-2 drinks. For Ray, it meant consuming half a quart of bourbon—on the rocks.

Around ten o'clock that evening Joe and Gene got Ray back in his room on the tenth floor. He was on the verge of passing out. Joe and Gene helped him out of the majority of his clothes while he abused them with snarls of 'I can get my own damn self ready for bed'.

About one am the following morning loud bells in the hallway began ringing. Joe felt as If he had hardly gone to bed when the awful racket from those bells began. He opened his door to the hall. Joe could see thick smoke filling the hall. The fire alarm was doing its job. Half the people on that floor were standing in the hallway in their skivvies. All of them quickly pulled on shirts, pants, shoes grabbed their wallets, and headed to the stairs. The density of the smoke was increasing by the minute. Joe couldn't tell where or what the smoke was coming from. Like the rest of the team, he decided to first save his own skin, determine the origin of the smoke later—preferably from some safe vantage point out of the hotel.

When they got to the lobby it seemed relatively free of

smoke. The hotel staff was passing out blankets for warmth. Joe took a quick inventory and found all their team in the lobby--except Ray. It was no stretch to imagine Ray lying passed out in bed from the half quart of bourbon he drank at dinner. The Fire Department wouldn't allow any of them back up to the 10th floor to check on Ray—nor did *they* seem eager to go looking for him.

Feeling a need to 'get eyes on' the situation, Joe and the team walked outside to the sidewalk. There were fire trucks and firemen lining the sidewalk along the entire block. They found a place on the sidewalk that gave them a view of what they guessed was Ray's window was on the 10th floor. Joe told several firemen he feared one of his party was still on the 10th floor. They looked up at the window Joe pointed to. They had no ladder trucks that could reach that high. The firemen discussed putting oxygen masks on a couple of firemen and sending them up to find Ray, if they could get by the fire—which still hadn't been located.

Wrapped in thin blankets that offered no more comfort against the cold than a bath towel, the team was staring upwards when a window opened on the tenth floor. The screen over the window flew outwards and whirled down to the street like a Frisbee. A man's head and shoulders came out of the windows--with no clothes on. It was Ray. With his hands on the window sill, he stared down at the fire trucks and us as if we might be part of a nightmare.

One of the firemen misunderstood Ray's intentions as he hung out that window. He cupped his hands to his mouth and yelled to Ray.

"Doonnn't jump!"

With a cynical look that was almost a fixture in his face, Ray looked down at the fireman who advised against jumping from his 10th floor window.

"Don't jump?? You think I'm 'freakin' crazy?" yelled Ray before he pulled his head back in the window.

Two or three minutes passed without further sightings of Ray. Joe was so cold he was shaking, and suggested they go back in the lobby. Maybe, he thought, we could get one of the firemen in the lobby to go up and get Ray. "Even if they refuse, wouldn't it be better", he said, "to face their refusal in the comfort of the lobby than suffer death by freezing on the sidewalks of Syracuse?"

The team hadn't been back in the lobby more than three minutes when the door leading to the stairs opened. Out walked Ray—completely nude— except for a wet towel wrapped around his head with only the smallest slit for his eyes. That was a sight you don't see every day in hotel lobbies. He had gotten his underwear off after Joe left him, earlier that night, and passed out on his bed—nude. When he woke up, the electricity was off, he couldn't see anything but smoke in his room, he didn't know where his clothes were, and some fool fireman was telling him not to jump to his death from a 10th floor window. He wrapped a wet towel around his head so he wouldn't inhale smoke and walked down 10 flights of stairs—still soused enough to make his walk unstable.

Except for the small white streaks down his abdomen where the rivulets of water had run down his body from the wet towel wrapped around his head, Ray's entire body was covered with black soot.

Fortunately, there were no children among the hotel guest gathered in the lobby. There must have been 60-70 people in the lobby when Ray walked into it--half of them were women. Joe could hear comments and sounds from women standing closest to him.

"Omigod! –"WOW—look at that!"—"Is he nuts?"— "Well—that guy's livin' proof they don't have all the 'loonies' locked up!"

The hotel manager rushed to Ray with a blanket.

"Sir! Sir! Cover yourself with this blanket, please! There are ladies present!"

Ray wrapped himself in the blanket and dropped the wet towel on the lobby floor. Joe walked over to Ray and spoke to him. Joe later swore he would never forget Ray's answer to his question if he lived to be 100 years old.

"Ray--why on earth didn't you wrap the towel around your *waist*?" Joe asked quietly.

"Well—", said Ray, "for one thing, these cheap bath towels aren't big enough to go around my waist. More importantly, I figured if I wrapped the towel around my head, came into a lobby full of people, none of them would recognize me—except a *'close friend'*."

For the rest Joe's 36 years with the company, he wondered if that was Ray Hanson talking, or the bourbon.

THE DREAM HOME

Brad and Dee Woodward came to Virginia by way of a company promotion. Brad was a born salesman and a natural leader. His company recognized his talents, worked him up the promotion ladder until the top sales job in Virginia came open in the mid 80s, and then named him Virginia State Sales Manager.

As far as Brad and Dee were concerned, this job was to be nothing more than a stepping stone to company officer ranks in Home Office in their native state of Georgia. They were in Virginia less than a year when the beauty of the land, the easy-going life style of Virginians, the mild climate, the low cost of living, the ease of the job, and his generous salary—it all persuaded them to spend the rest of their lives there.

Dee was a gourmet cook. She and Brad delighted in hosting dinner parties in their home, entertaining interesting people, and basking in the compliments of those who enjoyed the succulent delicacies prepared by Dee. Dee was becoming recognized as a 'ranked' gourmet cook.

Entertaining on Brad and Dee's level called for a home custom tailored to their needs and lifestyle. Up to this point, they had leased a nice home in the Oakwood section of town. But—spending the rest of their lives here—entertaining wealthy and influential people at lavish dinners—nothing less than a home custom designed to support such a life style would do.

They decided to locate a lot in just the perfect place, hire the area's most sought after builder—Les Addison—, describe to him their unique requirements in a home, have detailed drawings committed to paper, and within 12 months they would be in their one-of-a-kind— *DREAM HOME.*

There is a school of thought which contends every soul on this earth will a pass through a day in their lives when the collision of certain events or things produces negative, unforgettable, life-altering, results. Those who experience this wretched low point in their lives usually refer to this particular day as *'the blackest day of my life'*.

Some months after hiring him to build their home, Brad and Dee would call the day they signed a home building contract with O. B. Johnson, Jr. 'the blackest day of our lives'. Ironically, in the final stages of the construction of the Woodward home, O. B. Johnson, Jr. would, bitterly, claim that **same** day to be 'the blackest day of my life'.

O. B. Johnson, Jr., or 'Junior' as he was popularly known, to his displeasure, was the only child of Mr. & Mrs. O.B. Johnson, Sr. They were life-long residents of the Riverside section of town. As did most inhabitants of Riverside, they believed themselves to be above the masses, impervious to error, superior in intellect, and exempted from the rules and trials that burden the lives of lesser mortals. Except where business and common courtesy dictated the need for minimal verbal interaction, they spoke only to family, peers of equal or greater wealth, and God. They perpetuated this myth of pseudo-Rayalty by raising their off-spring to adopt similar attitudes.

O.B., Sr., by shrewd investments, support of Riverside peers, and paying his employees very nominal wages, enjoyed financial success as an Optometrist. He expanded his optometry business from a single shop in town to four satellite offices in the growing county suburbs.

They doted on O.B., Jr., denied him nothing in his youth, and sent him to one of the better private colleges. The one thing they could not remedy for Junior was his withered left arm. The result of a congenital defect, there was nothing medicine could do to repair the smaller left arm. While usable, the shorter left arm limited his physical capabilities.

Determined that Junior would assume his 'rightful place' in town's society, O.B., Sr., sent him to a recognized Optometry school, kept him there until he graduated, had some business cards printed with the name of Dr. O.B. Johnson, Jr. on them, and made Junior the head of his largest suburban Optometry office.

Most people who met or dealt with Junior thought he was an arrogant little prick. His condescending attitude and arrogance did not endear him to potential optometry customers. An hour with Junior was more like a treatment than a treat. After one visit to Junior's office, a good number of patients changed Optometrists.

For several years, O.B., Sr., and Junior, lived in denial of Junior being a 'square peg in a round hole'—as an Optometrist. Oddly enough, for one with a handicapped arm, Junior was a 'fair'—not great—draftsman. He had taken a course in drawing building plans in high school. Bred to believe his family's 'station in life' exempted him from failure or accountability, Junior decided to leave the field of Optometry for a career in custom home building/development. He planned to develop whole neighborhoods of up-scale, custom, expensive, brick homes.

Even O.B., Sr.'s, bankroll wasn't fat enough to buy an entire tract of land for development. He and Junior had to be satisfied with buying 6 one-acre lots in the prestigious Black Watch neighborhood, just west of town.

On these six lots, Junior planned to design and build custom houses. He would design and build custom 'spec' homes. If the prospective buyer so wished, he would draw plans from their description of the home they wanted on one of his lots. His custom built homes would be the launching pad his reputation as the area's *'primo'* master-builder of luxury homes. After all, he was O.B. Johnson, Jr.—of Riverside. How could he fail? 'Who *wouldn't* want *my* name on their home', he reasoned.

Brad & Dee found the perfect lot for their dream home. Located in Black Watch, it had a stunning view of Sharp Top—the highest peak in the Blue Ridge Mountains, home to a National Park, and the famed Skyline Drive. They would sit on their porch with guests, have after dinner drinks, and watch the sun set behind Sharp Top. The lot was owned by Junior.

They quickly learned there was <u>no</u> chance of getting that choice lot away from Junior—even at double the price he paid for it. However, not to worry, he told Brad and Dee. He could and would design and build any type of home they wanted on the lot—and it would be the envy of Ivy Knolls. Their home, he promised, would be one other people rode by on Sunday afternoon drives—the one they admired— the one they envied—the one they fantasized as theirs— and the one they bought tickets to see during the annual Home & Gardens Open-House tour.

They really wanted their home built on that lot—and ol' Junior did *talk* a 'good game'—as a home builder. When he finished his spiel, Junior had them believing he possessed a wealth of experience as a home designer/builder. Top of his class in drafting, he told them. Then, alas, he dropped out of the craft to get his doctorate in Optometry and help his aging father manage his vast and growing optometry empire. Now, he was returning to his first love. He showed them some drawings of homes he had done—and they looked impressive. He might have omitted a few details— like telling he had taken pre-existing blue prints belonging to others, and adding a few *very minor* touches of his own to them.

Dee and Brad inked a contract with Junior. He would build

them a 4000 square foot, two story, Colonial Williamsburg style home on a once acre lot for $255,000. This was a lot of money for such a home in the late 70s—top dollar in most anybody's book. The customized extras Brad and Dee demanded in the house raised the price a bit. No matter— this was to be a 'one-of-a-kind' showplace. "You get what you pay for", Junior told Brad. Months later, Brad would amend this cliché to "You get what you pay for— when you put Junior on the *application* end of a ball bat".

Spring time arrived in Black Watch. Junior broke ground for Brad and Dee's home. Their lot gently sloped, downhill, across the two hundred foot frontage of the lot. Somehow, ol' Junior never learned how to draw plans for a house built on a sloping lot. Dee would later tell dinner party guests she didn't know whether Junior had trouble with elementary math or skipped class the week his instructor taught drafting plans for houses on lots that slope.

Brad and Dee were out of town for several weeks. During this time, Junior's workers built the basement walls and laid out the first floor of the home. Dee was almost giddy when they drove up to the site the day after they returned home. Actually, it may have been this visit which gave them their first hint that construction of their home would not go smoothly. Imagine their surprise—well, more like shock— when they found the entire first floor of their home built on *three* different levels. No Colonial Williamsburg house Dee had ever seen included multi-level ground floors— certainly not *their* Colonial Williamsburg style Dream Home plans.

The first floor den-library, a hallway, entrance foyer, and garage were located on one level. Two steps down put them in their first floor formal living room and dining room. Down another two steps, on the east side of the dining room, there was their first floor kitchen, breakfast nook, pantry, and Dee's study. According to Brad and Dee's understanding of the house plans, all of these rooms were all to have been on a ground floor—of the *same* level.

Junior was not at the building site when they got there. Brad had to be content with talking to wall studs and floor joists as he bellowed curses, and threatened physical and legal action against Junior. He paced up and down the various levels of the 'first floor' of their house as he vented his anger.

Between sobs, Dee screamed words that a 'proper' lady doesn't normally use. She clung to the bare, wooden, wall studs for support during bouts of hysterical crying. She wailed to Brad, several times, that she was fully involved in a nervous breakdown. Brad, nodding his understanding, told her—when she checked in at the psychiatric ward—to look around for the 'nut-case' who was building their home. As they walked away from the house, Dee hysterically wailed an oath to slice off Junior's manhood before the sun sat again.

Brad and Dee's meeting with Junior the next day took a drift that pretty much set the tone for most of their future meetings with him. They shouted questions, accusations, referenced their house blueprint, and demanded answers.

Junior <u>never</u> admitted an error—of any kind—at any time. Condescendingly, he explained his actions; he expressed shock at their failure to grasp the logic of everything he had done; he offered to let them break their contract with him—saying he could sell the house to someone else before the next day had passed; before they had time to consider and actually accept his offer to nullify the contract, he offered a monetary concession on his contract price for building the house—to serve as a marker of his generosity and good faith intentions to 'do the right thing here'.

Warming to the sound of his own voice, Junior expounded on his reasons for inclusion of multi-level floors in their house. Had they read their Virginia history, he purred, they would know most all original colonial houses were built on multi-levels. This was true, he said, because the original Colonists were poor. They could only afford to build one room of the house at a time. The ground was uneven. When they added an *addition* to the house, it had to be built on another level, with a door cut through an exterior side wall, with a step up or down, to the *original* room. Moreover, Junior extolled the value of owning a home with 'sunken' floors. It added 'character and individuality', he said. Actually, Junior beamed, it cost more to build a house with 'sunken' rooms.

Not wishing to start over, they grudgingly decided they could live with the 'sunken' floors. They accepted the monetary concession Junior offered—along with his solemn promise all would go well with the remainder of the construction.

The house was under roof, and things seemed to progressing nicely. Brad and Dee went out late one afternoon to see how the grand staircase from the entrance foyer to the upstairs looked in its completed state.
The massive oak, front door had been hung. The heavy, solid brass door handle felt good in Brad's hand as he swung the door inward—right into the face of the carpenter stepping down from the last stair step onto the entrance foyer floor.

Brad felt a solid thud as the door made contact with something. He heard a quick yelp of pain, a curse, and a loud crash of something falling on wood. Brad and Dee looked at each other in puzzlement. Brad quickly stepped into the foyer and looked behind the big entrance door. There was the carpenter—lying on the stairs, his tool bag beside him, holding his head in his hands.

"For Pete sake", snarled the carpenter, "don't you b'lieve in knockin' before you open somebody's door?"

"Knock? Why would *we* knock? This is *our* house." Snapped Dee

"Oh—sorry, thought you were just people lookin' at new houses."

Brad was mute during this exchange. He stood in the middle of the foyer, his hands on his hips, his head slowly shaking back and forth, staring in disbelief at the scene before him. His lips began to move as he struggled to speak in coherent sentences.

"Who in the name of—how can *anybody* build—if I wasn't standing here—Jesus Christ —this must be a sick joke—the queen mother of all nightmares!"

"Hey fellow, you ok? What you're sayin—don't make good sense. You havin' one of them strokes, or somethin'?" said the carpenter.

Brad stared at the carpenter for a long moment, pointed to the staircase, and began to speak.

"*I* ain't acting right'? *I* appear to be acting 'oddly', you say? Did you hear the man, Dee? He says I'm not making any sense. I apologize, sir, for causing you concern. If you can offer some *reasonable* explanation for what I'm looking at—then, maybe, I could speak in *reasonable* sentences" said Brad.

"Why, I'm wondering, does this staircase end within 6 inches of the hinges of my front door? Really—*look* at youself, lying there on the steps! *Anybody—anybody* coming down those stairs stands a darn good chance of getting their teeth knocked out when someone, outside, opens the door into their face! Can you shed any light on why a designer, builder, planner—hell, anybody at all— would design and build a house with a staircase and front door positioned like that? Any thoughts on that matter? Any thoughts—at all? Listen—whatever your name is. If this door/staircase thing is a <u>joke</u>, dreamed up by some sadistic s.o.b, I can handle that. I think it's in poor taste, going too damn far—but I can handle it. What I'm going to have one hell of a hard time handling—is you telling me these stairs and that door were <u>deliberately</u> put where they are!! So—if you can *explain* this—this— lunacy—I'd just love to hear it!"

"Naw—I can't help you, fella'—not me. Me—I thought the placement of them stairs was a mite odd. But, I just follow the blueprints—just build whatever they say. Not my place to ask questions. I get paid to work, mind my own business—do what I'm told, ya' know", said the carpenter as he picked up his spilled tools from the stairs.

"Ah, of course—the blueprints. Why bother with logic when you've got blueprints. Well, let's forget the staircase—for the moment. Since the stairs are where they are—why hang the front door so it opens to the <u>left</u>—right into the stairs? Huh--? Doesn't that seem—a bit—oh—how do I say this—a bit backwards to you? Think about that—please. Do take your time—don't let me rush you into a hasty answer. Wait—don't tell me! Let me guess! The blueprints called for the door to open to the left! Am I right?"

"'That's right! Tell you the truth", said the carpenter as he leaned forward and spoke in a conspiratorial whisper, "I personally thought hangin' that door like that was crazier 'n hell. But—it's not my house. I just—".

"We know", mumbled Dee as she angrily walked out the

door, "You just follow the plans. Sorry about your head. C'mon, Brad. Get me out of here before I throw up."

Two days later, Brad and Dee met Junior at the house for their second stormy meeting. Junior fixed a condescending smile on his face as they vented over the stairs and door. He was the picture of control as they unloaded their anger and frustration on him. Finally, after a demand for an explanation for the stairs and door, they stared at Junior.

"Mr. Woodward, you're an insurance professional. No doubt, you are well aware of the large number of burglaries which take place in the *finer*, more expensive homes. Now, sir, I knew this. I anticipated your concern that this same frightening form of criminal invasion might occur at your lovely home", said Junior with an air of concern in his voice. "So—I built your staircase to end right at your front door. Then I hung your door to open into your staircase, to help you good folks protect hearth and home."

Brad and Dee exchanged totally confused looks, and turned back to Junior as he continued his reassuring explanation.

"You see, when a burglar comes through your front door, he won't be able to see you standing right behind the front door on your stair step. You take a baseball bat, or whatever your weapon of choice is, and just pop him right upside the head. He'll be laid flat out on the floor, without ever knowing who or what hit him. You call the cops—they haul him off to the slammer—and you don't lose a thing to the thieving rascal. Damned thieves—they're everywhere, you know."

Brad stared at Junior for a few seconds. He was sure Junior was making a poor joke to cover his mistakes, would laugh at his joke, and offer to correct the entire, ridiculous, mess at his own expense. When Junior gave no indication of expecting anything less than their applause for his explanation, Brad leveled an angry stare at him. In a quiet, determined, tone of voice he told Junior to tear out the stairs, re-hang them away from the door opening, and hang another front door, which would open in the opposite direction.

Unhappily, Junior agreed to install another door, which opened in the opposite direction. With dread in his voice, he pointed out the design of the house would not allow the stairs to be, practically, moved back from the front door. If he moved the bottom of the stairs back three feet from the door, as they demanded, the stairs would be so steep it would be akin to climbing a step ladder to get up or down them.

Junior countered the screams of outrage from Brad and Dee with the same offer to let them break their contract with him—"No skin off my nose—I can sell this house tomorrow, to a half dozen people—". Before they could accept his cavalier offer to cancel the contract, he, quickly offered a second monetary concession—to salve their disappointment with the stairs. Again, they felt they the most reasonable alternative at this stage would be to accept a change in the *direction* the door opened—live with the present position of the stairs—and accept Junior's offer of another monetary reduction in the contract price of the house. Seething in disappointment, they agreed to continue with the construction of the house.

After the door was re-hung, the progress of construction was routine for a week. Now making daily trips to monitor Junior's work, Brad and Dee were walking upstairs when Brad looked down to see a light on-off switch mounted on the wall about 18 inches above the stair tread he was standing on. He had to bend down to reach the switch, but found it actually turned on the ceiling light at the top of the stairs.

"Junior, do you want to tell me why this light switch is mounted on the wall only 18 inches above one of the stair treads—where I have to bend down or squat to reach it?"

"Mr. Woodward, let me ask you something—man to man. Do you take a drink, from time to time?" said Junior with a smug smile.

"Yeah, I like a good Scotch now and then. What has that got to do with this light switch being mounted so low I have to bend over to reach it?"

"Well sir, I put that light switch down there for a very good reason. If you come home one night when you've had one-too-many drinks of Scotch—you're so drunk you have to *crawl* up these stairs—you'll be able to reach that light switch to turn the lights on—so you can see where you're going", said Junior with a grin that split his entire face.

"Junior, you're killing me!" said Dee, "Just—freakin' killing me! Change that light switch to the correct height—and do it before I come out here next week! "

Two weeks later Brad & Dee came out to view their 'finished' back porch. It was finished—screened in, nice fan-light in the ceiling. Trouble was, the floor of the porch had rough, deck flooring instead of finished, tongue and groove, red oak flooring as specified in the plans. As with all deck flooring, there were cracks between each of the flooring boards. Brad took two minutes to get his emotions under control and then called Junior to the porch.

"Junior, as you know, our house plans specified a back porch, not a deck."

"Mr. Woodward, this is a porch. Screened in and everything. What's wrong with it?"

"What's wrong with it? This porch has deck flooring, not tongue and groove oak flooring—that's what wrong with it."

"I say again, I don't see anything wrong—both kinds of flooring are made from wood."

"The problem, Junior, is deck flooring has space between each board. I had you screen this porch in to keep the insects *away* from us. With spaces between the porch *deck-floor* boards, insects will come up through the deck-floor spaces and be, literally, screened inside *with* us—to bite and torment the life out of us! You understand that—don't you, Junior?"

His well-worn, condescending smile crept across Junior's face. He draped his good arm across Brad's shoulder in a fatherly manner.

"Mr. Woodward, you're from Ohio—right? Well, sir, not being from Virginia, you probably don't know *insects can't fly* <u>uphill</u> *in Virginia*. No sir! They could <u>never</u> fly upwards through the cracks in that flooring. Why—you could have the air around the *outside* of your porch screen literally filled with skeeters and gnats –and not a one of them could fly <u>up</u> through the cracks in that deck flooring to gnaw on you and the Missus."

"Junior, tear out the decking—put in the tongue and groove flooring—or I will not sign off on the next twenty five thousand dollars due to be paid at this stage of construction."

Angrily, Junior told the carpenter to tear out the deck floor of the porch and replace it with tongue and groove. He was so angry he was mumbling to himself—out of Brad's hearing.

"I swear –these people have me so upset I feel like hell is flying through me a mile wide. At this point—I've made so many concessions to these Yankee-fied people—torn out and rebuilt so much of this friggin' house—I'll be lucky to break even on it, let alone make a single dollar of profit!"

The Woodwards, he fumed to himself, were just being doggone unreasonable. What's more, by gosh, it just wasn't right! A *Johnson* from Riverside being ordered around *ordinary* people—like those Woodwards! Even worse, he raged, they were from up north! Hell, they'd never be invited to dinner in *any* home in Riverside—let alone give orders to a *Johnson!*

It was a world gone mad, he bitterly concluded. Let some low-bred Yankees get a little money in their pockets and they forget their place. Get all snotty—think they can order their 'betters' around. Well, he declared, they weren't going to do it to yours truly, O.B. Johnson, Jr. He was a man of breeding, civility, forbearance—but his tolerance and charity had their limits. And those Yankee-fied Woodwards had pushed him to his limits!

From here on in, it would be strictly business between them! No more Mr. Nice-Guy Johnson! No more favors! No more rolling over and taking their abuse! No sir—strictly business. Let's see how they like it that way! When they walked by him from now on they would get frost bite instead of a smile!

A few days later Brad and Dee visited their home to find the concrete masons putting the finishing touches on their curved patio in the rear of their home. Brad uttered profanity as he looked down from the rear porch—to see a concrete patio. The plans called for a brick patio—not concrete. Once again, Brad had Junior meet him at the house--immediately.

"Junior, look at these plans. What kind of patio floor do they call for?"

"I know—the plans call for brick flooring—but, we've run out of brick. I was afraid the brick might not be the same color if I ordered another load from the kiln 3 months after the original bricks got here. I know you folks are particular—you want all the bricks to match. So, I just had the patio floor poured in concrete."

"And saved $2000 in the cost of brick and labor by going with concrete instead of brick?" said Brad.

"Well, there was some savings—yes. But that wasn't my reason for doing it."

"Junior, we want a brick floor on the patio. Tear out this concrete and put in bricks as the plans specify."

"Tell you what. I'll just have the brick mason lay brick on top of the concrete. How about that?"
"No—if you do that the surface of the brick will be 2" higher than the bottom of the patio sliding doors. Every person who walks through those doors to the patio will be tripping on the raised brick and falling on their faces. Tear out the concrete, put in the brick floor correctly, or I won't

sign off on the work."

"Mr. Woodward, it's time for me to tell it like it is! Time for me to talk to you, straight up! I've just been too good to you. You folks have taken advantage of my good nature. You and the Missus are just too demanding! I've virtually built this whole house <u>twice</u>—just to keep you two satisfied! As it stands right now, I won't make a dime on this house. Not one damn dime! I tell you, sir, you've driven me half out of my mind! I mean every word of that! Just last night my wife told me so much of my hair has fallen out since I started this house I am almost bald! You hear me— bald! Bygod, sir, I just can't take any more hassling from you and the Missus! Not another thing! That's it! Over and finished! And while I'm clearing the air, stop calling me Junior! My name is O. B. or Johnson—*Mr.* Johnson to you folks!"

"Don't be so melodramatic, Junior. Every change you've had to make was because of *your* mistakes, or you wouldn't have voluntarily made the first change. Please have this concrete removed and replaced by brick before the end of the week."

Junior felt his blood pressure shooting sky high. He could feel his pulse pounding as the veins stood out on his forehead. He feared he would suffer a major stroke any second now. He couldn't wait to get away from this house and these pretentious little Yankees—telling *him* what to do. What the hell ever possessed him to get tangled up with these people on a house-building deal, he asked himself. Junior just didn't have any money left in this house's budget to make more corrections. He was into his own pocket now.

"Curse the day I agreed to build a house for the Woodwards", he mumbled aloud. "It has to be the blackest day of my entire life. Worse than that, it has turned into an unending nightmare. I have been verbally whipped, without end—and financially ruined by their ridiculous demands for costly and unnecessary changes. Well, I'm damn sure not paying skilled masonry labor rates to tear out that concrete patio, he told himself."

The next morning Junior drove his truck down to the corner of Fifth & Federal Streets. This was the hang out for winos looking for just enough work to buy another bottle of $1.89 wine. He picked up four minimum-wage winos, hauled them out to the Woodward house site. He gave them sledge hammers, shovels, and a wheelbarrow. He told them to break up the concrete patio and haul it around the house to the dumpster. Unable to stand being around the Woodward house another minute, Junior left for another job site after telling the men he would be back to pay them at five o'clock that evening.

Feeling uneasy about Junior's attitude when they parted the day before, Brad drove out to the house site at noon of the next day. As he walked through the front door he could hear odd sounds coming from the back of the house. A muted 'whump-whump-whump' sound drifted through the still air.

He quietly walked out on the back porch and looked down to the patio below. The four laborers were beating the gum-like concrete of the patio with sledge hammers. The concrete hadn't hardened enough over night to break apart. Every time they swung the sledge hammers down into the concrete the head of the hammer would bury itself four inches deep into the concrete. With some back and forth motions, the laborers would work the hammer head loose and pull it out of the doughy, gummy, concrete— leaving an indention in the concrete where the hammer head had buried itself.

There were indentions and imprints of hammer heads over the entire concrete patio floor. One of the laborers placed the edge of a shovel against the concrete, stood on the metal part of the shovel, and succeeded in gouging the shovel several inches into the rubbery-like concrete. Still, the concrete refused to break apart into pieces. Four hours work had resulted in no more than two half loaded wheelbarrows of concrete being transferred from the patio to the dumpster. At this rate, it would take an entire week to remove all the concrete from the patio.

The smile on Brad's face spread until it dissolved into hysterical laughter as he walked back to his car. He regretted not having a camera with him. What he had just seen was the equivalent of Hollywood's best slapstick comedy. He wondered if anyone would believe his tale of what he has just witnessed. He knew this patio incident was right in keeping with the history of Junior's construction miscues at this house. Still, sane people just didn't stand for hours, hammering at gummy, half-cured concrete, making no progress at all in its destruction. Nah, he told himself, no ordinary person would ever buy into this tale. No point in even telling it. I should have had a camera, he thought.

Things didn't get a lot better as construction of the house staggered toward the 'finished' stage. While the painters and paper hangers were applying paint and wallpaper to the interior walls, an odd thing began to happen to the house windows. The glass in nearly every window throughout the entire house took on a foggy, milky appearance.

Brad had Junior install insulated windows in the house. Each double-hung window frame had two panes of glass— separated by a quarter of an inch. This space between the glasses was a sealed vacuum. The vacuum acted as a barrier, to keep cold or hot air from transferring from the exterior to the interior of the house. The windows were expensive, but billed as the latest and greatest thing in controlling the cost of heating and cooling a home. The installation of these windows required an experienced and skilled installer—to avoid breaking the vacuum seal between the glasses of the windows. It said as much—right on the installation instructions taped to each window. Toward the end of the construction of the house, Junior cut some corners—to recover some of the money he had lost on this house. As far as he was concerned, a window was window. Rather than pay the going rate for skilled window installers, he put several of his minimum wage laborers to work installing the windows. The laborers, jamming the windows into the brick openings with wedge-bars and hammers, broke the vacuum seal on nearly every window in the house. With the vacuum seal broken between the glasses, moist, cool air seeped between the two glasses of each window. The warmer air of the interior of the house against the interior glass of each window cause the cool air between the glasses to condense to a moisture form, creating a virtual white fog between the glasses.

When someone drove up in the driveway of their house, Brad or Dee would have had to raise a window or open the front door to see who it was. They couldn't see a thing through their fogged windows.

This incident was the final straw. It triggered the end of their relationship with Junior. They insisted he use a qualified installer to remove and replace every window in the entire house. To remove and replace all of the windows with skilled labor would cost $5000. Junior flatly refused to do it. He told *them* to get rid of the 'fog' in the windows by turning the heat of a hair dryer on each window—each and every time they wanted to see *through a fogged up window*. He refused to spend another dime to tear out and replace *anything* on their house.

Brad refused to release the last $30,000 payment Junior was due for completing construction of the house. Junior threatened litigation to get this money. Eventually, the matter was settled out of court. Junior gave up his rights to $10,000 of the last $30,000 due him upon completion of construction of the house. Brad and Dee agreed to hold Junior harmless for any present or future construction flaws or defects.

Brad used the $10,000 to hire another contractor to correctly replace the windows, and correct other minor mistakes Junior had made. In truth, both Junior and Brad lost money on that house. Junior built only one other house before leaving the construction trade and returning to the Optometry business.

Mr. O. B. Johnson, Sr. furnished the money to hire a law firm to draw up the final 'quit claim' agreement between Brad and Junior. Being a true protector of the myth of infallibility and superiority of the Johnson name, he had his Attorney include a confidentiality clause in the 'quit claim' agreement. It forbade Brad and Dee to discuss the terms of the settlement or defame Junior's skills as a home builder in any way.

Brad and Dee took the 'speak-no-evil' clause of the contract lightly. Two years later they regaled dinner guests with stories of Junior and his construction—*DEstruction*, Dee would say—of their *Dream Home*. They felt Junior owed them a laugh for every *Dream Home* agony endured.

THE PIANO MAN

We were working out of an office above a wholesale grocery and tobacco warehouse store in northern Virginia. There were 7 of us, counting the secretary and Manager. We were handling claims for one of the largest Auto-Home-Owner-Commercial insurance companies in the country at the time. One of the Claims Reps was the incomparable John Sawyer.

John was one of the hardest working Reps in the entire company—and one of the least effective. The reason for his weak results? In short, John was in the wrong job. Those more eloquent would say, 'even a genius in the wrong job just looks average'. Choice of words aside, John was an affable fellow, and intelligent too. Everybody in the office liked him—enjoyed his company—counted him among their sincere friends.

John Sawyer was also one of the greatest, gifted, natural, piano players we ever heard. He had an undisputed, God-given talent for coaching unrivaled sounds, melodies, and **arrangements** from the keyboard of a piano. Songs like *St. Louis Woman*, *St. Louis Blues,* Cole Porter's *In The Still of The Night,* Gershwin's *Someone To Watch Over* Me—or Pachelbel's *Canon in D Minor* they just took on new meaning with John at the keyboard. He could do things with Jazz music that few could. When world Jazz greats, like Dizzy Gillespie, came to the Washington, D.C. area to perform, they called John, right in our office, and invited him over to some D.C. club to jam with them.

On the other hand, John handled 'conflict resolution' miserably. His fear of rejection left him in a virtual state of panic when it was time to make an offer of money to people for settlement of injury claims. As if that wasn't enough to cope with, John's organizational skills—his capacity for using common sense in problem solving—his ability to separate relevant from irrelevant info—well, his command of any or all of these skills was somewhere between weak and poor. Add these things together and you have a classic list of character traits that guarantee a miserable work life, if not outright failure, for anyone earning a living as a Claims Rep—for any insurance company.

The burden of these characteristics was compounded by John's unwillingness to admit he was in wrong line of work. His insistence on plowing into each new day on the job with some irrational tactics led to some riotous results and stories. Here are but a few of the stories that made John Sawyer legendary, and infamous, in the world of insurance claims.

THE BACK PORCH SETTLEMENT

John had been assigned an automobile injury claim of a lady which he had failed to settle for almost a year. There was nothing extraordinary or complicated about the claim.

It should have been settled with 3-4 months of assignment to John. The woman's treatment by her doctor had been concluded within 2 months of her injury. The woman had furnished John with all her medical bills and doctor's reports regarding her injuries within 3 months of her injury.

Had John offered the woman $2500 to settle her claim for pain and suffering stemming from her injuries, it would have been a fair and generous offer. Nine times out of ten, the woman would have accepted the offer— the claim would have been closed and off John's list of pending claims. Nearly any other Claims Rep in the office would have settled that claim in 3-4 months—no problem. BUT— not John.

John was reluctant to make a monetary offer of settlement to the lady—because he was afraid she would reject his offer. Fear of rejection of any settlement offer was crushing to John. He took it as a personal rejection—of him. Even worse, he feared she might verbally abuse him for making her an offer she felt was too low and insulting. She might, he worried, be so enraged by his offer she would retain an Attorney to file a legal action on her claim. Suppose, he agonized, she even called his boss and filed a complaint against him for an 'unfair' offer. Having a legitimate 'complaint' about our work lodged with our boss, Woolford Wilson, was a 'cardinal' sin—the 'un-holiest' of 'un-holies'.

Out of earshot, Woolford was aka 'Woolie'. Within earshot, as he instructed, we called him 'Boss', 'Sir', or 'Mr.Wilson'. Ol' 'Woolie' had little use for informalities around the work place.

The things John feared about his settlement offers very rarely happened in reality. Regardless, John's <u>fear</u> of rejection and adverse reactions to his offers led him to put off making offers on nearly every injury claim assigned to him. In reality, having an <u>old</u>, <u>unsettled</u>, <u>soft-tissue</u> injury claim on your pending claims list—and John always had 15-20 of them—was far more apt to bring down the wrath of 'Woolie' than an unjustified complaint of undervaluing an injury claim by a few hundred dollars.

Truth was, two thirds of *first* offers *all* Reps made on injury claims were rejected by the injured person. People always assumed you would pay more than your first offer. All Reps knew this, and seldom made a first offer for an amount the claim was truly worth. We allowed the injured party to 'negotiate' a second, and slightly higher, offer from us—making them the 'victor' in the negotiated settlement amount. Everybody, except John, understood this was the way claims were settled and accepted it.

'Woolie', the very personification of a Marine Drill Instructor, came into the office one summer day to scan all unsettled injury claims. When he looked over John's list of pending injury claims he saw the year old unsettled, minor claim of a Mrs. Hardin Ellington, III—wife of the President of the Bank of Remingway. Remingway, a small, rural, town 35 miles from Washington, was home to financially comfortable, educated, and politically connected people. They were used to be being treated with deference.

Throughout the office, we could hear 'Woolie' when he bellowed for John to come to his office. He raked John over the coals for not having the Ellington claim settled—long ago. He pointed his finger at John and bellowed at him.

"John, you're KILLING me—just by-god KILLING me! Now boy, you listen to me—every word I say! You get in your car, and you go out to this woman's house—right now! You heard me right, boy—you heard me right! Your shadow better not darken this office sixty seconds from now! No sir! And, sir, don't you come back here until you settle this woman's claim and have a signed release in your hands!"

John created 95% of his problems with 'Woolie'. Still, he never stood up to 'Woolie'—talked things out with him— man to man. John always took out his frustrations with 'Woolie' by talking to himself—out of 'Woolie's' range of hearing. John always began his 'Woolie' rant by prefacing 'Woolie's' name with the "F" bomb vulgarity—followed by the same frustrated, angry sentences. He did it this time too.

"F-ing 'Woolie' Wilson! Ol' s.o.b.! Not suppose to be like this! The man is driving me to my grave—just driving me to my grave! I'm on my way—right into the grave! Hope I never turn out to be like Woolie—so dam mean everybody hates the ground you walk on! Oh—the tension—my neck is already stiff—and the day just starting—".

Mumbling curses at Willie under his breath, John hustled out to his car and raced off to Remingway. The easy way out of this claim would have been to make the lady an offer for a little more money than the claim was worth—just to get rid of it quickly. But, John—he never reduced any problem to its simplest terms. His lack of common sense caused him to believe the solution to every problem was to be found only at the end of a complicated path of action.

Mrs. Ellington was going through her usual daily routine in her colossal, white, two-story, impeccably restored farm house when she heard a noise on her back porch. Opening the back door, she saw John putting something together on her back porch. She recognized John—but hadn't been expecting a visit from him today and couldn't grasp what he was erecting on her back porch.

"Mr. Sawyer—good to see you, as always. I wasn't expecting you today. Uh—excuse me. What is this—this thing you're putting together on my back porch?"

"This is an Army field cot—used for sleeping in the field. I got it at a good price, at an Army surplus store. Works well enough—fairly comfortable—for a something made out of a bunch of canvas stretched between wooden legs."
"Very well—if you say so—but why are you putting it together on my back porch?"

"Uh—I'll just get right down to brass tacks on this matter, Mrs. Ellington. My boss told me to come out here—and not come back until I had settled your bodily injury claim. Now, I don't know how long it's going to take me to get you to sign a release on your claim. You might not want to accept the amount of money I offer you to sign this release. If you won't accept my offer—well, I've told you what my boss said about *not coming back* until I settle your claim. There's just no way I can go back to the office until you accept my offer, and sign a full release on your claim. So—I brought my sleeping cot with me. The weather is good—I can sleep right here on your back porch. If you could just let me use your bathroom from time to time—maybe give me a little water occasionally—I can live right here on your porch until you sign this release. I can give you $2500 to sign this release—today—or I've got to live out here on your back porch until you give up and take the $2500. Sooo—what's it gonna' be, Mrs. Ellington?"

Mrs. Ellington's face contorted in disbelief. For a few seconds, she appeared not be breathing. Regaining her composure, she turned, stalked into her house, slammed the door, and left John standing on the back porch beside his cot. Shaking his head in disappointment, John sat down on the army cot and pondered his next move. He felt his offer was generous. He wasn't going to offer her one dime more than $2500. He was afraid she might reject his offer, but had hoped his demonstration of willingness to camp on her back porch would convince her that $2500 was his top offer—and she should accept it. Instead—she slammed the door in his face. There was just no reasoning with some people, he thought.

Hugh was in 'Woolie's' office when Mrs. Ellington's call reached ol' 'Woolie'. Hugh could hear the sound of her voice as she bellowed at 'Woolie' over the phone. 'Woolie' was trying to understand her complaint, but she was almost incoherent as she angry screams came over the phone.

"Oh come on, Mr. Wilson! Don't insult my intelligence by pretending you have no knowledge of what's going on out here! And stop saying you can't understand me! Don't you DARE say that another time! You hold <u>ME</u> hostage—engage in EXTORTION—send this half-wit out here to CAMP ON MY PORCH—to get my signature on your damn injury release form? He told me <u>YOU</u> told him to do this! You want me believe you had NO part in this ridiculous stunt? Do you actually think I'm that naïve? If you do, you have less brains that that fool you sent out here with an army cot? After all, this man Sawyer does work for you—or do you deny that too?"

"Mrs. Ellington, I did instruct John to make you a monetary offer to settle your injury claim. I know *nothing* about an army cot—or him threatening to 'camp' on your porch. Neither the company, nor I, would *ever* condone such an act—let alone encourage it. I swear to you—as God is my witness—I had no part in or previous knowledge of this 'stunt'—as you call it. I know you are upset, and I don't blame you. If you will let me talk to Mr. Sawyer, I believe I can resolve this matter to your satisfaction—quickly."

Mrs. Ellington put John on the phone. In a low voice, seething with anger, 'Woolie' told John to "Pack up that idiotic cot—apologize to that woman—get your butt off her property in the next 60 seconds—and get th' hell back to this office in the next 60 minutes. And another thing,

Sawyer—I'm gonna' make you pay for this army-cot stunt! You've gone too far this time—and you're gonna' pay! I don't care if it comes down me to whipping your ass— you're gonna' pay. Now put her back on the phone and get th' hell out of there!"

'Woolie' got Mrs. Ellington back on the phone. He spoke in soothing tones—verbally prostrating himself to her. He told her he was, immediately, re-assigning her claim to another Rep—that another offer would be made to her within 24 hours. He assured her the offer would be one she and her husband would find *very* generous. Mrs. Ellington calmed down some—but was still giving 'Woolie' an earful when she hung up the phone. She didn't buy a word of 'Woolie's claim of having no part in John's little 'back porch sleep-over'.

'Woolie' gave the claim to Hugh, with instructions to make an appointment to see Mrs. Ellington at once—and pay whatever it took to settle the claim. His voice was mixed with anger and apprehension as he talked to Hugh.

"You just listen, I'll do the talking. You take this claim—I swear to God—Sawyer and his—I could lose my job if this woman calls Home office and tells them this cock-eyed story. You know I had nothing to do with this—but—well, here is what you're going to do. I want you to put this whole mess to bed—no ifs, or buts about it! You go out there—you get on your knees for that woman if that's what she wants! You go through her door with an apology on your lips. If you have to 'brown nose' her—do it—even if you wind up wind up with a brown ring around your face clear back to your ears! You make that woman an offer—no negotiating now—that will get her signature on a release and have her smiling when she does it. When you leave there, I don't want her to even *think* about calling Home Office with this sorry story about Sawyer— gonna camp on her porch—Jesus—why would he—never mind—just go."

Hugh met with Mr. & Mrs. Ellington the next evening. He settled her claim for $5000—which was about twice as much as it was worth. They were all smiles when he handed them our check for $5000. John's 'sins' were forgiven—and Hugh had a release with both their signatures on it.

'Woolie' kept poor John in his office for a half hour—berating him over his un-orthodox, irrational, tactics. Not that it made any real difference. Tomorrow, the next day, and all the days in the months to come—John would be John. He wasn't going to change. As far as he was concerned; Mrs. Ellington had abused his good-faith offer, Willie was a tyrant, and Hugh was insane for paying $5000 to settle her claim.

THE ICE BREAKER

'Woolie' Wilson called a meeting of all Reps in our office. He had just reviewed our ratio of claims assigned to our claims closed on '<u>first call</u>' for the previous month. He wasn't happy. He was steamed over our 'first call' results. The company expected Reps to close small, trivial claims, quickly, during our <u>first</u> contact with people. Claims for minor bumps, bruises, aches—we were expected to offer them $50 to $500—give them a check—get their signature on a release—close the claim.

On average, we closed about 33% of our assigned claims on 'first call'—month in-month out.Whatever the reason, our total results in 'first call' closings were less than 33% for the past two months. Some of us had met our goals on 'first calls', but others did not. As 'Woolie' was prone to do, he painted us all with the same brush. In the meeting, he chastised every last one of us—pointing out the cause for our failure to meet our 'first call' goals.

"You know what the problem is with you guys? Huh? Do you have any idea why you aren't closing enough claims on 'first call'? Of course you don't. Let me tell you what your problem is. You don't take the time to gain the trust and confidence of people before you make them a monetary offer of settlement! You guys—you just get on the phone, or walk up to people, and say, 'Hey, you want this check for $50—sign this release—take it or leave it' ".

'Woolie' glared at us in silence for a few seconds before he gave us his 'solution' for our failures.

"You guys don't know how to use '*Ice Breakers*'. Yeah— that's right! I said, Ice Breakers! Look, guys. You can't take control of people, take control of what they will or won't don't do—until you have gained their *confidence*. Once you have their confidence— they'll allow you to control the settlement of their claim!"

"Listen—here are some examples of how to use *Ice Breakers*. You walk up to a guy's house—if he has a nice lawn, you say something like, 'Gee, Mr. Smith—your lawn is fabulous! Do you take care of this lawn yourself? Where did you learn how to grow a lawn like this?' Or you go in his house—you see a deer head mounted on his wall, you say something like, 'Wow! That is a big deer—and a beautiful rack of antlers! Did you bag that deer yourself? How long did you hunt it? Have you been hunting long?' "

"Now you have *'broken the ice'*. They are proud to share their accomplishments with you. You have gained their trust and confidence. Once this is done—THEN you can ask them if they want $50 to sign a release for you. Nine times out of ten—they'll do it, with a smile—because, now, they like and trust you."

"Now—I want you guys on the phones or ringing door bells, first thing in the morning. I don't want any offers made until you have used an *'Ice Breaker'*. Use those ice breakers and I KNOW you'll close more claims on first call."

The next morning John Sawyer walked resolutely into the office and plopped down at his desk. Without a word of greeting to us, he picked up the folder on a newly assigned injury claim. It involved a Mrs. Bolger—who turned out to be a crusty, earthy little ol' lady of some 73 years of age.

Even though it was only 7:45am, and we usually didn't call people before 8:00—9:00am, John rang up Mrs. Bolger. Knowing John, my knuckles turned white as I gripped the edge of my desk. The phone conversation began.

She: (cough-throat clearing)-Hello (cough). "Hellooo. Who's this?"

"Hello. Mrs. Bolger—a good morning to you, Mam'! John Sawyer here—with the insurance company. How are you feeling this morning?"

"What? What are doin' callin' me this early? I'm still in bed! How am I feelin'? Some fool hit me with a car! I'm black and blue all over my body! Every bone in my body aches! How th' hell do you think I feel?"

"Yes—well, accidents do happen. That's why—"

"Accidents happen? If people kept their mind on where they're driving accidents wouldn't happen! You act like it wasn't that other fool's fault! Let me tell you right now, if you start that stuff—you ain't gonna' talk to me! I'll hire me one them blood-sucking lawyers— he'll bleed your company dry!"

"Of course. What I'm trying to say—", said John as he tried to break into the conversation.

"You think you can just jerk an old woman around? Think I don't know what I'm doing? Think I can't stand up for myself? You're barking up the wrong tree, Mister! I know how to handle someone like you! I haven't lived for 73 years without learning to recognize an 'insurance crook' when I talk to one! It'll be a frosty day in July when you put one over on me! I know your kind—you ain't gonna' take any skin off my—".

"Mrs. Bolger, what I'm trying to say is---."

Once again, Mrs. Bolger interrupted John with a torrent of crusty comments and obscenities that you wouldn't expect from a little gray haired senior citizen. John kept trying to break into the conversation to use his 'ice breaker'—gain her trust and confidence—as 'Woolie' had promised he would. Despite his efforts for several minutes, the limited words John could get into their conversation before Mrs. Bolger cut him off with another tirade were little more than:

"Yes, but—", "Well, perhaps—", "If you will just—". "If you would—", "You see, what I'm trying to say—".

Mrs. Bolger, despite the early hour and her aches and pains, was doing all the talking—shouting obscenity laced threats—damning all insurance companies—giving John no chance to use his 'ice breaker'. Five minutes into their one-sided conversation, John decided to use his own method of gaining control of the conversation.

As Mrs. Bolger railed on and on, John reached down and picked up the metal waste can beside his desk. The thing was about two feet tall, circular in shape, with corrugated ribbing all the way around its sides. John took the phone receiver in one hand, the waste can in the other, and vigorously swung that phone receiver round and round against the inside of that metal waste can. He did this as hard as he could for about 2-3 seconds. It made a horrible racket—just deafening. When John put the phone receiver back up to his ear there was complete silence for a second or two. Then Mrs. Bolger slowly spoke.

"My God! What th' hell was that? Hello—are you still there?"

"Yes, I'm still here. I didn't hear anything, Mrs. Bolger. Must have been on your end of the phone", said John. Then, before she could start ranting again, he put his version of an 'ice breaker' to work on Mrs. Bolger.

"Now—Mrs. Bolger—let me ask you something. What do you see when you look up an elephant's trunk?"

"What—up an elephant's trunk? I—how would I know?" she snorted.

"A six foot booger—that's what you see! Ah-hah-hah-hah. Good one, huh? Now listen Mrs. Bolger, I'm coming over to your house to see you. I'm going to bring my check book— I'm going to write YOU a check for $150—you're going to sign this release I have—and your claim will be settled. See you within the hour, dear. Bye-bye, dearie."

John truly believed the elephant joke was an 'ice breaker', rather than the barroom joke that it was. He drove over to Mrs. Bolger's home with a check already made out to her for $150. She greeted him at the door with another barrage of verbal abuse, profanity, and the announcement that she had hired Lou Koulalaris as her Attorney—right after he laid his 'elephant joke' on her.

Ol' Lou was an infamous bodily injury lawyer with a phenomenal success rate in the court room. John eventually had to pay Lou $1500 to settle Mrs. Bolger's very minor claim—to keep him from taking it before a court room jury.

John came back to the office from Mrs. Bolger's home, complaining bitterly about the uselessness of Willie's **Ice Breaker** theory. In his mind—he had used the 'ice breaker' approach perfectly. And it 'didn't work worth a damn', he said.
 In his estimation, he would have been much more successful, 'Had I taken my trash can, a baseball bat, a check for $150, and a release form to that filthy-mouthed ol' hag's house. I would have run that bat around the inside of my trash can—right in her ear—until she begged to sign that release for $150. That's how you settle claims'.

SAWYER MOMENTS

John supplemented his income from our company with occasional paid music 'gigs'. Most of his music gigs took place in the evenings— too close to the end of the company's normal business day for John to return home, dress appropriately for the 'gig', and return to the place of his band's appearance. So, John would, once every couple of weeks, show up for work at our claims office fully decked out in his 'musical band' tuxedo.

His Tux included a snow white shirt with a fetching lacey front, black studs, a striking maroon cummerbund, and shiny black patent-leather shoes. You can imagine the effect it had on some of our policyholders when they answered John's knock on the door to find him standing there decked out like someone on their way to a formal 'black tie' event, a wedding, or a funeral. More than one person's reaction to John's appearance at their front door was to growl something like, 'You got the wrong place— Baptist Church is two blocks down', and slam the door in his face—without giving John a chance to say a word.

Not all of the people placing claims with our company were totally honest with us. Some tried to 'pad', or illegally inflate their claim—to rake in 'free' money. This was seen by most Claims Reps as just 'part of the business' of insurance claims—people giving in to temptation. We corrected the dollar amount claimed to the properly documented amount –paid that amount—and let it go at that. Most inflated claims didn't involve enough money to bring police into the matter on a charge of fraud.

John didn't see it that way. With him, everything was black, or it was white. There was no in between. Stealing was stealing—even if it involved no more than a dollar and twenty five cents. He found bogus claims for theft of household property particularly offensive. Discovery of an entirely bogus theft claim would lead most of us to write a letter denying the claim for lack of proof of theft. If the Insured insisted on pressing the claim, we wrote a legally correct letter to him/her suggesting he/she pursue his/her claim in a court of law. The fear of using the legal system for fraud was enough to cause the claim to be dropped in 99 and 4/100% of the bogus claims. That was the end of it—we forgot the claim—moved on to other work.

John—he never saw it that way. Once he determined an Insured had submitted a bogus/inflated theft claim, no matter how small the dollar value, John would deny the claim to the Insured in a letter that was more of a scathing indictment of the Insured's morals than a letter of denial. His letters on such matters usually read something like this.

> Dear Mr. Smith:
>
> This letter is to inform you of our denial of coverage for your recently submitted claim for the theft of your TV and Stereo.

We don't pay claims of people who lie about theft claims. Our investigation reveals the items you claimed were never stolen from you. Indeed, submitting this claim makes you a thief yourself. You should be ashamed of yourself.

Disgustedly,
John Sawyer, Master Claims Rep

Every time John wrote a denial letter and dropped it in the 'out' box, one of us would quietly intercept his letter—read it—and re-write it if it was inappropriate. It was our way of saving John from himself.

Our investigation of claims often included the need to take a statement from people setting forth their versions of events surrounding the claim. In those days, we had no recorders to use in taking a person's statement. We had to write down what people told us on paper, and then get them to sign it. Nothing complex about it. You simply asked people questions about their role in the claim, wrote down their answers, and got them to sign their statement. You did it in narrative form, with the only thing on the paper being their words of what they said happened. We were trained to never put anything on the paper except what people told us—in case the statement had to be used in court proceedings at some later date. We were also taught to leave out profanities.

None of us had any problem with this—get their version on

paper—get them to sign it—and it was done. None of us—
except John. John had this thing about 'completeness' or
'comprehensiveness'. John felt everything a person said *or*
did while he took their statement should be memorialized
in the statement—and that's literally what he did. Here is
an example of 'taking a statement' by John.

"My name is Joe Smith. I was involved in an auto accident
with Jack Jones on 8/7/64 at the intersection of Rt. 50 and
Gallows Rd. The weather was hotter than hell that day. I
was on my way to---you want a beer?" (Policyholder offers
me a beer—I decline—policyholder opens a can of beer for
himself). "Anyway, this guy comes flying down Rt. 50—runs
the stop sign—and plows into the side of my car. I mean, he
just wasted my car—totaled the damn thing." (Mr. Smith
crushes the empty beer can in his hand and throws it in the
kitchen sink—then opens another beer for himself). "Well,
neither me nor that guy in the other car could move for a
while. Then somebody called the cops and a meat wagon
came and took us both down to the hospital for a check-up.
Cops gave that other asshole a ticket—don't know what
for". (Mr. Smith crushes second beer can, throws it in the
sink). This is my statement, freely given by me, this 9th day
of August, 1964"—signed, Joe Smith.

Anybody but John taking that statement would have left
out (1) the offer of a beer (2) the fact that Mr. Smith had
two beers while giving his statement. We would have
written the guy's exact words relating to the accident—
minus the profanity—and asked him to sign his name below
his statement—and that would be the end of the matter.

John—he looked on a statement as more of an all-inclusive missive. *Every* word and action was needed to insure the full impact of the statement. On more than one occasion, our Attorneys had to re-depose a person involved in John's cases that found their way to a court room. That some of his statements had to be re-done to make them legal—didn't bother John. Far as he was concerned, any re-write of his work was something less than the 'whole' truth.

John also believed a statement from a person, regardless of whether it contained relevant information, was essential for a 'complete' file. For example: John would show up at 7:00 a.m. —at a given intersection in Washington, D.C—to investigate an accident which had occurred at this intersection at 7:00 a.m. several days prior.

John would approach pedestrians, at random, as they waited to cross the intersection.

"Excuse me, mam. My name is John Sawyer. I worked for an insurance company. I'm investigating an auto accident which occurred at this intersection three days ago at 7:00 am. Do you walk by this intersection every morning—at approximately 7:00am?"

"Yes—I walk this way to work."

"Did you see an auto accident that occurred at this intersection 3 days ago—at approximately 7:00am?"

"No—no, I didn't."

"Really—OK, what is your name, please?"

"Why do you need my name?"

"For the record—our records on events have to be accurate."

"Well—my name is Opal Johnson."

"Very well, Mrs. Johnson. Give me just a moment, please."

John would take a piece of lined paper and write as follows:

'My name is Opal Johnson. I live at 4376 NW 33rd St., Washington. D.C. I walk by the intersection of New York Ave. and 9th St. NW every morning on my way to work. I walked by this intersection on August 7, 1964 at approximately 7:00a.m.—and I did <u>not</u> witness an accident occurring at the above intersection on that date and time.'

"Now, Mrs. Johnson, please sign your name at the bottom of this statement, please."

A puzzled Mrs. Johnson would sign a written statement confirming she had <u>not</u> seen an accident. John would give her a carbon copy of her statement, thank her, and approach the next pedestrian arriving at the intersection. He would do the 'statement' thing all over again. By 7:45

that morning, John would have a half-dozen statements from people who had <u>not</u> seen the accident he was investigating. John would dutifully include all 6 of those statements in the file on that accident. Not one of those statements confirmed or denied the facts of that accident—but John had six irrelevant, useless, statements in the file—to satisfy his need for file 'completeness'.

SAWYER'S SUNSET

Life with John went on this way for a 1-2 more years. John was always one step away from 'Work Performance Probation', but managed to hang to his job. One evening there were 10-12 employees gathered in the old ball room of the once famous Chamberlain Hotel on Old Point Comfort. We were there for an overnight business meeting. There was nothing for us to do in the evening. For want of anything better to do, we wandered up to the top floor of the hotel and into the once legendary Chamberlain Ballroom. The ballroom was empty—save for 20-25 old chairs, 4-5 tables, and a magnificent old Steinway Grand Piano with a dust cover over it.

Without a word, John pulled the dust cover off the piano, sat down, and played 2-3 pieces of classical blues music—as only John Sawyer could. The only light in the room was on a small lamp on the piano. Not one of us in the room made a sound—just sat there breathing in the music that John coached out of that piano.

After a half hour or so, John finished a song and turned away from the piano for a breather. From behind us, out of the dark, came a voice.

"Good Lord—John, you ought to be playing the piano for a living. Not working for an insurance company."

It was the voice of 'Big Bill' Whiting, a company Senior Vice President who was in town for our meeting. John looked toward the sound of Bill's voice in the dark, struck one chord on the piano, stood up, bowed toward Bill, and said.

"Bill—you're right. I quit!" John turned and walked out of the room without another word to anyone. Two days later, on our first day in the office since the meeting, John walked into 'Woolie's' office and laid his resignation on 'Woolie's' desk. He was gone in two weeks—but certainly not forgotten. You don't forget people like John Sawyer—*ever*.

John formed the **JOHN SAWYER TRIO**—a sort of Jazz/Blues band. His band was a hit in the Washington, D.C. scene, right from the start. His popularity grew by the week. Those of us in the office used to go into Washington some evenings to catch him and his band at the Hi-Hat Lounge of the old Ambassador Hotel on 14th St. When his band took a break he would buy us a drink and talk with us. He was obviously happy. In a few months, John's band 'moved up' on the Lounge circuit. He was hired to play at the

Windjammer Lounge of the Hilton Hotel, just on the Virginia side of the Potomac River, across from Washington. They were paying John and his Trio $50,000 a year to perform 5 nights a week—5 hours a night. This was 'big time' money in the 1960s. John had been paid $5000, annually, when he worked for with us—and was unhappy most days.

Two years later, the **JOHN SAWYER TRIO** had grown to a band of 4 people—and had become a fixture at the Evans Farm Inn. This was a pricey place in McLean, Virginia where numerous politically powerful and wealthy people lived. Among them were family members of President John Kennedy. Getting reservations at the Evans Farm Inn was tough. They started John's band off at $90,000 a year plus a percentage of the income from the Inn's Lounge. His band was a fixture there for nearly 25 years before they retired. I haven't the slightest notion what they were paying John to play when he retired—but a good guess is it was more than the entire payroll for our old claims office—and John was in the perfect job for him.

THE PUZZLE PALACE

Doing a 'tour' at company headquarters was virtually mandatory, if you had any plans of climbing the corporate ladder beyond entry level management jobs. The company was the world's fourth largest insurance company. It had operations, offices, and subsidiaries across, most states east of the Mississippi and some west, Puerto Rico, and even owned a subsidiary in Germany. Company employees numbered around 15,000 people. The company's home office was located in a south-west state.

Most employees began their careers in some state operation. However, it was an unwritten company rule that no one would rise to a management job, beyond entry level management, without serving in some *staff* job at Home Office—where you would be observed and evaluated by high level corporate officers. A staff job in home office was the 'gate' to promotions and higher paying jobs. It was also a 'gate' that swung both ways.

One side of the gate led to invaluable mentoring by successful senior officers, opportunities to see and solve corporate operational problems, development of decision making skills based on facts rather than intuition, and learning the all-important difference between leading people and managing them.

The other side of the 'gate' involved performance of duties not reduced to print in the staff job description. The last few words of the last sentence of the staff job description '—and all other duties *as assigned*—'covered a lot of *'unspecified'* duties. In truth, the unnamed duties fell into one of four categories. (1) *Unconditional* loyalty to your boss (2) Do <u>anything</u> you were told to do—and <u>always</u> keep your mouth shut about it (3) Get any job assigned done— no excuses (4) give your boss full credit for any successes achieved—claim personal responsibility for any failures.

It was my 'duties' that fell under the heading of '—all other duties as assigned—'that gave birth to some unique stories of life on corporate staff. They aren't meant to imply that I worked for a bunch of bunglers. For the most part, I worked with some very savvy corporate officers. Rather, the stories offer a glimpse into '—all other duties assigned— 'close to the *helm* of corporations. Truth be known, I suspect these sorts of things went on in most *all* major corporations To borrow a signature line from one of America's legendary radio newscasters, Paul Harvey, *"Now—here's the **rest** of the story"*—on *'other duties as assigned'*.

'MURDOCK'S BOOK, MANURE SPREADER, CABIN, and RAY GUN

The founders of our company were led by the legendary Murdoch Craddock. Murdoch was born in a cabin, or one room house, on a New England farm around 1900. According to him, his early life was filled with hard work on this rocky, poor-boy farm. The experience had a lasting impact on him. With persistence, hard work, and very little money, he graduated from college with a major in Agricultural Science and a minor in Business Finance.

Murdoch saw little humor and small ease in life. He believed job success was only to be found on the other side of a serious commitment to long, hard, hours and an unending quest to save money.

He got the officers of some Farm Cooperatives to sign a loan note for $10,000 to start their own insurance company—so they could insure their farms, businesses, and homes cheaper and make a little profit in the bargain. This was in the mid 1920s. By the mid-1960s this little 'Farm Co-op' insurance company had grown into the fourth largest insurance company in the United States.
The company employees numbered close to 15,000—with Murdoch as Chief Executive Officer. He had become a larger-than-life figure to company employees, policyholders, local and national politicians, and other insurance company executives—all the way from the Atlantic Ocean past the Mississippi River.

When I was promoted from a state operation job to a job in Home Office in the mid 1970s Murdoch was already in his late 70s. While respected for his accomplishments, he was little loved and much feared. He had no real friends in the company—and wasn't looking for any. Some in the company felt he should have turned over the CEO reins to someone younger in the company when he hit 65 years of age—but he didn't. Further, he gave no indication he would retire any time in the near, or distant, future. He lived in denial of the toll age and work had taken on him. He truly believed his absence from the helm of the company would result in swift, total, and irrevocable failure of the company.

Murdoch had garnered much power over the years—in and out of the company. A lot of people, important and un-important, owed the jobs they held to his patronage. More than a few people, in and out of the company, feared his power. No one was going to suggest to, god forbid *tell*, Murdoch it was time for him to step down from his job as CEO. Not if they were reasonably secure in their job and wished to remain so. There were tales of employees, some in high positions, who fell into disfavor with Murdoch. These unfortunate souls were swiftly 're-assigned' to a dead-end job in one of our subsidiary companies located in a remote area of a northwestern state—and virtually never heard from again. Some of these tales *may* have been exaggerated. Be that as it may, no one I knew was about to test the truth of the stories by irritating Murdoch. Just a glare from Murdoch was known to causesome employees to increase their dosage of tranquilizers and blood pressure medication—or possibly consider 'taking the gas pipe'.

My introduction to Murdoch Craddock was through a temporary assignment to his staff to help write 'his book'. He had reached the point in life where he felt compelled to share, in book form, his secrets for becoming and remaining a successful corporate mogul. Over twelve months, off and on, two other staff 'temp assignees' and I helped him write his book. He dictated an outline of what he wanted to say— impact of 'key' decisions— a list of obstacles overcome—competitors bested—refusal to have 'defeat' or 'failure' in his vocabulary—and early-life experiences to support his belief that his years on a hard scrabble farm provided the toughness necessary for survival in the corporate world.

Using his vernacular, we fleshed out his major points for success, built in details to support his recipe for survival, and *tried* to breathe a little entertainment or 'happy ending' into his methodical prose of a Spartan life throughout his rise to corporate success. We were careful not to take license—go off on a tear and start re-writing his story in a vein *we* thought would read well. No sir. You didn't do that with Murdoch—no matter how uninspired and plodding you thought *his* narrative of events was. His idea of our obligation to him was organization and fleshing-out of his material, checking the grammar, add punctuation where needed, and polishing his 'self-made-man' image. As I recall, his instructions were, "Don't get too damn flowery—stay away from big, fancy words—remember *whose* story this is".

For the title of his book he chose, *MAN IN CHARGE OF*

REVOLUTION. Not a one of us could see how that title was related to the story line of the book. The book, for the most part, was a glorification of his rise from a poor beginning on a rocky farm field in New England to the office of CEO of a major insurance company. His story stressed self-denial, hard work, long work days—all while working for wages worth little more than hand full of dirt. To accept his version of his life—you may as well petition the Pope to canonize him—on the spot—make him Saint Murdoch 1st.

Well—okay—give credit where due. He *did* devote some print to the company employees. Specifically, he referred to his philosophy of 'earning employee respect through fear'— never letting the employees feel too secure in their jobs. Fear was a sure-fire cure for work-place laziness—so he said. He claimed Biblical scripture as the basis for that philosophy, but offered no specific scriptural reference.

No, nowhere *in* the book was the word *revolution* mentioned—let alone <u>inviting</u> a work-place revolution. Murdock didn't even tolerate employee *opposition* in any form—let alone a revolution. He would have considered an insignificant lunch-break 'gripe session' between two janitors in the office sub-basement as the opening round of a full blown servile insurrection.

Moreover, any perception by him that you weren't enthusiastically supportive of his views could lead to you being the 'sacrificial lamb' in one of his patented 'relocation shuffles' to the 'back of beyond' in some northwestern state. His title for the book—it was what it was. We were *his* voice—nothing more. So—in the interest of job security—we embraced his selected book title with enthusiasm. Not to put too fine a point on it—better to have the fleas of 100 mangy dogs infest our hair than get on Murray's bad side.

As the book grinded to completion, Murdoch was convinced it would be a *BEST SELLER*. In truth, the book was anything *but* a sensational, gripping, page-turning, best seller. You could have found more entertainment and motivation by looking at some soul lying in state. Those of us that worked on the book were grateful our names weren't mentioned in the book. In self-defense, we sucked up to Murdoch. To him—we said the book would wind up on the register of 'classics' in our society. To anyone else— we denied having any part in the book beyond proof reading the manuscript and adding a punctuation mark here and there. We feared concession of even those minor contributions left us open to ridicule and mockery by our peers.

Being the devout cowards we were, we lauded the finished manuscript and agreed with Murdoch's suggestion that we order a first printing of 5000 copies of the book—at the company's expense. He vowed all proceeds from the sale of the book would, to the penny, be deposited in the company coffers. No sir, he didn't want one dime. He had dedicated his life to the company—and he would sacrifice the financial benefits from the sale of his book to the company as well. What an example of self-sacrifice! A life just short of taking a vow of poverty! Right—and he was a bowl of

Rice Krispies too.

Murdoch's mental faculties were already giving way to the ravages of age and work related stress. It had become increasingly difficult for him to keep track of plans and the actual chronology of events. His attention span had grown short. He didn't keep close tabs on the sale of his book. His mind became occupied with other matters. Every 3-4 months he would ask, 'How's the book sale going?' We provided positive but vague updates.

We had a Home Office sub-basement storage area filled with cases and cases of that book, stacked floor to ceiling. We were giving away copies of the book as 'awards' to employees for any reason we could think of. Every visitor or politician who came by Home Office was given a copy of the book. Most of the company's employees had a copy on their desk. We had Murdoch autograph the books he personally handed to his business guests. We also gave the books to employees who completed *any* kind of training course—as an achievement award from the 'Great Man' himself.

We shipped out 10-15 cases of those books to every state operation. To encourage them to actually read the book, we suggested Murdoch might want commentaries from state managers on the details in the book. When we could, we gave away the books to public libraries.
By the time this book 'distribution' ran its course, almost a year later, all copies had been removed from the basement storage area to 'somewhere'. You could find more copies of

it on the desks of employees than our company's 'Bible'—better known as our Standard Operating Procedures manual. I never asked how many thousands of dollars were spent printing the book. I'm not certain, but I doubt if one copy of this book was ever actually *sold* to anybody.

THE MANURE SPREADER

The first time Murdoch's 'Senior Moments' became public, outside the company offices, was during an address to a group of young men from a half dozen nearby colleges. It was planned as an informal gathering in a local college's Social Hall..

Murdoch would make some opening comments on the 'dos and don'ts' for success in private industry, the ups and downs to be expected, his biggest successes, one or two disappointments, how to lead people to their full potential—and then take questions for 30-35 minutes.

A couple of us put together some 'talking points' for him, based on the topics his remarks would cover. We estimated the entire evening wouldn't last more than 60-90 minutes. Murdoch's long time Executive Assistant knew Murdoch's powers of recall were going south—that he might have need of an 'Aide' at the meeting. You guessed it. I drew the short straw on this detail.

Murdoch smiled all through his glowing introduction at the meeting—written by yours truly. The audience of 60 young men expected to be handed a sure-fire recipe for guaranteed corporate success from a legendary corporate head. To vigorous applause, he took his place at the podium—and I watched the world unravel right in front of me.

Murdoch smiled warmly, looked around the room, and never glanced once at his prepared notes lying on the podium. His smile slowly dimmed until his eyes reflected a vacant, far-away look. He held up his hands in front of him, slowly turned them over, and examined them closely—for a full 10 seconds. Those 10 seconds seemed like 10 minutes to me. Then he spoke, with more passion and emotion than I had *ever* heard him display. His voice was strong, deep, and boomed over the room.

"I've worked hard all my life! It's the only way of life I've ever known! You can tell by looking at my hands—they are no strangers to hard work. Just look at these hands!", he thundered as he held them up to the audience.

"I was born and raised on a farm. So I can tell you, hands and a strong back, alone, won't get the job done on the farm! Not even working from sun-up till sun-down! You have got to have some good *tools* if you are going make any money from farming!"

Beads of sweat began to cover my forehead. I wondered if his mind had finally 'broken' completely. As I desperately contemplated some way—any way at all—to graciously get him from behind that podium and out of the building, he began to speak again.

"If you don't remember another thing I say here, remember *this!* The single most important tool a man can own is a *Manure Spreader!!* Yes sir! If you don't own a manure spreader—and I mean a good one—you're not going to make it as a farmer. You can pour your heart, your soul, and your sweat into that land—but you'll get a lot less out of it than you will if you spread a good load of manure on it. You've heard the old expression, 'Nothing + Nothing = Nothing'? Well—it's true! *Crop* land *without* fertilizer on it is pretty much 'nothing'. If you put 'nothing' on it—and by 'nothing', I mean if you don't spread *manure* on the land— that land will yield, 'nothing' when harvest time comes around. 'Nothing + nothing= Nothing'. Normally, I'd be inclined to say 'You can take that to the bank'. However, in this case, I know it would be more accurate to say a farmer without a good manure spreader won't be taking much of anything to the bank."

Murdoch paused—as if searching for the right words to arouse in his audience a passion for manure spreaders to match his own. He certainly had the attention of every person in the auditorium, mine included. My fingers had curled into fists so tight my finger nails were cutting into the palms of my hands.

'Where th' hell is he going with this sermon on manure spreaders', I desperately mumbled to myself.

As he gazed over the audience, a puzzled look came over

his face. He looked off stage at me. His expression told me he knew who I was. What disturbed me was the look of confusion and fright on his face, just for 2-3 seconds. Over the months I worked with him, his range of emotions never came close to confusion or fear. Those two words weren't in his vocabulary. It didn't take a licensed doctor to know something was wrong with Murdoch. As I stood up, off stage, to walk toward him, he blinked rapidly and his eyes refocused. His discreet wave of dismissal told me to stay where I was. He looked at the audience, smiled, stretched his arms to them with palms upturned, and said.

"Well, gentlemen, that's what I have to say. If you have any questions, I'll try to answer them." That told me he was 'hedging' on his answers. Murdock Craddock didn't use the word *try* when he spoke of *his* intentions. He would either 'do' or 'not do' something—depending on his feelings about the subject matter.

I saw in his face he was fairly certain he had been talking, but—about *what*—he didn't know. He didn't have the slightest notion what he had said in the past few moments. The way he looked down at his notes, I was betting he thought he had been speaking from the 'talking points' we had prepared for him. Of one thing I was dead certain. Murdoch had no memory of having just delivered an impassioned support of cow manure as earth's Elixir of Life. One of the college students in the audience spoke up.

"Mr. Craddock, how does farm work prepare you to successfully run one of the largest insurance corporations in the world?"

Praises be to the Almighty for not leading the kid say 'What has owning a manure spreader got to do with running a major insurance company?' Still, I figured it would only be a matter of time before one of the young men brought up the relevance of a manure spreader—or questioned Murdoch's lack of comments on actual problems and solutions in the corporate world of today.

I anticipated a public relations nightmare when word of this got out—with me standing at Murdoch's elbow during his little 'Farmer-in-the-Dell' fantasy trip. Without a doubt, I would be held responsible. No one was going to buy my explanation of 'Murdock had a *senior moment*'. Even if he had suffered an on-the-spot epileptic seizure, I would have been expected to make it look like a hiccup and usher him through the issue without a 'blemish' on his image. Impossible!! No one could have anticipated his rabid spiel about manure spreaders! No two ways about it—I would be moved to the head of the line of upper-management candidates to be 'disappeared'—for life! I was on the verge of surrendering to a major case of panic. Then, God intervened—and Murdoch gave the perfect answer.

"Young man, if you can make a farm feed your family, pay your bills on time, show a profit at year end—then sir, you can be success in *any* business. There is nothing tougher than making a living as a farmer! You have to be a good planner, a good manager of money, make good long range decisions, and be totally committed to hard work."

From this opening answer, he segued into details of character traits found in *farmers*. Self-denial, commitment to overcoming adversity, a willingness to take on the most thankless job with fervor, never wasting a minute of the day, think twice before spending a dollar that won't be returned to you with a profit—the same traits, he said, found in successful corporate heads. He opined that one's early life experiences, possibly as much as formal education, play a major role in developing one for his or her chosen profession. He shared poignant and touching stories of back breaking obstacles faced in rising from a meager subsistence on a farm to a college degree—and related how they had served him in his successful climb up the corporate ladder.

After setting the stage for personal traits needed to survive in a tough corporate world, he proceeded to discuss problems he had faced in the dog-eat-dog day-to-day corporate world and how he had addressed them—some with success—some with something less than success. He emphasized how his early life of facing and meeting disappointments had schooled him for 'getting back up and working harder than ever to learn from failures and disappointments and turn them into a success the next time around'. He gave *fact* to his comment by offering by offering problems he had face—solutions he had used— and the profitable results he achieved.

 For ninety minutes of talk and discussion with these young men, Murdoch never once looked at his notes. He was speaking from experience—and from his heart. For the first time in the two years I had known Murdoch, I found myself admiring him. I actually felt pride in learning from him that evening. Things I would use years later when I face adversity and challenges. Looking and listening to him that evening made me re-evaluate him.

Yes—he was now a hard-nosed executive; could be vindictive if provoked; a tyrant at times; exhibited signs of increasing mental fragility. On the other hand, seeing him that evening told me he was, possibly, a different person and leader 30-40 years ago. Maybe even a likeable and inspirational leader. Between the stress of 40+ years of building a major insurance company out of virtually nothing—the strain of surviving as its head—going toe-to-toe with competitors to maintain his corporation's place in the 'pecking order' of major insurance companies—staying too long in a job that involved almost inhuman demands at times---. Perhaps his mind eventually told him survival could only be found by totally subscribing to the old cliché—'you gotta' be the biggest and meanest rat in the house'.

When he walked away from that podium, he heard loud and long applause from a standing group of young men. Me—I was applauding with them. And it was from my heart.

When the evening was over, I knew three things were true. Those young men heard remarks they could understand, relate to, and take encouragement from—albeit by way of

a Manure Spreader testimonial; Murdoch's mental
condition was more fragile and advanced than any of us
had realized; It took a man like Murdoch to turn a $10,000
loan from some farmers into one of the major insurance
corporations in this country.

For a couple of months after Murdoch's 'manure spreader'
speech, I put up with a barrage of notes and phone calls
from colleagues. Zingers like, 'How are you going to make it
in this company without a manure spreader in your
driveway?'--- 'Does Murdoch know you are buying food for
your family when you don't yet own a manure spreader?'

THE CABIN

A few months later another 'dark' moment descended on
me. I was temp-assigned to Murdoch's staff for another
'project'. My plea for exemption from 'Murdoch Duty' this
time, since I recently served on his 'Manure Spreader'
speech, was dismissed with, "You should be proud to be
requested by our CEO".I didn't have the courage to
challenge my boss's suggestion that I should take pride in
working for Murdoch.

Notwithstanding my recent glimpse at what Murdoch may
have been like 30-40 years ago—via his 'Manure Spreader'
speech—the Murdoch we *all* were dealing with now was a
potential nightmare—of the worst kind.

On the long walk to his office I muttered, "*Proud*—I should be *proud*? Ridiculous! Proud to particpate in a nightmare? Every moment I spent in servitude for Murdoch was like being a member of a firing squad—arranged in a circle."

Murdoch's actions and directions became more bizarre each succeeding time I was assigned to him. When I heard his proposal this time, I figured he had gone too far. This time I was sure an Officer or Director of the company would face off with him— put a stop to his 'off the wall' fantasies.

Murdoch had recently purchased his old family home place, as well as the New England farm which went with the house. If rocks had any real value, that farm would have been worth a fortune. Under 10-12 inches of top soil, the entire 120 acres was nothing but a bed of rocks. His old home place was a very small, one room, unpainted, clap board siding house. The walls of the house were originally made of hand hewn logs. At some point, many years ago, clap board siding had been nailed over the exterior log walls.

Clap board siding or not, Murdoch was fond of telling people he had been born in a 'log cabin'. He decided the 'cabin' was a historical structure. He, the venerable Murdoch Craddock, had risen from a birth in that humble 'cabin' to become a nationally respected corporate head. He drew an analogy between himself and 'Abe' Lincoln, our late President—another self-made man—pulled up by his own boot straps—the ultimate boy-makes-good success story.

Murdoch had our company President propose to the Board of Directors that they show (1) gratitude for all he had done for the company (2) an interest in the preservation of historical structures (3) a sign of their undying gratitude and interest---by footing the bill to have his birth-place home dis-assembled in New England, moved to corporate headquarters, and reassembled next door to his working office on the 40th floor of our Home Office building.

Nobody was looking for trouble. The corporation was financially healthy and growing fast. Moving the cabin for a 'good cause' was the easy way out. If Murdoch wanted his cabin moved half way across the country—why not? My eager anticipation of watching Murdoch getting his house-moving scheme shot down by our corporate hierarchy? Forget it. That fantasy crashed and burned on take-off.

Those of us assigned to assist Murdoch in this his restoration project were to act as a facilitators and liaisons between him and (1) carpenters who would tear out existing home office walls to make room for the cabin (2) employees whose office walls were summarily torn down to make room for the cabin (3) the contractor hired to disassemble the cabin, move it to Home Office, and re-assemble it on the 40th floor of Home Office—more than the length of a football field above street level..

His expectations of us were brief and direct—"There better not be one board of that cabin broken!" What a peach to work for—our careers held hostage for undamaged old boards on an old house—with the boards in the hands of a third party carpenter—over whom we had little if any control. We felt we had a better chance of success at playing 'Pick Up Sticks' with our fingers cut off up to the second knuckle than we did of getting that old building moved from New England to Home Office with no broken boards.

It took 10 months to finish this job. When was all in place, Murdoch could open a private door in the rear wall of his office, walk right into his old family home—which had been totally reconstructed right against the back wall of his private office on the 40th floor. He could, and often did, walk into the living room of that old cabin and take his afternoon nap on the same antique sofa that graced the living room of the old family 'manse' where he grew up.

How he could rest on that old sofa was a mystery to all of us who worked on that project. The sofa was like most living room furniture from the late 1800s—early 1900 hundreds—more for show than use. The upholstery in the seat of the thing was so hard it was like sitting on a bed of rocks. Well—Murdock found no problem in napping comfortably on it—and, as usual, he didn't really care what the rest of us thought.

I never asked about the cost of dismantling and moving that cabin from New England to the top floor of home office. Nor did I ask in which budget line item we buried the cost of relocating the cabin. None of my business. Having a job that I needed to keep—a family I needed to feed—I did what I was told to do, kept my mouth shut, and enthusiastically forgot about the entire project once it was completed.

After the 'cabin' project was over, the group of 'Temp-Assistants' I worked with on 'Murdoch Projects' changed our closely guarded nick name for Murdoch. After the 'manure spreader' speech, his name became 'Mur-nure' Craddock. After the cabin re-location project it became 'Abe Lincoln' Craddock. No—none of us ever called him that to his face—or within 5-6 floors of his office—or within earshot of *anybody* but our small group. None of us wanted our innocent, comic relief to get us moved to the 'front of the line' for Murdoch's 'Involuntary Relocation Plan'.

THE RAY GUN

It was late one spring when I was, once again, detailed to Murdoch's staff. I hadn't seen him for a year—praises to all the Saints. Not to belabor the issue—but my freedom from abnormal levels of stress was directly proportional to the length of time between calls to me from his secretary. Just receiving a call from that woman was enough to trigger a neurotic episode in a 'Temp Assignee'.

Murdoch's secretary didn't give a big rat's rear end if any or all of us had just suffered loss of bladder control; were battling a terminal illness; had just received news of a death in our immediate family, or had fallen prey to any one of the other 97 most dreaded human fates. When she called and said 'Come up to Mr. Craddock's office at once'—she meant literally.

When I walked into Murdoch's office I was stunned by the severity of his physical deterioration since I last saw him. He appeared smaller in height—as if he had literally shrunk. His hands trembled. He walked slowly, with a shuffling gait. His physical impairments were now outpacing his mental decline, but not by much.

His irascible attitude remained the same. His snarling, impatient, commands were ever present—but delivered more slowly. People still walked on egg shells around him, being properly deferential. There was a noticeable decline in his alertness. For ages, his sensorial powers had been legendary. Some swore he could see through walls and hear through concrete ceilings.

His grip on matters was more tenuous. His eyes—the ones that used to melt glass with a glare—were dull orbs that occasionally stared past you to some vacant spot. Too often, he turned away in mid- sentence and gazed absently out the window at Holt Street—40 floors below him.

Murdock focused on the blue print on his desk and laid out his plans for his latest ground breaking project. His memory of life on the family farm had 'kicked in' again.

"Beetles, worms, and numerous other parasites are almost as big a challenge in farming as the weather itself", he said in a halting voice. "Well, God is still in control of the weather", he conceded, "but, through determination and good fortune, I have discovered a cure for the plague of insects and similar pests!"

After witnessing a dramatic demonstration by its inventor, Murdoch had purchased a 'Ray Gun'. His acquisition of this deadly piece of weaponry included the exclusive right to its usage throughout the entire south-western United States and the whole of the Atlantic seaboard. This 'Ray Gun' came complete with instruction for assembly, installation, and operation. Once it was mounted on the roof of Home Office this 'Ray Gun', with nothing more than longitude and latitude coordinates entered into its aiming mechanism, could shoot a deadly ray of light in an arc through the air, around the curve of the earth, to the farm located at those coordinates. Upon touch-down at this designated location, this light ray would kill every last living bug or parasite laying waste to that poor farmer's crop—without even a hint of damage to so much as a leaf of one plant of the entire crop—spread over hundreds of acres. The crowning attraction of this marvelous tool was its *indefinite* life span.

Further, he had the gun's inventor's word that our company was the first and only insurance company in possession of a weapon so far ahead of its time. Such a marvel of science wouldn't be a secret long, he warned—so it was our task to, immediately, put this 'Ray Gun' to work.

"Do some good' for our farm-owners policyholders! Make hay while the sun shines! Garner Invaluable publicity for our company! Make us the *first* insurance company in history to offer this marvelous service, at *no* cost, to anyone insured with *us*", he thundered as he slammed his fist down on his desk.

Murdoch was breathing hard. He had worked himself into a fever pitch while sharing this ground-breaking news with us. He paused to catch his breath and give us a chance to applaud his genius, his flair for innovation, his charity for mankind.

We glanced at each other for about one second. Was the old man testing our ability to weed out a joke from serious matters of business?

First off, Murdoch had no sense of humor. At least, not one that anybody had seen. Secondly, the ability to think analytically was not a skill he credited *us* with—nor anyone else in the company whose name we could call to mind. We were there solely to do his bidding. Third, the smile on Murdoch's face broadcast his sincere pride in being the first to put his lasso on this 'Ray Gun'.

Not a chance in this world that Murdoch was joking. To a man, we 'Temps' sprang to our feet and applauded him. We tumbled over each other to give voice to—his skill as a visionary—his courage for embracing new ideas—and his compassion for those in need. It was enough to make you sick—watching we grown men verbally validate the fantasy of a sick, demented old man.

Murdoch waved off our applause and ordered the 'Ray Gun' installed on the roof of Home Office—pronto. He wanted procedures written for locating and serving farmers in need of the Ray Gun's' killing beam, and records kept on each and every successful use of that deadly gun. Finally, he wanted an all-out introductory PR campaign worked up for both print and broadcast media. As he shuffled out of the conference room he growled one final order.

"Just so we're on the same page, gentlemen, I expect all aspects of this matter to be operational no later than one week from today."

What a model of charity—this man! It was Monday morning. That left us 6 1/2 days to make a silk purse out of a sow's ear. Of all the assignments involving Murdoch, this was the first time he had come up with a cockamamie scheme involving *active* participation by people *outside* the company. It left we four 'Temp-Assistants' with a critical 'first task' question—should we shoot Murdoch, or ourselves. We knew this sounded like a sick joke—unless you were there and in our shoes.

There was just no way we were going to phone working farmers, or anyone else, and invite them to be the beneficiaries of the power of a remotely located bug killing ray gun—courtesy of their insurance company. At best, they would hang up their phone without a reply—laugh at us—or threaten to report us to police. At worst, word of this lunacy would spread to newspapers or TV stations.

Either way—a story of a 'Ray Gun' being 'operated' from the roof of Home Office would quickly reach the company President and Directors —probably through some TV reporter's call. Regardless—we, 'Temp-Assistant' toadies, not Murdoch, would pay for letting word of this science fiction get outside the office walls.

We knew the logistics of putting a bogus 'Ray Gun' into play, developing bogus feedback 'success' stories for Murray, all while keeping this lunacy from getting to the company officers and Board of Directors— it just wasn't doable. There could be no 'ray gun' trials—no calls to farmers—no media knowledge of it—let alone company involvement.

After 2 days of discussion and debate, the only viable solution we could come up with was 'delay'— for years, if need be. We hustled up to the company's in-house legal department—better known as Office of General Counsel.

There were some 30-40 lawyers in General Counsel. Their hallmark, besides being excellent corporate lawyers, was performing exhausting research on any question or matter before offering an opinion on it. Some issues in the General Counsel's office stayed under 'consideration' for months, possibly years. Why?. No corporate lawyer wanted to be found to be on the wrong side of a legal opinion— which could cause bad publicity, a sizable verdict against the company, and the soiling of their reputation.

Mike opened the meeting by saying we were seeking advice on a matter *personally* involving Murdoch Craddock. As we anticipated, this was enough to cause the single *junior* attorney stuck with listening to our story to ask 2 *senior* attorneys to join our meeting.

When all were settled Mike told them there were only 9 people, including Murdoch's secretary and them, in the entire company, who had knowledge of the information we was about to share with them . In the strongest terms possible, he suggested any search for 'loose lips' would be confined to the 9 of us if one word of this secret got into the wrong hands and bathed Murdoch or the company with the harsh light of bad publicity. Further, he speculated, even if Murdoch, or our company officers, never found out *precisely* who leaked the information—it was entirely probable *all* of us would be held accountable, involuntarily relocated to some remote subsidiary, and given jobs worse than being in Hades with a broken back.

He must have made an impression. The senior attorney in the room jumped to his feet—vowed he spoke for everyone in General Counsel when he swore an oath of silence.

Nodding, I laid out Murdoch's plan to install and operate a bug killing 'Ray Gun' on the roof of Home Office. I said he was compounding the lunacy of this proposal with his insistence on involvement of the print and broadcast media. To complete the disaster, he was insisting on the involvement and testimony of farm policyholders who were delivered from pestilence—courtesy of the 'Ray Gun'. He expected to see these farmers on TV—giving testimonials about the thousands of dollar in crop damages they were spared—all the glory to Murdoch and our company.

The attorneys stared at Mike in disbelief as he laid out details of Murdoch's 'Ray Gun' plan. Their faces pale, eyes wide, mouths open—they seemed to want to say something, but no words came. They looked at each other, back at us, and then up at the ceiling. I wondered if they were begging the Almighty for deliverance. From the looks on their faces, it was far more likely that they were pleading for Divine intervention, in the form of a lightning-fast deliverance of Murdoch and we 'temp aides' to Hades. They sat there silently—for so long I was beginning to wonder if the news of Murdoch's latest adventure had caused the entire lot of them to stroke out.

I asked them about finding legal means and reasons for delaying implementation of this fantasy for an indefinite period of time—years, hopefully. Murray's memory was short and getting shorter, I mused. Perhaps he would forget about the entire matter in time, I suggested. If Murray did raise the issue, at future intervals, I said, perhaps Counsel could offer a legal issue that was keeping the matter in limbo.

Having laid out the only viable course of action we could think of, we sat there and looked at the attorneys for their concurrence—or a better suggestion. They sat there—saying nothing—looking at us like we had asked them to assault the gates of Hell with nothing but a thimble of water in their hands.

Mike told the attorneys he could read their eyes. He tried to add a little levity to the situation by saying he knew we would be taken off their Christmas card list for the next decade. He knew they felt we had dumped *our* problem on *them*. I offered to consider any suggestion <u>they</u> had. One of them suggested that Murdoch and I both drink a glass of strychnine. With a lame smile, I asked for a suggestion more reasonable than swallowing a glass of rat poison.

After a long 4-5 minutes, they began formulating plans to go through reviews and research of FCC and FAA regulations, license requirements, EPA involvement, patents for existing 'Ray Guns', etc. They would file periodic 'progress reports' on their 'Ray Gun' legal review. If Murdoch asked for an update, we would tell him the legal work on the matter was 'on-going'.

General Counsel did put one attorney to work on the matter. He worked on it infrequently, along with other assignments, for over two years. Oddly, the review revealed one or two interesting legal questions about Ray Guns— had there been a *real* one. Mercifully, for the 9 of us, Murray eventually forgot the 'Ray Gun'. It was never put on the roof—its operation was never tried. It was stored in one of our sub-basements pending completion of legal review of the matter. I have no idea what eventually became of the thing.

I got a promotion to Field Operations about a year after the 'Ray Gun' incident. I had been in our Maryland Headquarters for a year when I was called back to Home Office for a management seminar being held at our Corporate Training Center complex. It was three weeks before Christmas. As I walked across the campus to the meeting room, a soft snow was falling. Murdoch's company limousine rolled past me on its way to the building reserved for meetings of top corporate officers.

His car eased to a stop. There was an inch of fresh snow on the asphalt. Two assistants lifted him out of his limo. They stood him up on his feet, put his arms around each of their shoulders, and literally carried him the short distance to the building where his meeting was being held. He couldn't walk. He couldn't even move his legs—but he wouldn't let them put him in a wheel chair. I looked down at the asphalt behind Murdoch's feet as they carried him to the meeting room. There were two small trails in the snow covered asphalt where the toes of his shoes drug along. It was a piteous sight—and one that reminded me he was still too powerful to be removed from office.

That was the last time I saw Murdoch. His health forced him to retire 6 months later. He didn't live long after he retired. When the company memo regarding his death hit my desk I wasn't quite sure how I felt about his passing. Some sympathy for his family—they must have felt some loss; resentment that one person could hold so much control over the lives of others, with no restraint from anyone. On the other hand, time can give things a different perspective. Some things I had to do with or for Murray didn't look or feel a darn bit funny when I was doing them. With the passage of time, and with my career no longer ransomed to Murray's whim, I found myself actually chuckling over some days of my life spent with him.

THE BOSS

My boss at corporate headquarters was Senior VP, Mike Murphy. He was a good guy, taught me how to handle sticky corporate problems, the very important difference between leading people and managing them, and that a 10-12 hour work day normal in management. I was responsible for doing numerous other things for Mike—like writing his speeches—ghost writing his magazine articles—trouble shooting proftiability problems in our regional operations—auditing work performance in our state operations—and handling social receptions he held to entertain visiting corporate guests.

Vic DiNardo, who was also on Mike's staff with me, sometimes caught 'step-n-fetch-it' duty with me at social receptions Mike threw for high level officers from other companies.

Most receptions were held on the campus of the company's Training Center, near Home Office. The place was nice—almost like a small college campus. The rooms used for receptions were large, professionally decorated, adorned with expensive furniture, with crackling log fires in season. In short, a room fit for corporate heads taking their ease with 'restoratives' while sharing stories of trials and triumphs at the helms of the corporate world.

When Mike wanted to host a reception, Vic and I did the 'grunt' work. We reserved the room, had the kitchen staff prepare hors d'oeuvres, boogied over to the liquor store for the whiskey-wine- mixers, hauled the booze to the reception room, and sat up a nice bar for the reception. During the reception we served as bartenders. We committed to memory the drink of pleasure for our company officers, and, once told, that of their guests. We used only mixers of their preference, and poured only their favorite brands of whiskey.

Mike had a standing rule. He only drank Haig & Haig Scotch whiskey—"none of the rest of that rot-gut some people call Scotch". Usually, we kept a good supply of Haig & Haig in the whiskey inventory we kept in a locked cabinet, hidden away in an obscure closet.

As luck would have it, far more guests than usual ordered Scotch one night about three weeks before Christmas. I don't know—maybe it was the dozen or so unexpected guests added to the guest-list at the last moment. Maybe the festive Christmas atmosphere—the air of gay camaraderie—the free booze— whatever—it moved them to empty their glasses more than usual. We ran out of Haig & Haig. We were about an hour into the reception and Mike was well on his way to being 'sloshed'—which wasn't out of ordinary. As host, he felt compelled to match his guests—drink for drink. With a big swallow, he emptied his glass, looked across the room at Vic, and growled.

"Hey—Vic—another Scotch."

"Yes sir, Mr. Murphy—right away, sir", said Vic as he

hustled across the room to take Mike's empty glass.

All we had left on the table was a bottle of low-end Scotch with a brand name of TEACHERS emblazoned across the bottle label. Neither Vic nor I had a clue how that bottle of TEACHERS got on the table—but, it was the only Scotch we had left, period.

I kept my eye on Mike as Vic poured him a glass of TEACHERS Scotch. I saw Mike him watching, out of the corner of his eye, every move Vic made. He knew Vic wasn't pouring him Haig & Haig scotch. I could sense trouble coming, but what was I going to do—TEACHERS was all we had.

Vic trotted across the room, gave Mike the glass of TEACHERS. Mike didn't say a word—pretended he hadn't seen Vic pour his drink out of that bottle of TEACHERS. He sucked in a big mouthful of TEACHERS' Scotch—then spat it out with enough force to spray it half way across the room.

"What th' hell—what did you give me to drink? Hell fire— that wasn't Haig & Haig! What did I say about pouring me anything but Haig & Haig? Huh?" bellowed Mike at Vic. Looking first at Mike, then me, Vic said nothing. He stood there, trying desperately to think of an answer that would placate Mike.

"What—you can't hear me? Huh? What's the matter with you?" said Mike as he glared at Vic.

I hurried across the room to Mike and grabbed what was left of that glass of TEACHERS Scotch out his hand.

"Mr. Murphy, I apologize. You are exactly right—the error is ours. Give us one moment, please sir. I'll take care of this right now! We'll be right back. Vic, come with me, quickly please."

On the way past the bar I grabbed up the bottle of TEACHERS and the empty Haig & Haig bottle. We shot through the back door of the reception room and flew down the hallway to a room used for teaching auto repair techniques. I found a small, plastic funnel. I had Vic hold the funnel in the empty Haig & Haig bottle, while I poured the TEACHERS Scotch into the Haig & Haig bottle. I pushed the cork top back into the Haig & Haig bottle as we hurried back down the hallway to the reception room.

When we entered the reception room I held the Haig & Haig bottle up high so Mike could see the whiskey in it. I grabbed a clean glass, dumped a few cubes of ice in it, and filled it with the TEACHERS we had put in that Haig & Haig bottle. I trotted across the room to Mike, who had been watching my every move.

"Here you are, sir", I said with an apologetic look. "I am so embarrassed by our obvious mistake. I have no excuse— none at all. I believe you'll find this Scotch to your liking. Just give this Haig & Haig a try, if you will—see if it meets your satisfaction, sir."

Mike took a big gulp of that cheap TEACHERS scotch whiskey—rolled it around in his mouth—swallowed it—smacked his lips—smiled, and said.

"Now—that's better. That's real Scotch whiskey. Don't you *ever* repeat that mistake, Mister!"

"Oh—no sir—you can bet on it. We'll be on our toes from here on out, sir", I said as I smiled at him.

He never knew the difference between one Scotch and another that evening because he was already so 'soused' his body was swaying where he stood. Vic and I never told a soul about that little trick until years later when both of us had retired. As a rule, Mike was a great guy to work for. On the other hand—you just never knew when he might take exception to our 'switching' with his whiskey of choice and decide he, and the company, no longer had need of our services.

The Chinese have a saying, 'May you live in interesting times'—or something like that. I could never decide if it was a 'blessing' or a 'curse'. Regardless, I think working those receptions for Mike were certainly 'interesting times'.

After several years of working for Mike, a job became available in one of our biggest field operations. It involved the management of over 140 employees— multi-million dollar budgets—all strung out over two states and that cauldron called Washington, D.C. A bunch of guys in the company wanted that job—all of them were qualified. I applied for the job, but, with competition for the job being really tough—I wasn't at all sure I would be selected. The list of candidates was pared down to four people. All of us went through multiple interviews over several weeks. I got the job. No one ever said so, but I'm guessing Mike had a lot of input in naming the appointment to that job. I like to think he thought I had earned it.

WRONG WAY

'Wrong Way' was the nickname given to Gary Donovan, a Manager for the insurance company we both worked for. He was, originally, from South Philadelphia. He worked his way up the ladder and arrived in Virginia via a promotion to the job of Division Manager.

He was dubbed with the name of 'Wrong Way' because many felt if there was a wrong way to do something—Gary would find it—including driving in the wrong direction on a one way street or road.

As do some people transplanted from north to south of the Mason-Dixon line, Gary came off as assertive—maybe a little pushy—a bit inclined to manage instead of leading people. Those things aside, he was still a likeable fellow, an honest man, devout to his faith, a good boss, and a good family man.

Gary had a wife, Penny, and 6 children—four boys and two girls. The youngest of the children, Lisa Anne, was 'special'. She was a lovable child, outgoing, engaging, about 6-7 years old. Her mental age, according to medical specialists, would probably never progress beyond that of a child 7-8 years of age.

Temperamentally, Gary and Penny were perfectly matched. Neither of them seemed to worry about anything. They lived by the creed 'everything will work out okay'.

Adversities, trials, and bad luck that might drive most people to bouts of swearing, frustration, anger, depression, and tears seemed to roll off their backs. With six kids, one of whom was 'special', maybe they had to be that way—to survive each day with their sanity intact. Even after the older boys grew up and left home, when something went awry in their lives they called Gary to bail them out. He usually found a solution for them without complaint. Below are some events involving Gary, Penny, and Lisa Anne over the years I knew them.

~~~~~~

Occasionally, Lisa Anne would wander out of the house and take a 'walk' through their neighborhood. Gary or Penny would, eventually, miss her, be unsure exactly how long she had been gone, or where she might be. They would marshal their other kids into a search party, begin walking, running, or driving up and down streets in the neighborhood, and call neighbors who may have seen her wandering past their houses. Sometimes the police were called to join the search.

Lisa Anne was always found—sometimes a quarter-mile away from the house—sometimes no more than 3-4 blocks, and always unharmed. A week, a month, or two months later, they would go through the 'Lisa Anne search party' routine again. A year's span might witness 5-6 Lisa Anne 'tracking parties'. Gary and Penny just brushed off these 'searches' with an 'oh, things happen' attitude and went on with life.

~~~~~~

The company assigned a new Chevrolet to Gary, as his company car. It was an impressive car—midnight blue outside, deep navy-blue velour seats. Lisa Anne put their white cat in the car and shut the door—which was far less distressing to the cat than the time she put it in their clothes dryer and turned it on. The cat spent the night in the car, peed on the car's floor carpet, and shed white cat hair all over the dark blue seats. The following morning the interior of the car reeked unbearably of the strong, acrid smell of cat urine—and there wasn't a square inch of navy-blue seat fabric without white cat hair on it.

As it happened, Gary was supposed to drive his boss to a distant company meeting that day. He couldn't get all the cat hair off the seats—nor could he get rid of the stifling odor of cat urine. Being 'Wrong Way' Donovan, he tried a remedy without thinking it through. He mixed ammonia with water and wiped down the car's floor carpet with it—certain that would neutralize the odor of the cat pee. It didn't. The combined fumes of ammonia and cat pee in the car were so overwhelming it made your eyes burn and tears flow. Many people would have reacted to a mess like that by getting rid of the cat or disciplining Lisa Anne. Gary just waved it off, and asked his boss to drive them that day—in the boss's car. His boss was irritated by the situation. Gary just waved off his boss's displeasure—confident his boss would eventually accept the incident as 'just one of those things that happens to everybody now and then'.

A month after the 'cat pee' incident, 'Wrong Way' locked his car keys in the trunk of his new company car. Instead of calling a locksmith and getting a ride to work with somebody else, he used a hammer and screw driver to knock the lock mechanism out of the car's trunk lid. In the process, he ruined the lock, dented the trunk lid, and was left with no practical way to keep the trunk lid closed (except using of half roll of duct tape) while driving the car. He had to have a body shop repair the trunk lid and replace the lock. Any of the rest of us who did that to our company car would have had the damage and lock repaired quietly, and paid for it out of our own pocket to keep the boss from finding out we had pulled such a stunt. Not 'Wrong Way' Donovan. He turned the repair bill in on his weekly expense report and trusted our boss to approve reimbursement of the expense under the premise of 'just one of those days— we all have them'.

'Wrong Way' had a well-worn, big, 6 year old Plymouth sedan for a personal car. He and I were working together out of our company's Home Office in the south-west. Our work took us to states all over the country where our company had operations. We would often fly out of town in the company jet—which meant a pre-dawn take-off time. We would take turns driving to the airport. It was Gary's turn to drive. The temperature was below freezing when I arrived at his home at the pre-dawn hour of 5 a.m.
I parked my car, threw my luggage in his trunk, jumped into

the front seat of his old Plymouth—and dropped through a hole in the seat of the car to the floor. With me cussing and Gary laughing, I opened the door and crawled back out of the car. I saw a small piece of house carpet mashed down in a hole where the seat bottom was supposed to be.

'Wrong Way' had forgotten to tell me he had taken his dog with him to the Division of Motor Vehicles the previous afternoon to renew his driver's license. He left the dog in the car. He was in the DMV for an hour. When he got back to the car the dog had clawed and chewed away the entire bottom of the front passenger seat. Nothing was left of that seat bottom but a few wire springs and the metal frame.

A lot of people might have given the dog away—right on the spot. Not 'Wrong Way' Donovan. He just stopped at a home carpet store, bought a small, cheap, door-mat piece of carpet, and threw it over the hole in the seat. The piece of thin carpet did nothing to keep anyone who sat on it from falling through the bare seat springs to the floor. It never crossed his mind to fore-warn me before I fell through the seat bottom. He expected me to handle it as he would have— just brush it off and be glad I didn't tear my trousers or injure myself on the seat springs.
~~~~~~

Gary's children adopted Gary and Penny's 'laid back' attitude—concerning nearly anything or anyone. Penny approached people of power, position, wealth, importance, just as she would an old friend or next door neighbor. She called the President of our company, Robert Donald, and left word with his secretary for 'Bob' to give her a call at home concerning a donation, in the name of our company—one of largest insurance companies in the United States—to her favorite charity, a school For the Deaf & Blind.

There were somewhere between 15-16,000 people working for our company. Without a doubt, 10% of those people would never—not even in a lifetime with the company—*see* President Donald personally. Even at a distance. A conservative estimate of the number of employees who would never personally talk to the President would come in around 25%. Even to say as much as 'hello'. The guy was just too busy and occupied running one of the largest insurance companies in the world. This meant nothing to Penny. To her, he was just a person she needed to talk to. So, she reasoned, give him a shout—leave word for him to return her call.

Defying reasonable odds, President Donald decided to return Penny's call. Maybe her comment about a charity benefiting handicapped kids did it. When his call came through to 'Wrong Way' and Penny's house, she was in the driveway washing their car. One of their teenage kids grabbed the wall phone in the kitchen and answered it with, 'Yeah?' President Donald identified himself, and asked if he could speak to Mrs. Penny Donovan. The kid mumbled into the phone, 'Yeah—hang-on'. Then, with the phone receiver near his mouth he leaned out the kitchen door and yelled to Penny in the driveway, "Hey Ma, I got Ronald McDonald on the phone here—says he wants to talk to you. Prob' ly trying to button-hole you for money for that Ronald McDonald House. You want I should just hang up on him?"

Most people would have been mortified. Not Penny. She took the phone—laughed off President Donald hearing her son call him 'Ronald McDonald'—and asked him to make a $1500 donation to her charitable cause. Unbelievably, President Donald did agree to a $500 donation. Penny told Gary, when he came home that day, that their son had called our President 'Ronald McDonald'.

That *was* one thing 'Wrong Way' didn't blow off. For two weeks after that ill-fated call, he climbed the stairs to our 27th floor office to avoid a possible meeting with President Donald in an elevator car carrying him to his 38th floor office.
~~~~~~

Penny, inadvertently, got involved in a phone conversation with 'Wrong Way's' boss, the legendary 'rough-and-gruff' Director, Ray Hanson. She got Ray on the office phone because 'Wrong Way' was at lunch. Ray told her as much. Most wives would have quickly apologized for disturbing the boss and terminated the call. Not Penny. She blithely told Ray, "Give Gary a message. Tell him to bring home a gallon of distilled water—the Guppies in our fish tank have the pink eye", then Penny hung up.

Ray did give 'Wrong Way' the message. He also filled his ear with a gruff reminder of, "I'm not your damn secretary—I don't take messages for you!" Wrong Way nodded his agreement and quietly backed out of Ray's office. When he got to our offices he laughed it off and shared the story with us. That was vintage 'Wrong Way' Gary.

~~~~~~

SAINT PATRICK'S DAY PARTY

Gary & Penny, being of Irish descent, decided to throw a St. Paddy's Day dinner party. The guests were 'Wrong Way's' co-workers. That meant twenty people—counting their spouses. This many people tightly filled their home of comfortable but modest dimensions.

St. Paddy's Day, being in March of each year, always means 'iffy' weather—especially where we were stationed at the time. The temperature the night of the party was in the low teens. The wind, as usual, was blowing. Several inches of frozen snow was on the ground.

As guests arrived, 'Wrong Way' and Penny welcomed them and stored their outer garments in a rear room. About half the guests had arrived when Art and Cheryl Trevell breezed through the door. Lisa Anne, despite her mental challenges, could, and did interact socially with people—on limited levels.

As Penny put their coats away, 'Wrong Way' brought each guest a mug of Irish beer and showed them to seats in the living room and the adjacent dining room.

Most of the 20 guests spent the majority of their time sitting or standing in that area—with occasional circulation to the kitchen and recreation room in the rear of the home. 'Wrong Way' and Penny saw to the comfort of people in the living/dining room, and moved on to guests in the rear portion of the house. They hadn't been out of the living room a full minute before Lisa Anne, now 10 years old, took their place as a self-appointed 'Hostess'.

She greeted each guest by looking them straight in the eye, holding up her hand while saying 'Hi!', grabbing up the guest's beer mug from a table, and quaffing down a couple of deep swallows of their beer before the guest could react. There were repeated cries of, 'Oh—no-no, sweetheart', followed by swift moves to reclaim their mug. Lisa Anne easily surrendered the mug to the guest, wiped her mouth with the back of her hand, belched heartily, smiled her way through a satisfied sigh of, "Aahhhh"—and moved on to the next guest. This went on throughout the evening.

Gerry Keller gently pulled her beer mug away from Lisa Anne. While Gerry contemplated the mannerly thing to say to Lisa Anne as she pulled the mug out of her hand, Lisa Anne sidled around to the other side of the room. She eased up to a coffee table and picked up the beer mug of Cheryl Trevell, who was fully engaged in a conversation with another of the guest. When Cheryl noticed Lisa Anne belting down her beer, one fourth of the mug's beer had made its way down Lisa Anne's throat.

"Ohmigod! Please don't do that, Sugar. It's not good for you. Ohmigod—she has drunk almost half of my beer!" gasped Cheryl as she used both hands to pry Lisa Anne's fingers from her mug.

Basking in the warmth of the alcohol copped from 4-5 different mugs, Lisa Anne smiled broadly and dropped to her knees in front of Cheryl. This feeling of 'good cheer' left her in the mood to expand her duties as Hostess. She was floating on the equivalent of, roughly, 2 bottles of beer downed in a 30 minute span. She began to undo the spaghetti straps of Cheryl's high-heel dress shoes. Cheryl, with a helpless smile, graciously tried to stop her.

"Oh—honey—you don't need to do that. No—wait— sweetheart –that's okay—I'm comfortable with my shoes on—why don't you—."

Lisa Anne softly swatted Cheryl's hands away, happily babbled "you be comf-r-bul", and continued to undo the shoe straps. She pulled Cheryl's shoes off her feet. Cheryl looked at us, shrugged, and said,

"Oh—what th' hell. If it makes her happy--. I'll get 'em when I leave. More comfortable without 'em on anyway." Lisa Anne disappeared with the shoes— we assumed to the designated cloak room in the rear of the house.

The hubbub of conversation between a dozen people had just returned to an even flow when we heard the frenetic sound of rapid foot-falls coming down the hallway. We heard Penny yell,

"Caesar—Brutus—no! Come back here! Gary—shit—Lisa Anne let the dog and cat in the house! Get 'em—quick!"

Not even Superman could have reacted quickly enough to stop Brutus the dog from chasing Caesar the cat around the corner of the hallway and into the living room. Caesar raced across the living room floor. With the graceful agility all cats have, he leaped 2 feet off the floor, sailed through the air, and passed neatly between two potted flower plants on the three-shelf high, stand-alone, metal, flower pot-holder— which served as a room divider between the living room and dining room. There must have been a dozen potted plants setting on the three shelves of that divider.

Brutus followed suit in his pursuit of Caesar. He launched himself through the air in an attempt to follow Caesar's flight between the plants on the middle shelf of the divider. Brutus was a full grown Labrador weighing in at 40 lbs. He didn't have a chance of threading his way between the shelves of that divider—let alone two closely spaced, large, potted plants. Half of his head made it through the shelves before he knocked the entire three foot high metal divider and all twelve potted plants across the dining room floor. The metal divider came apart—pots broke—black dirt and flowers flew in all directions over the carpeted floor.

This all happened so quickly not one of us had time to grab the dog or cat before their destruction of the metal divider and the flowers it held made the room looked like the end product of a tornado. We sat there, mouths open, eyes wide, as the chase between Brutus and Caesar continued through the dining room, into the kitchen, around a corner, and down the hallway toward the front door.

The hallway floor was hardwood oak—highly polished. By the time Caesar rocketed to the area of the hallway nearest the front storm door he was traveling at 'warp' speed. Brutus, with dirt and flower leaves still clinging to his body, was right behind Caesar. At the last second, Caesar dug his claws into the cloth doormat on the floor in front of the storm door, jerked his body to the left, hit the carpeted stair landing, and raced up the stairs.

Brutus, carrying 40 pounds, traveling at his max speed, and not having the claws of a cat—well, he gave into the laws of momentum and gravity. He sailed straight ahead, through the air, into and right on through the glass of the storm door.

There was the sound of 'whummpp', followed by the sound of shattered glass, a yelp of pain from Brutus, door hinges ripping from the door frame, and another 'whummpp' when he landed on the frozen concrete of the front porch and rolled to a stop on the front walk.

Again, Brutus' second meeting with a fixed object happened so quickly no one had time to do anything except watch the event unfold. Several of us leaped to our feet and hustled out to the hallway to see if Brutus was fatally injured. When we looked toward front door we saw a badly damaged metal storm door frame, a few small shards of broken glass hanging to the frame, and the metal door frame hanging to the wall by only one hinge.

Brutus was standing on the concrete walk way shaking the dirt, snow, and glass off himself. Satisfied he had rid himself of the dirt and glass, Brutus trotted back to the front door. 'Wrong Way' ran outside and began checking Brutus for cuts or injuries which might call for a quick trip to the vet. Amazingly, there wasn't a cut or scratch anywhere on his body.

After checking Brutus over, 'Wrong Way' examined the destroyed storm door. Hanging on one hinge, it swayed in the winter wind. From his vantage point on the front porch he looked through the frame of the storm door where the glass had been—and into his house at the wreckage between his living and dining rooms. His gaze took in his dirt covered carpet, broken clay pots, flowers, twisted metal shelving—all strewn over the dining room carpet. He gazed to the Heavens and grabbed his head with both hands.

"Jesus Christ! Look at this mess! I swear—Penny, did you see—ah, what th' hell ya' gonna' do? Dammit, you let a dog and cat get together—what th' hell can ya' expect? Well—we're here for a party, not a funeral. Let's get the dirt cleaned up. Penny—break out the vacuum! I'll get a broom and shovel out of the garage and clean up the glass and flower pots. Shut the front door before we all freeze to death. Anybody want another beer? Huh?"

That was vintage 'Wrong Way. In the flash of an eye a cat and dog had wrecked the house— 'Wrong Way and Penny Ann just let it roll off their backs. Clean things up—get back to the party—just one of those things.

The 'cat-and dog' disaster didn't happen until around 8:30 pm. Just before the cat and dog got in the house Penny had quartered a couple of heads of cabbage and thrown it all into a huge skillet with some corned beef. She put it on the stove, and turned the heat on under the skillet. Here were 20 people—invited to their house for dinner—and Penny hadn't started the first preparation toward dinner until just before the cat-n-dog saga started around 8:30pm. Again, this was vintage Gary and Penny. No sense of urgency—no need felt for pre-party time preparation of food. Just have a few more drinks—let the food cook whenever.

Around 9:00pm, with guests helping with the clean-up of dirt, flower pots, door glass—we had the mess cleaned up as well as could be on a short term basis. 'Wrong Way' and Penny celebrated the clean-up by sticking another bottle of beer in the hands of every guest. Penny raised her mug, shouted an Irish blessing of 'God bless all in this room'— and 'Wrong Way' shouted, 'everybody drink up'.

Feeling badly about the destruction of his home, we all raised our mugs and bottles to him. Conversation had barely returned to a normal hub-bub when one of the guests standing near the kitchen yelled.

"Hey—Donovan! Something's on fire! There's smoke and I can smell something burning!"

Penny reached the kitchen first and found smoke so thick above the stove top it made seeing much of anything difficult.

"Christ—Gary! The corned beef and cabbage is on fire! Shit! I forgot about it—cleaning up that mess from the dog and cat—gimme' a towel—out of the way people!"

Penny grabbed a towel, wrapped it around the handle of the flaming skillet of corned beef and cabbage, raced to the kitchen door, yanked it open with her free hand, kicked open the rear storm door—and slung the flaming corned beef, cabbage, *and skillet* through the air into the back yard. That done, she slammed the door shut, threw down the towel on the kitchen counter, stretched a big grin across her face, and bellowed, "And that's the end of that! Who wants some cake for desert?"

Sounded like a punch line—out of some black humor routine. Not so. Not a word of it. Penny meant just what she said. The main entrée had just burned up—there was nothing left to consume except Irish beer and a cake with green icing on it. Considering the way things had gone in the last 30 minutes, she probably feared the cake would complete the evening's destruction by self-combustion if she didn't invite us to eat it quickly.

I looked at the clock on the kitchen wall. It was five minutes away from 10 pm. The intended main course had just gone into the back yard in flames. Even if she had another skillet and replacements for the food, it would have been 11:00 pm before she could have, with all possible speed, put it on the table. No one in their right mind would have wanted to start a full course meal of corned beef and cabbage at an hour away from midnight.

Even though there were so many stomachs in that house growling from hunger it sounded like a pack of dogs fighting—no one wanted a piece of cake with green icing on it. Especially knowing it would have to be washed down with beer.

Most of us, by then, were standing in the smoky kitchen of a house that still had some dirt on the dining room carpet, and a storm door hanging from the front of the house by one hinge. The noxious odor of burned cabbage and meat permeated the entire house—and we were close to being in the morning hours of another day.

We all declined the gracious offer of cake, offered our regrets for the bad luck with the animals and food—and suggested it was time for all of us to be heading home. We bustled about retrieving our coats. One soul felt a pressing need to empty his bladder before he started home. He was trying to get into the 'powder room' just off the downstairs TV room.

"Uh—Gary. I can't get the door open to your bathroom. Is it stuck or something?"

'Wrong Way' walked toward the bathroom. As he did so, he looked at the dog cage in the corner of the TV room where Brutus was supposed to be locked up. Asleep in the dog cage was Lisa Anne. All the beer she had quaffed down been too much for her. She was out like a light in the floor of the cage—and Brutus was nowhere to be seen.

"What—where th' hell did the dog go? Penny—where's Brutus? Lisa Anne has locked herself in his cage, and he's gone! Christ—what next! Oh—here, Chuck, let me see why the bathroom door won't open."

'Wrongway' pushed hard on the door and it slowly opened. There was a sound from the other side of the door and then a bark. Lisa Anne had put Brutus in the bathroom and took his place in the animal cage. When Gary got the door opened enough to get the dog out he looked down to see the linoleum on the bathroom floor ripped and chewed to pieces.

Apparently, Brutus had gotten bored with being locked in that small bathroom. He had clawed and chewed on the linoleum until he broke through the finish on it. He used his paws and teeth to pull up most of it up in small pieces until a pile of it had almost jammed the door when the guest had tried to open it. You could see the bare wooden sub-floor that used to be covered by the linoleum.

Gary threw up his hands, again—moaned his exasperation—rolled his eyes upward, and asked God why he singled him out for all the crap that had happened to him that night. The rest of us were shaking our heads and laughing quietly. How, we wondered, did either 'Wrong Way' or Penny keep their sanity? How did they resist spiraling into depression over the cost of the evening's destruction? How did they control their temper and not end the lives of the cat and dog? There could be only one answer—they were 'Wrong Way' and Penny. Everything rolled off their backs.

The guests put on their coats, said 'thank you' for being invited to the party, and walked through the cold night to their cars. What more could any of them do or say. They couldn't very well say 'the food was delicious— thanks for a wonderful evening'. That would have re-defined the limits of hypocrisy.

Finally, there was no one left but Art, Cheryl, Bonnie and I. Bonnie and I wanted, badly, to go home. Cheryl had been in the room where the coats were stored for a long time. She had offered to bring out our coats along with theirs. Art went to find her. When they finally reappeared, Cheryl put the crowning touch on the evening. She had been in the back room searching for her shoes for a good 5 minutes— with no luck. She had given up looking for her shoes when Art found her.

Art asked Gary and Penny Ann where Lisa Anne might have put Cheryl's shoes. They didn't have a clue. Efforts to wake

Lisa Anne and get an answer from her were futile. She would awaken only for a few seconds and then fall asleep again. While she was awake it was obvious she didn't have any memory of those shoes—let alone where she put them.

After 'Wrong Way' and Penny searched the house from top to bottom for 15 minutes with no sight of Cheryl's shoes, we convinced them to call off the search. Art started the motor on their car, Cheryl ran across the snowy walkway and street—barefoot—jumped into their car, and waved as they drove off.

After Bonnie and I drove out of sight of the house we both laughed, hysterically, over the whole evening until there were tears in our eyes. I could hardly see to drive our car. This party took place over 30 years ago—and I can still see it as if it was last night.

It was the last party 'Wrong Way' and Penny hosted—that any of his peers were aware of. Maybe the events of that night got to even those 'optimistic' friends.

THE BIRD IN THE WALL

'Wrong Way' Donovan and I were currently assigned to Claims Staff in Home Office. One of our primary duties was auditing the work performance of our insurance company's Claims Reps working in various states around the nation. We would audit the work files of Claims Reps, compile and summarize our findings, schedule a personal visit with the company's state Officers, and present our findings and recommendations for the employees of the state being audited.

We had completed our review of work performance by the Claims Reps in the state of Connecticut. We scheduled a personal meeting with Connecticut company officers in Hamden, Connecticut to review our findings. We flew into Hamden the night before the meeting. Our long tested routine was to check into a motel, freshen up, go out for dinner and any sight-seeing we wanted to do, and get a good night's sleep. The premise was, we would be well rested and at our best for the day long presentation, and discussion, of our findings with state officers.

'Wrong Way' had some distant relatives living in Connecticut. He said he had visited them in years past— was familiar with notable historic areas around Hamden— and would serve as our guide for the tour and dinner. I had never been in Connecticut before, so I let 'Wrong Way' rent a car, pick the spots to tour, and choose a place for dinner.

I should have known better. We weren't 15 minutes away from the Howard Johnson Motel before 'Wrong Way' was obviously lost. He refused to ask directions. We drove for 45 minutes, stopped at a random bar for drinks, got a few general directions, and continued our wandering drive around Hamden, Connecticut. About 8:30 that evening—two hours after the time of our planned dinner —we found the historic seaside town of Mystic, Connecticut. It was also home to famed seafood restaurants.

It was a pleasant meal—with drinks before and after dinner. We left there at 10:00 that evening—only when I insisted we do so. An hour later we were, again, lost and driving and around Hamden—passing some places twice. When I threatened to get out of the car and find a cab, 'Wrong Way' stopped and got directions. The directions were wrong or 'Wrong Way' didn't follow them correctly. At midnight, we were still lost.

I was irritated and more than a little concerned. I could see us driving around Hamden when dawn broke the following day. I envisioned us appearing before a company Vice President in rumpled clothes, with blood-shot eyes, and incoherent from lack of sleep. Our credibility, and possibly our jobs, would have been history.

Then the Gods smiled on us. We pulled up beside a police car at a traffic light. 'Wrong Way' gave up any pretense of knowing where he was, told them he had been lost for hours, and was desperate to find our motel. The two policemen let us follow them back to our motel. Actually, we were no more than 7-8 minutes from our motel when we met the policemen—but we didn't know that. We had begun to wonder if we were still in the city of Hamden.

Our rooms at the motel were next door to each other.

When we got to the door of 'Wrong Way's' room I said goodnight to him and continued walking for 8 feet or so to the door of my room. 'Wrong Way' yelled after me.

"Hey—. You wanna' come in my room for a night cap? I got some really great Scotch. Good stuff."

"Thanks—but, no. It's almost 1 am—we have a long hard day ahead of us. We've already had more to drink than we should have—and we ate too much. I just want to take a shower and get some sleep."

'What! Aw—don't be a party pooper! We've had a good time tonight! Let's finish it off with one more drink—put a cap on the evening."

"Not me, Gary. I'm beat. I don't want any more to drink. You should get some rest too."

"Aw—tuh' hell with yuh! Be that way. You wanna' miss out on some good Scotch—it's your loss."

"Goodnight, Gary. See you in the morning."

I went into my room and heard Gary slam the door to his room. I shook my head over his insistence on drinking more whiskey and staying up even later when we had a tough day ahead of us. But—that was 'Wrong Way' Gary. He never worried about anything—he expected you to follow suit. I felt he would forget about the matter by the next morning. I took a quick shower and jumped in the bed. I was almost asleep when I heard a beating, thumping sound on the wall against the head of my bed.

I sat up in bed and listened. I knew 'Wrong Way's room was right on the other side of that wall. The beating, thumping sound began just to the left of the head of my bed and continued to the right of my bed on the dividing wall between our rooms until that wall hit the exterior wall of my room about 20 feet beyond my bed. Once the 'beating' noise reached the point where the wall hit the exterior wall, the noise stopped abruptly. Then there was quiet.

I thought 'Wrong Way' was still ticked because I wouldn't join him for a drink and was beating on the wall to keep me awake until I joined him. My head hit the pillow. I was almost asleep when the 'beating' noise started again—moving all the way down the wall of my room to the *exterior* wall of the motel. Then, another period of quiet.

This went on for ten minutes. I was determined not to go to his room, even if he beat the wall all night. The beating stopped. It was replaced with the sound of finger nails scraping up and down on the wall—all the way down the wall to the *exterior* wall. It was approaching 2 am when I finally went to sleep, despite the scratching on the walls.

The next morning I walked out the door of my room at 7:00 am, just as 'Wong Way' walked out of his room.

"Good morning, Gary. Sleep well?"

'Wrong Way' didn't look at me and didn't reply to my cheery greeting. He slammed the door to his room, turned sharply, and began walking away. I assumed he was still ticked because I didn't come over to his room for a drink—despite his beating on the walls. So be it, I thought. I got some sleep and was prepared for a busy day of conferences with company officials. With 'Wrong Way' up all night, hammering and scratching the walls, I doubted he would be able to organize his thoughts well enough to make any kind of lucid presentation to the local Vice President. Well, that was his problem—not mine.

With me trailing behind, 'Wrong Way' walked quickly to the office of the motel. He angrily pushed open the office door, told the desk clerk he wanted to talk to the motel manager, and stood there drumming his fingers on the counter top. He still didn't look at me—didn't say a word to me.

"Good morning sir. I hope you slept well last night. How may I help you?" said the manager as he walked up to the front desk.

"Odd that you should ask how I slept last night", said 'Wrong Way'. "In a word, I didn't get 15 minutes of uninterrupted sleep all night. There is a bird trapped in the walls of my room. It cried out all night long. I mean all damn night long! It was making a 'peep-peep' sound every few minutes. I mean, the freakin' bird never stopped—'peeping' once every minute—all night long! I don't know how the bird got in between those walls. I assume he found a crack or something out on the patio of my room—got in between the walls of my room—and couldn't find his way back out. Jesus Christ, man! What a nightmare! I was up **ALL** night long. I beat on the wall—I scratched on the walls—trying to scare the bird into moving back toward the patio—hoping he could find the hole he came through and fly back outside. Trust me—that bird is still in those walls this morning! I'm so exhausted I can hardly hold my eyes open. I emphasize my lack of rest because I don't want you to entertain any ideas of me to paying for that room! I hope we have that clear."

"Sir, I apologize for your discomfort. I can't imagine how a bird could have gotten in the walls of your room."

"Yeah? C'mon with me. Let's go to my room. You listen to the bird—and then you can tell me you don't believe there is a bird trapped in the walls!"

'Wrong Way' stomped across the parking lot to his room with the Manager and I following close behind. We walked in 'Wrong Way's room and stood there quietly. We hadn't been in the room more than ten seconds before we all heard a distinct, short, shrill sound. Sure enough, it did sound like the 'peep' of a bird.

"There! You hear that? Wha'd I tell you! Huh?"

The Manger looked upward toward the ceiling. I thought he was simply staring upwards while he pondered the 'peep-peep' sound. He looked down—stared at 'Wrong Way' a second, and said.

"Mr. Donovan—that sound is your smoke alarm. The battery is about is about to expire. The smoke alarm is, by law, set up to give a 'beep-beep' signal when the battery that supports the alarm is about to go dead. It serves as a warning, so you can replace the battery and not lose the protection of the smoke alarm."

It was all I could do not to collapse in hysterical laughter. 'Wrong Way'—up all night long—chasing a 'bird' in his walls—which turns out to be a smoke alarm. 'Wrong Way' looked at the smoke alarm, looked at me as if to say 'don't say a damn word'—and glared at the Manager.

"Either way, I didn't get any sleep last night. It's your fault the battery in the damn smoke alarm battery wasn't replaced before it expired. And I'm still not paying the room charge!" said 'Wrong Way' as he stomped out of his room.

Later on, as we drove the few short blocks to the local company offices, 'Wrong Way' spoke to me for the first time that morning.

"If I hear one word about this from anybody in Home Office, when we get back to Columbus—one, I'll deny it. Two, I'll know you told them. Three, I'll watch for *any* little mistake *you* make—and I'll see that word of it is spread over the entire home office."

Still trying to keep a straight face, I listened to 'Wrong Way' deliver his ultimatum to me. It was more a plea than a threat. Gary 'Wrong Way' Donovan and I traveled about the country together for another 2 years before both of us received promotions and were transferred out of Home Office. He was sent to, of all places, the Hamden, Conn. Office. I was sent to Annapolis, Md.

I never mentioned a word of the incident to anyone while both of us were still employed by the company. I seldom saw 'Wrong Way' again after the company transferred us to different states. On the occasions I did see 'Wrong Way' again, he never brought up the 'bird' incident—neither did I. But, it didn't dim my memories of that 'bird in the wall' incident one bit.

Made in the USA
Middletown, DE
06 May 2018